Fleur McDonald lives on a large farm east of Esperance in Western Australia, where she and her husband Anthony produce prime lambs and cattle, run an Angus cattle and White Suffolk stud and produce a small amount of crops. They have two children, Rochelle and Hayden. Fleur snatches time for her writing in between helping on the farm, and chats about her life on the land as a writer, mum and farmer on Facebook, Twitter and her blog. *Crimson Dawn* is her fifth novel.

www.fleurmcdonald.com

Also by Fleur McDonald
Red Dust
Blue Skies
Purple Roads
Silver Clouds

FLEUR
McDONALD
Crimson Dawn

ARENA
ALLEN&UNWIN

Arena Books, an imprint of
Allen & Unwin
83 Alexander Street
Crows Nest NSW 2065
Australia
Phone: (61 2) 8425 0100
Email: info@allenandunwin.com
Web: www.allenandunwin.com

Cataloguing-in-Publication details are available
from the National Library of Australia
www.trove.nla.gov.au

ISBN 978 1 74331 531 6

Set in 13/17.5 pt Adobe Garamond by Post Pre-press Group, Australia
Printed and bound in Australia by Griffin Press

10 9 8 7 6 5 4 3 2 1

The paper in this book is FSC® certified.
FSC® promotes environmentally responsible,
socially beneficial and economically viable
management of the world's forests.

*To the girls who are 'ordinary girls' but,
like Laura in this book, making waves,
breaking new ground and bridging the divide—
Amanda Salisbury, Gemma Lee-Steere and
Catherine Marriott, to name only a few.*

Chapter 1

2000

Laura stared at the thin white stick. Nothing.

Flipping the toilet seat down, she sank onto it, waiting for the blue lines to appear. Waiting to see what her future held.

Please, let there only be one, she prayed over and over.

She stared so hard her eyes began to play tricks. First there was only one. Then, maybe, a second began to show, but the colour didn't seem to get any stronger than a faint now-you-see-it-now-you-don't.

Holding her breath, Laura focused carefully for another few seconds. Then she breathed out in a *whoosh*. Surely that dreaded second line would have shown up by now if it was going to? She must have made a mistake. Perhaps she got her dates mixed up. Whatever it was, she was thankful she wasn't pregnant. She'd had a fright. It was a warning to be more careful.

Of course, she wanted children, but not yet. She still had so much to do before she settled down. She had dreams. Plans. Things she wanted, no, *needed*, to achieve.

Laura placed the test on the vanity and got up. She still felt sick, but maybe the breakfast bacon had been off. Or perhaps it was the stress of the last few days. Shearing was a demanding time.

Pulling her long blonde hair back into a ponytail, she noticed the telltale signs of a pimple at the corner of her mouth. It was a bit sore. Maybe, *maybe* her period was on its way.

She bent down to grab the towel she'd left lying on the floor and, as she did, focused on the stick once again.

Her heart stopped.

Two blue lines.

Clear and strong against the white background.

No, the voice in her head screamed. *No!* It couldn't be. There had only been one before.

Laura felt a mixture of disbelief, horror and, despite everything, happiness. This could be life-changing.

She looked away then back at the stick, hoping, by some miracle of miracles, something was different. But it wasn't.

Her heart began to thump and she felt a sweat break out all over her.

She was pregnant.

❧

Outside, the wind gusted around the gum trees and rain rattled on the roof, but the icy air couldn't penetrate the farmhouse or dampen the spirit within. Laughter and the clinking of cutlery rang out in the enclosed verandah where Laura and her family were gathered. Despite the weather, the room was pleasant and cosy, with floor-to-ceiling windows, comfy chairs around a roaring fire, and a long dining table that today was set for lunch.

Laura loved these get-togethers, but after her recent discovery she was finding it hard to act normally. She wanted to shout from the top of the shearing shed that she was having a baby, but at the same time she didn't want anyone to know. She didn't want to be judged if she decided she couldn't keep it.

Her half-sister Nicki walked past, holding the salt and pepper shakers. She was singing to herself, and she flashed Laura a grin as she did a couple of dance moves in the middle of the room. Laura made herself smile back, recognising the song as one she'd been hearing with regular monotony on the local radio station. Nicki's sweet voice was low and unobtrusive, and Laura noticed Papa look fondly on as his granddaughter danced. Laura decided she'd ask for a concert from the sixteen-year-old before she and the others returned to Adelaide. Her stepmother, Georgie, was quite a pianist, and the music mother and daughter created together was beautiful.

Laura knew she had to savour the day. These gatherings didn't happen with the frequency they should, not since her dad and Georgie had left Nambina.

Today was even more special, though. Her Papa, Howie, had asked Laura to organise it, saying he had an important announcement to make. She didn't know what he was going to say, and the rest of the family appeared to be as much in the dark as she was.

Laura played with the champagne glass in her hand, feeling nervous. Her own news was big enough, let alone whatever Howie was going to drop on them.

She'd picked up the phone to call her boyfriend, Josh, about a hundred times since yesterday. She wanted to tell him he was going to be a dad. But she kept disconnecting before he'd had a chance to answer.

She was so mixed up. Her dream was to have an impact on the agricultural industry and to farm at the same time. And she was already making a difference, she felt, as a member of several local committees. But could she do all she wanted and planned with a baby in tow?

One moment she was sure she'd manage, and she'd imagine taking a pram into a meeting and the baby playing quietly or sleeping while she helped with something important and useful, like having trial plots on Nambina, liaising with research and development companies, offering her stock as guinea pigs for the good of production. There could be field days on Nambina, with her show-casing the results. But of course, babies didn't always do what their parents wanted, and in the next moment she'd be positive she couldn't do it. She'd envision the baby screaming and being unable to settle it, while her colleagues looked on with disdain or sympathy. At these times, she wondered whether it would be better for all concerned if she had a termination.

And then there was Josh. She shook her head. In her mind she'd had the conversation with him a million times—and it never went well.

A recent incident at the pub hadn't helped. Laura and Josh were eating dinner with Josh's half-sister Meghan, who happened to be Laura's best friend. Also there that night was a family with a newborn baby. The little boy was crying and the mother, who looked exhausted, couldn't calm him down. Meghan had gone over to help and brought the baby back to their table.

To Laura's surprise, the normally understanding Josh was annoyed. 'Don't bring that screaming bundle of noise over here,' he'd said.

'Can't you see how tired that poor woman is?' Meghan had answered. 'Someone needs to give her a break, even if it's just for five minutes.'

'Shouldn't come out in public if they can't stop it crying,' Josh responded, taking another slug of his beer. 'Wrecks the whole night for everyone else.'

Meghan had shaken her head with an exasperated smile and rolled her eyes at Laura. Her grin changed to triumph when the little boy burped long and loudly then stopped crying. His eyes fluttered, and within minutes he was asleep.

'There,' she cooed. 'That's better, isn't it? You can go to sleep now.' She took the baby back to his mother, settled him in the pram and waved away her grateful thanks.

Laura pulled herself away from the memory. She knew Josh could react either way to her news. Maybe he would be angry, but maybe he wouldn't. After all, he helped create the child.

And what would Howie say? What would her family say?

She glanced around the room. Howie, at the ripe old age of seventy-eight, leaned on his walking stick, warming his bones by the fire as he talked intently to Sean, Laura's father. Nicki had joined them. Not far away sat her youngest sister, Poppy, headphones jammed on her ears. Laura could hear the pumping music from where she stood, many metres away. A trip to the country didn't suit the fourteen-year-old, and she seemed determined to block it out as much as possible.

Laura knew with certainty that her family wouldn't judge her. So what was she worried about? The fact she wasn't sure she wanted to keep the child? She wasn't ready? She gritted her teeth, furious at herself. How could she be thinking along those lines when she had such a supportive family? She knew they would juggle their lives to make things work for her, just as she would for any of them.

Turning to look out the window and down the winding drive, Laura caught sight of a dark blue ute racing towards the house. Butterflies started in her stomach.

Josh.

He parked next to the garage and she felt her heart beat a little faster as his familiar long frame unfolded from the cab.

They'd been together for a couple of years now, and were as in love as the first day they got together. Josh was good-looking and clever, and they shared a passion for the land.

But when they first fell for each other it had surprised everyone, including Laura. Josh had never been on her radar, even though he was only two years older and his sister was her best friend. They'd attended the same primary school, but he'd left for boarding school in Adelaide while she'd gone to the local high school in Mangalow, the nearest town.

Laura had heard snippets of Josh's life from Meghan, but at first had only taken a passing interest because they were friends.

That all changed in 1998 during the AFL grand final. Laura had gone to the golf club with another close friend, Catherine, to watch Adelaide play North Melbourne. She'd been surprised when Josh had walked in. Last she'd heard, he was at ag college in Geelong.

She'd caught him looking at her a couple of times. The third time she boldly met his gaze. At half-time, he bought her a drink. At full-time he asked her out to dinner, and by the end of the weekend, they were an item.

Meghan was thrilled.

Now Laura's stomach flipped again as Josh walked up the path. Unsure if it was morning sickness, nervousness or excitement, she put down the glass of champagne she'd been pretending to sip and opened the door, letting a blast of wind blow in.

'Hi! You made it. Shocking day.'

Josh dropped a swift kiss on her lips, shook the water from his Driza-Bone before peeling it off like an unwanted skin. 'Bloody awful day, but I'm liking the rain. Sorry I'm late. Had to pull a calf.'

Laura took the jacket and hung it just inside the door, ignoring the slow drips onto the floor. 'Okay?' she queried.

'Yeah, fine. Just a mis-presentation. Leg back.' He lowered his voice. 'Do you know what this shindig is about yet?'

'Nope, you're in the dark just as much as me.'

'Well, I've brought this, in case it's needed.' Josh pulled the cover off the camera that was slung around his neck. 'Smile!' He pointed the camera at Laura and snapped.

She poked out her tongue and crossed her eyes in a silent protest.

'G'day, Josh.' Howie limped forward and Josh quickly crossed the space between them, his hand extended.

'I see you're here to document events, as usual,' Howie said. Josh was a keen photographer and always had his camera at the ready.

'Of course! Howie, how are you?'

'In top form, lad. Top form.' Howie clapped the younger

man on the shoulder, and Sean came forward to shake his hand. Georgie rushed over in a mist of perfume and kissed his cheek. Josh was always welcome.

Nicki smiled a shy hello but Poppy studiously ignored him until Laura walked past her little sister and poked her with her toe. She gave an unwilling wave to acknowledge his arrival.

'Good to see you all,' Josh said, accepting a beer from Laura as he greeted them.

'How are things on the farm, Josh?' Sean asked.

He filled them in, then asked Sean about his medical studies.

'Three more exams, mate, and I'm done. Really looking forward to getting out there and practising.'

Sean had tried farming. He'd tried lots of things. The couple of years after he left school he'd spent on Nambina, but he hadn't enjoyed it and Howie had known it would only be a matter of time before his son moved on. One night, Sean was drowning his sorrows at the pub when he met a girl. Lee had been visiting in the area but would soon be travelling back to Queensland, where she lived. After an evening of laughter and companionship together, Sean took up Lee's offer to travel with her.

Two days later, they were on their way.

'Only as friends,' Sean had said. 'Be good to have company.'

Howie had nodded knowingly.

It was only supposed to be a twelve-month travelling holiday. But a year turned into five—and parenthood.

When Sean arrived home with a babe in arms, not once, he said later, had Howie admonished him or given him a hard time. Howie just helped care for Laura, making sure Sean found his feet.

The only time Howie showed any anger was when Sean explained that Lee had made it clear she didn't want the child. Couldn't handle being a mother, she'd said.

Sean told Laura that Howie's disgust had been palpable, and there had been times they had both wished his mother, who'd died years before, had been alive to help. 'We just coped the best we could,' Sean said. 'And we wouldn't have had it any other way.'

Sean began working on Nambina again, and Laura grew up in and out of the sheep yards and paddocks. She'd loved every moment. Sean, however, had spent the time attempting to find the passion Howie had for the land, for the stock, for wool, and for crops. But it just wasn't there. Instead, he found Georgie and took solace in her arms.

Finally, six years ago, he'd plucked up the courage to leave, and leave for good.

Howie had been unsurprised by Sean and Georgie's move to Adelaide. But what had astonished him was his middle-aged son going back to study medicine. Sean had thrived on the adrenalin and frenetic pace of his prac time in Emergency. Having finally found his niche, he knew he had made the best decision of his life.

It had caused much gossip around the community, but Howie had been steadfast in his support of, and belief in, his son. He understood that living on the land without loving it was no living at all.

Laura had been in year eleven when Sean and Georgie moved. She was settled in a school bus routine—it was only fifteen minutes to the local school, which gave her plenty of study *and* Nambina time. With Howie as much a father figure as Sean, they all knew she wouldn't be going anywhere! Laura was as allergic to the city as Poppy was to the country.

'Well, now we're all here,' Howie began, 'some of you will be wondering why. You shouldn't be. It's been too long since we were together.' He frowned over his glasses at Sean, who grinned sheepishly and held his hands up in mock surrender.

'So, let's sit down and I'll explain after we've had lunch. Laura, can you serve?'

'I'll help.' Georgie and Nicki spoke in unison and followed Laura into the kitchen. Poppy didn't move.

Grabbing the oven mitts, Laura opened the oven door and pulled out plates she'd dished up earlier. Steam rose from the roast lamb and vegetables.

'That's Papa's, Dad's and Josh's,' she directed, before picking up a couple herself.

As the family ate, the conversation was upbeat and the laughter loud, but Laura could feel an expectation hanging over the table. What would Howie be announcing? As she swallowed her last mouthful, she felt Josh's hand on her leg. It slid towards her thigh.

Hoping it wasn't obvious, she carefully moved her hand under the table and grabbed Josh's, holding on tight, with a not-now shake of her head. She gazed ahead, ignoring him as best she could. She wasn't embarrassed by his show of affection, just too wound up.

Her fingers strayed to her stomach and she let them rest there for the briefest of moments. Then, realising everyone had finished, she jumped up and began to clear the dishes. It was hard to stay still.

When everyone was seated again, Howie tapped on his

wine glass with his fork. The family quieted immediately; Papa commanded respect. Grasping his walking stick, he struggled to his feet, refusing help from his son.

'Nambina has been in our family for three generations,' he said. 'Despite droughts and fires, too much and too little rain, we've prospered and gone forward.'

There was a quiet 'click' and Laura looked around to see Josh taking a photo.

Howie ignored him. 'Good management,' he continued, 'is part of the key to staying viable in today's farming world, as is marketing and production levels and many other buzz words I don't understand.' He smiled and Laura looked down at the table, grinning too. They'd had this conversation only two days earlier.

'And I believe, no matter how much you love something, there's no point in outstaying your welcome.' He paused and Laura's head snapped up. She drew in a quick breath. 'It's time to pass it all on to someone who has as much passion and drive as I did when I was young.'

Howie's watery eyes fixed firmly on Laura and she felt a rush of heat to her cheeks.

'Would you care to finish, son?'

Laura turned to look at her dad.

Sean cleared his throat and stood up. 'Laura, we know how much you love farming and Nambina. It's that sort of love I have never understood or had, and it's why today we are passing the reins of it over to you, darling girl. Howie will still live in the house, but the farm's yours to run as you see fit. Of course, we'll keep an eye on the cheque book!' He chuckled. 'Dad, Georgie and I believe you are destined for greatness within the ag industry. After all, you've achieved so much already. Look at the Young Farmers' Association that you've overhauled and got pumping! It's just the tip of the iceberg.' He paused, smiling at her, his face glowing with pride. 'You've got an incredible career in front of you and we can't wait to watch and see what happens and where it ends up.'

Laura sat still, eyes wide, unable to think of a word to say. Her whole family was watching, waiting to see her reaction. She opened her mouth. Shut it. Opened it again and said: 'Uh . . .'

The table erupted with laughter.

'It's not often you're speechless, Laura,' Georgie said above the noise.

'I think you'll agree, there is no one better suited,' Sean finished.

Chatter broke out but Laura couldn't distinguish what was being said. She felt Howie's rough hand patting hers. Her stepmother was smiling at her from the other side of the table and her sisters whispering to each other, throwing weird glances at her. Her stomach heaved a little as she rubbed it gently. Would Papa have made the same decision if he'd known she was pregnant? Sure, Sean had brought home an illegitimate daughter, but that was Howie's *son*—it was different for boys. The woman always got judged, not the bloke. She banished the notion. Of course he would have made the same decision!

She turned towards Josh, who leant forward to kiss her.

'Let's raise our glasses to Laura and the new era of Nambina,' Sean said.

Josh jumped to his feet and began to take photos.

'I, uh, I don't know what to say.' Laura turned to Howie, her cheeks red and her face taut with anxiety.

12

'You don't have to say anything. We already know your answer.'

Laura had to look away. Howie's smile showed how proud he was of her. How excited he seemed to be at this new venture, and she should be too. This was all she'd ever wanted. To be on Nambina, to run it as well as she could, to learn and improve things. To be a leader.

Howie and Sean understood her drive and passion and had just granted Laura her dream.

The problem was, she didn't know if she was up to it now.

∽

As the day's light faded, Laura walked Josh out to his ute. The rain had stopped, but the breeze still came in bursts. Laura's arms were crossed over her chest, trying to ward off the chill.

She looked towards the shearing shed and further on, to the grazing land. Nambina was red gum country and despite being reasonably flat, the loamy soil ensured it was well drained. When the season broke, strawberry clover and rye grasses grew in abundance and the large gum trees dotted throughout the paddocks stood tall and proud. In the distance, on a hill, the crumbling mansion of the disused asylum stood alone and empty, making Laura shiver.

'Well, that was unexpected,' Josh said, standing by the door of the ute. He reached out, slipping his arms around her waist and holding her tightly.

Laura smiled up at Josh and ran her hand over her long hair, trying to stop it from whipping around their faces. 'You're telling me.' She turned into the bitter wind, thankful for the coolness on her burning cheeks.

'Aren't you pleased? I was sure you'd be jumping for joy.' He put his cold hand on her face, keeping the other one firmly on her hips and kissed her. Then he let her go.

Laura touched the place on her lips where his had just been. 'It's just really taken me by surprise. I . . .' She stopped and ran her finger over the chrome badge on the side of the ute, trying to work out what to say next.

'Come on, Laurs. It's a great opportunity. I can't think of anyone else who would just get a farm handed to them.' He tilted his head meaningfully.

'I know.' She straightened her shoulders and looked him in the eye, knowing he had mistaken her hesitation for being daunted at the prospect. 'Josh,' she started, but he had already rushed on.

'You'll be able to buy some of those White Suffolk rams you and Meghan have been talking about. Man, won't she be pleased! She's always been so proud of you. As am I.' He kissed her again. 'And Catherine. She'll be happy too. I can just see you all dreaming and scheming.' He smiled at her and ran his fingers over her cheek. 'Be happy about it, not scared. It's a challenge!' Opening the ute door, he climbed in and wound the window down.

Laura gathered her hair into an untidy bun at the nape of her neck. She needed to tell him now.

'I got some great photos today. I'll get you some prints made.'

Right now.

Before he left.

Laura tried to form the words but her voice remained stubbornly quiet, the words stuck in her head.

'Come here,' Josh said, gently tugging on her wayward hair to pull her to him. 'Congratulations, baby,' he muttered against her lips. 'You deserve this. See you soon.'

Laura tucked her arms around her stomach as he started the engine and gave the accelerator a couple of jabs. The V8 rumbled.

'Josh, I really need to talk to you.' But between the wind stealing her words and the noise of the engine, she knew she hadn't been heard. The ute jumped forward and Josh drove away down the dirt road.

As the sound of the vehicle faded into the distance, the sun showed its face for the first time that day. A crimson ray shot through the cloud and reflected off the shearing shed roof.

Laura stood and watched, confusion whirling within her. She still wasn't convinced she could manage everything, even with Josh by her side. So where did that leave her?

Chapter 2

2000

'Doctors! Surely it can't be *that* hard to keep appointment times! I mean, really, we all have lives and things to do.' Meghan raised her coffee cup to her lips and stared at Laura over the rim.

They were sitting in a cafe on the main street of Mangalow while Meghan waited to see a doctor at the surgery across the road.

'You, being a nurse and all, would understand the delays, wouldn't you?' Laura asked mildly. 'Aren't there times when one patient needs attention more urgently than another? Maybe that's what's happening at the moment.' She took another sip of her water and felt her phone vibrate. Talking and reaching for it at the same time, she continued: 'Anyway, it's given us a chance to catch up. I'm not sure when I'll be able to get a spare hour again. You should see my diary!' She looked at the number and saw there was a message. She dialled into her message bank.

Meghan was quiet for a moment. 'Gah! I know you're right. I'm just nervous. Impatient,' she said finally.

Laura giggled. 'You? Not possible.' She shook her head to emphasise her words.

Meghan broke into laughter and punched her gently on the arm. 'I need another coffee. Do you want one?'

'I'm fine with the water,' Laura said. The truth was, she was having trouble keeping even *that* down. Just the thought of coffee made her almost dry retch.

Meghan squinted at her. 'Why, aren't you drinking coffee? You live on the stuff.'

Laura held her hand up, listening to the message on her phone. She took her diary out of her bag and started to take notes. When the message ended, Laura stayed on the phone for a few moments, more in the hope that Meghan would go and order and forget her question.

But Meghan had gone nowhere. Laura looked at her notes and reached for her glass again. 'Health kick,' she finally answered.

Meghan snorted. 'Why? You're almost too skinny as it is.'

Laura changed the subject. 'Can you believe this? You know Neil, the president of the Young Farmers' Association? He's changed the meeting time again! How can I plan anything if he keeps changing when it's supposed to be! It's so frustrating.' She stood up. 'You order. I'm going to the loo. Be back in a sec.'

'Ha! You were just saying that sometimes things crop up,' Meghan said to Laura's back as she walked towards the restrooms. 'Now it's your turn to take a chill pill!'

Pushing open the door into the stall, Laura flipped the lid

down and sank onto the seat. With her head in her hands, she tried to fight the tears, but they were threatening to spill over. She really didn't care that the meeting had been postponed. She was trying to stop her best friend from finding out she was pregnant to her brother, trying to keep up appearances and act as if nothing was wrong. As if nothing had changed in her life. That she was grabbing the opportunity of Nambina with both hands and going for it.

But things had changed. The mixed-up, churned-up sick feeling never left her, no matter the time of day, and the need to tell someone was overwhelming.

Laura didn't understand why she still hadn't told Josh, and she knew she couldn't tell anyone before she told him. Not even Meghan. Taking a deep breath, she wiped her runny nose on a piece of toilet paper and dabbed at her eyes. She couldn't go back out like this. Meghan would know something was wrong for sure.

She stood up and threw back her shoulders. 'You're going to have to get a handle on yourself,' she told herself.

Catherine's voice entered her head as Laura imagined what she'd say if she knew about the baby. 'Cowgirl up, honeybunch. It's all good! You're fine. But maybe tell him today, huh?'

She thought of her practical, lovely friend. They'd met at a field day, eight years before, and bonded over the muddy plot of barley they were learning about. The energy changed when Catherine walked into a room. Her positive attitude and refusal to see a setback as a bad thing were just two of the things Laura loved about her. Catherine's dream was to bridge the gap between city and country by teaching the farming community how to communicate with their city cousins about their jobs, treatment of animals and producing food. She was the most likely person to succeed whom Laura had ever known.

Finally she splashed water on her face and went out into the café. Josh was sitting in her seat, breakfast in front of him, and she smiled without thinking. She walked over quickly and put her hands over his eyes.

'Hey there, sexy,' Josh said. It was their standard greeting.

She leaned forward and kissed him on the head then sat down in the spare chair. 'Hi, yourself. What're you doing in town?'

'Came to pick up some drench for the ewes. Found barber's pole in one mob. Took the opportunity to pick up some of the photos I took at lunch the other day. I've got them in the ute for you.' He shovelled the bacon and egg sandwich into his mouth. 'Have you been around your ewes?'

She nodded. 'I'm not surprised. I'd been thinking the conditions were pretty perfect for that type of worm. But we're all good.' She turned to Meghan. 'Have they rung yet?'

Meghan shook her head. 'Still waiting.'

Laura really hoped this new doctor would be able to pinpoint what was causing the crippling pain her friend was suffering in the pelvic area. The last doctor had put it down to a urinary tract infection. Laura was sure it was something more serious. Whatever it was, it needed to be sorted out. Meghan had been worrying about herself so much it was affecting her mood. Usually cheerful, she had become despondent and seemed unable to see the good in things.

Josh reached over and patted his half-sister's hand. 'I know this new bloke will get to the bottom of it,' he said gently. 'Laurs was right to suggest you go.'

Meghan nodded and was about to speak when Laura's phone vibrated again. Laura looked at the number and excused herself. 'Hi, Jim,' she said, walking out onto the street.

'Laura,' the president of the Rural Action Group said. It was yet another committee Laura was involved with. 'I've had an email from a cropping organisation in Western Australia wanting to tour our area. You in?'

'When is it and what do they want to see?' she asked.

'Next year, June-ish. Crops mostly.' Jim spoke in short sharp bursts—she could tell he was excited. 'They're making a trip of it. Coming over on a bus, stopping off on the west coast, detouring down the east peninsula, footy in Adelaide and then down our way.'

'I'm in, if they want to look over Nambina, but we don't have a lot of crop.'

'That's fine. I'll write you down. And Laura?' he paused. 'They've invited us back there in July. Be a brilliant opportunity to forge some good contacts.'

'Yeah,' she agreed, but her heart sank. By then she'd have a tiny baby to care for. There was no way she'd be able to go.

'Catch you later.'

Laura walked back into the café just as Meghan stood up. 'The surgery just rang. There's only one patient in front of me now,' Meghan said to Laura's questioning look.

Laura held out her arms. 'I hope it all goes as well as it can.' She hugged Meghan tight. Josh stepped up and put his arms around both of them.

'It'll be fine,' he murmured into their hair.

They broke apart and Laura could see Meghan had tears in her eyes. Impulsively she grabbed Meghan's hand. 'Do you want me to come with you? I can ring Neil and put our meeting off for an hour or so. It's only the two of us, anyway. He won't mind. He's already changed the time twice. I don't think it will matter if I do, as well.'

Meghan shook her head. 'No, I'll be okay. This is something I need to do myself. But thanks.' With a look of apprehension on her face, she left the café.

Laura and Josh watched her cross the street.

'I hope they find out what's wrong,' Laura said softly. 'I'm beginning to worry.' She pulled out her diary and wrote a reminder to ring Meghan the following day.

'Me too,' Josh answered.

Laura felt her emotions begin to get the better of her again and grabbed Josh's hand. 'Come on, I've got something to tell you,' she said, dragging him towards the door.

As they walked out onto the street, Laura noticed that Josh seemed angry.

'What's wrong?' she asked as they walked to his ute, where he handed over the photos. Laura stuffed them into her back pocket and they headed towards the park.

'Nothing,' he answered shortly.

Laura raised her eyebrows. 'Doesn't sound like nothing,' she countered.

'Who was on the phone to you?'

'Which call?' Laura asked, forgetting he hadn't been there for the first one.

'The one you just answered. How many did you get before I arrived?'

'Oh, that was Jim. Jim Munday. You know, the president of the Rural Action Group. Feels like the phone hasn't stopped today. I don't think I'd be able to remember everything without my diary.'

They reached the park and stood beneath a large tree. Laura didn't know what kind of tree it was, but she knew that the same trees grew around the house on Nambina. When she was a kid, Sean had shown her how to pick the pods and stuff them with painted cotton wool. They looked like robin red breasts and he'd taught her a nursery rhyme: 'Little Robin Redbreast sat upon a tree'. They'd used the seed pods as Christmas decorations.

I'll be able to do that when this little one is born. All at once, she was baffled by her reasoning, which seemed to turn 180 degrees at any given moment. Just this morning she'd been thinking again about terminating the pregnancy.

'I think he's got his eye on you,' Josh said, turning to face her.

'What?' Laura didn't understand what he was saying.

'Jim. He's got the hots for you.'

Laura was silent, not sure where the conversation was heading. 'So what?' She shrugged. 'I don't have for him. Anyway, I'm sure you're wrong. He's never given me any sign that he has.'

'You shouldn't put yourself in situations where people can get the wrong idea.' Josh folded his arms, staring at her intently.

'I'm not!' Inexplicably, tears welled up. 'How dare you, Josh Hunter!' She turned away.

'You are.' Josh persisted. 'He rings you and you answer. Talking to him, sitting with him at meetings. You should be distancing yourself from him.'

Anger flared now. 'And how do you propose I do that? He's

the president and I'm the bloody secretary. It's pretty normal we should have conversations. I can't believe you're even thinking like this.'

'Well, I am. And you need to listen to me. I can see how it looks to everyone else. And I've seen how he looks at you. I'm sure you don't want to be the talk of the town.' Josh stuck out his chin and Laura had the unexpected urge to hit him.

'If you don't trust me, Josh, why are you going out with me?' She stared straight into his eyes.

'I trust you, but I don't trust Jim. The best thing to do is take yourself away from the situation.'

'This is ridiculous,' Laura exploded. 'The whole conversation is bloody stupid. You sound just like your mother!' A thought struck her. 'Oh,' she nodded her head, 'that's where all this is coming from. Glenda. She doesn't like me. Never has.' Josh's stepmother had all kinds of pretensions. Who knew what the socialite farmer's wife thought of their relationship? Laura crossed her arms. 'Let me tell you, I don't care what the town thinks about me and I really don't care what your mother thinks. I'm not resigning from my position just because she doesn't approve.' She began to walk away.

'Laura! I didn't mean for us to fight,' Josh called.

'Well, I don't know where you thought the conversation was heading, bringing up that sort of rubbish. I have to go. I have things to do.' She looked over her shoulder with disbelief on her face. 'When you're ready to apologise, call me.'

'Me? Apologise for what?'

Laura didn't answer. She kept walking back to her ute. She put her handbag on the roof of the car and dug her keys out of her pocket. Forgetting her bag, she drove off, her cheeks red with anger. At some point on the journey home her bag blew off the ute roof. It wasn't until she got home to Nambina that she realised what had happened, and that her precious diary had also gone for good.

∾

'Come on, Laurs! If you don't get off that farm, you're going to turn into a sheep.' Meghan always overstated things. That's just the way she was.

Laura laughed. 'Don't be dense! Anyway, I was at the Young Farmers' meeting a couple of nights ago. I'm still going out, not welded to the yards just yet.'

'But tomorrow's Friday. You've got to come to the pub. We always go.'

'I know, I know, but I'm just so tired, Meghan. I really need an early night.' In all honesty Laura couldn't think of anything worse than going to a smoke-filled, beer-smelling, yahooing pub. Even with her best friend. And how would she explain not drinking?

Meghan lowered her voice and Laura imagined her friend glancing around to make sure her mother wasn't about. Laura now had a clear idea how Glenda felt about her relationship with Josh, and it wasn't good. She'd obviously been in Meghan and Josh's ear.

Howie had implied as much when Laura, ashen faced, told him about her argument with Josh in the park.

'Doesn't sound like the Josh I know,' he'd said. 'What's got into him? Or *who* has?'

'That's not the point. How could he stand there and accuse me of something I haven't done?' Laura had fumed.

With a little placating Howie had managed to calm her, but Laura still felt uneasy. Something wasn't right. The two phone calls she'd had with Josh since had been stilted and she wasn't sure she could forget it until he apologised.

Now Meghan was talking in hushed tones down the line. 'Josh is worried about you, and I am too,' she said. 'You're so tired all the time. Josh said you overreacted to something he said last week and you look pale. Are you sick?'

Laura ignored the jibe about her so-called overreaction and closed her eyes, wishing with all her might she could tell Meghan. That she could halve the load. In fact, she got as far as opening her mouth before stopping herself again. Josh had to know first.

'I'm fine,' she said. 'Just a little rundown. After all, it's not just the farm, it's all the other things I'm involved in.' She took the opportunity to change the subject. 'Did you know I'm on five different committees? I counted them.'

'Don't doubt it.'

'I've been trying to arrange to get Catherine back down here. She runs empowering and communications courses for women now. But she's so hard to pin down. So busy! I'd love to be able to do something like that, wouldn't you?'

'Not really, Laura.' Meghan determinedly turned the topic back to what she wanted to talk about. 'You haven't even got time for Josh or me these days.' Her tone was whiny, laced with reproach.

Laura sighed inwardly and rubbed her forehead. Lord, she was exhausted and the gruelling schedule she had created for herself since she took over Nambina hadn't helped. Of course, neither had the little one inside her. The doctor had, in a loving way, described an unborn baby as a 'parasite'—a being that leaches all the goodness out of its mother. Apparently it wasn't unusual to feel the way she did.

As much as she loved Meghan, there was no doubt she was needy at times. Today, Laura wasn't sure she had the energy. 'Look, how about we have a lunch at Nambina on Sunday? I've got an Agricultural Society meeting in the morning, but I'll be home by eleven.' She hesitated. 'Well, that's if Jason hasn't had another fabulous idea that needs ten hours of discussion, as he usually does.' Laura tried to remember what was in the freezer. 'I'll do a roast in the Weber.'

There was a pause. 'I'd like that. I . . .' Meghan broke off. 'I need to talk to you.'

Irrational fear shot through Laura as she wondered if there was any way Meghan could know she was pregnant. She was a nurse, after all. Maybe she'd noticed *something*.

'What's up?' Laura said.

'I've finally got a diagnosis.'

'Oh hell, Meghan. What a bloody awful friend I've been. I forgot to ring you and ask. Damn, I don't know how that happened. I'm so sorry. I've been so caught up in my own stuff, I completely forgot that you'd been to see that doctor.'

In fact, Laura knew exactly why she'd forgotten—the argument with Josh and the fact she'd lost her diary. When she arrived home and realised what had happened, she'd spent the rest of the day buying a new phone and trying to track down what meetings she had over the next month. It had been a nightmare.

Josh hadn't thought to mention Meghan in either of their conversations, either.

'What did Dr Jones say?' she asked gently.

'He's pretty sure I've got endometriosis.' Meghan's voice cracked and Laura listened as her friend took a breath before going on. 'They've got to do more tests, but he's just about certain I can't have children.' Meghan sniffled. 'You know how much I love kids—that's why I trained as a paediatric nurse. It's why I help at the kindy on my days off. I couldn't wait to have my own, when I met the right guy, Laurs. And now, maybe I can't.' Her voice broke.

Laura choked down a gasp.

Chapter 3

2000

It was always amazing to Laura how quickly the weather could change. When she'd risen, the sun, still below the horizon, was throwing crimson rays on the leaden clouds. There were patches of blue and a hope that the day would see the clouds lift.

'Red sky in the morning, shepherds' warning,' she'd said to herself as she glanced uneasily around the sky. 'What will today hold?'

It would hold a new beginning, she'd decided. She'd spoken with Josh the previous evening, both of them concerned about how Meghan was taking the news of her diagnosis. They'd also made plans to catch up that evening, and she was determined, this time, to break the news to Josh, whatever happened.

Now the wind had picked up, the blue sky was hidden by clouds and a light rain was falling. Laura squelched through the sheep yards, her rubber boots sticking. She wasn't complaining, though. Howie always said there was money in mud, not in dust. There was definitely some mud this season.

Laura climbed up onto the loading ramp, and spotted Rusty, the dark red cat, silently regarding the movement in the yards from a dry spot under a bush. They were the only farmers she knew of who had a yard cat instead of a yard dog. Rusty chose to walk behind the sheep as they were being brought into the yards, casually winding his way from one side of the mob to the other, just as a sheep dog would. It made Laura laugh every time she saw it.

She'd found Rusty as a tiny kitten, eyes barely open, in the middle of the yards during a hot summer's day. The kitten's mother was nowhere in sight. Feeling sorry for the tiny creature, Laura had taken him home and cared for him. But there was a built-in wildness in Rusty's little frame and he'd fought her, not wanting to be confined inside the house.

As he grew, there had been days he'd disappeared and nights he hadn't returned, and Laura had feared he'd been bitten by a snake or injured somehow. But, like a homing pigeon, Rusty always reappeared and in time they came to an arrangement that suited them both. He never slept in the house and Laura stopped trying to encourage him. She knew now he lived in one of the sheds, and would always turn up at the sheep yards whenever there was work to be done.

'Hello, Rusty,' she called now. She smiled when she saw how the cat ignored her, looking away to wash his paw. 'Hello to you, my life saver,' she said, her sarcasm evident.

She whistled to her black and white border collie, Dash, and called him to heel. The ewe lambs were skittish today and pushing them hard would make them worse.

'You won't ignore me today, will you?' she asked the dog. 'Come on, come behind, Dash.' She leaned against the fence, trying to catch her breath. 'Don't reckon we'll need you much today, mate. Not that you're much good in the yards. The paddock is more your style, hey? Now, go and sit down.'

She was still feeling squeamish from breakfast and the morning sickness was getting harder to hide. Her usual coffee routine had changed to a cup of tea—if, in fact, she could stomach anything at all—and her choice of beverage to accompany her nightly discussion with Howie had gone from a glass of wine to an iced tea.

And she was so tired. So tired.

If he was aware anything was different, Howie wasn't letting on. But she'd caught him looking at her with concern this morning as, pale faced, she'd tried to walk calmly from the kitchen to the toilet, when she really needed to run. He must suspect something, she thought.

In a rush of clattering hooves, the ewes pushed down the raceway and squashed up against each other. Clanging the gate shut behind them, Laura leaned over to inspect the first one. Using her thumb and pointer finger, she parted the wool on the sheep's hip and looked at the crimps. Brushing it back together, she repeated the process in three other spots of the fleece and gave the animal a once-over. Good feet, no under-shot jaw. The ewe needed to have a good size and frame about her.

She ran her hand over the head, checking for the layout of the wool. If there was a chance crutching would be late, she didn't want any of them getting wool blindness.

'I reckon this one's a keeper,' she said to Dash, who was now curled up out of the wind.

She moved on to the next ewe and the next. By the time

she had reached the last one, there were only two culls with red marks on their heads.

Glancing at the four hundred sheep she still had to check, she unchained the gate. She'd have to work more quickly. She gave a short, high whistle, then waited for Dash to hunt the ewes. The dog barked and, with a leap, the flighty animals charged towards the opening.

'Whoa there, you lot. Settle down,' she muttered.

Concentrating, and looking for the redheads, she counted the ewes as they ran towards her and within moments there were none left. The two culls were drafted off into a smaller yard and the others milled around in a larger one, sniffing each other and calling for their mates.

Laura turned around and started all over again. With only fifty or so left, she finally had a break and drank deeply from her water bottle. She closed her eyes, trying to rest for a moment. She felt Rusty wind his way around her legs.

'Oh, feeling social now, are you?' she asked, reaching down to pat him. Her smile widened as his purr started and his eyes shut. Her fingers traced his chin and cheek, and she marvelled that an animal could be so soft. She took her hand away and stretched, back aching. Rusty reached up onto her calf with his two front legs and dug in his claws.

She let out a squeal. 'Ow! Rusty, don't *do* that.' Laura pushed the cat away.

With a haughty look, Rusty leapt onto the yard rails and stalked off. 'Yeah, well, if you weren't so bloody nasty . . .' she began and felt a cold, wet nose touching her hand. She looked down to see Dash's eyes, one blue and one brown, staring at her.

'Glad you haven't got claws like that.'

He pushed at her again.

Automatically, she touched the flat spot between his ears. 'Jealous, are you? Need a pat?' She looked across the yards. 'We're not doing too badly here. I reckon there're only about forty culls out of four hundred and fifty. I'm happy with that. Those new rams Papa and I bought from Sharpe's last year have pulled this breeding program into line.'

Dash didn't say anything.

Laura laughed quietly as she looked at the bliss on his face. 'I wish I had your worries, Dash-a-dog. Only caring where your next feed or pat comes from. You think you'll be able to babysit for me, later? Tell me if the baby is crying?'

She looked across the green paddocks and saw the misty shadow of another light rain shower approaching. She pushed herself off the fence. 'And while we're talking about it, have you got any idea how I'm going to tell the three most important men in my life?' She stared down at him. 'Okay, sorry. Four, but you already know. Come on, let's finish up before we get wet.' She looked around and saw that the cat had well and truly disappeared. 'And that's probably the last we'll see of Rusty today, so I won't be telling him.'

The clanking of the chain on the iron gate scared the last of the sheep and they piled on top of one another against the fence.

'Man, you guys are feral,' she muttered. Turning to the dog, she raised her voice. 'Get out, Dashy. Out of the yards. I don't think we need any extra force.'

Dash barked loudly, ignoring her instructions.

'Shut up!'

Quietly she walked back along the fence, reaching down to turn their heads with her hands. One ewe saw the narrow race and cantered towards it, taking her friends with her. Laura pushed the last one in with her knee and shut the gate, yanking the chain hard.

'Must be the weather,' she said, as the pitter-patter of rain started on the tin roof covering the raceway.

Laura grabbed the red rattle from her pocket and marked a ewe with an undershot jaw. Startled at the force, the ewe reared up, planting its two front feet on the animal in front of it. The ewe's head had caught Laura under her jaw and the thump of skull on bone made her see double for a moment. She let out a screech. Tears welled and she grabbed at her head.

'Bloody hell!' she gasped, trying to shake the pain in her teeth away. 'Bitch!' She turned away from the race and stood still until the pain had eased slightly.

She had to keep going, even though the throbbing was still there. Only another eight ewes and she'd be finished. Cranky at being hurt and unable to yell without her head ringing, she yanked opened the gate and gestured to Dash. 'Go back. Fetch 'em up.'

The sheep started to run. *Nine, ten, eleven*, she counted. Laura saw the red mark and waited until it was nearly at the end of the race, then pulled the drafting gate across to make the ewe run out into the other pen.

Realising her escape route had been closed off, the ewe began to slow down, her feet sliding along the ground. And then she jumped. She'd tried to clear the barrier and follow her mates, but the ewe jumped straight into Laura's stomach, knocking her flat on the ground.

The next thing Laura knew, Dash's warm body was curled up next to her and Rusty was sitting heavily on her chest, his rough tongue licking her chin.

And there was a cramping agony rippling through her abdomen.

Chapter 4

1937

Thomas breathed heavily against the cold air that had snuck into the enclosed verandah between the glass louvres. He touched the spot on his cheek where, only hours before, his father had smashed his fist. Gently he rubbed at it, trying to brush away the pain and all the emotion that went with it.

Staring down at the man who was supposed to love and protect his children, Thomas could feel nothing but hatred. Ernest lay across the sun lounge, mouth wide open, large belly shuddering with each alcohol-infused breath. A pig-like snort came from his nose.

Near the sun lounge stood an old and nearly dead pot plant. Thomas loved that plant. It was the only thing belonging to his mother that his father hadn't destroyed when she left, and Thomas had done his best to keep it lush and green. He hadn't done a very good job.

As Thomas checked his rucksack, Ernest rolled over before falling off the couch and onto the floor. The snoring stopped for a moment and so did the boy, terrified. Then it started again. Even louder than before.

Thomas closed his eyes briefly and made a hurried inventory of what he had grabbed from the room he shared with his brother. He was taking very little, but not because he was travelling light. He didn't have much to take. Just a few clothes, some food from the pantry and the chain his mother had given him. It was wrapped up tightly, right at the bottom of the bag.

Thomas glanced again at the lump of a man and knew he wouldn't move any time soon. This scene had played out many times before. The boy felt sick with revulsion: it made him tremble, made his stomach roll, made him want to hold a pillow over that ugly, bearded face and put a stop to everything. He shook himself. There was no place for those sorts of thoughts.

Placing the bag on the floor behind the pot plant where it wouldn't be seen if Ernest did wake, Thomas knew this was it. There was no time, no options left.

He went into the bedroom, where Howard was asleep on a thin mattress. Leaving his younger brother was his only regret. With just a year between them, he knew it might be only a matter of time before Howard made the same decision Thomas had made tonight.

The brothers' argument the day before removed some of the guilt Thomas felt for leaving him on his own. To maybe become their father's punching bag.

Deep within him, Thomas harboured a hope that his brother might just be okay. Howard didn't look like their mother, not the way Thomas did. Up until now, it had given

36

his younger brother some kind of protection against Ernest's beatings and sharp, cutting tongue.

'Take care, mate,' he muttered as he shoved an envelope under the bedding. Thomas had saved hard for the pound note that was inside, along with a letter.

Howard didn't move.

With a final glance over his shoulder, Thomas went into the hallway and stood in front of the grandfather clock.

Tick-tock, tick-tock. It was mesmerising.

'I'll be back,' his mother had said right on this very spot three years earlier. 'As soon as I can. Keep this and know, *know* I will be back for my boys.' Jessie had pushed the silver necklace into his hand and closed his fingers around it, kissing him and then his little brother.

There were days when Thomas thought the necklace still felt warm, the way it had been when his mother had pulled it from her neck. And when he closed his eyes he still could see every movement of that day: how they had stood there, silent and watching, as Jessie picked up her suitcase, pulled the front door shut behind her, walked down the path and got into the waiting vehicle.

Thomas had never seen a car so flash. And he'd never seen such kindness as the driver showed his mother. The driver had stood next to the car and held the back door open for her. When settled at the steering wheel, he'd leaned over the seat to offer her a handkerchief before grating the gears and leaving with a jerk.

Despite her promises, her reassurances, Thomas's mother had never returned. He was sure she wasn't alive. She couldn't be, because if she were, Jessie would have moved hell and high water to come home to her boys.

Why had she left them with this violent man in the first place? Thomas had so many questions.

The clock chimed two and broke his reverie. A grunt from Ernest was all he needed to spur him on. It was time to go.

The door closed with a click. Thomas moved into the night, stopping only to pat Flea, who was straining at the end of his chain.

'Sorry, you old mongrel. You can't come. Howard'll look out for you.'

The darkness was waiting, so he set off without looking back at the house that held both sweet and bitter memories. 'Every scar has a story,' he muttered, gently touching his cheek once again. 'And there won't be any more from him.'

∽

Thomas pulled his meagre coat tightly around him. There really wasn't any point; he was wet through. The shelter from the broad gum tree only broke the wind. It didn't stop the sleeting rain or the cold drips that fell from the leaves when there was a break in the weather.

It had been only a day since he left Nambina and already the autumn weather had turned nasty. The weather in the south-east of South Australia could be like that. Fine one day and incredibly horrible the next.

Still, he had not once questioned his decision to leave—not that he had got far at this point. He was free of his father, and being wet and cold was better than being beaten, he told himself.

He glanced over his shoulder. Behind him he could just make out the asylum, a brooding pile barely visible in the darkness.

What if there was an escapee on the loose? He shivered, from fear this time. It was scary enough being so near the gloomy building, let alone coming face to face with one of its inmates.

He peeked around the tree to see if there were any cars coming. Someone would surely take pity on him.

Finally, he saw two pinpricks in the darkness. Headlights. Taking a breath against the biting cold, he walked onto the road and stuck out his thumb. 'Please,' he prayed. 'Please, please stop.'

The car pulled up and the passenger's door was flung open.

A man in his forties peered from the driver's seat, his brow creased with concern. 'What are you doing out here, young man? Get in, get in! Goodness me, you'll catch your death.'

'Thank you, sir, thank you,' Thomas gasped as he scrambled inside. He was hit with a blast of warm air and within moments, his cold fingers and cheeks started to burn as the blood surged back into them.

The man reached over the seat and handed Thomas a towel. 'Dry yourself with that, lad. What's your name?'

'Thomas, sir.'

'Now then, Thomas. Where're you off to on such a miserable night?'

Thomas looked at the man's flushed cheeks and kind face, and clenched his jaw. 'Away,' he answered.

From the corner of his eye, he saw the man's gaze rest on the fading bruise.

'I see. Will anyone be missing you?'

'No.' The word pushed from his mouth as he banished his brother's memory from his mind. 'No,' he repeated, softly this time.

'Right.' The man stared at Thomas for a moment, then pushed the column gear into first and let out the clutch.

The car smelt like lanoline and sheep, and as Thomas's clothes and hair started to dry under the hot air blowing from the vents, the air grew humid.

After half an hour of silence, Thomas's rescuer spoke again. 'Looking for work, then?'

'Yes, sir, I am. Do you know of any?'

'You'd better call me Mac. What can you do?'

'I grew up on a farm. I can turn my hand to most things.'

'Ah, a jack of all trades and master of none.'

Thomas nodded, face expressionless. His mother had often used that turn of phrase. 'Yes, sir.'

'Mac,' the man reiterated. He lifted one arm up above his head in a stretch.

Instinctively, Thomas raised his shoulders and hands to ward off the blow, then, realising it wasn't coming, tried to relax.

Mac eyed him briefly. He lowered his arm and tapped on the steering wheel for a moment or two. 'Must be your lucky day, Thomas,' he said. 'I'm on my way north to a shearing shed. Wool classer, by trade. You can come with me and learn the ways of the shed. The pay isn't much, but it'll be enough for you, for the time being.'

Thomas's stomach constricted. There was compassion in the man's voice and the boy hardly dared believe what he had just heard. There must be a catch. He waited to hear what it was.

'Well? What do you say?' Mac asked, turning in his seat to look at him.

'Yes,' Thomas answered, with the ghost of a smile. 'Yes, please. Thank you.'

Mac laughed and reached across to clap his shoulder, but quickly withdrew his hand when Thomas flinched. 'Here's to new beginnings, mate,' he said.

'New beginnings,' Thomas echoed, wondering how he got so lucky.

Chapter 5

2000

Within a few minutes the cramping agony in her stomach began to subside and Laura managed to drag herself upright and hang on to the rails.

At the same time, her hands were on her belly, trying to feel the baby. Gently touching, poking, prodding. She knew it was a silly thing to do. There was no way the baby would be big enough to feel, but she had to do something.

Her breath quickened as another strong pain hit her. Grasping the rails, she steadied herself. After a few slow calculated breaths it passed.

'Don't panic,' she counselled herself. 'Just breathe and feel.'

With her eyes closed, she assessed herself. There was no wetness between her legs and almost no pain now. Still hanging on to the yards, she looked around and pulled down her jeans just to make sure.

Definitely no blood.

'Lucky,' she mumbled. She took a few unsteady steps with

Dash at her heels and Rusty walking behind her. 'Think I might have a spell at home,' she said.

She managed to get to the ute and drive herself back to the house.

Howie looked up from reading the paper next to the fire, knowing something was wrong the moment he saw her. 'What?' He grabbed at his walking stick to help him to his feet. 'Laurs, what's wrong, love? Are you hurt? Let me ring the doctor.'

Laura shook her head. 'I think I'm fine. Just a bit sore. Got barrelled by one of those flighty ewe lambs.'

'Where'd she hit you?' Howie limped closer and put his hand on her shoulder.

'Stomach.'

'You haven't bled? Miscarried?'

Laura felt shock run through her. 'You know?'

'Of course I know,' he said impatiently. 'You haven't lost it, have you?'

Laura shook her head. 'I don't think so. I'm not sure, but I don't think so.'

'Not good enough. Come on, we're getting you to the doctor.'

Laura had always known her grandfather had an accelerator fetish. He liked to drive fast and today was no exception. Within ten minutes they were at the local hospital.

'You stay there, love,' he said, as he struggled out of the car and limped towards the emergency door. 'I'll get a wheelchair.'

A nurse returned with him and helped her into the chair. Quickly they wheeled her inside, all the time peppering her with questions.

'How did it happen?'

Laura told the story.

'Any pain?'

'Not now. But I had some cramping while I was still in the yards.'

'How much time has passed since?'

Laura shook her head. 'I'm not sure. Maybe an hour? Hour and a half?'

'Right. We better have a look at you. Mr Murphy, are you coming in?'

Laura could see Howie looked uncertain. He'd always been a bit that way when it came to 'women's secret business'.

He looked at the nurse and started to back away. 'No, no. She'll be in good hands with you. I'll wait in the waiting room.' He walked towards the sliding doors. 'But tell me the second there's any news.' He stopped and shook his finger at the nurse.

'Of course,' she answered.

Two hours later, the doctor still hadn't seen Laura, and Howie was ranting like an angry bull. 'Where's the bloody doctor? He needs to see my granddaughter right now. Does he know she's here?'

'Of course he does,' the receptionist answered. 'She's not in a life-threatening situation. He'll be here as soon as he can.' Her soothing voice did nothing to pacify him.

Laura, who was lying on a narrow bed shielding her eyes from the bright lights above, could hear him through the doors.

'Sorry about Papa,' she said weakly to the nurse, whose name she had learned was Gillian.

'Oh, he doesn't scare us. We get worse than him in here.'

Laura watched as Gillian squeezed clear gel onto her stomach and smoothed it around with the wand of the ultrasound machine. She waited for the nurse to say something, but she was staring at the screen intently.

Minutes passed as Gillian ran the wand around her stomach. It was soothing and Laura closed her eyes, waiting for her to speak.

But she didn't. Finally, after what seemed like hours, the movement stopped. She opened her eyes in time to see the nurse put the wand back into the holder and switch off the machine. Handing Laura a towel to wipe her stomach with, she stood up. 'Okay, well, I've got the information the doctor needs, so I'll give him a ring and tell him to come in.' She pushed a few buttons and a printout began to emerge from the machine.

'What does it say?' Laura asked tersely.

'I'm not sure how to read these,' Gillian answered, tearing off the printout and putting it in the folder marked with Laura's name. 'The doctor will tell you what it says when he comes. Are you in any pain?'

Laura shook her head.

Gillian smiled. 'Okay, well, I'll be back to do your obs in—' She checked the paperwork on the end of the bed. '—twenty or so minutes.'

'Thanks.' Laura traced her stomach with her fingers, certain the nurse knew more than she was letting on. To take her mind off the unanswered question, she kept talking to the baby in her mind. 'Come on little one, hang in there. Please hang in there.'

After a long wait, Dr Jones finally walked in.

She knew there was something wrong as soon as she saw his face.

He smiled kindly. 'Had a bit of a knock, Laura?'

She nodded. 'Got hit by a sheep.'

'I'd like to do another ultrasound.'

'The baby?' she asked. 'It's okay?'

'Well, there were a couple of things I couldn't see on the printout. So let's do another one and see what we can see.'

It was then that Laura understood there didn't need to be another ultrasound. She knew and Dr Jones did as well. He was just double checking.

Her baby was dead.

'Is that your grandfather out in the waiting area?' he asked.

Pulling her eyes away from the doctor's face, she nodded, unable to speak. The lump in her throat had grown so big, she couldn't make any sound.

Laura waited, hoping she was wrong. All the worries she'd had about not wanting the child because she had too much to do flew out the window. How could she have been so selfish? A child was a gift. Made in love, and Josh *did* love her. Why had she waited to tell him?

She shook her head and the doctor queried if she was in pain.

'No, no,' she managed. She stared at the wall so she could shut out the sight of him staring at the ultrasound screen. Her eyes snapped back to his when she felt him stop and heard him hook the wand into its holder.

She peered at him, hopefully.

Dr Jones shook his head. 'I'm sorry, Laura . . .' he began.

She didn't hear any more. The world receded for her. She could see the doctor's mouth moving, but there wasn't any sound coming out of it. When he touched her shoulder and asked her a question, she had to ask him to repeat it. Vaguely she heard him say she'd need a curette and would have to stay overnight.

He mentioned something about counselling, but all Laura did was nod. Whatever. She didn't care what happened now. The baby was gone.

Soon Howie was beside her, smoothing back her hair. Telling her he loved her and it would be okay. But how could it? The baby she'd carried, that she and Josh had created, was dead. Laura swallowed the tablets the nurse gave her and slipped into the welcome darkness of oblivion.

❧

'You bloody bitch.' A bitter tone filtered through Laura's sleepiness. She tried to open her eyes but they felt heavy.

Her mind raced.

'How dare you,' the male voice spat. Laura could feel the fury, even though she couldn't open her eyes.

'What? Josh?' Finally her eyes opened and she focused on the angry face in front of her.

He moved in close and looked into her eyes. Laura recoiled, seeing the hate in them.

'How. Dare. You.' His tone was measured now. 'You couldn't even tell me you were pregnant?' His voice rose a notch. 'What sort of fucked-up woman are you? I'm the father. I have a right to know. Oh, I know what they're saying. You were hit by a sheep and lost it. But I know the real story. You aborted it, didn't you? Why?'

47

He stopped and pulled back as if something had sparked in his mind. Then a twisted smile spread across his face and he nodded. 'Of course. It wasn't mine. You were pregnant to someone else. Who? Who was it?' His eyes narrowed. 'Jim, maybe. Or some other man you've had "business" dealings with.'

Laura shrank against the pillows. 'No,' she whimpered. 'That's not true. I was in the sheep yards . . .'

Now the attack started from the other side. 'We've heard what Howie's side of the story is. Trouble is, we don't believe it. You're a whore,' Meghan said menacingly. 'Not his baby? You've been sleeping around with someone else. I should have realised. That's why you haven't had time for us. Why you've been avoiding us. You've been too tired because you've been fucking everyone else and you got caught out by getting yourself pregnant.' She glared at Laura.

'It's not true,' Laura, still groggy, tried to defend herself but couldn't find the energy or the words. She was confused. It was like everything had left her when the baby died.

Gillian appeared and put her hand on her hips. 'What the hell is going on here?' she asked suspiciously. 'Meghan, you should know better than to be in here upsetting a patient. You're a nurse!'

Laura saw Meghan open her mouth, but Gillian held up her hand. 'I don't care what beef you have with her. Save it until she's out of hospital. Now you'd better leave.' She pointed towards the door.

'Don't worry,' Meghan answered, moving around the side of the bed. She reached for Josh's arm and dragged him with her. 'We're going.'

She had just about disappeared from sight when Meghan stopped and turned back to Laura. 'I can't believe you would break his heart and mine at the same time,' she called through the open door. 'I can't have kids and you can. Fact is, its life ended, by your own hand or not, it doesn't matter. You put yourself in a situation where its life was in danger. As if it didn't matter. You'll rot in hell for that. And I'll be laughing,' she spat towards Laura.

Chapter 6

1937

Thomas grasped the handles on either side of the Ajax wool press and cranked them up and down, forcing the steel plate onto the wool. As the fleeces compressed, the handles became harder to pump. That was the signal to grab the thick pins and force them through the pack to hold them down.

Deftly, Thomas folded the flaps over, pinned them and opened the door to let another bale thump heavily onto the wooden boards.

Today they would finish the sheep for this station. Five weeks of shearing and he had survived. Improved, learned, grown. The first two weeks had been tough, though. Who knew that working as a roustabout could be so hard? Mac had kept up his encouragement. 'You're doing well, son. Look, you're hardening up already,' he'd say. He'd give Thomas's upper arm a squeeze to show his muscles were developing.

Thomas knew how lucky he was that Mac had found him that stormy night. But with this job almost done, an inescapable feeling of uncertainty pressed on him as surely as the Ajax pressed the wool. What would happen to him when the final sheep was pushed down the chute, when the last bale was pressed and his new-found friends went their separate ways?

Every night, after dinner, while the shearers sharpened the combs and cutters, rolled smokes and yarned, Thomas had listened to their stories of shearing thousands of sheep in places he'd never heard of. The adventures they spoke of had sent his mind into overdrive. Days on the dusty roads. A sea of ewes, contained in yards, stretching as far as the eye could see. Freedom to choose which shed, which fork in the road. Hard work, sweat and flies. Teams of twenty men. Creamy white fleeces. Independence. Cold beer at the end of the shed.

Then, the same all over again.

Thomas wanted to be part of it, to see the country, to work hard and be as far away from Nambina as he could. These weeks had been the best of his life. Being treated as an equal had meant so much. The only harsh words spoken had been on a Saturday night, when the rattling mail van brought bottles of beer in a wooden crate packed with hay to keep them from breaking.

Clarrie had drunk a couple too many that night and had been sure he could belt the living daylights out of his mate, Tez.

'I gonna fight!' Clarrie had yelled, spinning around, fists raised. 'Whack! Whack, one, two!'

'Yeah?' came the lazy response. 'Who ya gonna fight, Clarrie?'

'You. Carn, you yellow excuse for a man.'

'You're a stupid bastard, Clarrie.' Tez's voice had been low and calm, in contrast to Clarrie's.

'Call me a bastard?'

Thomas had slunk into the shadows, trying to make himself invisible, too many memories pushing their way up. He'd heard the thump of a body hitting the ground, a muffled groan as Clarrie fell forward, the effect of the drink too much. Tez, sitting next to the fire, had shaken his head. A few moments passed before he got up and hoisted Clarrie over his shoulder, then carried him towards his swag. 'Stupid bastard,' Thomas heard him mutter. 'Should leave you here so the dingos can piss on ya.'

Tez had seen Thomas hiding in the darkness. 'Can't handle his grog, young fella. Never has. He always falls asleep on his feet when he's had too much and he hits the bloody deck. I know it's gonna happen the minute he talks about havin' a fight.' He'd flung the unconscious man unceremoniously onto his swag and invited Thomas to have a game of cards.

In the shed each day, the raised voices hadn't been to belittle or abuse, but to be heard above the noise of the engine, to hurry or to advise. Thomas had begun to feel safe. He wasn't going to be belted here.

Mac kept the team running like a well oiled machine. He didn't tolerate tardiness or a bloke not doing his job properly. Rudeness and bad behaviour were grounds for instant dismissal.

Wool classers seemed to be held in high esteem, by both the landowners and the shearing teams. Mac ate and slept at the main homestead. The rest of the blokes slept in swags or on hessian bags stuffed with the wool they'd shorn. The owners didn't mind, just as long as the wool was returned to the right bin before the end of shearing.

It was Mac with whom the landowner discussed the day's tallies and the quality of the shearing job. If it wasn't up to scratch, it was Mac's reputation that was on the line.

Now this shed was nearly done. 'Last ones are in the pens,' called Gecko, the bloke whose job it was to keep the sheep up to the shearers.

Those words sent a hum of expectation around the shed and the pace picked up. Thomas spun about, grabbed the wool hook, stabbed it into the bale and pulled. He thump-thudded it over to the bales near the loading ramp. Heaving it from the bottom, he managed to stand it up all by himself. When he'd first started, he'd needed help.

Another achievement.

He looked around and saw Mac wink at him. Thomas grinned and flexed his arms, before pointing to his newly defined muscles.

'Wait 'til you get to town. The girls'll love those muscles, mate!' Mac yelled.

Frankie and Jock hooted. Thomas blushed. He grabbed another hessian wool pack, ignoring everything except his work.

Mr Hampton, owner of Carpoole Station, was standing near the engine, waiting to shut it down as the last sheep was pushed into the chute. When the motor died, the absence of noise took some adjustment. Even though there was general chitchat among the team, what stood out most to Thomas were the yells and shouts from the yards outside. He'd seen many dogs and up to three men working the freshly shorn animals. The frantic barks and whistles from the men made it clear there was still much work to be done. But not by the shearing team.

As the blokes stretched and packed up their gear, Thomas peeked over the swinging doors and saw nothing but an empty shed. It really was finished. Sadness hit him as he watched the rest of the men pack up their gear.

'Righto, you fellas. Once you're ready, I'll see you at the office to pay your wages,' Mr Hampton called.

Thomas tried to shake the nostalgia away. A wage! He couldn't wait to see how much he'd earned—his first real pay as a man.

'Come on, Thomas, no dilly-dallying,' Mac reminded him. 'The rest of this wool still needs to be pressed. We'll start with the pieces.'

Mac was there waiting as the last bale was closed. Normally, it was the bits and pieces—the bellies, pieces and locks—that were baled last. But Mac had saved enough fleeces for a different type of bale. He was to brand it AAAM—the best-quality line of the shed. The wool was soft and creamy and, despite the tough season the year before, Mac told Thomas it would make good money.

Mac pulled out a piece to show him. 'See how the crimps in the wool are wide?'

To Thomas it looked like there were ripples going through it.

'Now see this one? The crimps are closer together. It's a finer fibre than that one, and will make more money.' Mac held up the hand containing the better quality one and shook it. 'This is tougher country on the sheep than, say, around the

54

south-east, where I picked you up. Wool down there is finer, because the seasons are kinder—there's usually something to eat. Not like up here. It's harsh, especially during summer. There is often a break in the wool, which makes it tender. It breaks easy and the buyers don't like it as much. And it can be full of dirt, burrs and prickles.'

Thomas nodded ruefully. His arms were covered in little red pinpricks and scratches where the prickles had pierced his skin. Each night, the team got out their needles and went to work on their hands, removing any splinters that had got under their skin during the day. If they didn't they would fester.

In the many days and hours of driving it had taken to get to Carpoole Station, Thomas had learned that Mac was a wool judge at the Sydney Royal Easter Show. It was no wonder he was held in such high regard. Mac also judged at other shows, including the Royal Adelaide Show, which, being in his home town, was his favourite.

By now the rest of the team had vanished to the homestead to receive their pay. The boys were talking about the next place they were headed, while they slugged at mugs of tea and ate the cake Mrs Hampton had made.

Thomas's nerves got the better of him and he dropped the pin he was holding. He wasn't sure what would happen now. Would he have a job with Mac when he moved on to the next shed? He'd worked as hard as he could to prove himself, and he could feel the change in his body.

He still flinched if anyone came too close but, just like the bruises had, the memories of his previous life were fading.

'Nothing like the last bale,' Mac said softly, patting the corner of it. 'Hoist it up over there with the others.'

Thomas picked up the pin and threw it onto the wool table, then did as instructed. He stopped for a moment, drinking in the sight of his labours. Line after line of bales stood tall and proud, waiting in the dim light to be carted to market.

'Righto, Thomas, ready for your money? We'd better head down and see the boss.'

'What happens now, Mac?' Thomas blurted out, unable to hide his anxiety anymore.

'You get paid.'

'After that?'

'Do you still want to keep working?'

'Bloody oath.' Thomas looked at his mentor with an expression that he hoped implied he never wanted to leave Mac's fold.

'You'd best come along with me to the next job, then. You can use some of your money to buy a bedroll and some food when we go through the next town. I'm in demand as a wool classer. Wherever I go, I can make sure there's a place for you.' Mac started to pack his stencil and wool books into his kit. 'You've worked hard. Proved yourself. I'm happy to take you with me.'

Thomas couldn't contain his smile.

Chapter 7

2001

Laura switched on the kettle and threw a teabag into her cup. 'Tea or coffee?'

'A glass of water and a tea, thanks, honeybunch,' Catherine said before walking into the lounge room to look at some recent photos that had been hung there. 'Holy crabsticks!' she exclaimed then. 'Look at Nicki and Poppy! They've grown up so much. What year are they in?'

Laura gave a half-hearted shrug. 'Nic has just started year twelve. She turns seventeen later this year, and Poppy's in year ten.' Her voice was dull and lacked enthusiasm. She was pleased Catherine had taken the time to come and see her, but she certainly didn't have the energy for her friend's zest for life.

Catherine was staring at a photo Josh had taken during the afternoon Howie handed Nambina over to Laura. 'I can see some similarities between you and Nicki,' she said. 'Poppy looks more like Georgie.'

Laura glanced over her shoulder at Howie, who was dozing

in a chair by the window. 'Shh,' she whispered and put her finger to her lips.

Catherine took the hint and walked back into the kitchen.

'Sorry. I hope I didn't wake him.'

'He sleeps a lot during the day now.' Laura dunked the teabags with extra force, then slopped some milk into one of the cups and handed it to Catherine. 'Let's go onto the verandah,' she said and turned to go out the kitchen door.

Catherine caught her arm. 'No,' she said. 'Let's go for a drive. Let's go somewhere you'll actually become the person I knew last year, the person I could always talk to.'

Laura stared at her friend for a moment and then shook off her arm, before storming outside and walking to the ute. As she reached to open the ute door, she stumbled, and scalding tea slopped onto her hand. Letting out a yelp, she dropped her cup. It smashed as it hit the stones.

Catherine came running.

With great, heaving sobs, Laura turned into her friend's shoulder. She felt Catherine's arms around her, holding her, shushing her and stroking her head like she was a baby.

A baby? Laura's sobs became louder. For her baby's lost life.

She didn't hear Catherine say anything. Her friend just held her until the sobs subsided and she could talk again.

'I'm sorry,' she stuttered finally through a few breaths that grabbed at her throat. 'I didn't know that was there.'

'Of course it was, honey. You haven't let it out since it all happened. You came back here and worked that little tush of yours into the ground. You didn't let yourself heal. That's such a dangerous thing.'

Catherine flashed Laura a smile and fondly pushed her friend's hair back from her face and behind her ear.

Laura couldn't think of anything to say. The ache that was still inside her was not just an ache. It was a bloody great gaping hole. She knew she'd tried to work hard to forget about the baby. She'd pulled out of every committee she was on and had concentrated on Nambina. No blokes could get the wrong idea that way. It was just her and Howie and Nambina and Sean when he came to visit or rang. That was the way she wanted it forever.

She took another shuddering breath.

'Come on,' Catherine said, moving to open the door of the ute. 'Let's go for a drive and see what we can see, see, see.'

'At the bottom of the farm, farm, farm.' Laura smiled. Maybe Catherine was the medicine she needed after all.

They drove in silence for a while. Finally, Catherine got out to open the third gate. Leaning against the bullbar, she looked out over a pasture paddock that was ankle-high with clovers and rye grass. 'From everything I'm seeing here, the season's been pretty good,' she called to Laura.

Laura got out of the ute and stood beside her friend. Nambina's best mob of ewes were out grazing, their lambs playing in a group. The two women watched as the lambs appeared to play chasey: one would pigroot and the others would follow. Another would take off flat out along the fence line and the others would chase it. They were happy and it made Laura feel better just watching them.

'Tell me why you've dropped out of everything you're good at?' Catherine asked seriously. 'Why did you resign from every committee? What made you stop wanting your dream?'

Laura was silent, still watching the lambs. She sighed. 'Geez, you're hard-hitting today, aren't you?'

'You're rotting out here by yourself. Most people don't drop out of society when they've had a miscarriage.'

The lambs had noticed them now and were advancing towards the ute, curious to see what it was.

Laura was quiet for some time, trying to compose the words in her head. She expected Catherine to ask again, but her friend just waited.

'You know what they said to me, don't you? That it wasn't Josh's child.'

Catherine nodded.

'So I keep thinking somehow, just maybe, it was my fault.'

She stopped as she heard Catherine's sharp intake of breath, then continued. 'No, no, I'm not playing the victim, okay? I've turned this over and over. Why did Josh suddenly act like he did? Maybe I did do something to earn his distrust, but I didn't realise. Maybe I *did* give off signs to other blokes and that's why he acted the way he did. It doesn't excuse what he said or anything like that, but it's a question I've got.'

'That's total bullshit, Laura, but we're not going to argue about it.'

Laura spoke over her friend. 'So, I figured the best thing was to bow out of anything that put me in close proximity with men—working with them at night and that sort of thing. I don't ever want to be in that situation again.' She paused. 'I've never told anyone this.' She stopped again and let her head fall backwards, taking in the large open sky. 'I almost chose not to have the baby.' Once it was out, it hung between them.

Catherine slowly turned to look at Laura, who pretended she didn't notice. She kept her eyes firmly on the sky.

'The question of keeping the baby or not should never have crossed my mind. I was too selfish. I had too many things still to do. I guess that's why I never got around to telling Josh, or anyone. I hadn't made my mind up. But when Meghan rang and said she couldn't have kids, I realised that what I'd been thinking was horribly wrong. I was ready to tell Josh—and then the accident happened.'

The lambs had come closer. Without warning, Catherine sneezed. The animals reacted like a bomb had gone off, racing back to the safety of their mothers. Neither girl smiled.

'A horrible misunderstanding.'

Laura nodded. 'I didn't want to have anything to do with either of them after what they did in the hospital. I mean seriously, Catherine . . .' Confusion mixed with anger showed on her face. 'How can you claim to love someone and then do that to them? Accuse them of doing things there is no way in the world they would? Neither of them would accept what had actually happened. Chose to twist it to what they wanted to believe.' She crossed her arms. 'Josh isn't the man for me, if that's how he thinks, or reacts. Or lets himself be led.'

'But didn't Howie try to sort it out for you?'

'Yep. I asked him not to, but he insisted. He went over to see Josh and Meghan and tried to get them to understand what had *actually* happened. Thought we could work through it all.' She pursed her lips and narrowed her eyes. 'But what they had concocted between them . . . That wasn't going to happen while my bum pointed to the ground. Stuff Josh. Stuff 'em both.'

'Okay, I get all of that. I'm still trying to understand why you've isolated yourself. Why you're still sad. Is it because you lost the baby?'

'Yeah.' Laura's voice was barely audible. 'Feel so guilty. So angry with myself. How could . . . Anyway.' She dismissed the conversation. 'That's it. Don't want to talk about it anymore.'

'Okay.'

Laura noticed the ewes and lambs had moved further away now and she sat down on the grass.

Catherine sat down beside her. 'So, would you like me to tell you about the little plan I've dreamed up for you?'

Laura looked over questioningly.

'You reckon I don't think about you when I'm not here? Not on your life! I've been scheming. And I've come up with a plan.' Catherine grabbed Laura's hands. 'Now listen, I don't understand why you're cutting yourself off from the outside world. I don't like it, but I know how pig-headed you can be. I'm guessing whatever I say isn't going to change your mind, so . . .'

Laura interrupted her. 'Thanks so much for the compliment,' she said sarcastically. 'So pleased you've come to support me.'

Catherine continued on as if she hadn't heard. 'And since you're too proud to patch it up with Josh—' Catherine held up her hand in case Laura was about to explode. 'I'm not saying you should. He acted atrociously. However, everyone's entitled to make a mistake. If you actually *talked* to him instead of avoiding him, and Meghan, for that matter, it might help.'

'Never.' Laura's tone brooked no argument. 'I have nothing to say to either of them. I'll cross the street rather than walk by them.'

'So, since we've clarified all of that, I'll continue to tell you about my plan, shall I?'

Laura held out her hands in a 'go ahead' sign.

'Since you don't want to be lobbying and so on, as you were, how about you help young kids get into farming? Start up a school that teaches all the practical things of the industry. Fencing, shearing, wool handling, stock husbandry, cropping. All that sort of thing. Give them the experience to get out there and get a job. There are so many kids who want to farm but don't have the skills. They might not have been brought up on a farm or don't like asking questions because they're not confident enough. I'm sure you'd be brilliant at creating a safe environment so these kids can learn. And it could work for you too. You'd have a small labour force.'

Laura plucked at the grass next to her knee, trying to hold in her shock. It was a way-out-there suggestion. Still, she shouldn't be surprised. That was Catherine all over. Outrageous, smart, forward-thinking. Full of energy.

She knew Catherine was watching for her reaction. Her mind raced. There were so many good things that could come out of Catherine's idea: labour for Nambina; help to do the jobs that needed more than one person; and she'd be back contributing to the agricultural community.

'You know,' she said, nodding, 'it's a brilliant idea. Maybe it *could* work!'

A huge smile spread across Catherine's face. 'I knew you were down but you weren't out, honey!'

'It'd be a huge job to get it off the ground, though,' Laura said, thinking out loud.

'Nothing you couldn't handle. Now, while you're at it, I have another idea for you. Why not show some of those gorgeous boys you've been breeding?'

'What, the rams?' Laura scoffed. 'Take them to an actual show?'

'Yeah.' Catherine nodded, her face serious. 'Look, I was at the Keith field days last week and you've got sheep every bit as good as the recognised studs around here. I think you should have a go. Get your fellas out there. Show everyone what you're made of. You obviously think they're good enough to use over your flock, because that's what you're doing. You're not going to jeopardise financial returns by using a substandard product. So get out there and have a go.'

Catherine paused to take a breath. 'Why don't you try one of the smaller shows first and then lead up to the Adelaide Royal?'

'What?' Laura screeched. The show idea tipped her over the edge. 'You're out of your mind. That's not what I'm about, and you know it. I love mucking around with genetics, checking out the wool, improving the mob, but putting myself out there to be judged? No way, friend.'

But as she said it, she felt something inside reacting. Something she couldn't put her finger on. She remembered how excited she was when she'd sat in the stands at the Royal Show watching an old bow-legged judge sash a proud-looking ram with a silky blue ribbon. The owners' faces showed how satisfied they were that their hard work had paid off. Laura had approached them afterwards to ask if she could buy a semen package from them.

Could she really do something like that? Would it actually be possible to set up a farming school on Nambina? To show sheep?

Maybe it was.

For the first time in a year Laura could see a future.

Chapter 8

1937

Thomas slowly became aware of his surroundings. He felt stony earth beneath him. There was a noise he couldn't quite place, but as his senses sharpened he recognised it as raucous laughter.

His face throbbed. He breathed heavily against the pain and gently tested his arms, legs and torso. Nothing seemed broken, but when he pressed his right leg, he let out an involuntary gasp as the sting of a deep bruise made itself felt.

'Bloody hell,' Thomas croaked as he struggled into a sitting position. He pushed cold fingers into his cheek and probed. Nothing but a bit of gravel rash and another big bruise, he surmised.

'Come on, mate. Up ya get.' Firm, strong hands grasped Thomas under his arms and helped him to his feet.

'Geez,' he exclaimed. 'What happened?'

There was another burst of laughter. 'Sorry 'bout that,'

one of the station's jackaroos said. 'Didn't think you'd go and knock yourself out.'

'Haven't you been taught which side to mount a horse?' another of the men drawled.

'It was good for a laugh, that's for sure,' someone else said.

'Reckon you could get a job in a circus riding horses with that effort!'

Thomas brushed himself down and looked around, taking in the jackaroos and their grinning faces, wondering what joke they'd just played on him.

'This is how you do it, boy.' This time it was Donnie, the jackaroo who'd offered him the ride and caught the horse Thomas had just tried to mount. Donnie gathered the reins, went to the off-side, swung himself up and, after a quiet word to the animal and a touch of his heels into the flank, the horse leapt forward and cantered out into the paddock.

The gathering of station employees whistled and cheered. One nudged Thomas. 'See, that's how it's done. You leave it to us experts, shed boy.' His tone implied anything but friendliness.

If Thomas hadn't been humiliated and wasn't feeling completely self-conscious, he would have enjoyed watching the display between horse and man. But with his face still stinging and all of him aching, he turned to go, knowing he'd been part of a prank he didn't understand.

Leaving the jeers and laughter behind him, he walked back to the safety of the shearers' quarters.

'Don't worry, mate,' Mac said when Thomas told him what had happened. 'There're plenty of blokes out there who've been asked for left-handed screwdrivers or some other mythical thing. Some people find it amusing poking fun at another's ignorance. That Donnie in particular. He's a piece of work. But just remember: they had to learn once too and more 'n likely they had something similar happen to them when they were starting out. Don't give it a second thought.' Mac nodded for emphasis then moved on. 'Come on, it's just about grub time.' He turned back. 'But stay away from those jackaroos.'

⁀

'Another day, another pound,' Mac said to no one in particular. He stretched, then reached into a pocket for his tobacco.

Already up, Thomas stood silently watching the sky change colour before his eyes. Sunrise in this part of the country could be spectacular, and on this particular morning the clouds smouldered a deep crimson. Thomas had to drag himself away from the magnificent sight to fill the billy. Raking the coals of the camp fire to level them out, he placed the blackened billycan onto the still-glowing embers.

Around him the team was beginning to stir. Frankie sat up in his swag and coughed, hacked and spat onto the ground.

'Nothing but a gentleman,' Gecko said, as he pulled his boots out from under the tarp of his swag and put them on.

Thomas threw a few handfuls of tea into the boiling water and set the billy back on the fire. A few minutes later, he tapped the can to shake the leaves and then grabbed the handle and expertly swung it in a circle so nothing spilt, gravity keeping the liquid inside. Finally he set the billy down on the makeshift table and poured it into the pannikins.

'Tea's up,' he called.

He collected his own mug and took it over to a fallen branch and sat down. Moments later, Mac sat down beside him.

'Start the last shed of the season, tomorrow.' Mac broke a stick from the dead tree and stirred condensed milk into his tea.

'Yeah, I know.' Thomas was subdued. When, back on Carpoole Station, Mac had offered him a job, Thomas never contemplated that it would end.

But now his future, once again, was uncertain, at least until the next shearing season.

'There was a telegram waiting for me when we passed through Broken Hill,' Mac said casually as he took a slurp of his tea.

Thomas waited, sensing Mac had more to say.

'I'll be heading back towards Adelaide after we finish here,' Mac said. 'To judge at the Royal Show.'

'Right,' Thomas said.

'Guess you'll be wanting to come along too.' It was a statement, not a question.

Thomas took a sip of his tea, his mind suddenly full of questions. 'Yeah, I'd like that,' he answered. 'But where would I live and what would I do while you're at the show?'

'You can stay with me. I've got a small house right near the showgrounds. I want to teach you how to class. How to judge. You've got a feel for wool. For sheep. Haven't seen it in a young lad before. Think you could be a wool classer in your own right, one day. If it's what you want to do.'

Thomas felt himself tingle at the generous praise. He knew his face would be red, the blush rising high on his cheeks. Over the many months he'd been with Mac, he'd learnt an amazing amount. At first it had felt like a different language, a different world. It had been a steep and hard learning curve, one which Thomas had greeted head on. Anything to keep him away from the memories of home and why he'd left.

Mac had explained how a shed was run and the process that had to happen before shearing could take place. He'd taught Thomas that nutrition was as important to the quality of the fibre as the genetics used. Thomas now understood the different lines of wool, how AAAM was the highest quality a shed produced, and AAM was the second. The difference between the two had to be two micron—those crimps that Mac had shown him in the first shed. He'd learned about brightness, texture, colour and density.

Mac had shown him how, every time the shearer nicked the skin, the wool retained a piece of skin that would have to be cut off before it rotted. Thomas had grown used to the shout of 'tar boy' when there was a cut. Mac would stride over to inspect the wound and clip the flesh from the wool. Once done, he'd hand out a bit of advice about keeping the shears on top of the skin, not in it.

Mac had been quick with praise during the first few sheds. It was as if he knew Thomas had never received any. But as time had gone on, his expectations had risen and Thomas had been keen to meet them. He'd made mistakes, as everyone did, but there hadn't been a beating to follow them. There had been kind and consistent encouragement, and an explanation of what he'd done wrong.

And now Mac was doing it again.

Thomas opened his mouth to thank his friend and mentor, but Mac had already stood and drained the last of his tea. 'Come on, you lazy buggers,' he called to the crew. 'If you want more than a dingo's breakfast you'd better get a hurry on.

I'm leaving in twenty minutes. If you want me to cart your packs, then get 'em in the car. I'll see you all at the shed.'

Thomas knew a dingo's breakfast was a piss and a good look around. These fellas would be riding their bikes to the next shed so would need much more than that.

Mac always went ahead in his car. He liked to talk with the owner about the season and conditions of the sheep. Hear what the Boss Man expected from his wool clip and get a feel for how everything would flow. He also had to settle into his bedroom in the main house and, as he disliked putting the mistress of the house to any trouble, he would slip in when it was best for her. It didn't bother the rest of the team. They were happy camping under the stars or in the shed. Only a few places had shearers' quarters.

Frankie groaned. 'I'm glad this is the last time I gotta ride me bike. Next time I come, I'll have saved enough money to buy a car, I swear. Ruts as deep as mine pits, yesterday, there were. And I got a flat.'

'At least it's a good season and there's plenty of grass to stuff in the tyres. Imagine ridin' on just the rims.' Gecko, who'd helped himself to another mug of tea, dunked a piece of damper in his cup then ate it.

Thomas was looking forward to the shed on Kilkenary Station. He'd heard stories of free-flowing beer and lamb chops on a barbecue to celebrate the end of the season. Not that the beer interested him, but a decent meal did.

Four other stations were near Kilkenary which made for a more social time, when the others jackaroos visited. Mac had told Thomas that the women were kind and the ringers much more sociable than the bastards back on Rochden Downs.

They tolerated the blow-ins so long as they didn't drink too much of their grog or get in the way or upset their women folk.

But none of that explained the main reason for his excitement. The boss had a daughter whose reputation went well and truly before her. Apparently Elizabeth was pretty, but she also loved wool and sheep. She was different. Special. Although some blokes thought she was out of line taking an interest in the station, Mac thought it was the way of the future.

They would only be on Kilkenary for fifteen days. Fifteen days and four or so thousand sheep. And then the season would be over. Thomas was torn between wanting to stay with the team and going with Mac to Adelaide. Thanks to Mac, he now had money in his pocket as well as options, something he'd never had before. He didn't want to let his mentor down in any way.

Mac broke into his contemplation. 'Come on there, Thomas. We haven't got all day. Help load these packs up.'

'Here, Thomas. Fill this waterbag for me, will you?' Clarrie held out a hessian bag and Thomas refilled it from the stores of water they had with them. Within the twenty minutes Mac had given them the camp was packed up and the fire extinguished. As the men prepared for the ride, they joked and laughed. It was the same every time they were about to start on a new shed. The excitement was contagious—Thomas had to admit it was one of his favourite times. Because every shed was different it meant every start was new. Of course, within a couple of days the humdrum of normality always set in.

'Righto, see you there!' Mac called out of the open window as he started the car.

'One day I'll get there before you, Mac,' Tez said. 'I swear I will. I might even get up in the middle of the bloody night, just to do it.' He grumbled as he threw a leg over his bike and settled down. 'Calluses on me arse, that's what I've got.'

Thomas laughed as he got into the passenger's seat, thinking how lucky he was he didn't have to ride a push bike. As they drove away, Thomas heard Clarrie answer that calluses on his arse were better than chilblains.

Mac snorted.

The team made a strange sight, Mac's car out front with five men on bikes behind. Well, it had seemed strange to Thomas to begin with, but the more he travelled with these blokes he'd come to call friends, the more he realised there were plenty of other men just like them. Fellows on their way to, or looking for, work. Some were on bikes, some on horses. A few were lucky enough to have cars, but many only had shanks' pony—their feet. But they were all on the same mission—to put a pound in their pocket.

The journey was a quiet one to begin with. Thomas was turning over the possibilities of Adelaide in his mind. He'd only ever been to a small country fair before, nothing like what he imagined the Royal Adelaide Show would be. He could only picture it from the stories Mac had told him during their long stretches in the car. The lines of ewes and rams and two-tooth wethers in single pens, there to be judged on their wool growing and conformation. The people milling about, making their own calls on the quality of the animals. The laughter and the talking.

'So what do you think about Adelaide?' Mac asked after a while.

Thomas took his time in replying. 'I'm looking forward to it.'

'Ever been to a big show?'

'Nah.'

'Smaller one then, maybe?'

Thomas didn't want to think about the time his mother had taken him and his brother to the local show. 'Yeah.'

'What do you remember about it? The sheep? The smells? The music?'

Thomas knew why Mac was pestering him with all the questions. In the last couple of months, he'd been on about contacting Thomas's family. Letting them know he was okay. Even mending the rift between them.

Rift? That rift was a million bloody feet wide and couldn't be fixed. Wouldn't be fixed, if he had anything to do with it. He was prepared to never set foot on Nambina again. But Thomas hadn't said that. He'd nodded, agreed to nothing, and Mac finally dropped it.

Without his wishing for it, he suddenly remembered his mother lifting him onto a horse on the merry-go-round. Howard was beside him. Jessie rode next to them, her smile wide and her hair blowing out behind her. It was a memory he hadn't even known he'd possessed until now, and as he dwelt on it, he knew that his mother had been truly happy in that moment.

What had happened to her?

'No,' he whispered aloud.

'What's that?' Mac looked at him.

'Uh, no. No, I don't remember anything about it.' Thomas shook his head emphatically.

Just my mother's smile.

'I'll fill you in. I know I've told you about the sheep showing and wool judging, but there's much more. The food, the rides. There are merry-go-rounds for the kids, Ferris wheels . . .'

Thomas continued to nod, although he wasn't listening. He was still thinking of his mother's smile. The gentleness of her hand on his as she encouraged him to hold the horse's mane. The sound of Howard's chuckle. The joyful innocence of that day.

Chapter 9

2003

If someone had told Laura that Howie would be dying just three years after he'd handed her Nambina, she wouldn't have believed it possible. Now, here she was, sitting with her father on opposite sides of Howie's hospital bed, waiting.

Of course she understood the circle of life—she just didn't want to be experiencing it right now. Not with her darling Papa.

Sean and Laura each held a sun-spotted, bony hand. The time between each rattling breath seemed to increase and Laura waited, praying that each breath wasn't Howie's last, although deep down she knew she was only hoping to prolong the inevitable.

She felt Howie's fingers tighten around hers. He was trying to say something. Father and daughter leaned towards him in an attempt to hear the few whispered words. Laura looked at Sean, hoping he'd caught what Howie had said, but Sean shook his head. Now they both leaned closer.

'My brother. Thomas.' Howie's voice was stronger this time, his need for them to understand visible on his face. 'Thomas. Ran away. If he comes, if his family come, you must help them. Look after them.'

He looked intently at Laura with weepy eyes and tried to tighten his hold on her hand. 'He never forgave Dad. Or me. It's gotta be you, Laurs.' He leaned back then. 'There mightn't be any of them left. But there might. Promise me.'

Laura kept her eyes on Howie's face as she nodded. 'I promise, Papa. I promise.'

Did Howie know what he was asking? Still, it didn't matter. She would have agreed to do whatever he asked of her at that moment. If her word meant he went into eternity content, then she would do it.

Howie was clearly exhausted by the effort it had taken to talk, and he slumped back on the pillows. His eyes closed and never reopened. It wasn't long before he drew his final breath.

Laura and her father sat still, shell-shocked for a moment. Then Sean reached over and placed his fingers under Howie's nose. There was no breath.

Laura felt a searing grief mixed with fear. 'No, Papa, you can't go! You can't leave me. I *need* you!' she wanted to scream.

But she didn't. And neither did Sean. They reached across the bed for each other's hand, their fingers colliding in a clumsy grip.

They stayed that way for many minutes, Howie's last words hanging in the air.

☙

Shakily clutching a sheet of paper, Laura was unsteady in her high heels as she made her way towards the pulpit. To get there, she had to pass Howie's coffin and she paused for a moment to touch it. Then, straightening her shoulders, she ploughed forward, desperate for her part in the service to be over. Her throat was constricted and she wondered whether she'd be able to make her voice work. She'd have to, she told herself as stepped up onto the platform.

She looked out into the church. Seated in the front row was her family. Georgie was dabbing at her eyes, while Sean sat ram-rod straight. Laura could see his tightened jaw working overtime as he tried to stop himself from breaking down. Nicki and Poppy sat next to each other, holding hands, both pale faced, eyes large and red. It was the first death they'd really experienced.

Everyone in the church was silent, watching her. The only sound was a shuffling of the order of service.

A movement caught her eye. Catherine. A tiny signal. Two thumbs up. A wink. It was like she was trying to channel strength to Laura.

The minister stepped forward, ready to take the eulogy and read it, if needed. But Laura opened her mouth and, as she did, she knew she could do it. 'Howie Murphy was an extraordinary man,' she began.

From that point the words flowed freely. Her voice was strong and clear, and as she spoke she hoped that, with every word, Howie would be proud and that somehow she would keep his memory alive.

Laura was nearing the end when she faltered. 'As you would all know, Papa helped raise me. And the way he brought me up was to always believe I could do anything I put my mind to. And so when I told him a couple of years ago that I wanted to set up a farming school, he didn't laugh. He encouraged it. He always encouraged everything I did and I couldn't have asked for a more accepting and supportive person to be in my life. I'm just grateful that Howie saw the idea off the ground. And while he never lived to meet the students, they'll know about him when they do come. Hopefully, I'll be able to pass on the same kind of encouragement Howie always showed me.'

Laura's voice cracked and once again the minister stepped forward, but she shook him off and turned to the coffin. 'Papa, thank you. Thank you for everything, but thank you most of all for always being there. I'll miss you more than you could possibly imagine.'

She stumbled from the pulpit and sat next to her father, who patted her knee and gave a wobbly smile. Georgie reached out her arm and slipped it around her shoulders.

After the burial, the family went into the hall. The church ladies were serving cups of tea and coffee with homemade sandwiches, sponge cake and scones.

This was the part Laura hadn't been looking forward to. Having to smile and pretend she wasn't broken-hearted.

Catherine reached her before anyone else could and dragged her into a corner. 'I'm so proud of you,' she said softly, giving Laura a hug. 'You did really well. Shit of a job.'

'Thanks.' They looked around at the people who had come to Howie's funeral. 'He touched so many, Catherine. Look at all these people. They're here to honour his life and memory.'

'Yeah, but don't forget they're here for you and your family too. Look, there's Tim Burns. I met him at one of the seminars

I held a few weeks ago. He's our age and I'm sure he's here to show his support for you too, not just Howie.'

Laura glanced across at Tim, the local vet. She'd never seen him in a suit before.

Catherine gave her shoulder a nudge. 'He's pretty hot in that suit!' she said, as if she'd read Laura's mind.

Laura was saved from answering when Mrs Johnson came up and pulled her into a lavender-smelling hug. 'My dear girl,' she said. 'You must be feeling so lost.'

Laura tried to smile. She nodded.

'Oh, you'll be so lonely out in that rambling old homestead all by yourself. You make sure you call me if I can help.' Mrs Johnson patted Laura's shoulder then left them alone.

'Honey, I have to run,' Catherine said. 'I've got to get back to Adelaide so I can catch the plane to Perth. I've got three events to run over there. Ring me any time of the day or night.' Then she smiled. 'Still, you already know that.' Catherine gave Laura another hug. 'I'm so proud of you. Only a few more weeks and your first lot of students will arrive. They'll be a distraction.'

Heat pierced Laura's eyes. Even though she was sure she'd shed all the tears she could she suddenly found more. 'Wish he could have seen the school's first day, the first intake arriving, though.' Her voice caught. 'I'm going to miss him so much.'

'I know, honey. But you're strong too. And I believe he'll be watching down and see the students arrive. You never know, he might even come back to haunt them.'

Laura gave a watery smile. 'Oh, hell no! He was always a bit unorthodox in his methods. I can't teach the students the way he would have done things.'

Catherine took hold of Laura by the shoulders. 'You'll make a great teacher and I'm so pleased you've got something to absorb you. You've worked too hard to get this off the ground to let it fail now.' Catherine smiled, gently punched her shoulder then took her leave.

'Laura.'

She turned at the sound of a soft male voice. It was Tim Burns.

'Hello,' was all Laura could manage.

'I'm so sorry for your loss. If there's anything I can do . . .'

Laura swallowed. 'Thanks.'

The vet was one of many who passed on their condolences that afternoon, and Laura found herself being constantly hugged, kissed and wept over. It was exactly the scenario she'd dreaded.

Finally, the church hall was empty and the family made the drive back to Nambina. But with Howie gone, it was a sad gathering. The house seemed empty, even with all of them there. They kept expecting to see Howie sitting in his chair, or standing by the fire.

How Laura would keep going without his love and encouragement she had no idea. And when her family left in the morning, she'd be alone, well and truly, for the first time in her life.

Chapter 10

1937

'Tar boy!' Gecko held a ewe between his legs. She twisted and thumped her back legs on the board.

There was a chorus of 'Hang on to her!' and 'Get a grip!'.

Thomas looked up from branding a bale as a young Aboriginal boy who worked on the station ran over with a small billy and brush to paint on the thick tar.

Thomas could see that the ewe had been cut on the long blow and the gash went from the top of her shoulder and around her rib cage. Mac wouldn't like that, he knew. He quickly turned back to his work before anyone could see him watching. Wiping his brow, he used the black ink and stencil to mark the bale number and the type—AAM.

'Thomas!'

He turned to see Mac hurrying towards him.

'Mr Ford would like to take another load of wool to town. Have you got enough to fill his truck?'

Thomas quickly ran through the morning's efforts. He'd

pressed fourteen bales this morning and there were another three from yesterday. Ford only needed twelve.

'Yeah. There's plenty.'

'Good. Help Jacko load it, will you?' Jacko was the head stockman.

'No worries.'

Thomas grabbed the wool hook and began manoeuvring the unwieldy packs. He slid open the iron door and was blinded by sunlight.

Once his eyes adjusted, he could see the rusty red flatbed truck reversing towards the shed. Four dogs were running around on the tray, barking loudly, their ears pricked and eyes keen. Thomas grinned at the sight of their obvious love of life then stopped as, in his mind's eye, his childhood dog, Flea, chased a rabbit. Flea's expression and how he'd cowered when Ernest's voice rose had mirrored Thomas's feelings every time.

Quickly he grabbed a bale, pulled it onto its side and flipped it over and over, rolling it towards the loading ramp. He wouldn't let memories get in the way of his new life. He couldn't understand why they were beginning to plague him now, months after he'd left home. He wished the memories would just go away.

'Here, boy!' A harsh voice called out. 'This way.'

The tone reminded him of his father and at once anger surged inside him. But, as always, he kept his mouth shut and did as he was asked.

'No, no, no! Not like that.' The head stockman roughly took the bale hook from him and turned the wool on its end, rolling it all the way to the front of the tray. Here, he wiggled it until it was just right and strode back to get the second bale.

Thomas moved to help him.

'Get out of me way. You're too slow and don't know how to stack them well.'

Thomas found his tongue.

'Show me, then.'

'Haven't got time. Mr Ford needs to get his daughter on a train back to Adelaide.'

Mac, hearing the impatient tone above the noise of the shed, came out onto the landing. 'What's going on?'

'Your green presser has no bloody idea how to stack bales. Look at this higgledy-piggledy mess. No point getting him to help me load. Mr Ford's in a hurry.'

'Do it yourself, then,' Mac said shortly and nodded for Thomas to go inside.

Feeling embarrassed and hoping he hadn't let Mac down, Thomas walked quickly back to the wool bins and grabbed an armful to throw in the press. He would prove to Jacko he could do his job well.

'Pay no mind,' said Mac, appearing at his shoulder. 'He's a grumpy bugger at the best of times.'

Thomas looked over his shoulder, watching Jacko roll and flip the bales as if they weighed nothing. The man pushed and pulled until they slotted against one another, unable to move. 'Get away with you!' he yelled at the dogs, which were happily trotting around his feet.

'Ah, look at that, would you?' Mac nodded towards the homestead. 'A vision splendid. Miss Elizabeth Ford. Or Lizzie, as her parents call her.' He turned back to the rest of the crew. 'Ducks on the pond, my friends,' he called. 'Ducks on the pond.'

Two figures walked towards them. Thomas knew Mr Ford. He'd seen him out in the yards, looking at the wool on the sheep and drafting the young ewes into lines. He'd heard stories of the daughter who accompanied him often, a girl who knew as much as her father did when it came to breeding sheep and growing wool, but he'd never set eyes on her before.

She was blonde and slim. As she drew closer, Thomas could see her face was beautiful, her hair tied back in a bun. She wore a long skirt, a tucked-in blouse and low, sensible shoes, but judging by the way she strode confidently through the small scrubby bushes and rocky ground, Thomas knew she wasn't a fashionable lady. She was a woman who had grown up on the land and understood its moods.

'Ford's daughter,' Mac confirmed. 'Best catch going around here. She'll be heading back to boarding school. She's been home helping look after her sister—she's been ill. Her mother needed the extra help with shearing on. Lizzie really should have been in school.' He sighed. 'I tell you, Thomas, she'll make a man a fine wife in a few years' time. She's practical and sensible. Certainly doesn't suffer fools. Just the sort of lady a man needs . . .' He broke off. 'But still, I'm sure there'll be many suitors when the time comes. She's about your age.' He raised his eyebrows at Thomas and nodded.

Thomas was silent. They both looked a bit longer and then Thomas turned away. No point in longing for something that could never be his. He grabbed another armful of wool and threw it into the press.

The bale was full so he grabbed a handle either side and started to jack them up and down. He could hear Jacko cursing and the shearers' call of 'sheep-o' or 'tar boy', but he concentrated on his work. If Jacko looked in, he would have no cause for complaint.

The small door at the side slid open and Mr Ford stood, silhouetted in frame. Thomas glanced up then went straight back to his work.

When he heard voices he looked up again, and stared straight into the vivid blue eyes of Miss Ford.

He was suddenly aware of his appearance as he'd never been before. Sweating, filthy, and greasy from the wool. His clothes were threadbare and covered in the dirt from the day's toil. He wished he'd mended the tear in his shirt last night, as he'd planned. He'd ended up playing poker instead.

Quickly he looked back to his task.

'You'll see here, Mr Ford,' Mac was saying. 'This is the line I'd like you to put up for sale first. It's consistent in micron and strength. Because of the good season, there's little vegetable matter, and I believe, of all the wool I've seen so far, it should top the first sale you're able to get it into.'

From the corner of his eye, Thomas could see that Mac was showing the owner and his daughter the samples he'd kept out from each bale. It was a habit not many classers had, but Mac liked to have a physical piece of fibre to refer to. He would follow every line, from every station he'd been on. When he returned the next year, he'd know what the wool had sold for and what results had been achieved. The owners liked the way he did this, Thomas knew—he'd overheard Mr Hampton at Carpoole Station saying so. It was one of the things that put Mac at the top of his profession.

Thomas glanced up again and found Miss Ford still staring at him. He bravely held her gaze for a moment, then placed the flaps of the bale over each other and closed it up. The door of the press groaned as it open. Thomas pulled the finished bale out and thump-thudded it over to the wall, where he heaved the nearly 400-pound bale onto its end. He knew the girl was watching and wished she wouldn't. Why was she?

'Truck's all loaded, Mr Ford.' Jacko was now standing at the boss's side and he touched a finger to his forehead. 'Miss Ford,' the stockman acknowledged with a wide smile, all his previous agitation gone.

'Mr Jackson.' Miss Ford nodded and turned back to the wool her father was holding. 'Mr McDougall,' she said. It took a moment for Thomas to realise she was talking to Mac—he'd never heard his full name used before. 'After helping my father class the ewe hoggets, I believe the purchase of the ram from Boonoke Stud has helped our yield. How many pounds of wool per sheep are we averaging this year?'

Thomas's eyes widened at the question. He'd heard she knew her stuff. Elizabeth must know everything there was to know about breeding sheep.

This could have been him if his father hadn't been a drunk. If Ernest had bothered to teach instead of hit. They could have taken an interest in wool, increased their mobs. Thomas hadn't realised how much he loved wool until he'd joined Mac's team, and he'd been told more than once he had a natural ability to judge it as it came off the sheep's back. He could still be living on Nambina, would have inherited it one day . . . But there wasn't any point in thinking about it. He had a new life. New friends. New everything. Still, there were times when he couldn't help but feel angry. This was one of them. He bit down the fury, which was rising like bile in his throat.

Nambina was another world and at least four hundred miles away. He needed to let it go. Breathing deeply, he jabbed the hook deep into the bale, wishing it was his father's heart.

'Well, Miss Ford, the weights are easily up about half a pound on last year,' Mac answered.

Thomas was unfolding a new pack to put in the press as he heard Mr Ford laugh, and he glanced over. Mr Ford was looking proudly at his daughter. 'Taught her everything she knows, Mac, so I did!'

'Miss Ford, I have to admit, you know your subject well,' Mac answered. 'As we discussed last night over dinner.' He nodded to emphasise his point.

She graciously inclined her head and glanced towards Thomas again.

'Well, we must be on our way. Elizabeth has a train to catch.'

'Back to the humdrum of boarding school,' she laughed. 'I'd much rather be here.'

'I'm sure you would, Miss Ford. But you can't have much longer to go now before school's over for good?'

'One more term after this one, Mr McDougall. Truth be told, I can't wait to finish. I've been happier here helping out than I could ever have been in the city. There's a life to be lived out here.' She smiled and Thomas felt his heart change rhythm.

'Come now, Lizzie,' her father said. 'It can't be all that bad. You'll be seeing Mr McDougall and the wool again at the show. You don't have long to wait.'

'I'm looking forward to it.' She held out her hand to Mac, who shook it gently. 'May I look at the wool book before I leave?'

'Certainly.' Mac indicated the bench, where the book lay open.

Elizabeth nodded and walked over. She had to walk past Thomas to do so and she stopped for a moment. 'You make throwing those bales around seem very easy,' she said admiringly. 'I know from dinner table conversation, you'll be with Mr McDougall in Adelaide. I'll look forward to making your acquaintance then.' She moved on, ran her finger down the book where Mac kept his records, then walked out of the shed through the loading ramp door.

Thomas, his face beetroot red, didn't know what to do. So he just turned away and said nothing.

಄

'She's got her eye on you, young fella.' It was the end of the day and Gecko was at the trough, throwing water on his face. 'I could tell. An experienced bloke such as meself.'

Tez snorted with laughter. 'Reckon you wouldn't know a woman if you fell over one on the city streets.'

Gecko looked offended. 'I've had girlfriends. I can always tell if they're keen and I'd bet me next week's wage the boss's daughter has an eye for young Thomas here.'

'Don't reckon,' Thomas said quietly, not enjoying the attention. He dipped his hand into the water and threw it over the back of his neck. The cold water made his skin crawl with goosebumps.

'You're such a young'un, you wouldn't know. What you need is the advantage of wisdom. I can give yer that. You just need to stick with me. I know what women want and how to get 'em. I'll show you.' Gecko spoke solemnly, believing every word he said.

'That's why you're out here, with us, and not a woman

in sight,' Clarrie crowed. 'But that's good, Gecko. You keep telling yourself that.' He slapped his friend's shoulder and walked towards the shearers' quarters.

Thomas grinned and finished washing up.

Then Mac appeared. 'Jackaroos are running the last of the sheep through the dipper,' he said. 'Seen it done before?'

'Nope.'

'Head up into the shed and have a look through the window. I'll be up in a moment or two.'

Back inside, Thomas looked through the grimy glass at the freshly shorn ewes running down the raceway. They were vivid white and, now free of their wool, they had more energy than before. They ran towards the big wide tank, pushed by the men and dogs. Plunging into the water, which had been laced with chemicals to stop lice, they swam to the other side then clambered out, their hooves sometimes slipping on the damp cement. Then they raced off into the paddock, shaking like dogs as they went.

What a sight. It made Thomas want to get out there and be involved.

Mac stood beside him. 'Something just makes you feel good when you see men and dogs who know what they're doing work sheep. Ford's employees are good stockmen, and good ones make it look easy.'

'They do,' Thomas agreed. They were silent for a moment. 'Lice decreases the value of the wool, you said?'

Mac nodded. 'Left untreated the wool clots together. If they don't treat for it, the product is of little value.'

'But those sheep have produced excellent wool. I didn't see anything that would stop it making good money.'

'Mr Ford likes to prevent lice. He dips them every year, whether they need it or not. It's good farming practice and it doesn't let them get a start. Once you've got lice they're hard to get rid of, because you need to treat every sheep you have. If you don't get a clean muster and the one animal you leave behind is lousy, it'll infect the rest of the mob in the paddock.' He stopped and looked over at Thomas. 'Ever had nits?' he asked.

Thomas remembered a time when Howard hadn't been able to stop scratching and his mother had doused his head with kerosene and wrapped brown paper around it. His brother had got to have time off school when he didn't. Well, good for Howard.

He shook his head. 'My brother had them once.' The words were out of his mouth before he could stop them.

If Mac noticed that Thomas had just let some personal information slip, he pretended not to.

'You're lucky, then. Lice are similar to nits. They're blood-sucking mites and they make the sheep itch. You can always tell if a place has lice before you see the sheep.' He took his tobacco pouch out of his pocket and started to roll a cigarette. 'They rub, you see. Rub against trees, bushes, fences. And when they do that, the wool is torn out and stays wherever they've been.' He put the cigarette in his mouth and fumbled for his matches. 'If you don't get rid of them, they just keep on biting.'

'Right.' Thomas committed the information to memory.

'Miss Ford knows all this too. Like I said earlier, she'd be a good catch.' Mac lit his cigarette, then turned from the window to look at Thomas.

Thomas slid a sideways glance at his friend. 'If I didn't know better, I'd think you were match making.'

'One of my many talents.' Mac laughed.

Thomas shook his head. 'She won't be interested in the likes of me. I have nothing to offer her.'

Mac slapped him on the shoulder. 'Come on, you've got to beat Frankie at cards tonight. It's about time someone did!'

Chapter 11

2008

Laura leaned over the rails inside the shearing shed and listened to the rain on the tin roof. One of the merino rams she'd reared came over and nuzzled her hand.

Laura stroked his soft velvety nose. 'What's up, Boof?'

He tried to nibble her fingers and she yanked back her hand. 'Don't do that! It hurts. You can't be hungry, I just fed you.' Laura glanced down into the feed trough and noticed that the special blend of grains, salt and molasses she'd mixed earlier had all gone. 'Guts,' she said affectionately.

The three other rams that were also kept in the shed milled around, sniffing and tossing their heads at her gently. Now it was Random's turn to get a pat.

'So, you boys ready for tomorrow?' A thrill of nervousness and fear shot through her. It all came down to tomorrow, when she'd be taking her rams to the Royal Adelaide Show.

Catherine had been right about showing her 'boys' and she'd begun to have a few successes. The first couple of country shows Laura had attended hadn't netted her much except a 'Highly Commended' award. The year after, however, she managed to get a champion ribbon at one of the local shows. And the year after that, she'd taken a team to the Royal Adelaide Show and struck gold, winning the class with a fine-wool two-tooth ram.

Making the victory even sweeter was the fact that she'd beaten Meghan's best ram. However, Laura would never forget the look of hatred that crossed her former friend's face when her ram was sashed. Of course, Meghan had immediately rearranged her expression into a tight smile before shaking Laura's hand. 'Don't think it will ever happen again,' she'd hissed. 'We're better than you. Always have been, always will be. This is nothing but a fluke.' Meghan had turned away and was gone an instant later, leaving Laura feeling sick to the core.

She shook her head in an effort to put her former friend out of her mind. Meghan really was ridiculous. How they could ever have been best friends Laura would never understand. Meghan had turned out to be uncaring and vindictive. And as for Josh, and where he fitted in, she still didn't understand.

The warm breath from Random's nose touched her fingers. She looked down at the animal and had to stop herself from opening the wool again to view the luxurious fibre. It wouldn't have changed from the previous ten minutes, but it was hard to stop looking at what she hoped was the best wool she had produced. Ever.

She had a lot to thank Catherine for. This had been all her idea. And the farming school that her friend had first dreamt up was also now a reality.

It still made her heart ache that Howie hadn't lived to see

the school get off the ground. He'd seen all the work go into it, the red tape and all the snares Laura had encountered. He'd been there to talk to at the end of a bad phone call and to celebrate with her after a good one. It was Howie who'd suggested she take a girls-only approach, even if it was deemed politically incorrect, and Laura had jumped at that idea. She could remember how, surrounded by blokes at field days, she'd been too scared of sounding silly or uneducated to ask questions, worried that she might become the target of condescending comments. Laura knew she could give the girls confidence in their ability and make them stand tall among the men.

The idea of enrolling the students for a year had been a good one from her father. It let the girls see the whole cycle of farming, from seeding to harvest, mating to lambing, marking to shearing and all the boring things in between, like fencing. The course ran from June to May, so the students had graduated and were out looking for work as harvest approached. This gave them the chance to pick up some casual work. Hopefully the owners would see how good they were and offer them a job.

But, as Catherine had foreseen, it was a two-way street. Laura taught the girls all the things she'd learned from her Papa, but with a more modern approach, how she'd come to understand the job. She mentored the students and instilled poise and conviction in their decision making. In return, they kept her smiling and eager to get up and go to work every morning, as well as giving her the labour force she needed to keep Nambina running.

And they kept the loneliness at bay. Since her acrimonious split with Josh she'd kept the promise she'd made to herself. There'd been no more men.

All at once the rams looked in the direction of the shed's open door. Laura turned and saw the outline of an old and decrepit Rusty limping towards them. The cat's wildness had taken its toll. He'd had fights with other cats and more than one dog, and he bore scars and walked with a hobble, his left ear torn in two. One day, she knew, she'd come into the shed to find him gone forever.

She watched as the cat slid through the railings and, tail in the air, padded over to Boof. Ram and cat eyed each other for a moment, then Rusty took the few steps that separated them and wound his way in and around the ram's legs.

Boof leaned down and sniffed him. Rusty nuzzled back with his nose.

Boof's front knees buckled and the ram sat heavily on the grating. Laura watched in amazement as, with one swift movement, Rusty jumped onto the ram's back, paced in a circle to make a bed, then sat down and began to wash his paw. Boof didn't move.

'That's so funny,' she whispered, not wanting to break the spell. 'I knew you were mates, but I've never seen that before.' Certain no one would believe her if she told them, Laura had half a mind to take a photo with her mobile phone, but she didn't want to disturb the friends so, instead, she just watched.

A clattering noise spooked the rams, and they darted away to the far side of the pen. Rusty had to leap quickly to the ground so he wasn't thrown off.

'Morning, Laura,' called Tegan. The students had arrived.

'Hi, girls,' she answered and watched as they shook raindrops from their hats and coats. 'Cool enough for you?' Spring had supposedly sprung but the weather was unseasonably cold.

95

Allie held up her gloved hands. But for the blonde curls framing her face, her hair was hidden by a thick knitted beanie. 'It's freezing! It took me two goes to get out of bed this morning. I love my electric blanket! Better than a bloke, I reckon!'

'Speak for yourself,' Robyn snorted as she ripped off her cap and let her long auburn hair fall. 'I'd rather a man keep me warm any day.'

Tegan shot her a sideways glance. 'Yeah, a man called Will Scott, methinks.'

Laura hid a smile.

Robyn blushed and turned away. 'Maybe,' she answered coyly.

It was the students' youth and enthusiasm, laughter and teasing, that made Laura love the new direction her business had taken. It kept her feeling young and excited about farming—something she needed. It did her soul good to know there were plenty of young women coming into the agricultural industry, that the industry would be left in good hands when she no longer worked within it.

And this group of students was different to the others. Previous ones had been from towns or the city, with only the odd farm girl thrown in. Some of the city girls had grand plans to marry men with large acreages. Those girls never lasted long, something Laura had been thankful for. They frustrated her with their romantic notions of how the land should be worked and animals cared for.

The farm girls often needed experience away from the family farm before going home for good. As Laura's reputation grew, more of the students were genuine want-to-learn girls, girls like Tegan, Allie and Robyn.

These three were all from farming backgrounds and their personalities were as different as the places they came from.

Tegan had crossed the border from Victoria, and Laura loved how much she laughed. Hard work didn't worry her, and she was usually the first to pitch in and have a go.

Robyn was the quietest of the group. She didn't need many words to say what she needed to, rarely speaking unless it was important. She'd grown up in the Flinders Ranges, and she was forever marvelling at how different her home up north was compared with the country around Nambina, especially in terms of rainfall.

Allie worked hard. She asked lots of questions and was always on time, but Laura had the feeling that Allie wouldn't end up on a farm. She seemed more interested in the financial side—gross margins and returns per hectare. Laura thought she might get into banking or an agribusiness, which wasn't a bad thing. As far as she was concerned, the more financial institutions understood the vagaries of farming, the better.

'Will Scott?' Laura queried, a small smile playing around her lips as she recalled the tall farm lad from the other side of town. 'Really?'

'Possibly.' Robyn dismissed the question and focused on the rams. 'Are we ready to load?'

'That's a deflection if ever there was one,' Tegan said, laughing.

'Okay,' Laura said. 'I've bagged up all the feed the boys will need for the three days at the show. Do you remember why I told you they couldn't run out of the feed they're used to?'

'Because it'll upset their tummies and they'll get the shits,' they recited together like schoolchildren.

'Good, and that's why we need to take our water with us as well. I've got five bags of mix already on the ute. Everything else is over there. Robyn, you want to load up the drums of water? Allie, can you check it all off this list as we throw it on?' She handed Allie a clipboard. 'Don't want to leave anything to chance.' Laura smiled. 'Tegan, can you help me tarp up the crate?'

'Sure.'

They worked together until everything except the rams was loaded and ready. Every time Laura looked across at the boys they were watching, seeming to sense something was different about today.

Finally, it was time. 'Here are the halters. I'll grab Boof, you girls take the others.' Expertly slipping a rope over Boof's nose and under his chin, Laura yanked on it gently before leading him out of the pen and down towards the loading ramp. His hooves clattered on the wooden grating and she took a quick look at his feet. The trimming she'd given him a couple of weeks ago had been worth it. They were in good shape.

Random was next, followed by Jack and Mr Darcy. One by one, they were all transferred into the back of the ute and the tarp tied down.

'Do you know, there was one family who took their show team to a field day in the mid-north,' Laura said as she made sure the rope was tied tight. 'It's always hotter up there than here so they opened the back flap to let air flow through. When they got to the field day they discovered the rams' faces were all sooty from the diesel fumes.'

'Oh no!' gasped Allie. 'What a waste of a year's work! They would have lost a heap of money, wouldn't they?'

Laura nodded. 'They had to pull the exhibits out and that wasn't the worst of it. There was an oily film all over the fleeces. It made them look like they were under-prepared.' She turned back to them. 'I've told you about the five Ps, haven't I?'

'Preparation prevents piss-poor performance,' they all chimed in together.

'Ah,' said Laura. 'I might have to get some new lines.'

'Imagine that,' Robyn said, dragging the conversation back. 'Blade shearing, getting a beautiful amount of wool on the animal, all the feed and care you've put into him, let alone the time spent making sure he's fit and healthy, or trimming his feet or whatever, just to pull out. That's insane!'

'Bloody disaster,' Tegan agreed. She bent down to grab another water barrel.

Laura nodded. The care factor with these girls was right where it should be.

'Okay, you guys all packed?'

They nodded.

'Righto, well, I guess we should be off.' She dug in her pocket and came out with a fuel card. 'You can use this to buy your diesel, since you're taking your own car,' she said, handing it to Robyn. 'I've written the PIN number on the back. Make sure you lock the gate and I'll see you in Adelaide at the showgrounds. And girls?' She turned back to look at them. 'Make sure you look pretty. The people get judged too.'

Chapter 12

2008

Laura was still streets away from the showground but she could hear the music and loud disembodied voices booming over the PA system.

After unloading the rams into their pens in the shed and parking her ute close by so their feed and water were handy, she had walked the short distance to the motel she had booked into. She'd slept restlessly, with dreams of Howie judging the classes and her rams losing.

From where she was now, if she looked up, she knew she'd see the Ferris wheel. But she didn't look up. In fact, she'd be avoiding sideshow alley and the rides. To Laura, the show was about letting people know what was out in the community. It was a shop window for the state, so to speak.

Laura hadn't been joking when she told the girls they'd be judged too, and this morning she was dressed in a striped shirt that had been ironed within an inch of its life, her best RM Williams boots and crisp clean moleskins. In her jacket pocket, her fingers closed on the small pin Howie had given her before he died. Laura took out the badge and looked at it for a moment before pinning it to her lapel. With a deep breath, she straightened and threw her head backwards, wishing just for one moment Howie could be beside her.

Can you see, Papa? she wondered silently. *Do you know what I'm doing? Do you approve?* Then she dismissed her musings: he'd support her no matter what she did.

She thought about the email she'd received that morning. Where the name of the sender would usually announce itself were the words: 'Don't come.' There was nothing written in the body of the email.

Laura was pretty sure Meghan had sent it, but could hardly believe it herself, it seemed so petty and immature. She put it out of her mind. Meghan wasn't going to spoil her day, she was determined.

At the entrance to the showgrounds, she pointed to her badge and held up an exhibitor card. The elderly man on the gate smiled and waved her through. 'You're too much of a whipper-snapper to be a life member of the Agricultural Society,' he said with a knowing wink. 'Pinch it from your dad, did you?'

'No! It was my Papa's.' She glanced down at the pin again. 'Before he died he had the membership transferred to me somehow. I've got the papers at home. Sorry, I didn't think to bring them.'

'Only pulling your leg, love. Happens a lot. Sorry about your granddad. Who was he? Been on this gate for nigh on forty years. Mighta known him.'

'Howie. Howie Murphy.' She took the program he offered

and glanced at the line-up behind her, not really wanting to get into a conversation. She was too nervous.

'Howie! I knew Howie. Lot of people knew him. But I didn't know he'd passed.' He looked at her with kind eyes. 'Sorry for your loss. He was a good man, he was. Always spoke to us gate-men.' He touched his hat and smiled again. 'You have a good day, young lady.' Then he turned to the next person. Laura hurried away, thankful the exchange hadn't lasted any longer.

As she drew closer to the pavilion, she could smell coffee and bacon and eggs. Those farmers who'd slept the night outside the shed, not willing to leave their animals alone, were having breakfast.

Her stomach lurched as a man emerged from the back of his ute, his eyes sleepy and hair tousled. From a distance, he looked like Josh.

It wasn't, she realised a moment later, before reminding herself that he'd never spend a night roughing it, anyway, no matter how valuable his sheep were. That wasn't the way his family did things. Nothing but five-star all the way for them nowadays.

Inside the shed, she moved quickly to check the rams. They weren't really sheep to her, anymore; they were pets. She'd fed, watered and talked to them every day for thirteen months, so they'd grown used to her too.

She could tell they were pleased to hear her calming voice in the strange environment. She spoke softly and Boof gently bunted his head up against her hand. Mr Darcy and Jack had both been sitting down but opened their eyes and stood up, coming to the rails to greet her. Random had his back turned, ignoring her. Laura looked him over but saw nothing unusual. Random could be a bit like that. Social one moment, aloof the next.

'It's a bit weird, isn't it, fellas. But don't worry, you'll do fine.' She checked their feed and water trays, making sure they were clean, then gave each animal a once-over with her hands. They didn't seem any the worse for wear from the trip and, thankfully, there was no sign they were getting an upset tummy.

'They're fine!' It was Tegan's voice, and Laura looked up. The students were rushing towards her, smiles on their faces. Allie was eating a steak sandwich and Robyn held a brown paper bag and a paper cup filled with what Laura assumed was coffee.

'We've been here watching them. Robyn would have slept here last night if she'd been allowed,' Tegan said.

Laura had told them it was more important to have a good night's sleep, discouraging them from staying at the show grounds.

'Ha! Well, I guess they are boys and you said you'd rather be kept warm by a bloke,' Laura said drily.

'I'm not a New Zealander,' Robyn said. 'Hungry?' she offered the grease-stained bag.

'Those smells always make me hungry,' Laura said as she peeked inside. 'I *love* doughnuts! How did you get these? Usually nobody starts cooking until the gates open to the public.'

'We bribed one of the food vendors,' Tegan said.

Laura arched an eyebrow as she bit into the hot sugary treat. 'Should I ask?'

'No.'

'Right.' She looked around at the rest of the shed. There were only a few people other than stewards. The rest of the pens were filled with merino sheep, all in different categories. 'I'm usually the first one here. When did you girls arrive?'

Allie glanced at her watch and licked her fingers. 'About three-quarters of an hour ago.'

'Checked out any of the competition?' Laura posed the question casually, while casting around, trying to get a gauge on the quality of the animals displayed.

'Not really. We didn't know if we were able to go and look without the owners around,' Robyn said. 'But we did walk down the aisles with our hands tucked firmly behind our backs.'

The other two nodded.

'And,' she drew out the word, 'obviously we're not the judges . . .'

'And obviously we're biased,' Tegan added.

'But we're in with a chance,' Robyn finished.

'Well, then, let's go and have a look and you can tell me why you think so,' Laura said, putting her teaching hat back on.

As they made their way around the pens, Laura quizzed the girls on the pros and cons of each animal. She felt a great sense of satisfaction at their answers and the ease with which they handled the wool.

They'd only started with her four months ago, and now here they were acting like professional judges. Their confidence made her smile with pleasure. She knew she'd made a difference in their lives. When they left next year, they'd be ready and able to hold good jobs and start to make their way up the ladder.

'Hey, Laura, have you seen this one?' Allie was bent over a hindquarter and spoke in a whisper.

Laura followed her and saw her hands were on the animal's testicles.

'Problem?' she asked.

'One's bigger than the other. Only marginally, but I can still tell.'

'That's not good for a show ram.' Laura quickly ran her eyes over the rest of the body and noticed a slightly undershot jaw. 'Look at this.' She pointed with her eyes to the head.

The girls nodded to show they understood and they moved on.

When they were a safe distance away, Laura explained why it was unprofessional and bad stockmanship to show an animal like that. 'You see, if you breed from poor genetics, you don't get quality offspring. That ram will throw undershot jaw lambs. They can't eat properly, which in turn means they won't fatten, and you won't get to sell them. It's a domino effect. Shit in, shit out. Simple. The bad ball? It won't matter so much in a commercial situation where all the ram lambs will be castrated and made into wethers, but there is no way you should touch that animal in a breeding situation.'

The girls nodded again.

They finished checking out the rest of the competition, then Laura decided it was time to get a coffee. 'I'll meet you back here in half an hour,' she said, digging around in her pocket for money. 'You going to stay or look at something else?'

'I wanted to see some of the cattle, so we might wander over there,' Tegan said.

'No worries. See you soon.' She flipped a wave as the girls left. Then, with goosebumps, she moved towards the wall where the board that boasted the names of past winners in all categories hung.

There it was. '1985. H. E. Murphy. Grand Champion, Two-tooth Ram.' She would have run her fingers over his name but it was out of her reach. She had to be content just to stare.

'You're just like a bad smell. You don't go away.'

Laura's jaw tightened at the sound of Meghan's voice. It was full of undisguised dislike. She turned to see a woman with her arms crossed and a sneer on her face.

Laura immediately noticed Meghan looked ill, with a red nose and eyes and untidy hair. Megan was also sporting a couple of pimples on the corner of her mouth—she certainly didn't look like her usual polished self. In fact, knowing how much Meghan took pride in her appearance, something her mother had drummed into her since she was a young girl, Laura was surprised she'd come, suffering from what looked like full-blown flu.

'Yes, Meghan. I'm here. Did you expect otherwise?' She put the challenge out there.

'Unfortunately, no. You have never known when to give up.'

'That's why I've been successful,' Laura pointed out. 'I'm like a dog with a bone. I just don't go away. Even if someone is trying to bully me. I assume the email was from you?'

'Oh, that's a dirty word, Laura. I like to think of it more

as a push in the right direction. We will win this showing, you know. There really wasn't any need to enter any of your, um, rams.' Meghan said the last word sarcastically. 'I was just giving you a little heads-up not to enter. I couldn't see the point in you coming.'

'I guess that's up to the judges,' Laura countered and turned away.

'And Laura,' Meghan said in a by-the-way tone. 'Have you realised yet? We're entitled to your land. By law. Did you know that?' Meghan gave a mirthless smile and tilted her head to the side as she spoke. 'No? '

Laura stood suddenly frozen with fear.

'Well, I'm not surprised. You really don't know much about your history, do you?'

Laura exhaled through her nose and counted to ten before she answered. When she did, she spoke slowly and deliberately. 'I have no idea what you're talking about. Stop trying to bully me. Stop trying to threaten me. Surely we can be adults and speak civilly to each other if we are in public, even though I'd be happy if I didn't have to talk to you at all. So, if you'll let me pass, I'll get out of your way.' She tried to leave, but Meghan still blocked her path.

'Oh, I've got proof. You don't know what I know,' Meghan said in a low tone full of intimidation. 'And when you do, you'll have no choice but to give Nambina to me.'

'Hit me with it, then,' Laura shot back, ignoring her trepidation. 'Tell me now. What's this so-called information you have?'

'I most certainly will. But only at the right time. Now, I must be off. Josh and I have to wash the rams.' Meghan turned to go. 'Been lovely seeing you.' She said it loudly, so people passing by would hear her friendly tone. But her last line was delivered in a whisper. 'And watch your mailbox.' She cocked her finger and thumb at Laura and made the sign of a gun.

Laura swallowed hard as she watched the other woman's swaying hips move towards the lockers lining the shed wall. With smooth hands and perfect fingernails, Meghan opened the door and brought out a bucket, rag and grooming brush before glancing back at Laura and giving her a knowing smile.

Laura's mind was racing. What was Meghan on about? Her family hadn't been in the district as long as the Murphys. They were only third generation. The Murphys were four. How could they take Nambina away from her? They bordered her every boundary—she was landlocked by them. But they had no right to Nambina.

Certainly they could *buy* her land. If it was on the market. Which it wasn't. But take it? Laura couldn't understand why Meghan was saying she could. Had she lost her mind?

Laura suddenly smiled as the realisation hit her. Meghan was trying to put her off concentrating on the show. On the rams. Hoping she'd make a mistake and stuff something up. Well, that wasn't going to happen either. She would never understand her former friend. Had Meghan been such a bitch in the old days and she just hadn't seen it?

'Dammit!' she muttered under her breath. 'She knows she's rattled me.'

'Look at her bloody hands.' A voice beside Laura made her jump. 'They've never done a day's work, no matter what she says.'

'Catherine!' Laura's surprise turned to delight, and they hugged.

'Here I am, honey! Just like I promised. I have to tell you, that witch hasn't gotten any nicer since I saw her last.' She shook her head. 'Some people just ain't got nice in them.'

'Got that right,' groaned Laura, still confused by Meghan's threat. She really hoped it was all about distraction. Surely it couldn't be anything else.

'Come on, let's get coffee, and then I want to meet your girls. That woman doesn't deserve a second thought.'

'And I need to hear all about what you've been up to. How was the last workshop you held?'

They linked arms and walked out into the bright sunlight, Laura desperately trying to banish Meghan's threat from her mind.

Chapter 13

2008

Laura straightened Tegan's jacket and brushed an imaginary piece of straw off her shoulders. 'You look so good, you might upstage this bloke,' she said, flicking her head towards the ram Tegan was holding.

Tegan flashed a nervous smile as she hooked the lead rope around one of the ram's horns, ran it under his chin and tied it to the other horn. 'I hope Random isn't random today,' she quipped.

Laura slipped her own hand through another rope then scratched the soft skin under Boof's jaw and tugged gently. 'Come on, Boof. Please be a good boy.' Her tone was half-joking, half-pleading. 'Okay, we right? Pen of two two-tooth rams. Let's see how we go.'

She pulled Boof forward and he ambled beside her at hip level. Once she was off and running without any problems, she turned back to see how Tegan was doing. Rams, especially on a rich diet, could be flighty, and Laura was just praying nothing would go wrong. She didn't want to give Meghan one ounce of satisfaction.

It was the last day of judging and, apart from the unpleasantness with Meghan on the first day, everything had gone pretty well. Mr Darcy had won Grand Champion for the fine-medium wool category, but Jack hadn't managed to win anything. It was down to these last two rams. This was the big one. Grand Champion for Fine Wool.

'Nervous?' Tegan asked from behind.

'It's always good to be a little nervous, because it keeps you on your toes. But I know I couldn't have done anything more. I've thrown my best at it and if it doesn't come off, it doesn't. I've done all I can do.' She would have feigned nonchalance except she was too busy pulling Boof towards the artificial turf of the judging ring. She couldn't tell her students she wanted this red, white and blue grand champion ribbon more than anything. That wouldn't be something a good mentor would say.

They waited in line until they were asked to lead their animals out into the ring. Laura scanned the crowd, hoping to see her dad and Georgie. They'd said they'd do their best to come, but Sean was on call so he couldn't promise. Catherine had stayed for only a few hours before she jet-setted off to another state for a public speaking engagement. 'I have a dream . . .' she said to Laura, 'where producers and consumers have an equal passion, respect and understanding for food production in our country.' It was the start of her speech and Laura had felt goosebumps erupt over her arms when she saw the fire and passion in Catherine's face as she started to speak.

A small crowd was seated in the stands, the faces mostly old and wizened. The old-timers wore the standard tweed jacket, tie and moleskins. Laura could see flashes of gold, as the men and women turned to look at each ram entering the show ring. It was their membership badges catching the light, she realised. Surveying them, Laura knew the people sitting there were one of the challenges facing the ag industry. Not the people themselves, but their age.

Laura believed there weren't enough young people encouraged to take up careers in the business she loved. Looking back at the fresh young faces of her girls, she hoped she was changing that.

A steward rushed past with a dust pan and broom with sheep poo in it.

'What a job, hey?' she muttered to Tegan. 'Keeping the turf clean.'

'Reckon,' the girl answered through clenched teeth, and Laura glanced around to see Random tossing his head in protest. She heard him stamp his front feet.

'You right?' she asked, worried. 'Don't let him get the better of you. It's not the done thing to have your ram get away from you, and especially not now. Hold him under the chin a bit tighter.'

Laura chastised herself. She should have taken Random. She hadn't because Boof was her favourite. A silly decision like that could be costly.

Laura looked again for her family. Instead her eyes came to rest on Josh. He was standing by himself next to the tiered-seat stands. As always, he had his camera around his neck.

She felt a tiny stab of regret and anger. The memory of the day in the hospital and the accusations he made were as fresh as ever, eight years on.

He shifted his gaze and their eyes locked. Neither of them smiled, but before Laura's gaze slipped away, she saw him nod slightly.

She turned. There was Meghan, standing on the other side of the ring, mouth in an unpleasant smile. Her arms were crossed and as she held Laura's gaze she slowly brought her hand up to her throat and slashed her finger across it.

Sweat broke out over Laura's brow and she looked away.

'Okay, Tegan?' she said to distract herself.

'I got him,' came the determined answer, but a couple of seconds later, Laura heard a gasp. She turned sharply. 'What's wrong?' but Tegan couldn't answer. Random had twisted his head back and forth and somehow the girl's hand had got caught in the rope. There were shouts and cries from the crowd as the harness twisted into his chin and, in an effort to avoid the pain, Random backed up, running into the other competitors.

Tegan let out a cry, and out of the corner of her eye Laura saw Allie and Robyn rush from the pens behind the ring to help. A steward ran over and tried to get a choke hold around the ram's neck.

Random wasn't having any of it, however, and with one final twist he managed to free himself from Tegan's grasp before running blindly towards the crowd.

'No!' Laura gasped. She was still holding Boof as firmly as she could, so she was powerless to do anything.

'I'll hold him,' a male voice called, and she felt a hand grab Boof's lead with certainty.

Without looking to see who it was, she yelled her thanks and ran after Random. The ram dodged the army of people trying to catch him, changing direction and heading towards the pens.

'See if you can herd him down the raceway,' she yelled to no one in particular.

Laura had seen this happen only once before and she knew that, while some people stood back, shock etched in their faces and their feet stuck to the ground, others would be running towards the ram, which would only make things worse.

She got a bead on Random and let out a moan of dismay as she saw him lurch into the air to try and clear a pen. There was a sickening thud as he landed on the other side.

At first, Laura thought everything was okay. Random was in a pen and contained. Her paced slowed. She didn't want to upset him any more by approaching him with sudden movements.

She heard someone call for the vet. Random was baa-ing loudly and pawing at the ground as if he was in pain.

Then she saw the blood.

'Bloody hell!' she shouted, and took off at a run again.

By the time she reached him, a crowd had gathered around the pen and a steward was holding Random by the head. 'Let me through, please,' she begged, and the people parted. When she got clear, she could see that blood was coming from Random's testicles. They'd been ripped in the jump.

'Oh no,' she moaned.

Allie, Robyn and Tegan arrived at her side, puffing.

'The vet's on his way,' the steward said to her as she took Random's lead.

'Thank you,' she muttered, unsure what to do.

'Righto, show's over,' the steward called. 'Back to the judging ring, please, everyone.'

Laura was grateful it didn't take long for the crowd to disperse, and the embarrassment she felt was soon overridden by her fear for the ram.

She looked at Tegan, who was pale and holding her hand. 'You okay?'

'I think so,' she answered. 'Laura, I'm so sorry.'

'Let's not talk about it now. Allie, I left Boof with someone, can you find him and take him back to his pen?' She was interrupted by a voice calling her name.

'Laura! Laura, love?'

She looked up to see Sean and Georgie hurrying towards them. Relief washed over her. She didn't have to be strong now. Then she shook herself. Of course she did.

'Dad.' Her voice cracked a little.

'It's okay, it's okay.' He hushed her as he'd done when she was small, except she wasn't crying now. She closed her eyes and when she opened them, Sean was inspecting the ram's nether regions.

'Looks nasty, Laurs. I reckon the spermatic cord is haemorrhaging. Can you get him on his back? Need to clamp it. I'll see if I can hold it together until the vet gets here.'

Laura had feared that since she'd seen the wound. She nodded and, as gently as she could, twisted the ram's head to make him sink to the ground. She craned her neck to see what Sean was examining and saw the exposed inside of the nut.

'Oh, you poor darling,' she said. 'I'm sorry, I'm sorry,' she whispered soothingly into Random's woolly head. She stroked her thumbs down his cheeks while the ram shifted with pain and agitation.

Sean was probing the wound with a look of concentration.

'Got it,' he said with relief. He turned to the stewards. 'Get that vet here as quick as you can. This bloke's in a bad way.'

'He's coming,' the steward answered, as he glanced towards the door. Nothing more was said until the vet ran in.

'We're over here!' Allie yelled, raising her hand.

The vet made his way over. When he was in hearing distance Sean called out: 'I'm a doctor, but I used to be a farmer. I know animals. It's the spermatic cord on the left side. Needs pressure and clamping.'

'Right.' The vet obviously agreed with the diagnosis because he dug into his bag for clamps and gauze. Sean moved out of the way to let him do his job, and Laura heard him ask after Tegan.

There was silence while everyone watched the vet work. Sean poked and felt Tegan's hand before proclaiming it was nothing but a bad sprain.

'Should get some ice for it,' he said, looking around as if hoping a bag would materialise.

'Don't worry about it,' Tegan answered in a low voice.

It didn't take long for the work to be completed. The vet finished by giving Random an injection for long-term pain relief. Then, handing over a packet of antibiotics, he told Laura to see her own vet as soon as she returned home. 'I haven't castrated him, because I don't think the testicle has been damaged beyond repair. You still might be able to use him with a small mob of ewes, but see what your vet says when he examines him.' He started to pack up. 'He'll be a bit sleepy for a while.'

'Thank you,' Laura said, sitting with the ram's head in her lap. She offered him her hand. 'Thank you *so* much.'

He shook it and nodded to the rest of the gathering, before leaving.

'Well, that buggered the trip, didn't it?' Sean sighed, sinking down next to his daughter.

'Too bloody right,' she said. 'You girls okay?'

They nodded mutely, but Laura could see the shock on their pale faces. 'That's the problem with showing animals. They become so much like our friends and then we're devastated when they get hurt. Sorry you had to go through that. I should have been holding him, Tegan, especially since he can be difficult at times. It was an unfortunate accident.' She took a breath. 'Are the other boys all right?'

Robyn nodded. 'They're okay. A couple of other breeders gave us a hand and we got Boof back in his pen. Jack and Mr Darcy are fine.'

'Okay, well how about we try to shift Random into the back of the ute where he'll be more comfortable. Good thing today was the last day. We can head home tomorrow and get him in a paddock so he doesn't catch anything from the dirty straw.'

Random was a dead weight and it took the help of four strong men to help shift him and settle him in fresh bedding.

'Sorry for your bad luck,' one of the men said as they moved off, and the others nodded.

'Thank you again,' Laura called out. The men waved. 'Well, then, that's finished. Is it too early for a drink?' she smiled weakly.

'No, it's certainly not,' Georgie answered as she put her arm around Tegan. 'Come on, let's head over to the Stockman's. I'll shout you all. You deserve one.' She shepherded the girls towards the bar opposite the ram pavilion and the others followed.

Sean fell in beside Laura. 'Don't worry, love. These things happen. It's not the end of the world.'

'I know, Dad. Just makes me feel horrible.'

'Yeah, I know.'

Then Laura stopped short. 'You guys go on. I just need to thank the stewards and the people who helped us. I didn't before. Allie, who was the man who helped you get Boof back into the pen? Did he tell you his name?'

Allie tried to remember. 'No, he didn't. But he did say he was from down our way.'

'Really?' There was only one other stud near Nambina.

'I know who it was,' Robyn piped up. 'I've only seen him at the golf club bar, though. Never talked to him. It was your neighbour, Laura. Josh Hunter.'

'Josh Hunter?' For a moment Laura couldn't speak.

Why had he helped out when Meghan was so openly trying to ruin her?

Laura left feeling very uneasy.

Chapter 14

1937

Thomas pushed hard on the brush, as Mac had instructed, scrubbing away any trace of the greasy lanoline on the shed floor so the wool wouldn't stick to it next time. His back usually ached doing this job, but today he didn't really feel it. Since Elizabeth Ford first made her appearance a week earlier, he could think of nothing else. Her knowledge of sheep and wool both fascinated and intimidated him, as did her beauty and confidence. He found himself looking forward to the Adelaide Show even more, but with apprehension. In short, he'd never felt like this before.

He tried to remain focused on the job at hand. They'd finally finished the shed and were planning to head off in the morning. Mac said you could tell it was the end of the season because all the blokes were getting a bit chirpy and excited about heading back home. The constant ribbing from his workmates had proved that point, but made him withdraw even further.

'Ignore them. They're only having a laugh,' Mac had said. Thomas knew that unless someone had been through the amount of ridicule and abuse he had, they wouldn't understand what the teasing did to a bloke. He'd rather just be invisible. Still, if Elizabeth was to notice him, maybe he needed to get up a bit of confidence, a bit of courage.

When he finished scrubbing, he stood and stretched. On a table were Mac's books, neatly stacked and ready to be packed away. He walked across and ran his hands over where Elizabeth's had been, then looked about the shed. This place had been his turning point. He'd learned more during his time here than in any other shed.

He straightened and tried to stand tall. If he was going to succeed, his desire for invisibility had to stop here. With one last glance around and a nod to the Aboriginal boy who was finishing the last of the sweeping, he walked out. He was ready to be a new man.

༄

'Sorry, boys,' Mr Ford called, after darkness had fallen. 'This is the last of the beer. Might be time to hit the hay.'

There was a chorus of disappointment from the men who were left at the camp fire. They'd been laughing at one of the ringer's kelpies. Jacko, the sullen head stockman, had a wonderful singing voice and the shearers had managed to get him to sing 'Danny Boy'. The trouble was, every time he opened his mouth and struck his first note, his dog broke into a howl.

Tez was rolling around on the ground, laughing so hard he could barely talk, while the rest of the men had given up reciting bushman's poetry and were trying to sing to get the poor dog howling again.

'Oh, Danny . . .'

'Oh, oh, ohhhh,' the dog wailed mournfully.

There was a fresh round of laughter and Thomas couldn't help but join in. The dog looked bemused at the attention.

'That's it, fellas,' Mr Ford reiterated. 'Time to wind it up for the evening.'

Gradually, the men made their way back to camp with calls of 'good night'.

'I got an idea,' Clarrie whispered to Thomas. 'You game?'

Thomas looked at him then, remembering he was supposed to be a new person, nodded quickly.

'Come on, Tez. Gecko, you in? We're going to the pub.'

'What, so you can get drunk and try to fight someone again?' Tez asked. 'I don't think so.'

'They'll be shut,' Jock said. 'It's well and truly after six.'

Clarrie just tapped the side of his nose and turned towards the track that led to a small siding not three miles away.

'Get away with you. You want another drink too, you know ya do,' he called over his shoulder. One by one they followed. Clarrie was right—they weren't ready for the night to end.

The pub was indeed shut, but Clarrie led them around the back anyway. 'Come on!' he cried. 'I'm damned thirsty after that walk. The publican won't mind. We've got an agreement.'

Thomas rolled his eyes but stayed quiet.

'What sort of agreement?' Tez asked.

Clarrie didn't answer. He'd found the back door unlocked and was now holding it open so they could enter.

Inside it was dark, but Clarrie seemed to know where he was going, so they followed him in single file. In the main bar he lit a gasoline lamp.

'Righto, who wants a drink?' he asked. 'Just leave the money on the bar for Bert to collect in the morning.'

He took a glass from the shelf and poured a beer, then another and another.

A door swung open and a man in striped pyjamas stood in the frame, holding a lantern.

'What the hell are you doing?' he asked.

Thomas noticed there wasn't any fear in his voice. It was as if he was used to unexpected midnight visitors.

'Nothing for you to worry about, Berty,' Clarrie answered. 'Just getting me mates a few drinks.'

'Clarrie? That you?' the man asked.

'Yeah, mate, it's me.'

There was a silence as Bert stood there, taking them in.

'Well, then, make sure you leave your money on the counter.'

'I always do. Now get outta here. There might be a blue heeler around here somewhere, waiting to yank yer licence.'

Thomas thought a policeman turning up was probably a long shot, considering they were miles from the nearest town and this was only a small railway siding.

'We're just here to have a few and play some cards,' Clarrie said.

The publican turned and left, shutting the door behind him.

Clarrie raised his glass. 'Don't worry, boys. As I said, previous arrangements.' He winked. 'Cheers.'

When everyone had a drink in front of them, Thomas pulled out a deck of cards and began shuffling them expertly. 'Who's for a game?' he asked.

'Where'd you learn to shuffle like that?' Clarrie asked, unable to hide his admiration.

Thomas shrugged. 'Don't know. Just always have been able to.'

'Reckon you should try and get a seat on a poker game in one of the pubs. You'd probably win a fistful of money.'

Thomas grinned. 'Don't reckon that's my thing.'

An hour later, Clarrie lay on the floor where he'd fallen after nodding off on his feet, and Gecko was slumped at the bar. Only Frankie and Jock still had drinks in front of them and they'd be the last, for everyone's pocket was empty.

'Bloody good cut-out,' Tez slurred, then he howled like the dog had earlier in the night. There were a few snorts of laughter, then everyone went quiet.

'So, Thomas. What's in store for you now?' Jock asked as he stared into his empty beer bottle.

Thomas shuffled the pack of cards and then put them in his pocket. 'I'm going to Adelaide with Mac,' he said. 'He's judging at the show there.'

Jock took another sip. 'So what's your story? Where did he find you? You've never told us anything about your life before here. We've travelled together for months and you're as much of a mystery as when Mac arrived with you.'

Thomas shrugged. 'No mystery. He picked me up down south and brought me with him. Nothing to tell.'

'Nothing to tell, my foot,' snorted Jock. 'You've got a history. I know you have. Everyone of us here has a history.

Why do you think we single blokes flit from one shed to another? We haven't got roots, we just ride on to the next shed. Take Clarrie here,' he nodded at the snoring man. 'Ever considered why he drinks until he falls asleep, even though he knows it's going to happen and he'll end up covered in bruises? And Tez. How he knows how to handle Clarrie when he does? And why he stays away from his family farm?' He waved his bottle around. 'Ah, yes, everyone's got a history. But I'll tell you one thing, Thomas, whatever your last name is. If you ever go wool classing and have your own shed, I'd work under you any day. You've a skill. I can see Mac's training you up. When everything is said and done, if you've been schooled by him, I'd work with you. Whatever your history is.' He drained his glass.

'I'm heading off.' Jock glanced around. 'Who's coming with me?' He laid the last of his money on the counter. 'Clarrie's got a good deal here. Wouldn't mind knowing how he got it.' He paused while he negotiated getting off the bar stool. 'See? History.'

With that he turned and swayed from the room, leaving Thomas feeling pleased at his words. He knew now he had a goal to aim for.

Chapter 15

2008

Laura sat at her office desk, reading an email from Tim Burns, the vet. It didn't make any sense. She'd started the day hoping to put the events of the previous week behind her. Until she received the email from Tim.

Trying to ignore the flutter of uneasiness in her stomach, she read the email for the fifth time.

> Dear Laura,
>
> I have examined Random, your merino ram, and can confirm that the treatment he received from the show vet was exemplary.
>
> On further examination, I believe . . .

Laura looked up as she heard voices, then knocking. The students stood in the open doorway, their faces bright with expectation.

'Morning,' she said and moved around her desk to sit in the meeting area.

The room was set up so that, when she sat at her desk, she had a view out the window. There was a small lounge space with a coffee table and four comfy chairs where she could chat with her students and any business visitors to Nambina. A whiteboard hung on the wall, with the farm outline drawn on it. Within the boundaries, the fences were marked and all the paddocks identified by name. The livestock living in each paddock were noted, as were the cropping paddocks. Whenever animals were moved into a different location or some other change occurred, the information would be recorded immediately on the whiteboard. This was the control centre of the farm.

'Morning,' chorused the girls.

'How's Random?' Robyn asked.

'He's a bit sore and sorry for himself, but he'll be okay,' Laura said, settling into her usual chair at the small table and gesturing for them to join her. 'It's early days, but Tim thinks we'll be able to breed from him after all. He's still an in-patient, though, at the vet's in town.' She smiled.

'Yes!' Tegan clenched her fist and punched the air.

'So what's on today, then?' Allie asked dully. She pulled off her hat and shook out her hair.

Laura noticed her skin had broken out in red blotches. *Bloody hormones*, she thought with sympathy, before looking over at the whiteboard. 'Have any of you been out into West Three?' she asked. West Three was the paddock that housed five hundred ewes and lambs.

'I was out there a day before we went to the show,' Robyn said.

'See any problems?'

Robyn shook her head, but her face tightened. Laura could tell she was wondering if she'd missed something.

'Okay. Good.' She smiled inwardly as Robyn relaxed. It wasn't that she meant to get the girls uptight, but she asked so that, when they were in the paddocks, they would be asking themselves the same questions. It taught responsibility and initiative.

'What about East Five?' she asked. East Five held the cows and calves.

'That was fine when I was there yesterday,' Tegan volunteered. 'The electric fence was working but I had to tighten the float on the trough. The adjustment wasn't quite right and it was overflowing.'

'Good work,' Laura commented, and then moved on to East Nine.

The girls looked at each other and Laura saw Tegan glance at the map. Hesitantly she answered, 'There's nothing in that paddock.'

'You're right,' Laura said. She looked around at the three girls. Allie was very quiet this morning, she noticed. Laura had heard her arrive home late the night before. Perhaps she'd had a big weekend and was still nursing a hangover.

She didn't expect her students to head out around the farm every weekend, but she'd often notice the girls would go out by themselves and check the stock or things they'd done during the day. It ensured they had extra information if Laura ever asked, and it was something she encouraged. 'That's where today's work starts. In East Nine. Fencing.' It was never a popular job and she let the word hang in the air, waiting for cries of displeasure. There weren't any.

She liked that about this group. She'd had some students who wanted to pick and choose what they did. On other farms she'd seen girls in skimpy tops thrust their chests out and make doe eyes at the closest male in the hope that the harder jobs would be done for them by the blokes. These young women weren't like that. They just got on with what they were learning and asked to do.

'Okay.' She stood and moved over to the map and ran her finger along the black line. 'See this bit of fence here? You'll know it's the boundary between the Hunters and us. Just along here,' she pointed to a shaded area, 'is an old fence line.' She turned back to the girls. 'Do you know where I mean?'

All three nodded.

'Right. There's a fair bit of rubbish along here—by "rubbish" I mean scrubby bushes, a few trees. There's a bit of native vegetation there, but not a lot. I want to cut this paddock in half from here,' she pointed to a spot on the fence and drew her finger across to the other internal fence, 'to here. So we're making one large paddock into two smaller ones I'll use as lambing paddocks next year. To do that, we need to clear this bit of rubbish away first, because we need easy access to be able to do the work and we don't want anything growing up through the new fence, or being too close so it can fall on it.'

'Won't you get into trouble over that?' asked Tegan. 'Aren't there laws against clearing now?'

'Yep, there are, but this is only about half a hectare and it's to make way for a fence so I'm sure it's okay. Bloody hell, there's so much crap about what we can and can't do on our own land these days, it's ridiculous. I might get a slap on the wrist, if anyone sees it, but it's a risk I'm prepared to take because the benefits will outweigh any problems. I'm really just cleaning up an old fence line.'

'Okay, so do you want me to take the front-end loader out there?' Allie asked.

'If you like. Robyn and Tegan, you bring the ute out and I'll bring mine. We'll need a chain too. Once we get the bush piled up, we'll bang in some steel posts and run a wire to make sure we're getting the fence in a straight line. Okay with all of that?'

'Yep,' Robyn answered, and the others nodded.

'Okay, I'll see you out there. I've just got to answer an email.'

The girls left and Laura returned to her computer. She looked at the screen saver—a faded photo of Howie and herself when she was much younger. Howie sat astride a motorbike with Laura in front of him. Both of them were grinning, although what they were laughing at, Laura couldn't remember. She couldn't recall the particular day either. But she loved the photograph. Howie had his hands on her shoulders and she was half-turned to look up at him. The love was apparent.

How she missed him! The worst time was coming home after dark. When he was alive, Howie would always have the fire roaring and dinner simmering on the stove. He'd be in his chair, sipping a glass of red wine while he watched the evening news. Now, with him gone, she came home to a cold and empty house every night.

Laura wondered what Howie would make of Meghan's latest threat. He'd be appalled, she was certain. And what would he make of Tim Burns's email?

She sighed and shook the mouse, watching as the computer screen came to life. The email was still open.

> . . . within time, he will be able to perform stud duties.
>
> You asked me to run some tests in light of his unusual reaction at the show. I can confirm that I found nothing to indicate any medical reason for his behaviour.
>
> However, I would like to discuss some other findings with you on the phone. Please give me a call on my mobile number when you get this.

Laura shivered involuntarily. Somehow she knew there was something more to this than met the eye. Hearing the roar of the tractor engine, she glanced out the window. There was still time to make the phone call before she was needed in the paddock.

The vet answered after a few rings.

They exchanged pleasantries and then Tim asked about the show. 'Sounds like it was quite eventful?'

'Yeah. I'm pretty sure he ripped himself on the steel post that was belted into the ground right on the corner of the pen.'

'Hmm. There shouldn't be anything like that in a stud pavilion,' he commented.

'I know that.' Laura fiddled with a pen. 'And he didn't end up back in his own pen. It was someone else's, and they'd obviously put it in because there was a feed trough hanging from it. Just really bad luck.' She left the last sentence hanging, in case he had something else to add.

'I'm not sure about it all being bad luck,' Tim answered

slowly. 'Obviously, I've known you for a long time and I know how you handle your sheep, Laura. I respect how you deal with your stock. It's always the best way for both the animal and the human. That's why what you're doing with those girls out there, teaching them how to work *with* the sheep or cattle, not against them, is such a good thing. So I know Random's reaction is unusual.'

Laura leaned her head against her hand. 'Yeah, that's right. But that was a completely different situation to what the rams are used to, Tim. After all, in a show environment it's noisy, there are different smells and loud noises.'

Tim gave a small laugh. 'Laura, it was you who said he responded oddly. Now you're trying to take it back?'

She wound the phone cord around her finger and was silent. She could make all the excuses in the world, but deep inside she knew something was not right. 'Okay,' she sighed finally. 'Hit me with it.'

'As I said in the email, there was nothing medically wrong, but I got to thinking about what you said and went a bit further. Tried to imagine what would cause him to suddenly lose it the way he did. What if someone passing had hit him with an electric prodder . . .'

'Seriously, Tim?' Laura interrupted. 'Someone would have seen that. There are stewards everywhere.'

'I know that, Laura. I'm not stupid.' Tim sounded irritated. 'Anyway, I sent a portion of his feed away to be analysed. You left a bag here, remember? So he had something to eat.' He didn't wait for her to answer. 'I've got a mate who specialises in putting mixes together for feedlots and so forth, so he's got all the gear.'

Laura nodded, then realised he couldn't see her. 'I remember,' she said softly.

'I only decided to get it tested because I wondered if one of your girls could have accidentally mixed it up incorrectly. Put in more protein than normal—that can hype them up.' He paused and Laura heard him shuffling papers.

She wanted to deny there could have been a mistake, but she knew she couldn't.

He didn't wait for an answer anyway. 'I found traces of methamphetamines in it.'

Laura was silent for a moment, trying to process what he was saying. She couldn't. 'I'm sorry?'

'Methamphetamines. Speed.'

'Drugs?'

'Yes. Drugs,' Tim confirmed.

'I . . .' Laura broke off.

Tim interrupted to explain. 'Speed is a central nervous system stimulant and when it's eaten . . .'

'Eaten? I was under the impression it was injected.'

'It can be. Or smoked or snorted. Let me finish. When it's eaten, it takes longer to react within the body. Sometimes up to twenty minutes. My guess is someone laced the feed, he ate it and reacted just as you were ready to go into the ring.'

Laura took in what Tim said, then shook her head.

'Drugs,' she said almost to herself. 'They each had their own bag of feed so that would explain why it was just Random who reacted.'

'Someone must have been pretty sure you were going to win,' Tim commented. 'To sabotage you like that.'

'Yeah,' she said slowly. But something didn't make sense.

She realised what it was. 'The timing. How could have they been so sure of the timing of it all?'

'Look, I can't give you all the answers you're looking for. All I can give you is the facts. The fact is his feed was laced.'

Laura was quiet again. This time the silence stretched out too long. 'Thanks, Tim,' she said finally. 'Will there be any long-term effects?'

'I don't think so. You'd be surprised at how many dogs I see who have ingested drugs—marijuana mostly—and they don't seem to have any problems after they've come down from their high.'

'Okay. I'd better be off then. Thanks again.'

'Laura, before you go . . .'

'Mmm?'

'In a couple of weeks, the golf club's holding a fundraising night for Jenny Spencer from school.' Tim sounded uncertain. 'You'd heard she was diagnosed with MS?'

Now Laura was on the back foot. Jenny was a single mum without any family support. Her diagnosis had been a shock to everyone in their community and Laura had heard that one of the churches had started a roster system to help Jenny out.

'Yeah,' Laura answered slowly, knowing what was coming and not seeing any way out of it.

'Would you like to come? It's sort of like a B and S ball for us oldies. They're calling it the Baggy and Saggy. Need to fill a table. Eight people. I've got three other couples we went to school with coming. You'll know everyone.'

Tim was talking quickly, more nervous than she'd ever known him to be, which was kind of sweet, she supposed. She had to admit he was a nice bloke. In fact, she'd wondered on occasion why he was still single. Probably too busy with his work, she'd figured, and, anyway, he could have been seeing someone, for all *she* knew. Laura had never bothered to keep up to date with local gossip. Obviously he wasn't now or he wouldn't have asked her.

'Sure.' She tried not to sound like a suffering saint resigned to her fate. 'Who came up with the name?' she asked, to change the subject. 'The Baggy and Saggy—that's horrendous!'

Tim brightened. 'Great! It's a good name! Where's your sense of humour? The idea is to wear something that shouldn't be seeing the light of day. Remember Katie? She's got a bridesmaid's dress that should have been burnt twenty years ago! I was looking through the Red Cross shop and found a purple suit jacket with leopard print lapels.' He let out a loud laugh. 'It's atrocious but my secretary told me it was perfect! Should I pick you up?'

'Leopard print lapels?' Laura echoed, her brow wrinkled. 'Okay.' She paused. 'Actually, Tim, I'll run myself in and meet you there.' She stopped before the unspoken 'so I can leave when I want' became too obvious.

'Seven o'clock. Golf club, two weeks on Saturday,' Tim reiterated, as if he was worried she might back out.

'Got it. Thanks again, Tim. Better run and make sure the girls are going okay. Catch you later.'

She hung up without listening to his goodbyes and sighed. 'Bloody hell,' she said to the empty room. 'What a phone call. Find out my ram's been doped and get asked out on a date. That's got be some sort of record.' If she wasn't so concerned, she could have giggled.

Looking across the yard, she realised the compound was empty. The girls would be waiting. Quickly, she shut down the computer, grabbed her esky and thermos, and headed out the door.

Chapter 16

2008

The front-end loader shuddered as it hit the trunk. The force caused Laura to jerk forward in her seat. She rammed the machine into the tree again, feeling a perverse surge of pleasure as she did so. Her rage disappeared for a moment. Then it was back.

Doping a ram?

Above the revving engine, she heard a crack. She looked up and saw the tree was beginning to sway. Quickly she jammed the machine into reverse and moved away. From the cab she could hear the ripping of the roots and, as if in slow motion, the ancient tree wavered a couple of times before succumbing to gravity. It hit the ground with a rush of leaves and splintering timber.

She clenched her fist in triumph and nodded. Then she gave a small laugh. Not because her anger had gone, but because she'd achieved something and it felt good. It made her feel in control.

Putting the tractor back into gear, she manoeuvred the bucket to the trunk of the tree and pushed with a little more *oomph* than was necessary. This was the last of five large wide-trunked trees that she was sure would have to be one hundred years old at least. She prodded it towards the pile, a cluster of entangled smaller bushes which would now dry and, when burning season started later next year, she would be able to put a match to it all. Then it would be gone.

She climbed out of the tractor.

'Wow, you're good,' Tegan said. 'How did you learn to drive a loader like that?'

'My Papa taught me the basics and the rest was just trial and error. You try different techniques—sometimes it works, sometimes it doesn't. You just have to keep working at it, honing your skills and getting better, even if it's only by a tiny bit each time.' She held her thumb and finger apart just slightly. 'Then one day it all clicks in.'

'Bit sad about those beautiful big trees,' Allie said. 'They must be so old.'

'Yeah, it's a bit of shame,' Laura conceded. 'But I've got heaps of shelter belts throughout the farm. Howie and Dad planted lines of trees everywhere so the stock had somewhere to go in bad weather. There are also plenty of native swamps fenced off. I don't think anyone will miss five trees and a bit of scrub.' She dusted off her hands. 'Let's have some lunch.'

They sat in the knee-high green grass and munched on sandwiches. Laura undid the thermos lid and watched as steam curled and rose. She wanted to ask the students if they'd seen anything strange at the show. If there had been anyone messing with the feed troughs or water. But she was pretty sure they'd have said something if they'd noticed anything unusual.

She poured her tea and listened to the girls chatter.

'That new band at the pub is amazing,' Tegan said, drawing out her last word. 'My legs are sore from dancing all night!'

Robyn nodded in agreement.

Allie turned, eyes sparkling. Laura couldn't help but notice how the blotches on her face stood out against her pale skin. 'I know. Saturday night was one of the best nights I've had here.'

Laura realised that Allie must have been back in Mangalow for the weekend, not in Adelaide, as she had first guessed. That probably explained Allie's hangover. Must have been a huge weekend.

'Who was the band?' she asked, knowing she had to show an interest in a world from which she was so far removed.

'Sinking Blizzard,' Allie answered. 'They're from Adelaide.' She swooned backwards and fell into the grass. 'The lead singer is sooooo gorgeous.'

'He thought you were okay too, from what I saw,' Tegan teased.

A coy smile snuck across Allie's face, but she didn't rise to the bait.

Tegan turned to Robyn. 'Will Scott still seems to think you're okay as well!'

Robyn laughed. 'He's not too bad himself. It's your turn now.'

'Oh no! Not me,' Tegan answered. 'I'm completely focused on passing this course and moving onwards and upwards in my career. No time for men. Not yet, anyway.'

The girls chatted on for a while. Laura decided it was now or never: she had to know what they'd seen at the show. Any little detail might contain answers.

The talk died down for a moment. 'I need to ask you a few things about the show,' she began.

'About Random?' Allie asked.

'Yes, about Random.' Laura began to tell them about Tim's email. 'So Tim couldn't find anything medically wrong with Random. There was no good reason why he should suddenly just flip out the way he did.'

'So, what?' Tegan shrugged. 'He just got scared with all the people around or something?'

Laura shook her head. She looked at each of them, trying to gauge what was going on in their heads. 'No. Tim had Random's feed tested. I left it with him so Random had his usual crumble. Tim found it had been doctored.'

'What do you mean?'

'It was laced with methamphetamines. Speed.'

'I don't understand.' Tegan looked confused.

This time, nobody said anything for a minute.

'Bloody hell,' Robyn said. 'That's crazy. Why . . .'

'I don't know,' Laura answered. 'I'd like to, though.'

'That goes without saying,' Tegan said, looking at the others. 'We'd like to know too, wouldn't we?'

'My oath.' Robyn nodded vigorously.

Only Allie was quiet.

'I guess my question is, did anyone see anything that was the least bit suspicious? Did you see anyone leaning over the rails, touching the ram? Ah!' Laura's frustration showed. 'It sounds stupid! Of course there are going to be people touching the sheep. They want to look at the wool, at the sheep's conformation.'

She threw her hands up, stood up and walked away before

turning back to face them. 'I'm furious that someone has done this on purpose. It's deliberate. Someone was trying to mess up my chances of winning a ribbon. And it's not just the ribbon. It's the prestige, all the sales of semen, financial gain. Not to mention the reputation you get as a breeder. It all goes with that bloody ribbon!'

'How much is Random worth?' Allie finally asked a question. She looked shaken.

The other two turned to look at her, horrified.

'Allie!' Tegan reprimanded her.

Allie held up her hands. 'No! No I didn't mean that rudely. I'm just wondering whether that was the reason it happened. If he was worth, like, I don't know, twenty grand and someone decided they'd be better off if he wasn't in the competition . . .' She broke off.

'Yeah, he's worth a fair bit, Allie,' Laura answered. 'You can never really tell until he's sold at an auction, but I'd like to think maybe seven thousand. But doping an animal because he's worth money doesn't make any sense.'

'Does if you're trying to kill it and claim the insurance.'

Laura started at Allie's comment, unsure how to take it. 'Well. Yes, I guess that's true. But . . .' She stopped. She really didn't know what to say. She decided honesty was best. 'I'm not really sure what you're getting at.'

'I didn't mean that's what you were doing, Laura,' Allie said quickly, obviously realising she'd said the wrong thing. 'Oh shit, sorry. Foot-in-mouth. I'm just saying it can happen. Or rather it could happen.'

'Allie, shut up.' Robyn looked at her crossly. 'You're just making it worse.'

'Definite mouth engagement before brain,' Tegan said.

'Sorry.' Allie looked suitably chastised. 'Just thinking outside the square. I didn't . . . I'll shut up now.'

'I know,' Laura said kindly. 'We're all upset about it. But did any of you see anything that could be classed as weird?'

What could have happened on the show day? Laura could tell they were trying hard to remember. The excitement and anticipation was still as memorable as the devastation and wreckage after Random's accident. Slowly Tegan began to shake her head. 'I can't remember anything that sticks out,' she answered.

'There was someone who came running across to help and then Josh Hunter grabbed Boof's halter,' Allie offered. 'But that's during, not before.'

'Tim said it could take up to twenty minutes for the drugs to work, so I guess the timeframe we're looking at is in the lead up to haltering and getting him out of his pen,' Laura explained. 'We were all there. It just doesn't make any sense.'

They fell quiet until the silence was broken by a magpie warbling and they watched as he flew down onto the pile of trees. He walked up and down the branches as if trying to work out why they were all on their side.

Allie suddenly let out a loud breath. 'Laura,' she said urgently. 'You've got it wrong. It didn't have to be within that twenty minutes. Think about this—if it was mixed in with the food, it would only react when he ate a bit of crumble. And I'd imagine that if he ate one tiny piece of crushed-up speed, it wouldn't react that much, but if it built up in his system over time, say a couple of hours, that widens the timeframe a lot.'

'Yes,' Laura said slowly, nodding her head. 'Yeah, and we all took off to get coffee and have a break, didn't we?'

The girls nodded.

'Well, then. Guess we won't be able to remember anything odd then, will we?' Laura was philosophical; she really didn't want to think about it anymore. Not for the moment, anyway. 'Righto. We'd better run a wire to make sure this fence is straight. Allie, can you grab my binoculars from the dash of the ute? I'll teach you the proper way to site up fences, not the way Papa did.'

'How did he do it?' Robyn asked.

Howie's unorthodox way of doing things was folklore on Nambina.

Laura grinned. 'He'd use the sights of a gun to help get a straight line. Nearly gave the neighbours a heart attack one day when they realised Papa had a gun trained on them!' She gave a wicked giggle. 'He swore it was for sighting the fence, not aimed at the very pretty widow who happened to be hanging out the washing without any clothes on.'

Chapter 17

1937

Thomas gazed out at the barren countryside, which seemed to go on forever. It had been a long trip on bumpy dirt tracks, and there were still miles to go before they would reach Adelaide.

Mac had a cigarette rolled and ready. Now he put it in his mouth and asked Thomas to light it while he drove. After a couple of puffs, he asked: 'Ever think about what's going on at home?'

'I don't have a home.' Thomas gave his standard reply.

'That's rubbish, and you and I know it.'

Thomas was silent, wishing the conversation would stop, but it never did with Mac. 'Don't bring it up!' he wanted to scream. 'Leave it alone. I don't want to think about it. Don't want to talk about it.' Unconsciously, he raised his hand to his cheek and touched the spot where the last fist had fallen. As his fingers connected with his skin, he realised what he'd done and quickly dropped his hand, hoping Mac hadn't noticed.

'Reckon you should think about it.'

Out of the corner of his eye, he saw Mac glance over at him.

'Maybe make contact with them. You never know what might have happened since you've been gone.'

'Nothing would've changed,' Thomas said tonelessly. Then without thinking, he said, 'It would still be as dark and frightening as it was when I was there. He'd come into our room, you know. When we were asleep. He was always drunk. Make me do things, like clean up after he'd puked—half the time he never made it outside. I'd have to cook him tea at midnight. And if I didn't do what he said, he'd lay into me. The day before you found me, I'd had it. I couldn't stomach the violence or abuse anymore. You saw the bruises.' He touched his cheek again.

'I sometimes think about my little brother. He was a good kid. I'm sure our "father"'—he said the word sarcastically—'wouldn't have touched him. He didn't look like my mother.' He broke off, horrified at how much he had given away.

'Where's your mother?'

Thomas shrugged. 'Who knows? Gone, anyway,' he answered bitterly. 'He's all front, you know. In public he's so different. Smiling, laughing, joking. I don't know what to call it. And he's on heaps of committees—he even helped organise the local show one year. He's very different at home. Don't know what people would think of him if they knew. He wouldn't be the good bloke and pub larrikin then.'

Mac was silent and Thomas went back to gazing out of the window. The landscape was covered in low scrubby blue bush and prickly-looking small grey trees. It was a world away from the lush green pastures of the south-east of South Australia where Mac had picked him up. The dirt here was a purple-red, whereas the soils down south were dark grey. There was rain there too, unlike here. Even if the season was good, there were only a few things that would grow on twelve-inch rainfall country. Lush green grass, like the lucerne he'd grown up with, wasn't one of them.

'You know,' Mac said at length, 'if you don't mend a rift, it plagues you for the rest of your life. It sorta gets inside you and doesn't let go—like a cancer. It eats away at you and as it does, the more resentful a bloke becomes. The more questions a bloke has, the angrier he gets.'

Thomas's head whipped around. 'It's not a bloody rift, Mac! I was used as a punching bag. Fathers don't do that to their kids. He *betrayed* me. Nothing I did brought this on me. It's *his* fault, not mine. I have nothing to mend, nothing to fix.' He folded his arms then turned his whole body away from Mac and stared moodily into the nothingness.

After a time, Mac said: 'Ah, but that's where you're wrong, mate. There's forgiveness. And then there's peace.' He said nothing more.

∽

Thomas rolled over restlessly. He was camped in a little dark room at the back of Mac's house in Adelaide. After months of sleeping rough, nothing had prepared him for the lumpy mattress and the sense of being walled in. It felt hard to breathe. It hadn't felt like this when he was working in the sheds, no matter where he slept.

He got out of bed and opened the door slightly, hoping for

a puff of breeze. There was nothing. Quietly, he slipped out of the room. The cement floor of the laundry was cold on his feet. He knew the night would cool the sweat on his body, so he opened the back door and went out into the darkness.

Thomas felt the breeze on his skin before he heard the leaves of the tree rustle. The forecast cool change had just arrived.

Above the silhouettes of pointed roofs, he could see the stain of dawn and he thought back to the night he left Nambina. For the umpteenth time he wondered whether Howard would have understood immediately what had happened. Had he cried? Felt alone?

Thomas's recurring dream had Howard moaning in pain, clutching at his head and crying for his brother, questioning why he'd been left behind. His mother was there too—a ghostly figure, flitting from room to room, her hands to her chest and tears on her cheeks. His father? He was stalking the edges of the sunroom, a bottle in his hand. Cursing Thomas, calling him all the names he could think of. Flea was trembling in the corner. Thomas broke out in a sweat just thinking about it.

Inside the house he heard Mac moving about and putting the kettle on the wood stove. Thomas had to let it go because today was the first day he was going to get a look inside the sheep pavilion at the Agricultural Society Royal Adelaide Show.

Mac came out onto the small verandah.

'Morning,' Thomas said.

'Ready for today?'

'Bit nervous, but excited at the same time.'

Mac lit a smoke and inhaled, glancing over at him. 'You look a bit rough there, mate.'

'It was hot last night. Didn't sleep well.'

'Unseasonably hot. And let me tell you, we'll be hot inside that shed today. It'll make you want to rip your tie off.'

'I'll want to take it off before I even put it on.'

Mac smiled. 'Gotta look the part. Be professional. Keeping up appearances is what this is all about.'

Thomas grinned and he knew he wouldn't take it off, no matter how desperately he wanted to, because Elizabeth Ford would be there—somewhere.

❧

Mac strode through the gates of the showgrounds, flashing his membership badge. 'He's with me,' he said to the man on the entrance, holding his arm out towards Thomas and ushering him through.

It seemed to Thomas that Mac commanded respect wherever he went. He wanted to be like that.

'Ah, now here.' Mac pointed to a small door and hustled him towards it. They entered a dim world, and the first thing that struck Thomas was the smell of lanoline. Immediately he felt like he'd come home.

The white fleeces, all contained in wooden display boxes, seemed to go on for a good fifty yards, and there was not an empty one to be seen. The stewards moved up and down the rows, tagging the fibres.

'Mac! It's good to see you again.' An older man in a bowler hat and thick moustache came towards them, his hand outstretched.

'John Banks! I'll be damned. You're still here!' Mac turned to Thomas. 'John's head steward. Has been for as long as I've been coming. He keeps threatening to retire, but it never happens. He turns up every year, just like a bad penny.'

He nodded at the man and shook his hand, his left one coming around into a double handshake. 'John, meet Thomas Murphy.'

'Pleased to meet you, Thomas. Have I met you before? Your face is familiar.'

'I'm sure you haven't, sir. I've never been to the show before.'

'Well, then, my boy, you're in for a fine day. A fine day.' He turned towards Mac. 'A lot of lovely fleeces in this year, Mac. The quality is definitely up and there are more entries.'

'That is good news,' Mac answered as he led the way over to the closest entry. He tucked his hands behind his back and leaned over, nose almost touching the wool, and looked at it intently. Thomas followed suit.

'See here, Thomas,' Mac said, without changing his stance. 'I can tell straight away this is from the north of the state. Crimps are a bit further apart, micron is stronger.'

Thomas nodded and Mac quickly walked further down the rows. 'And here,' he said, his finger jabbing at another fleece, 'the southern part. Can you see the difference?'

'Yeah,' Thomas said, understanding immediately. 'Yeah, I can.'

Mac nodded contently. 'Knew you'd be able to. We'll make a classer of you yet.'

'Where do you hail from, Thomas?' John asked.

'Oh, everywhere really. I work with Mac.' Thomas deftly avoided the question.

'Are you sure I haven't met you? I usually remember a face.'

'I'm certain you haven't,' Thomas answered.

'Come along, then. I'll take you through the merino pavilion. They also have increased numbers. I tell you, Mac, I'm excited about this show.'

Thomas grinned as John practically bounced on his heels in excitement. This wasn't how he imagined stewards to be. He'd assumed they'd look down their noses at him because he wasn't anyone. That's how stud people usually were.

He trailed behind, taking in the sights and smells, wondering if he would see Elizabeth, but all ideas of her vanished as John pushed open another door and Thomas saw rows and rows of merino sheep.

There were people combing fleeces and washing faces. Some rams stood in single pens with buckets of water and feed in them. A smell of ammonia rose in the air and Thomas's eyes watered.

'It's not open to the public today,' John said to Thomas. 'Judging only, both wool and animal. We start,' he looked at his watch, 'in about two hours, judging live. Later this evening, we'll look at the fleeces.'

'Righto, John,' Mac said. 'I'll get organised and see you out on the judging floor.'

John nodded and walked towards another steward, who held up his hand for attention.

'You go and sit up there, Thomas.' Mac pointed to the chairs around the edge of the shed. 'I'll get changed and come back for you in a while. Don't wander around on your own yet. Like John said, it's not open to the public today, so you'll need to be with me.'

Thomas did as he was told, and sat surveying the ewe hoggets in the pens in front of him. His fingers itched to open up the wool, but there was no way he would get Mac into trouble by leaving his seat.

Caught up in observing everything intently, he didn't notice the girl who sat down beside him, until she spoke. 'Hello there,' she said, and held out her hand. 'We weren't introduced properly last time. I'm Elizabeth Ford.'

Chapter 18

2008

Laura pulled open the screen door and walked into the sunroom. She was pleased the day had finished. She could be alone.

Already upset from the news about the ram, the trip to the mailbox on her way home had made her stomach churn. It had taken some moments to force herself to open the flap of the forty-four gallon drum that served as her mail drop-off point.

It had been like this since the show. Anxiety at every turn. What had Meghan meant when she said to watch the mailbox? Was she going to send her something that would irrevocably change her life? Laura had tossed and turned most nights, thinking, trying to work out how Meghan could possibly have a claim on Nambina. But no matter how many scenarios she considered, Laura kept coming up with nothing.

Zilch.

Just as, once again, there'd been nothing in the mailbox other than the normal bills and magazines.

Now, as she let herself into the house, she resolved to put those concerns behind her. She had to believe that Meghan had been bluffing and simply trying to shake her confidence at the show.

The smell of the pork roast she'd thrown into the slow cooker that morning hit her. 'Roast for one. Just what I feel like,' she muttered sarcastically. She wished there was someone to share a glass of wine and talk about the day with. She had so much to say. So much to debrief about.

The house had never been lonely while Howie had been alive. And years ago, she'd believed it would stay the same once she and Josh were married. She'd imagined laughter filling the kitchen as they cooked together and talked about what had happened on the farm, that they'd sip wine and sit on the verandah, watching as the sun sank below the horizon. She'd pictured them there in the mornings too, drinking coffee as the dawn broke and working out a plan for the day.

Now she knew it had all been a romantic fantasy she'd dreamt up when she was still naïve enough to believe that Josh was the man for her. As it turned out, aside from her father, Howie was the only man she could ever trust. But Howie was gone. She glanced over at the empty chair where her grandfather used to sit. The brown leather was the same as it had been that morning and every other day since his death. Worn and wrinkled. Much the same as its owner before he'd died. Catherine had suggested she shift the chair into another room, so it wasn't a constant reminder. But Laura couldn't do that, just as she couldn't clean out the bedroom Howie had shared with her grandmother. And Howie's office, which was a small room just off his bedroom, remained exactly the same as he'd left it.

Laura shook herself, trying to forget the disbelief and emptiness she'd felt during those first days after Papa died. The loneliness and sadness later. They could still ambush her after all this time.

Her unanswered questions about Howie's last words haunted her too, and was another reason why she couldn't ignore Meghan's threat entirely. But Meghan and Josh were Hunters, not Murphys. How there could be a link?

Laura went into the kitchen, took a bottle of wine out of the fridge and poured herself a large glass. Taking a slug, she checked the roast then pulled one potato from the pantry, cutting it in half then throwing it in the slow cooker.

She wanted to ring Catherine, but her friend had left for the States just after the Adelaide Show. She'd be gone for two months. Catherine wanted to learn about their agricultural industry and return with information that would benefit Australia. Laura wished her all the luck in the world, but knew she'd miss her terribly. Maybe Rusty would come in tonight. It would be nice to have another living thing beside her, even if it was only a grumpy old cat.

Distracted by loud laughter, she went to the window and looked towards the quarters where the students lived. Will Scott's ute was parked out the front.

As she watched, the door to the hut flew open and Will ran outside with Robyn over his shoulder. She was squealing and laughing at the same time. He gently draped her onto the bonnet of his car and kissed her quickly.

Tegan ran out and pretended to tug Will from Robyn, and two of Will's friends followed. All five were laughing. Allie came out with beer. Will went to the other end of the ute and opened the tailgate, where he and Robyn sat, his arm around her. The others stood around with beers in their hands and talked.

Laura couldn't help but smile wistfully. She and Josh had had that once. The same fun-loving, carefree relationship. But it had ended so suddenly and irrevocably. She couldn't forgive him for not trusting her and, well—she had no idea what he thought now. What's more, she didn't care. She'd sworn off men, off love, forever. Perhaps she was too cynical, but after everything that had happened with Josh she couldn't change. That's just the way it was.

As she watched out the window, she saw Allie slip around the side of the students' cabin and take something from her pocket. Then she put a hand to her mouth and leaned her head back against the cement as if suddenly relaxed to be away from the others. Laura wondered whether the girl was feeling as forlorn as she was. Always hard to be the third wheel, she thought.

She turned back from the window, pushing aside the loneliness that had engulfed her, and took another large sip of wine. From the office came a strange bleep. For a moment, she had no idea what it was. Then, realising it was the sound of Skype, she ran towards the computer, trying not to spill the wine.

'Hello? Hello, Nicki?' She grabbed the mouse and clicked on the icon that said 'Answer', hoping she'd got there in time to talk to the only person who ever Skyped her. 'Nicki?' She grinned as her sister's face appeared on the screen.

'Laurs! How are you, sis?'

'Nick! It's so good to see your face! How are you? How's it all going?' She set down her wine glass and reached over to pull out her office chair.

Her half-sister was staring at the screen, her brow wrinkled. 'What are you doing?' she asked. 'I can only see your boobs!'

Laura laughed and sat down, a huge grin on her face. 'Sorry, I was out in the kitchen. I'm sitting down now. You won't have a bad view anymore. How's London?'

'Oh, Laurs, you wouldn't believe it. I'm in Paris! Paris!'

Laura's eyes widened. Nicki had been attending a prestigious music school in London, but Laura had no idea she'd moved on.

'You're in Paris? How come?'

'Only for a few days. A couple of friends and I just popped over for a break. To sightsee and things like that. You can do that here. Everything is so close!' She grinned and shrugged.

'"Just popped over",' Laura teased. 'So tell me everything. How's school? Are you learning lots? Sung on any famous stages yet?'

Nicki laughed. 'No. No famous stages yet, but I'm learning so much. Not only to do with music, but culture, art. Everything. I'm loving it.'

Laura fingered her glass while Nicki talked about her life abroad. She'd been gone for a year and a half, and Georgie had said in her last phone call that she suspected the only time Nicki would return now would be for holidays.

'So what's happening over there? On Nambina?' Nicki finally asked.

'Nothing as exciting as what you're doing! I'm exhausted trying to keep up with you!' She took a sip of wine, wondering whether to tell Nicki about Random.

'Mum said you took a team to the show?' Nicki prompted.

'Yeah, we did. Didn't go too well.' Laura shrugged.

'Yeah, she said that too. What a bummer.'

'These things happen.'

There was a silence.

'Have you seen Josh or Meghan lately?'

Laura frowned. 'No,' she answered shortly. Then paused. 'Well, actually, I saw them both at the Adelaide Show a couple of weeks ago. We sort of acknowledged each other and that was about it.' She wasn't going to tell her sister about the threats Meghan had made. It would worry her, being so far away.

Nicki shook her head. 'You know . . .'

'You're beginning to sound like a broken record,' Laura interrupted. 'This is an old and tired conversation.'

'And I'm about to repeat it all over again,' Nicki said firmly. 'You gotta face this at some stage, Laura. Got to get over this rubbish and move on. I'm calling you at six o'clock on a Monday night. Your face is filthy, you're still in your work clothes and I bet you have no intention of going out. Come on, Laura! You can't just hide away on Nambina because of one horrible experience. You've got to get out, go dancing, have fun. Don't you miss their company? They were both part of your life! You didn't just lose a boyfriend, but a girlfriend as well. I'd be so sad if one of my mates didn't talk to me for years.'

'This is exactly where I should be on a Monday night!' Laura exclaimed. 'We farmers don't party every night of the week, unlike you muso-creative types, who only seem to come to life after the sun sets! And I'd like to know where I could possibly go dancing in town during the week. That's laughable! Anyway, who's the older and younger sister here?' Nicki had never been told about the scathing accusations Meghan and

156

Josh had hurled at Laura that night. There was no possible way Nicki could understand her disappointment and rage.

'Doesn't matter if I'm younger. I know I'm right.' Nicki sat back and crossed her arms. 'I bet you haven't even got a date on the horizon. Still sworn off men?'

'Actually I *do* have a date. So there.' Laura poked out her tongue childishly.

'Do what?' Nicki leaned forward again, eyes bright with anticipation. 'A date? With who?'

'Do you remember Tim, the local vet?'

'No-o-o-o.'

'Tim Burns. He's a vet.' Laura spoke in a slow voice, like she was explaining something to a child. 'We're going to a fundraiser next week. Together. Sort of like an oldies' B and S. Guess what it's called?' She didn't think it was a good idea to tell Nicki she was meeting Tim at the golf club. She had a sneaking suspicion her sister wouldn't class that as a date at all.

'I can't imagine.'

'The Baggy and Saggy.'

Laura saw her sister's eyes slip away, but a huge smile spread across her face. 'I'll be there in a moment. Give me five!' Nicki yelled to someone off screen. Turning back to the camera, she said, 'That's hilarious!'

'Are you going out?' Laura asked. She was peevishly annoyed with the idea of Nicki partying in Paris.

'Yep. We're going to climb the Eiffel Tower and then go and see the Arc de Triomphe. Got to make the most of the time we've got.'

'Who are you going with?'

Nicki rattled off three names that meant nothing to Laura.

'Well,' she said, with a small smile, 'have heaps of fun and take loads of photos. I'll want to see them when you come home.'

'I'll put them up on Facebook, so you can see them as soon as we've done it.'

'Ah, yeah. Facebook.' Laura remembered the account she had opened but rarely looked at.

'Yes, sister, dear, Facebook. Check it out. You might find it useful.' Nicki paused. 'Before I go, have you heard from Poppy lately?'

'Poppy? Why would she call me? She barely speaks to me when we're in the same room.'

'Something's going on with her. Not sure what it is . . . Okay, I'm coming!' she called over her shoulder before turning back to the screen. 'Sorry, gotta go. Try to call Poppy, okay?'

'Okay. If you think I should.'

'I do. Love you! Bye!'

'Love you,' Laura responded, but the screen had gone blank and she knew Nicki hadn't heard her.

Back out in the kitchen, Laura refilled her wine glass and switched on the TV. She checked the roast and turned off the cooker. With the newsreader for company, she peeled the rest of the vegetables and put them in the microwave. Deciding she couldn't be bothered making gravy, she sliced off a few pieces of meat and threw them onto a plate. When the vegies were done she arranged them on the plate with as much finesse as she had the meat. Finding her glass empty again, she replenished it before carrying it over to the table with her plate.

She looked critically at the setting. The table didn't even have a cloth covering it. Just bare wood with salt and pepper shakers, a bottle of Worcestershire sauce and a cutlery container sitting in the middle. She glanced around the room and saw nothing but evidence of a lonely existence.

If she'd had the baby, her fridge would have been covered in hand-drawn pictures. There'd be photos of her with Josh and the child, who'd be seven now. There'd be toys on the floor, homework on the kitchen table and reading books on the lounge. There'd be noise, bustle and activity, not this still, silent house she lived in.

Her phone beeped with a text and she grabbed it. Nicki.

'Play basketball again,' it read, and the words were followed by a row of Xs.

'You're a crazy lady,' Laura said out loud. 'Basketball? I couldn't run one hundred metres, let alone play a game of basketball.'

But it got her thinking as she ate her dinner. Maybe she did need to get out a little more. She'd played basketball at school, been good at it too. And eight years ago, she had been on every agricultural committee there was. Eight years ago, she'd been poised to become a successful agri-lobbyist. She'd had drive and a vision.

And in one moment it had all been snatched away.

Not only had Meghan turned her back on her friend, she'd turned Josh against her too. Her ex-friend's hatred had never faded over the years. In fact it had become more and more pronounced.

Would it ever be over? Would she ever be free of Meghan's loathing? Would she ever be free of the sadness she felt at her own loss?

Josh certainly hadn't stood still when it came to women. It seemed he always had one on his arm. They never lasted long, but they were there, although she noted he'd been alone at the show.

Then there was Meghan. Why hadn't she married? Laura guessed it was because she couldn't have children. Knowing Meghan, she wouldn't put herself in a situation that would cause her any heartache. She was too selfish.

And now Meghan was making threats of a kind Laura could never have foreseen. What had become of the three of them, she wondered. How could it have all gone so wrong?

She reached for the wine. Emptying the bottle into her glass, she drank the last of it.

Chapter 19

1939

Thomas straightened his tie and pulled at his collar. He was uncomfortable but Mac had taught him that clothes maketh the man, so he was making an effort.

He felt butterflies in his stomach as he checked the empty road for the bus once more. He glanced at his watch for the fifth time in as many minutes. The bus was late. He hadn't missed it, because he'd been waiting at the designated stop for half an hour before it was due.

Thomas kicked at the dirt with his toe then quickly bent down to clean away the dust. The boots had cost him two weeks' pay and he wasn't going to ruin them. With his handkerchief he rubbed until the shine returned and he could see the blurry reflection of his face.

At last he heard the distant sound of a vehicle and saw a rising cloud of dust. He relaxed. It was here.

Thomas dug into his pocket for the fare and picked up the battered suitcase he'd borrowed from Mac.

The bus pulled to a halt and the doors creaked open. 'Gawd Almighty,' the driver said to Thomas by way of greeting. 'I swear this bus will rattle to pieces by the time we cross the border.' He mopped his brow. 'Where're you going?'

'Portland,' Thomas answered.

The driver quoted a price and Thomas handed over the money.

'Throw your suitcase on the rack above and take a seat, young man. I'll see if I can get you there without this pile of rubbish falling apart.'

Thomas nodded and made his way down the narrow aisle, acknowledging the few other passengers as he went.

Finding a seat by himself, he sat and stared out of a window that was so dirty he could barely see the landscape. He pulled his shirt sleeve down and rubbed at the glass, but it made little difference. He settled back, closed his eyes and thought again of how he'd come to be there. He could see the grinning face of the steward from the show, John Banks, as he excitedly told Mac and Thomas how he thought he knew Thomas.

It was the third time he had attended the Adelaide Show with Mac and, each time, John had insisted he knew Thomas's face.

'You're related to the Granges from Victoria, aren't you?' John had asked as if he was in the presence of royalty. 'I know you are. That's why I thought I knew you, see? You look just like Mr Grange. I just couldn't shake the feeling and now it's finally come to me. You've got to be related.'

Thomas had let out a rare laugh at the man's excitement before shaking his head.

'I don't even know who they are,' he answered, but he noticed Mac turning to study him more closely.

'Surely, Mac?' John had looked to Mac for confirmation. 'Can't you see it? Anyway, if you're not related, I'll eat my hat. Go and check the photos on the wall. Mr Grange won the Grand Champion in 1929. I never forget a face.' He'd nodded towards the line-up of black and white photos of previous winners and left them to it.

That had been the last Thomas had expected to hear of it. But a couple of months later, Mac had handed him a letter. Thomas had grabbed it, hoping it was from Elizabeth—they had started up a friendship and Mac had been helping him improve his writing skills so he could correspond with her. Instead it was an unfamiliar hand with news that had shaken him.

Dear Mr McDougall,

I must say your letter has caused mixed emotions for my wife and me. We are pleased to know our daughter's son, Thomas, is fit and well and in your care, but we have to admit we were unaware and shocked that he had left his home of Nambina under such circumstances.

Unfortunately, we haven't had much communication from the family since our daughter left here to marry Ernest Murphy.

If Thomas wishes to come visit us, we would be very happy to have him stay for as long as he liked. If he is, as you say, handy with wool and is quick to learn, he will fit into our lives very well.

My wife is very keen to talk to young Thomas and find out what has become of his younger brother, Howard.

I guess it was fate that, when Thomas needed a ride, it was

you who was passing, Mr McDougall. Life, as they say, is full of twists and turns we least expect.

We thank you from the bottom of our hearts.

There was a heavily indented scrawl of a signature at the bottom of the page.

Thomas had spent a long time reading and re-reading the letter before folding it carefully and putting it in his pocket.

'How did you know?' Thomas asked Mac. His mentor was standing in the backyard, smoke curling from his cigarette.

Mac took a long drag on his cigarette before answering. 'I got to thinking about John's observations,' he said finally. 'I know your grandfather—William—and his wife, Dorothy. I've classed there. Only once mind, but I have been to their farm. It's in Portland, down the bottom part of Victoria,' he said when Thomas looked at him questioningly. 'They brought rams to the Adelaide Show once and swept the board clean. Won practically every category there was to win. But they never came back. "Quit while you're on top," was William's response when John asked him if he'd return the next year.' He took another drag from his cigarette and finally turned to face Thomas.

'I looked at the photos and I knew John was right. There was a definite resemblance to William. When I picked you up on the road that night, I knew there was something familiar about you, but I dismissed it. I couldn't think why I would know a ragamuffin with a black eye. Or cheek, as it was.' He looked over at Thomas with a small smile.

Thomas didn't know what to feel. He was conflicted. He had a family he knew nothing about. His *mother's* family! He didn't remember her ever speaking of them.

'So I wrote to them. I asked if they had a grandson and if you could be him. This is their reply.'

Thomas exhaled and sat down on the grass, staring at the fence. 'It's a bit hard to believe,' he said finally.

There was a silence.

'Do you think you'd like to go and visit them?'

'I don't . . .' Thomas stopped and turned to Mac. 'I want to know what happened to my mother! She left one day and never came back, even though she promised. She promised!' His voice was angry now and he stood up, agitated. 'She left us with *him*.' His disgust and hatred was obvious. 'I want to know why. Why she left, why she didn't come for us.' He stopped and tried to get his emotions in check. 'Maybe they know,' he finished more calmly.

Mac lit another smoke and sat down on the grass next to Thomas. 'Your brother?' he asked quietly.

'I don't know,' Thomas said. 'I've never made contact again. One night, when my father came home drunk, he said I looked like my mother. It was long after she left. Then he said he would change my face so I didn't look like her anymore. That he wanted to wipe the earth of every trace of her. He hit me. That was the first time, but not the last. Howard didn't look like her. There was more of my father's side in him—he even had a bit of a temper like him, although he hid it very well. He just used to go off by himself and let off steam somewhere. I think Howard would have been okay.' He added quietly, 'I hope he is, anyway.'

'I knew I'd picked you up from a bad situation, but I didn't realise how bad,' Mac said, clearly upset about Thomas's revelations. 'I'm happy I could help. But now you've got another option, other than me. To go visit them. They're good people. Good farmers. Excellent animal handlers. I'm sure they would welcome you warmly. They are also your *family*.'

The two men sat beside each other in the small Adelaide backyard, each lost in their reverie, each shaken in different ways. Finally Thomas broke the stillness. 'I think I'd like to go and visit them.'

'Then you should do it.'

Thomas turned to him. 'What about my wool classer's stencil, Mac? You're helping me get it and I don't want to let you down. You've done so much for me.'

'Listen to this piece of advice from a bloke who doesn't have any family to a bloke who does. Go and get to know them, enjoy their company. Ask your questions. There's time enough to finish that course and I know we'll see each other again.' Mac paused, seemingly to choose his words carefully. 'But go to your father too. Like I've said before, you need to see him, talk to him, before you can put any of this behind you.' He reached out and rested his hand on Thomas's shoulder, before getting slowly to his feet and heading back into the house.

It had taken Thomas another week to decide. Now here he was, on a bus, travelling to meet relatives he had never known. His mother's parents, no less. Clutching a hope that he'd finally have some answers.

He'd spent many sleepless nights thinking of this mysterious family. He'd tried to recall any memories his mother may have shared about them, but he'd drawn a blank. There had been nothing to indicate that Jessie had a family other than Ernest, Thomas and Howard.

What would they be like? Would he recognise himself in his grandfather's face?

The bus ground to a halt and another two passengers got on. Thomas glanced at his watch again. The journey would last for at least another eight hours, so he pulled out a pen and notepad and started to write in painstakingly slow strokes:

Dear Howard,

I guess I have to apologise for leaving you by yourself with Dad. The argument between you and me the previous evening, and the last fight with that man was too much. I hope you have forgiven me. I have never stopped wondering how you are or thinking about you. Have to admit, I have tried to forget you, tried to forget the things that happened on Nambina—I wanted to wipe those horrible few years away. But I can't. You're my brother and no matter what, we are tied by blood.

You're well within your rights to not answer me. After all, I know I left you without warning or word.

In case you are interested, I'm doing okay—I've been working in shearing sheds up north and enjoying it. It's different from our country.

During my travels I have found Mum's family. They live on a farm out of Portland and run merino sheep. I am going to visit them as I write this. I have to find out what happened to her. Mum, I mean. Once I have, I plan to return to Nambina and talk to our father. I doubt I will stay long, but if you like, you can come with me back to the shearing sheds.

With fondest regards,
Thomas

He looked at his writing—there'd been much scribbling out before he found the right words, but as Thomas read it back to himself slowly and carefully, he was pleased with what he'd said. He honestly had no idea how the letter would be received by Howard. He just hoped his brother would read it. It was now almost three years since he'd left Nambina. He couldn't help but wonder what may have changed in his absence.

He folded the letter and slipped it into his bag for posting when he arrived. He was reminded of Elizabeth, and he wondered whether she'd received his last letter, telling her of his plans.

The sky was darkening now. As the bus turned south for a moment he caught a glimpse of the sun's last rays barely visible to the west. He pulled out the packet of sandwiches he'd made for the journey and turned his back on the rest of the passengers. Slowly he ate, then he drew his shirt around him and closed his eyes. Maybe if he slept, the trip would pass more quickly.

Chapter 20

2008

Allie reversed the tractor towards the posthole thumper and Laura guided her with hand signals. When everything was lined up, Laura signalled her to stop and pushed the split pins through the lugs to make sure the implement was connected tightly to the tractor.

She gave a thumbs-up and motioned for Allie to drive back out into the paddock to where the new fence line was going to be built.

Tegan and Robyn where already there, throwing the pine posts off the back of the ute at measured intervals.

Laura watched as Allie headed down the two-wheeled dirt track, then checked the tray of her ute to make sure she had everything she needed. Wire spinner, hammers, staples, leather gloves, spirit level—that was the easiest way to make sure the posts were straight—and a cat.

'Coming fencing, are you?' she asked.

Rusty just looked at her haughtily and jumped soundlessly

onto the roof of the ute. He continued to watch so Laura stared straight back. She was too old for this game, but she enjoyed it. Finally the cat averted his gaze and, with a flick of his tail, he leapt to the ground and stalked into the shed.

Laura watched him go. Soon he'd be curled up in the wool bin, which had a couple of fleeces in it. She'd purposely left some wool lying around so he had somewhere comfortable and warm to sleep.

She knew she had about ten minutes before the tractor reached the paddock. It was mail day, so she decided to head down the driveway to check the mailbox. The idea made her heart beat a little faster, but she had decided that if Meghan was going to send something, the sooner she knew about it the better. She wouldn't bury her head in the sand. She'd fight whatever was coming.

She followed the gravel drive to where it merged with the main road. The mailman had been and there was a bundle of letters wrapped in an elastic band. Flipping through them, she once again breathed a sigh of relief. Nothing she wasn't already expecting, although she had to admit she didn't really know what she was looking for from Meghan.

As she approached the paddock, she could hear the wooden thud of the posts hitting the ground. She saw Tegan in the back of the ute and Robyn behind the wheel, driving very slowly. They stopped when they saw her.

'Going okay?' she asked, leaning out of the car window.

'Sure is,' Tegan answered with a huge grin. 'How could it be not so?' She spread her arms out and threw her head back, looking towards the sky.

Laura nodded in agreement.

Allie left the tractor idling and jumped down from the cab. 'So what's the plan?' she asked.

'Let's get a few of these in and then once you understand how the thumper works, I'll let you all have a shot at using it. Looks like you've got most of the posts out and ready?'

'There's about another fifty metres to put out, then we're finished.'

'Okay, you two do that, and Allie and I will start.'

Robyn and Tegan continued on their way.

She explained carefully to Allie what she wanted her to do, then the girl slowly inched the tractor back until the pine post Laura was holding fitted tightly into the thumper. She motioned for Allie to get out of the vehicle so she could show her how to use the new machine.

Allie jumped down, but as she did so, the tractor started to roll backwards, its large wheels turning slowly down the slope. Laura, who was standing right behind it, gave a squeal as the pine post was forced back by the pressure of the machine and thudded into her shoulder. She tried to duck sideways, away from danger, but the post entangled her legs and she tripped, landing on her knees. As quickly as she could, she got to her feet and took a couple of steps backwards, her eyes still focused on the turning wheels.

Unable to see behind her, she now stumbled into the line of wire running along the fence. The pressure made the steel strand snap and Laura fell backwards. The tractor kept coming. And coming and coming.

Allie, at last realising what was happening, yelled to the others then grabbed hold of the handrail to pull herself back up into the tractor.

Laura tried to crawl out of the way of the huge wheels. She had to stay out of the way of the massive tyres. Her heart was thumping like a bass drum and she fought the panic inside her. 'Stop it! Stop it!' she screamed in desperation.

The engine died and all was quiet, except for her laboured breathing as she stared up at the impossibly blue sky.

'Laura?' Allie's fear made her voice high-pitched and she fell out of the cab in her hurry. 'I'm so sorry, I'm so sorry.' Tears were streaming down her cheeks as she collapsed next to Laura.

Laura took a shaky breath. 'I think I'm fine.' She tried to wipe a wetness away from her cheeks and realised her hands were trembling badly. 'Oh, hell,' she muttered, then sat up and put an arm around the wildly sobbing Allie.

'It's okay, it's okay,' she comforted. 'No one was hurt. It's fine. Shh.'

The other girls had made it back. Robyn jumped into the cab and moved the tractor away, while Tegan found a couple of jackets and draped them around Laura and Allie's shuddering shoulders.

Allie was shivering uncontrollably.

They stayed that way for a while before Laura made a move to get up. 'Come on.' She held out her hand to Allie. 'Let's go back to the office and have a cup of tea. We'll regroup.'

They drove in silence except for Allie's loud, uneven breaths.

Inside the house, Laura boiled the kettle and made four cups of strong, sweet black tea and handed them out. She took Allie's cup and threw a shot of brandy into it.

'Drink,' she commanded before taking a gulp from her own beverage.

'I'm sorry,' Allie said again. 'I don't know what happened. I know I took the tractor out of gear.'

'First things first. No one was hurt and that's the main thing. But you *must* make sure that the tractor is in park, not neutral. If it's in neutral, it can roll the way it did, and I'm guessing that's what happened.'

'It wasn't in gear,' Robyn ventured, her hands wrapped around the hot mug. 'Not when I got into it, anyway. I think it was because it was on a small slope. It just rolled backwards.'

Tegan glared at Allie for a moment. 'Careless,' she muttered, getting up from her chair.

Allie stared at the table in silence.

Laura covered the girl's hand with her own. 'A mistake,' Laura corrected gently.

'You could have killed someone.' Tegan said it so quietly, Laura wasn't sure she had heard it.

∽

Later in the day, when most of the shock had worn off, Laura checked her mobile phone for messages.

There was one from Tim.

'Random is ready to be picked up when you've got time,' he had said. 'See you soon.'

Laura was keen to get Random home, so she'd just have to get over the self-consciousness she'd been feeling since Tim asked her out. She knew why she'd agreed to go with him, but the nerves attacked her whenever she remembered she had a date to go to the Baggy and Saggy Ball.

With Tegan and Robyn on a stock run for the rest of the

day, Laura decided she'd take Allie with her. That way, hopefully Tim wouldn't mention it.

The girl was curled up in a blanket on Laura's couch. 'Hey, Allie!' Laura called from the doorway. 'We can get Random. Let's go and bring him home.'

Allie turned slowly. 'He's okay?' she asked quietly.

'He must be. Tim wouldn't let him leave the surgery otherwise. Come on!'

They loaded a crate onto the back of Laura's ute and called the others on the two-way to tell them where they were going.

On the trip into town Allie sat silently staring out of the window. Laura wracked her brain for more words of comfort, but she'd already said everything she could think of. What was there to say, after all, when someone had almost killed you, other than 'it's okay'?

'Allie,' she began. 'I need you to understand that mistakes happen. Some mistakes are more serious than others. But listen, you can't dwell on this. All you have to do is learn from it and not make the same slip-up twice.'

'I almost killed you.'

'But you didn't and I'm fine. Now come on.' Impatience and a spark of anger flared in Laura's chest. For goodness sake, she was the one who should be shattered. She was the one who had almost been killed.

'Move on from it. You need to be stronger than this.' She looked out of her side window as they passed Josh and Meghan's mailbox and saw Josh's ute speeding down the driveway towards them. Quickly she looked away.

She drove past the 80 sign on the edge of Mangalow and

then the 60 sign. Flicking on the blinker, she turned into the vet surgery and parked.

Allie didn't move for a moment then straightened her shoulders. 'Okay,' she said more to herself than to Laura. 'Okay.'

Laura hoped that was the changing point for Allie and she would be all right. She knew how lucky they all were. How lucky *she* was. WorkSafe would have had an absolute ball with an accident like that. They would have shut down the school quick as a flash. Although, she noted wryly to herself, if the teacher wasn't alive then there wouldn't be a school anyway.

As they walked down the narrow path towards the surgery, a panicked male voice said: 'Laura? Excuse me. Can I get by?'

Laura felt her chest tighten as she recognised its owner without having to turn. Instinctively, she stepped aside, knowing there was something wrong. She pulled Allie with her.

Josh, face taut, raced past, carrying a black and tan kelpie in his arms. The dog was shaking and his tongue was hanging out. The animal looked in a bad way.

'Oh,' Allie began then stopped.

'Might be a bait,' Laura commented. 'Looks in a terrible state. Poor bloody thing.'

They waited a moment or two before following. Inside the clinic, Laura noticed one of the consulting room doors was closing and the vet nurse had a grim look on her face. She tried to smile a welcome when she saw them.

'Ah, Laura. You've come for Random?' she asked.

'Yeah, we have, Mel. Sorry, bad timing.' Laura nodded towards the door, feeling something like disappointment. She didn't think she'd be seeing Tim today after the way Josh had come in. Laura frowned and quickly refocused on Mel, pushing the feeling away.

'Always busy in the surgery,' Mel said. She motioned to the passageway that led into the backyard. 'Random's out there.' She grabbed an envelope and plastic bag and handed them to Laura. 'It's from Tim,' she said. 'All the instructions and antibiotics are in here.'

'Great, thanks. Here you go.' She passed everything over to her student, who almost snatched at it, she was so eager to help.

Mel showed them out into the yard. Two horses stood tethered to a holding rail and a vet was rasping one's teeth down. Dog kennels lined the back fence and most of the occupants were sleeping. Mel pointed towards a rusty iron shed. Inside, Laura let her eyes adjust to the semidarkness. Then she saw him. Random was standing tall and as they watched him, he sniffed the air.

'Hello there, beautiful boy,' she whispered and went over, hand outstretched.

Random nuzzled her fingers and made a small grunting noise.

'He's pleased to see you,' Allie said.

'He'll be happy to see you too,' Laura said without glancing at her. She tried to look at the injury without hurting him. She swung a leg over the railing and got into the pen. 'Can you hold his head?'

Laura put her hands on his back and leaned over. The stitches were still there, but the wound looked healthy. His balls weren't swollen and he didn't appear to be in any pain.

'Excellent,' she said more to herself than anyone.

'Want me to get the ute?'

'Yes, please.'

Laura watched carefully as Random walked quietly up and into the crate. 'Different animal. Look!' she said to Allie, remembering her role as teacher. 'See how his gait is steady and smooth? And there's no swelling anywhere around his scrotum.' She pointed.

Allie, standing at the side of the ute, looked up under his girth. 'Looks a damn sight better than it did that day at the show. Especially with all the bloodied wool clipped away.'

'Doesn't it?' Laura agreed.

'Ah, there you are.' Tim appeared, wiping his hands. 'Sorry I couldn't help you load him. Bit of an emergency.'

'We saw,' Laura said. She looked at Tim for a moment. It had been a while since she'd seen him and she'd forgotten how tall he was. His fingers were long and nimble, as a good surgeon's should be, but with his tanned face and muscled frame, he could be mistaken for a farmer. The memory of him in a suit at Howie's funeral made her smile at him more brightly than she'd intended.

There was no doubt she was now deeply indebted to this man—he'd performed a miracle. 'Thanks for everything, Tim,' she said sincerely. 'You don't know how much I appreciate it.'

'Very welcome,' he nodded. He gave her a huge smile, and brown hair flopped over his eyes. As he pushed it back impatiently, Laura noticed his smile made his eyes seem to shine.

'We'd better be off, but thanks again,' she said, confused at what she was noticing about him. She hadn't paid such attention to a man for ages.

'Got all the instructions? All the drugs for him?' Tim asked, leaning forward to look in the crate.

177

'Mel gave us everything, thanks.'

'Goodo. Any problems, you know my number.' He put a hand on her shoulder before turning away and walking towards the door that led into his surgery. 'See you at the Baggy and Saggy Ball, Laura,' he called. 'If you don't arrive, I'll come looking for you!' The door banged shut behind him. Laura was sure she heard him add 'and that's a promise'.

Avoiding Allie's eye, she climbed into the ute and started it up. Allie got in, a half-smile on her face as she looked questioningly at her teacher.

Laura said nothing, but as she drove out of the yard, a bubble of excitement began to form in the pit of her stomach.

Chapter 21

1939

'All passengers for Portland!'

Thomas woke with a start and realised he'd been sleeping for many hours. It was still dark, although there was a glimmer of light ahead. He rubbed his hands over his face, trying to get his bearings.

'Passengers for Portland,' the driver called again.

That was him.

Thomas stood and grabbed his bag from the rack above before stumbling down the aisle—a job in itself, with the bus lurching from side to side. His eyes peered towards the light and he looked around, eager to see where his mother had spent her childhood.

'Coming home, lad?' asked the driver as he negotiated the road.

Thomas shook his head. 'I've never been here,' he answered, realising the man couldn't see his movement in the darkness.

'That's the sea out to your right. Reckon the mist'll be in tonight.'

'The sea?' Thomas echoed. He hadn't known Portland was on the coast. He'd only seen the water once, when Mac had told him to catch the tram to Glenelg, a seaside suburb of Adelaide. He'd walked along the beach and not liked the way the sand had stuck to his feet. He hadn't ventured into the water. It held no interest for him and, after buying an ice-cream, he'd caught the tram back to Mac's home, where he felt comfortable.

'Here we are,' the driver slammed on the brakes and swung the wheel to the left, pulling up at the curb. 'Have a good night.'

Thomas thanked him and jumped lightly from the bus. He took a few steps forward to allow the bus to move on, then looked around.

The air smelt humid and he could hear a whooshing sound. *It must be the waves*, he decided.

It was dark, but for a pale illumination from the half-moon and the single globe light set on the side of the street.

He heard a car door slam. 'Thomas?' A voice called. 'Thomas Murphy?' An elderly man hurried towards him.

'Yes. Um.' Thomas stopped, unsure what to call this man who was supposed to be family.

The man stopped just short of him as if he, too, was unsure of the protocol in this sort of situation. Then he held open his arms and stepped forward.

Thomas jerked back, but felt the frail arms enfolding him and heard a choked voice saying: 'We're so pleased you're here. We would have helped if we'd known, my boy.'

Hesitantly Thomas patted the old man on the back.

છ૭

Thomas rose to the smell of bacon cooking. His stomach rumbled. The three sandwiches he'd eaten the day before had held the hunger at bay, but now he was starving.

He quickly rummaged through his bag and found a clean set of clothes. There was a mirror set into a dressing table and he stared at himself for a moment.

His skin was smooth and tanned from the long days on the road. Blue eyes stared seriously back at him and his hair stuck up in cocky little nests. Finding a small jug next to his bed, which had obviously been put there in case he was thirsty during the night, he grabbed yesterday's shirt and dipped the tail in. He dribbled the water over his hair and tried to pat it down. When he'd done the best he could, he knew there was no reason to stay hiding in his room. He needed to go and meet his family.

Thomas cracked open the door and looked out into the passageway. It was lined with polished wood furniture, and at the far end was an arched doorframe with a stained-glass window set above it. 'These people have money,' he whispered to himself, then immediately corrected himself. '*My family* have money.'

He stepped out into the passageway. His boots made a loud sound on the floorboards and echoed throughout the house. He knew his movements would be heard before he was seen.

Within seconds he was standing in the kitchen doorway. Sun streamed in through a large window, the light bouncing off the shining sink and clean glasses.

'Thomas,' a soft voice said. A white-haired lady was sitting at a long table, a delicate cup in front of her.

'Hello,' Thomas uttered in a morning voice.

'Come and sit down. Would you like tea? I've brewed a fresh pot.' The lady pointed to a porcelain teapot and an empty cup and saucer.

'Yes, please. Um . . .'

'I'm Dorothy,' she said, answering the unasked question. 'Jessie's mother, your mother's mother. Your grandmother. How would you like it?'

'Just black, please.' He searched her face. 'You look like her.'

A small smile touched her lips as she poured tea into the empty cup. 'Sit,' she said. She indicated a chair across from her and he took it, wondering why she was so restrained after the effusive greeting his grandfather had given him the night before.

'I see you've learned stockman's habits,' she said as she handed him the cup of hot tea.

He looked at her, horrified that his manners had failed him.

'Black tea,' she explained. 'It's hard to find milk and sugar in the bush.'

He almost laughed out loud with relief. 'Yes, it is. Mac, ah, Mr McDougall told me that from the start. Although we always had access to it on the stations, which had milking cows.'

'Are you hungry?'

'I'm starving,' he admitted.

'I'll get you some breakfast.' Dorothy rose from the table and went to the oven. She pulled out a plate piled high with eggs and bacon, toast and tomatoes. Thomas's mouth watered. After the bachelor's lifestyle that he and Mac led, this was a treat!

When the meal was put in front of him, Thomas waited what he hoped was the right amount of time before picking

182

up his knife and fork. 'Where's William?' Thomas asked after he'd swallowed his first mouthful.

'He's gone to check the water in the stud ewe paddock. He'll be back any moment.'

Thomas was silent, eating, but all the while there was a question on his lips. He wasn't sure if he could wait until William returned.

'Tell me about your childhood, Thomas,' Dorothy quietly prompted.

That was something he didn't want to do. He stalled, eating another few mouthfuls, but when he saw there was nothing left on his plate, he couldn't delay answering anymore.

'It was okay. We worked a lot, but with Mum around, it never seemed to matter. She made everything fun. But after she'd gone, everything always seemed much harder . . .' He searched for the right word. 'I don't know, dark, I guess. Dad used to order me around like I was a dog. Howard not so much. Dad hated that I looked like her. Like Mum.' He glanced up at Dorothy and saw she was staring into her cup of tea and sitting unnaturally still. He stopped.

'So you left?' she asked.

Thomas continued as if he hadn't heard her. Now he had finally cracked open the vault, it was a relief to talk about his childhood. 'He'd come home from the pub so drunk he could barely stand. Trouble was, when he was like that he was more dangerous than usual. You'd think his actions would be impaired by the drink, but they never were. He always knew just where to lay a fist or a knee.' Thomas winced at the memory of a knee going into his stomach when he least expected it.

Dorothy's hand flew to her mouth. 'Oh my Lord,' she muttered.

'I know if I'd stayed the beatings would have gotten worse. It wasn't just physical stuff. I had to clean the, uh—' He looked down at his plate, unsure whether to tell her. He rushed on to fill the void, '—up after him, after he'd vomited. He made me cook his dinner after he came home and then he'd throw it across the room if it didn't taste right.'

He drummed his fingers on the table, still not looking at her. The shame he felt in telling this story was immense. He still harboured a fear that something he'd done had caused his father to reject him. Surely, just looking like his mother wasn't crime enough.

'Then one night, I snapped. Knew it was time. I'd had enough. I'd toyed with the idea about leaving for maybe a year or more, but I'd never had enough money. During the weekends I'd done some extra work for our neighbour, getting firewood for the house, and he paid me. I saved until I had enough to leave Howard some and take a small amount for myself. Then I walked out. That was nearly three years ago.'

'Did he let you go without a fight?'

'He wouldn't have known until he woke up the next day. He was passed out on the couch when I left.'

The door swung open and William entered, his face serious.

Dorothy continued with her questions. 'It didn't bother you, leaving Howard?'

Thomas found her tone accusing and he bristled. 'No,' he said shortly. 'He never got the same treatment as me.'

William laid a hand on Dorothy's shoulder. 'Come on, Mum,' he said, a habit Thomas assumed he'd kept from the

184

time when Jessie had lived at home. 'Don't be cross with the boy just because we feel guilty.'

Smiling ruefully, Dorothy reached up to touch her husband's hand.

'Now, I believe it's smoko time,' William said. 'Is there a hot cup of tea for me?' He turned to Thomas. 'Good morning, young man. Welcome to our home. Your home for as long as you want. It's good to have you here.'

Thomas stood and held out his hand. 'Thank you, sir,' he answered as they shook.

'Just call me William,' his grandfather said. 'Like I said last night, we're probably a bit too far gone for you to call me Grandpa or something similar.'

He sat down at the table, and Thomas followed suit. There was a heavy silence until William cleared his throat. 'We know you've had a tough go at it, these last few years.'

Thomas just nodded. He could have agreed, but lately he'd come to feel that the whole experience had been some sort of rite of passage that had ended when Mac had picked him up. It shouldn't have happened, but it had made him who he was today and who he would be for the rest of his life.

'We wish we'd known,' William continued.

Dorothy looked across at him with pale, watery blue eyes. There was a pause and finally Thomas asked the question he had wanted to scream since he'd alighted from the bus. 'Do you know where she is? Where my mother is?'

The atmosphere grew even heavier and Dorothy covered her mouth with her hand, but not before a small sound of distress escaped.

With shaking hands, William held the cup of tea to his lips

and took a sip before answering. 'She's dead, Thomas. I'm so sorry.'

Heat pierced Thomas's eyes as soon the words left his grandfather's mouth. He swallowed hard. 'I was sure she must have been,' he finally said softly. 'She would have come back for us, otherwise. I know she would have.' The anger, which had been building over time, left him and was replaced with a deep sense of sadness.

Emptiness.

Relief.

With the relief came lightness. He knew. He finally knew.

'It's not quite the story you probably think,' Dorothy said, having gathered herself. She sat ram-rod straight and looked him in the eye. 'We didn't approve of Jessie marrying your father, Thomas. She was still hurting from the death of her fiancée, George, so she was vulnerable. Open to Ernest's charismatic ways and silver tongue.

'We made sure we visited as often as we could, but as I'm sure you'll understand, it isn't easy to travel these long distances unless one has a motor vehicle. We didn't back then, but we still tried. Especially after you boys came along. Jessie wrote us letters—happy ones. Full of the details of life on the farm, tales of you boys and what Ernest had been doing. She sounded happy and our misgivings were slowly put aside. We hoped we had judged him wrongly.' Dorothy shifted in her seat.

'Then we visited one Christmas—you lads were only small. Jessie had a bruise on her upper arm. It was obvious it was from a strong hand—you could still see the finger marks.' Dorothy stopped to take a shaky breath and William took up the commentary.

186

'We asked her about it, but she laughed it off, saying one of their horses had nipped her. We didn't want to pry. Even though we'd brought all of our children up to have close relations with us, there were still subjects that just weren't talked about.

'Over the years, there were small things that, when you look back, added up to one large thing. Her letters changed from wanting us to visit to discouraging us, and her happiness seemed forced.

'Then, one day in February, six years ago, we had a letter from Ernest saying Jessie was very run down. He was worried about her and had booked her into a sanatorium for a break.' He looked down at his hands before continuing. 'We were pleased. The last time we'd seen her, which had been in 1929, she had dark circles under her eyes and was thin. So thin.' His voice trailed off and he looked all of his many years. 'We were going to the Royal Adelaide Show to display our rams and we called in unannounced.'

It was Dorothy's turn to talk again. 'You were very young. Only eight, I think, and Howard would have been seven, which is probably why you don't remember us. We'd given her a necklace for her birthday that last visit. An expensive silver chain, thinking she could sell it if she needed to leave and get back to us.'

Silver chain? Thomas couldn't sit still anymore. He leapt from the table and hurried to his room. Throwing clothes and other items from his suitcase, he returned quickly to the kitchen with the chain in his hand. 'Was this it?' he asked, placing it gently on the table.

Dorothy and William reached for it at the same time then both sat back without touching it. 'Yes, it was.'

Thomas swallowed. 'Go on,' he whispered.

'The holiday was to be a surprise, so we didn't mention it in any of our letters and didn't expect her to. Then her letters stopped. It was six months before we contacted your father. The letter we got in return was full of threats and abuse.'

William reached out and covered Dorothy's hand with his own, then reached for Thomas's. 'Please understand how hard this is for us to tell you,' he said, tears in his eyes. 'He had . . . um, your father had Jessie committed.'

There was another silence, while Thomas tried to comprehend what had just been said. 'I don't . . . I'm sorry, I don't understand,' he whispered.

'He had her committed to an asylum. He pretended she was mad. Insane.'

'What?' Thomas exploded. 'That's ridiculous. She wasn't. There's no way . . .'

'We knew she wasn't, Thomas.' William's voice was gentle now. 'We can only assume it was because he wanted her out of the way for some reason. We really don't know why. You must understand, we looked for her. We tried.' The grief in his voice echoed what Thomas's heart was feeling.

'She was my daughter. I wouldn't let down my own *daughter*. But it ended up that I did. I was too late, Thomas. She'd been drugged and strapped to the bed for so long, she *had* gone mad. My dear Lord, I'll never forget that sight. Her eyes were dead—she didn't even recognise us. Her wrists were tied to a bed covered in filthy sheets. We wanted to take her home, but the law wouldn't allow us too. We fought the doctors, your father, everyone, just to bring her home and care for her. She died before we could. Just like that. I have always suspected they gave her larger doses of tranquillisers than they should have.

'We tried to see you boys as well, but Ernest wouldn't let us onto the farm. He threatened he would hurt you both, if we came. Seems that accepting what he said didn't stop that.' He fiddled with his teacup, before speaking again. 'I know Jessie would have tried to escape, whenever she could. Until they broke her, and they certainly did that. That's why she'd been tied down, you see. She tried to get back to you boys. You were the reason she kept trying to get away. So she could get home to you.' The bitterness in his voice was raw.

Thomas remembered tales of the crazy lady who had escaped from the asylum near his home, crying and screaming, her hair flying everywhere. Could that have been his mother? Had he been so close and not realised? He clenched his fists. 'There were stories,' he muttered. 'People who escaped from there.'

William shrugged, looking exhausted. 'Who would know, Thomas. It may have been her, but we'll never know.'

'I'll kill him,' muttered Thomas. 'The bastard. I'll kill him.'

Chapter 22

2008

Laura breathed a sigh of relief as she pushed open the door on Friday afternoon. The week had gone pretty smoothly if she discounted Monday, which had been a complete write-off—apart from getting Random home.

The four rams were now reunited out in the paddock. They hung together in a group, occasionally bunting each other's sides, and Laura liked to think they'd missed each other. A silly notion, she knew, but it made her feel good.

The fence was now up and all that was left to do was tie on the plastic batons—three between each pine post. 'That job's hell on your hands,' Tegan had informed her.

Laura had smirked. *Really? Like I wouldn't know*, she'd thought to herself.

She walked into the kitchen, took a bottle of wine out of the fridge and poured herself a glass. This was a repeat every night. Then, in her office, she checked the answering machine and leafed through the mail she'd collected earlier in the day.

Nothing needed her immediate attention. And there was certainly nothing from Meghan.

She checked her emails. Just the usual industry weekly reports and stock market updates.

She tapped the office desk with her finger and sipped at her wine. Outside she could hear Tegan and Robyn laughing as they piled into Tegan's dual-cab to head to the pub for the evening.

'I'll see you in there,' Allie called as the ute took off in a cloud of dust.

The lone voice made Laura look out and she saw a dejected look on her student's face.

'Odd,' she thought. 'They always travel together.'

Absentmindedly, her hand strayed to pat Dash, who would once have been at her feet. She found the spot empty, as it had been since last year. He'd been bitten by a snake while helping her muster. It amazed her that she still forgot some-times. She sighed again, then let her head drop to the desk and listened to the fading sounds of day: the ute disappearing down the driveway, a magpie calling from a tree. The frogs were beginning their nightly serenade, along with the crickets. Somewhere in the distance a sheep bleated.

It was dark by the time she got up from her chair. She switched on the lights and decided to make a fire. Even though it was warming up during the day now, the nights still held a chill that a fire would fix.

She went outside to gather pinecones and some small branches. When she had enough, she expertly laid them in the hearth of the tile fire. Placing larger logs on top, she unscrewed the lid of the diesel container and tossed a bit of the lighting fluid in. She struck a match and put it to the liquid, then sat back on her knees to watch the flare of orange light. It cast an eerie glow over the dim lounge room. After a moment or two and, satisfied the fire was going to take, she moved to get up but, instead, she settled into a more comfortable sitting position. She wanted to watch the flames a little longer.

She sipped her wine, watching the pinecones glowing and fizzing as the small flames licked around the edges of the kindling and larger logs. There were so many things a fire could be, she thought. They could be frightening when out of control on a summer's day. But they could be romantic too, as they'd been many times for her and Josh. She remembered the bonfire they'd had in the back paddock of Nambina for his birthday. It was on their common boundary and they'd met down there, laughingly calling it a secret rendezvous, even though their families knew what they were doing. It had been just her and Josh, a swag, a bottle of red, and the fire.

Fires could be warming and comforting—they seemed to hold a truth serum, creating an atmosphere where secrets came to light and, sometimes, hard questions were asked.

'Enough of that,' she said out loud. She got to her feet and went back into the kitchen. As she rummaged through the fridge to find something to cook, she heard the sound of an engine outside.

It was strange for the girls to be back so early. But then Laura remembered that Allie hadn't left with the others and figured it was probably her. She continued her rummage, but jumped when the door banged open and Sean walked in.

'Surprise!' he said as he put two plastic bags down on the table and opened his arms.

Laura knocked her head on the top of the fridge and gasped. Then her face lit up with delight. 'Dad!' She ran over and threw herself into his embrace. 'What are you doing here? You didn't ring! Are you staying? I haven't got the spare room made up. Is Georgie with you?'

'Whoa! What's with all the questions?' He let her go and stood back, looking at her with a cheerful expression. 'No, Georgie isn't with me. Yes, I'm staying, but I can make up my own bed, and I've forgotten what else you asked.'

'What are you doing here?' Laura asked, unable to keep the smile from her lips.

'I didn't know I needed an excuse to visit my oldest daughter! Surely not, especially when I bring Italian takeaway from her favourite restaurant in Adelaide!'

'Oh, serious? Excellent! I was just wondering what I was going to have. Do you want a drink?'

She walked over to the cupboard to get another wine glass.

'I brought a red.' He handed her the bottle so she could unscrew the lid and pour.

'So, really, why are you here?' Laura said after they'd toasted each other with a *clink* and sat down in the sunroom.

Laura saw her father glance at Howie's spot at the table, then through the doorway to his lounge chair near the fire. Neither of them ever sat in it.

'It's been too long, Laurs, that's all,' he said gently before taking a sip of wine. 'Hmm, that's good.' He closed his eyes for a moment. Laura could see he was tired.

'Things okay at the hospital?' she asked cautiously. Sean never did start his own practice, as he'd planned. An adrenalin junky to the last, he'd stayed in Emergency at Royal Adelaide.

'Yeah, fine. I'm on a five-days-on, four-day-off roster at the moment. It's good. Suits Georgie too. She can spend the five days doing her pottery and hanging around the house. Lord knows, Poppy makes sure there's enough for her to do washing-wise. Then we have the four days off together. It works well. And the break is enough time to get my energy back for the next round.'

'But you left Georgie at home for these few days. How come? I'd love to see her,' she said, shifting in her seat.

'Yep. She's been commissioned to make a couple of pieces of pottery for the Town Hall. Got a deadline of two months' time, so she's a bit under the pump. Plus it's good, dad-and-daughter time, don't you think?'

Laura flashed him a grateful smile and took a gulp of wine. 'Of course.'

'What about you?' Sean asked. 'How are the students going? And Random?'

'Oh! Random's home,' she answered, eyes lighting up. 'Brought him home on Monday. That was about the only good thing that happened that day. He seems fine and Tim thinks I'll still be able to breed from him, which is even better news. All four of the boys are together out in the paddock now, just waiting to be put to work.'

She took a breath but Sean got in before her. 'What happened on Monday?'

She screwed up her face. 'Allie forgot to put the tractor in park and it rolled back while I was putting a fence post into the thumper. Could have been nasty, but it wasn't.' She made light of it. The pain from the deep bruising had eased, and she didn't want to worry him.

'Shit.' He leaned forward. 'You okay, though?'

Laura nodded. 'Bit black and blue when I fell over, trying to get out of the way. Other than that, I'm fine.'

'Did you give her a good talking-to?'

'Poor Allie,' Laura said, remembering the tears. 'She was pretty shaken up, so I didn't go too hard. Just enough to make sure she'll never get out of a tractor and leave it in neutral again. Reckon she'll probably end up sticking the handbrake on even when it's only in the ute!'

Sean sipped his wine thoughtfully.

'Nicki called me on Skype the other day,' Laura said after a few moments. 'Doesn't she sound so happy? She was calling from Paris. To be honest, I can't believe she's twenty-four and living in London! It's doesn't seem that long ago she was getting her licence and doing her year twelve exams.'

Her father laughed. 'Nicki's the only one of my daughters I don't have to worry about! Happy, satisfied, working hard and forever broke.' He gave another chuckle. 'It's so difficult to find work as a professional singer, but I have to give it to her, she's a trier. Won't give up.'

'Nicki was always going to be a singer, Dad. She'll make it. I know she will.'

'Totally agree with you,' Sean said as he got up to stoke the fire. When he finished he walked over to Howie's chair and rested his hands on its back. He was silent.

'Do you think about him much?' Laura finally asked, not looking at her father.

'Mmm.' He nodded. 'I hear myself saying the things he did, when I'm talking to little kids coming through Emergency. His favourite, remember?'

195

'Oh, you silly sausage! How did you do that?' they chorused together, sharing a sad smile.

'I sometimes think about when he died,' Laura said, staring into the fire. 'You know, the actual day. It gave me the creeps for a while. Now I think it was kinda nice I was there. Just the three of us, the way it was when I was a kid. Do you remember what Howie said about his family coming back and how we have to look after them?'

Sean nodded.

'Why did his brother leave?'

Sean shook his head. 'I know very little. He didn't talk about his childhood much and when he did, only Mum got away with asking questions. I was under the impression it wasn't always happy. After Mum died, I knew better than to ask. He only opened up one night after a few too many reds.' He paused to take another sip of wine. 'Got to admit, I have thought about them on occasions. If I've got any cousins out there I don't know about.'

'Weird, hey? To have a whole family we know nothing of.'

'I doubt we've any relatives out there, Laurs. Given Thomas's age when he disappeared, it's likely he went to war and didn't come home. I think that's what Dad assumed happened. That night he spoke of him, Howie said he was sure Thomas couldn't just disappear into the middle of Australia and never show up again. Or at least not run into someone who knew him. At the time, there was a huge push for volunteers to sign up. You've got to remember, a lot of those lads would have never had an opportunity to see the world, so that was how the government sold it to them. It was a chance that might never come again. Thomas was young and free.' He raised his eyebrows as if to say, *you see where I'm going?*

'But wouldn't Papa and his father have been notified if he had been killed?' For a moment, Laura considered telling Sean about Meghan's threats. Then she decided against it. She was growing more and more certain that, after all this time, it really had been a hoax designed to scare her.

'Only if he put them down as his next of kin. And if my assumption is right—that Thomas ran away—I doubt he would have. I got the impression he left because he didn't get along with his father. But that's only filling in the gaps, you know? My take on the story Howie told.'

'That's so sad. Fancy leaving home because you didn't get along with your family. I couldn't imagine that.'

She got up from her chair and went to stand in front of the fire. 'I was so lucky with my childhood, Dad. I couldn't have had a better upbringing during those early years when it was just you, me and Papa. I never felt like I was missing a mum because you both made me feel so loved and secure.' She shrugged. 'So it's just never bothered me that my mother didn't want me. That you brought me home from that town in Queensland. I think it's so sad that Thomas may not have had the same experience.'

Sean was quiet for a moment. 'That's one of the best things I could hear, Laurs. It really is.'

He refilled their wine glasses and sat back down. 'Howie always said to me we had to make sure you were surrounded with love because if you were, you wouldn't want for anything. He told me he knew what it was like not to have a mum. I never really knew what happened to her, but she wasn't around and his brother shot through, so it was only him and his dad.

'He also understood what it was like not to have any softness as he was growing up. I'm sure that's why he realised it was important you didn't ever feel like that. He changed after I brought you home. Became sort of—' Sean tried to find the words. 'Oh, I don't know. Mellow, maybe. You were definitely the sunshine in this house!'

'You've never really told me the story, Dad. I mean, I know bits and pieces, but not from start to finish.' Laura looked over at him. 'Is it something I should know?'

Sean cleared his throat as he put his wine glass down. 'Well,' he drew out the word. After a moment's consideration, he said, 'Well, there's nothing in it which is a secret.'

He stopped and Laura waited him out.

'This is all very heavy for me, just arriving and all, Laurs! How about I give you the other present I brought with me, then we'll talk over dinner.'

He got up and Laura followed. 'I certainly didn't expect this when I decided to come for the weekend!' he joked.

'I guess it's my history, isn't it? I'd never really considered asking before. Talking about Papa's family has made me think . . . Maybe I've got other half-brothers and -sisters out there, people I don't know. From my mother. I've certainly got grandparents. And just because she didn't want me, doesn't mean the others wouldn't.' She paused. 'If they even know about me.'

Laura watched Sean's face and knew he was trying to keep it expressionless, the way he would when consulting with a patient. She knew him almost better than he knew himself and she could see he was wrestling with the idea. Maybe she should never have mentioned it, but it just seemed to pop out. *Bloody fire and its truth potion*, she said to herself.

She changed the subject. 'Not sure what Howie'd think of us now, two old winos!' She held up her glass and was glad to see her father smile.

'You know he'd be joining in! Now, come out to the car.'

Laura followed Sean outside. As they approached his car, she heard a high-pitched cry.

She stopped. 'What's that?' she asked, even though she knew.

Sean pulled up the rear hatch. Inside was an animal travel box. 'It's your new best friend!' he answered. He unlatched the wire door and Laura saw a tiny black nose and pink tongue appear. Then a tiny black head.

'He's not a replacement for Dash,' Sean said, reaching in to pick up the wriggling body. 'But he'll be good company and, I'm told, an exceptional sheep dog. He comes from a bloke who breeds kelpies in the Adelaide Hills. I really don't know how you've run this place since Dash died, Laura. It must make sheep work so difficult.'

'Oh-h-h,' sighed Laura as she reached for the pup. 'Aren't you just a little cutie?'

A thin puppy bark and a lick made Laura's heart melt. 'What about some dinner?' she asked.

'Good idea,' Sean answered and grinned when Laura gave him a withering look.

'I was talking to this little one. What will I call you, hmm?'

The pup shivered in her arms and barked again.

'Why not Howie?' Sean asked.

Laura considered the suggestion, then decided against it. 'I'm going to call him Rip.'

'He looks like a Rip.'

199

They went back inside, the pup tucked under Laura's arm. She got out some milk and heated it in the microwave.

'There you go, little one.' She watched as he lapped it up eagerly and turned back to Sean. 'Now I'd better get our dinner.'

'I'll heat it up,' Sean said. He opened a cupboard and got out some plates.

Laura went into the laundry and found a cardboard carton and an old blanket that would make a good bed for the pup. She brought it into the kitchen. Rip was sniffing at everything but when she walked in, he sat down and hunched over timidly. He looked tiny. She picked him up and cuddled him again.

'You're beautiful,' she murmured. 'But you'll have to learn to do as you're told. I don't want another dog being pushy in the yards and people getting hurt.' For a second she saw the ewe careering down the race at her, remembered being hit and the agony in her stomach. Laura shook away the memory of the loss. 'Yep, you'll have to do as you're told.'

Rip regarded her seriously before his eyes began to droop. Laura tucked him into his bed, gave him one last pat then joined her father.

'Thanks,' she said, leaning on her father as he spooned spaghetti and meat sauce into the bowls.

'You're welcome. I hope you become good mates.'

'I know we will. How's Poppy?'

'Fine as far as she lets us know. Studying, but probably not hard enough. Parties a bit too much. I'd hoped a 22-year-old would have decided what she wanted to do by now, but she keeps swapping and changing subjects at uni.' He gave a wry smile and held up his hands. 'Still, I don't suppose I can talk. It took me a while to find my calling too.'

'She's a strange girl,' Laura said without thinking.

'She's not, Laura.' Sean frowned.

'Sorry, Dad. I didn't mean to criticise her. She's just so different to me.'

'Bound to happen. Two different childhoods, different situations.'

'That's for sure. She's city, I'm country and never the twain shall meet.'

'You shouldn't be so hard on her,' Sean commented.

Laura crossed her arms. 'Dad,' she said firmly. 'She doesn't even try when she's on Nambina and she'd rather not come down here. And when I'm in the city, she thinks I'm a country hick and doesn't give me the time of day. We're too different. Doesn't mean I don't care about her, but I don't think we'll ever be great friends.'

'You know, when Georgie and I moved to the city we didn't think we'd stay forever. Just long enough for me to go to uni. We'd always intended to come back to somewhere in the country. Small towns are screaming for doctors. I honestly had no idea what a difference it would make for the kids, growing up in the city.' He shook his head. 'Neither of those girls will ever want to be in the country full-time. That goes without saying. But Nicki doesn't mind spending time here. I know Poppy finds it a little . . .' He searched for words.

'Primitive?' Laura offered.

'Boring, perhaps.' He took the plate she handed him and sat at the table, then looked at her. 'I wish we'd brought her up on Nambina. It's much cleaner living. Here there aren't the temptations that there are in the city. And I must admit I'm pretty worried about her, Laurs.'

It was then she wondered if maybe the tiredness she could see on his face was actually concern.

'Why?'

'Oh, I don't know. I don't like a couple of the girls she spends time with. They seem a little too, how do you say it? World-wise for my baby Poppy.'

Laura grinned. 'You sure you're not just being overprotective, Dad? After all, she's the last one at home.' She looked at him with a small smile and was pleased when he returned it.

'Maybe,' he answered with a little laugh. 'I hope that's all it is, anyway.' He shifted in his seat. 'I'll tell you a secret though.'

'What's that?'

'You are perfect for this place and I'm pleased Lee didn't want to be a mother, either. Georgie and I liked having you to ourselves!'

Laura reached over to pat his arm. 'I love you, Dad.'

'And I love you, Laurs.'

'Now, can you *please* tell me the story?'

Chapter 23

1940

Thomas stood by the front gate. Nambina. After so long away, it felt strange to be back. Memories came crowding in. Phantom voices screamed at him and he felt the crack of Ernest's fist against his cheek. It was all so real, he recoiled and held up his arm to ward off the blow. His heart beat faster and he had to reach out to the fence to steady himself.

The moon cast just enough light for him to see the two-wheeled track leading to the house. At first, it seemed as though nothing had changed—he wouldn't have expected it to. But then he noticed the freshly painted gate and next to it a sign announcing 'Nambina', the home of 'Ernest and Howard Murphy'.

There was no mention of Thomas, and certainly no mention of Jessie. His fury surged to the surface and he wanted to hit something, but instead he shut his eyes tightly and balled his hands into fists. Breathe, he encouraged himself. Just breathe.

He opened the gate, went through it, then refastened the chain. Thomas now stood inside Nambina's boundary for the first time in three years. Soon he could see the outhouses and sheds. They looked tidier and more cared for than when he'd lived here.

Maybe Howard was doing all the work now, as Thomas once had. It was hard to imagine 'little Howard' as the mainstay behind Nambina. One thing Ernest did know how to do was work. But not on the farm. He enjoyed being away from it and socialising with all the well-to-do farmers in the district. That's why he'd spent so much time on committees. Ernest was the one people relied on when there was a fundraiser or event coming up. He'd be the first one there and the last to leave. He was known for pulling more than his fair share of the weight. But not at home.

'Must be Howard's doing,' Thomas muttered. 'My brother was always tidy and proud.' In which case, Howard probably hadn't enlisted in the army. With all the propaganda encouraging young men to sign up, surely it had crossed his mind, as it had Thomas's, if only fleetingly.

There was no chance of Ernest enlisting—he wouldn't be fit enough.

Thomas tried to take another step forward but found he couldn't move. His heart beat faster and he wasn't sure if he was petrified as well as angry.

He stared out into the darkened countryside. He could hear the murmur of sheep in the paddock, and the familiar sound comforted him. It had been a long, hot summer, and the fact that the ewes were out grazing, even though it was dark, suggested feed was getting scarce, he surmised.

He made a quick decision. He wanted to create an element of surprise, and to know what was going on before he walked into the house. He'd spend the night in the shearing shed and watch them tomorrow.

Skirting along the edge of the fence, he made his way through the compound of sheds. If Flea was still alive or there were any other dogs around, they wouldn't hear or smell him that way. He was upwind.

Inside the shearing shed, he rolled out his swag in one of the wool bins. That way he wouldn't be easily seen if Howard came to the shed first thing in the morning.

He lay back, his hands behind his head, and stared at the tin roof, at last comfortable among the familiar smells and noises. He thought back over the past weeks he'd spent with his grandparents. He'd enjoyed their company and learned a lot about merino farming too. William and Dorothy hadn't wanted him to leave.

Thomas had hungered for information about his mother, and Dorothy had happily obliged. Her tales of Jessie's childhood had brought much laughter and, for Dorothy, some tears. Thomas just listened and kept everything he felt inside.

William had tried to draw Thomas out, to discover what he was thinking. He figured he'd probably frightened the old man when, after hearing about his mother's fate, Thomas had sworn to kill his father.

'There's no need for an eye for an eye and all that sort of nonsense, Thomas,' William had said. 'He'll get his judgement in good time. Leave it to our Lord. Just like this dratted war. Promise me you'll never fight. There's no need to.'

But Thomas had no intention of forgiving his father. Ernest had stolen the dearest person Thomas had ever known, and he would pay. Thomas's anger grew with every day until the need

205

to confront his father had consumed him and he knew they would face each other in a day of reckoning very soon.

The morning he left, he'd woken in a sweat. He'd dreamt he was pushing Ernest down onto the bed with a choke hold. It had frightened him but also spurred him on.

'Dorothy, I need to leave today,' he'd said without preamble when he walked into the kitchen.

He saw her shoulders slump and a look of resignation cross her face. 'We understand, dearie,' she said softly. 'But please, Thomas. Don't do anything rash.'

'I'm going to catch up with Mac,' he lied, but he could tell she didn't believe him.

Just before he left, William pushed a wad of rolled-up banknotes into his hand. 'For essentials,' he'd said, before clasping Thomas by the upper arms and staring intently into his face. It was as if he was committing his grandson's face to memory. As if he understood he would never see Thomas again.

And now here Thomas was. Back at Nambina. Ready to challenge his father.

Kill him? He wanted to. But there were things to think about, and his brother was one of them. Thank goodness he hadn't posted the letter he'd written to Howard, or forewarned him of his visit.

❧

The next morning Thomas was awake before the sun had risen. He'd slept fitfully, even though he was comfortable. Strange dreams and memories had crowded his mind, and now he felt sluggish and had the beginnings of a headache.

He rolled his swag and slid it down one of the chutes

underneath the shed and stretched. From his rucksack he took some dry biscuits, then ate them while he decided what to do. He needed to keep in the shadows today. To watch, to learn, to understand. Then he would confront Ernest.

The problem was going to be dogs. If Ernest and Howard still had any, it was likely the animals would sniff him out. Maybe he could get into the house? Yes, that was a better plan. The door from the garage led into the cellar. He could sit there and listen to the goings-on within the walls. Perhaps the conversations, grunted, yelled or otherwise, would give him an idea of the state of play.

Without hesitation, he started walking towards the house. The moon had sunk and it was only the glow of the stars and predawn light that showed the way.

By the time he was standing in front of the cellar door, the sun's rays were visible above the horizon. He'd only just made it. Thomas held his breath and slowly turned the handle. It opened noiselessly and he slipped inside. He paused until his eyes adjusted, then found the stairs. Slowly he climbed them until he was halfway up. He would wait here.

∽

That evening, hungry and stiff, Thomas laid his bedroll out in the wool bin again. But he couldn't lie down to sleep—he was too furious.

Angrily, he paced the floor. He'd left to make his life better. He, Thomas, had been the one with the initiative to get off his backside and make something of his existence. Not to get stuck in the rut of working, being beaten and abused. He had made decisions that meant transforming his world.

It had worked and he was happy. He was thankful and content. But not for one moment had he ever contemplated that things would be different on Nambina. He shook his head. He didn't understand.

When Howard had come out into the kitchen that morning, he was whistling. Thomas had instantly remembered the tuneless whistle and how annoying it had been.

When Ernest had arrived there had been cheery good mornings all round and a discussion about the day. There had been no sign of a hangover or surliness. Thomas hadn't trusted the change. It all sounded peculiar—too chummy. What was going on?

The two men had decided that Ernest would go into town for some supplies for the sheep. From the branches of a tree, Thomas had watched his father walk to the truck and climb in. The man looked well—not the sallow, pasty face from before nor the red-rimmed eyes. Had he reformed?

Howard looked fit and tanned. There was talk of his girlfriend, Mary, and Ernest had teased him about a wedding. Howard had said that wasn't happening any time soon, although he was going over to Mary's place for dinner that evening.

While Howard was shoeing a horse that Thomas didn't recognise (and when did his brother learn to shoe, anyway?), Ernest had sought him out and actually talked to Howard.

Thomas was so enraged he knew he couldn't contain it anymore. There had been no mention of his mother nor him. It was like they didn't exist.

An idea struck him. Had Ernest wanted to get rid of him? Had his father known he wouldn't put up with it and would eventually leave? As his grandfather had said, Ernest had wanted Jessie out of the way for some reason. But if this was the case, why had Ernest chosen to be rid of Jessie and Thomas, but not Howard?

Thomas looked out into the night and listened. All was silent. He checked his watch and saw it was 7 p.m. If they still followed the same routine, Ernest would have turned on the wireless and would be listening to the news.

'Now's the time,' he said to himself. There was no turning back. It had to be done.

Armed with nothing but his hands, he strode towards the house. Thomas could see one window illuminated and knew it would be the gaslight in the sunroom.

Moments later, he stood outside and raised his hand to knock. But his fist didn't connect. The door opened. There was Ernest.

'Evening, Thomas,' his father said in a hard voice. There was no smile on his face and no welcome.

Thomas said nothing, but his stomach flipped and turned with fear. How had he known?

'Did you think I couldn't see you sneaking around today?' Ernest continued in a low voice. 'I knew you'd come back one day and because of that I've never let my guard down. That's why I stopped the drinking. I've got you to thank for getting me off the booze.' He smiled coldly. 'I've been watching for you.' He stopped.

Now it made sense. No drinking. Thomas wouldn't have believed it possible. Because he had left, Ernest had managed to get himself together. The irony of it made Thomas want to smile, but he met the man's gaze, never once blinking.

Ernest leaned against the doorframe. 'So, to what do I owe this pleasure?'

Thomas was overcome with emotion and found he couldn't speak, even though he wanted to.

'If you haven't got anything to say, why are you here?' Ernest looked at him questioningly. 'It'd be better if you left. You made your choice when you walked out the door.'

Thomas pulled himself up straight and glared at his nemesis. As he did so, he realised he was now taller and stronger than Ernest. 'You killed Mum,' he stated.

'No, I didn't.'

'Yeah, you did. Not by your hand, but your actions. I know what happened. I know the truth and you have to pay.' He took a step towards him, but Ernest didn't move.

'Thomas, I'm not going to discuss this with you. I've changed and I'm sure you have too. I'd rather not think about the past.' Ernest shrugged. 'Unfortunately, both you and Jessie remind me of something I never want to think about again. She was crazy, and you?' He looked at Thomas for a long moment, his insinuations left unsaid. 'So why don't you be on your way?'

That gave Thomas pause. Changed?

He looked past his father and into the sunroom. The spot where Jessie's plant had always been was empty. Then rage packed every inch of Thomas's body again and he took another step forward, glowering down at the man who'd filled him with fear for so long. Ernest seemed to shrink in front of him. Whether it was his imagination or not, Thomas didn't care. He felt powerful. In control. He was here to avenge his mother. To avenge Jessie.

'How could you do that to her? How could you do what you did to me? You're my *father*!'

Ernest retreated but the insults kept coming.

'You're just like her,' Ernest said. 'Unstable, they call it. Split personalities. Something goes wrong and you lose it. Turn into a blubbering mess. Like that time I found you pissing yourself in a chair. Gah!' His disgust was plain. 'All I did was tap your face and you had to piss yourself. Scared, weren't ya?' he nodded. 'That's why you're not out fighting for our country. Why you're not wearing the Australian uniform with pride. You're too scared.' He tried to smile. 'What are you gonna do when they call you up, 'Fraidy Tom Cat?'

Thomas swung his fist and, despite never having thrown a punch before, managed to connect with his father's face and knock him to the ground. Ernest kept up a stream of taunts, though he grunted as he fell. Thomas loomed over him.

'Yeah, scared.' Ernest nodded. 'You won't ever come to nothing. You're weak! Weak, I tell you!' he yelled. 'Don't think I'll leave you anything. You've given up all your rights to anything I own by being a nothing. You're pathetic. Now just leave. It's best for us all.'

Ernest was breathing quickly now, and Thomas could almost smell his fear. The tables had turned. He was the younger and fitter one. The stronger one now, even though Ernest was clear eyed and sober.

Thomas stuck his foot out and leaned just enough weight on Ernest's stomach to make him grunt.

'I'm not weak and I will become something,' he said calmly. 'No. Thanks. To. You.' He pressed harder. 'I wouldn't want anything from you, anyway. It'd be blood money after what you did to Mum.'

He increased the pressure and Ernest grabbed at his ankle with both hands, but the grip felt like nothing to Thomas. 'You know,' Thomas said, changing tack. 'I came to kill you.' He took pleasure in seeing the man's eyes widen. 'But I'm not going to. I'm just going to make sure you remember I've been here and you remember this night forever. Believe you me.' He took his foot away and kicked his father's soft middle, then watched as the man curled into the foetal position. He drew his fist back and smashed it into the side of Ernest's face. He kept going until he heard a high-pitched cry.

Thomas stopped, breathing heavily. He looked down at the helpless man, who was bleeding from his nose and mouth, and watched as he clambered away. He looked at his fist and realised he was bleeding too. Their blood was intermingling. He wiped it on his trouser leg and ran his other hand over his face, clearing the sweat from his forehead.

'Do you feel better?' Ernest managed to whisper as he pulled himself away from the assault. He got to a chair and leaned heavily on it, trying to pull his battered body into a standing position. His legs gave way and he had to be content to sit on the floor, his back against the chair.

Thomas knew that, without a doubt, he could kill his father now, if he wanted. Ernest was beaten.

Then he considered the question Ernest had asked.

He'd always assumed he would feel content after giving Ernest some of his own medicine. He didn't, though. He felt empty and unsatisfied.

Studying the broken man before him, Thomas came to

understand something. Why he'd ever believed hurting his father would make everything right, he had no idea, because it didn't. Jessie was still dead. Howard was still out of reach and Thomas, himself, still bore the scars.

Coming to Nambina hadn't changed one damn thing.

Thomas shook his head. 'You're nothing but a worthless piece of shit,' he said. 'If I ever lay eyes on you again, it'll be too soon.'

Thomas walked out without a backwards glance.

Chapter 24

2008

Laura swirled spaghetti around her fork and breathed in the garlicky scent. Sean had refilled their wine glasses for the fourth time, which was probably just as well, given the story she was about to hear, she decided.

Her father took a breath. 'I'm sure you know I was a bit of a drifter when I first left school,' he began.

She nodded. 'But not in a bad way?'

'No, no. I just knew farming wasn't for me. Dad knew it too, which is why he was so patient with me when I kept trying different things. A lot of his care and easy-going ways stemmed from his childhood. He'd decided he wasn't going to be like his father—Ernest, his name was. I think they ended up with a reasonable relationship, in the end, but there was something . . .' He paused. 'I'm only guessing this, but there may have been some violence when he was growing up. There certainly wasn't any encouragement, that I'm convinced of. But you've got to remember, kids were brought up a lot tougher in those days. Everyone had to pull their weight and work, so maybe I'm reading too much into it.

'Anyway, like I said, I'm certain that's why he was so patient with me, despite my lack of interest in the farm. He said to me one day he was tempted to put roofing nails in my feet to keep me in one place!'

Laura smiled. She could hear Papa saying that, as clear as a bell.

Sean leaned back and looked at his daughter. 'One of the things I've learned working at the hospital is that kids seem to follow one path or the other. If they're raised in a violent household they either become violent themselves, or they shun it and become gentle and caring. They don't want to end up like the person who abused them, I guess. I'm pretty sure that's what happened with Howie.

'I tried to stay on Nambina—as soon as I left school I spent a couple of years here. That was 1970 to '72. When Mum died in '68 the place just didn't feel the same. I guess that was when I realised that farming wasn't for me. The most enjoyment I was getting out of life was on the footy field every Saturday.'

Sean picked up the wine bottle. 'Top up?'

Laura shook her head.

He poured the last of the wine into his glass then continued. 'Reckon it was Mum dying that made me unsettled. I couldn't think straight for a while. Anyway, it was Howie who suggested I leave the first time. I'd mucked up something—boxed some sheep up I shouldn't have, I think. Trying to keep his temper in check, he said: "Your heart isn't here, son. Maybe it's best you take off for a while to see if you can find something you really like doing."' Sean laughed. 'I couldn't believe the timing.

215

A couple of days earlier, I'd met your mum at the pub. Lee was from out of town—had come to visit relatives or something. She'd been travelling for a while and made it sound so exciting. No responsibility, so many things to see, a whole wide world to explore.

'I talked to Dad and told him I wanted to travel for a year or so, and that then I might be ready to come back to Nambina. So Lee and I hitchhiked to Queensland—she lived up there and was heading home—and bummed around for a while. I always worked, though. Needed the money.'

'Were you, um, together then?' Laura asked.

'Not to start with. I saw her as a good chick. We clicked that night at the pub, but I never looked at her as a potential partner. She was such a free spirit.' He looked into the fire. 'Lee was really confident and content within herself—something I wasn't. I guess that's what drew me to her in the first place.

'Anyway, I cooked at a roadhouse and stacked shelves at a supermarket. Then a bloke put me on as a mechanic. Not a real one, but I could change oil in cars and basic stuff I'd learned on the farm, so I did the smaller jobs for him. I enjoyed it—there was plenty of contact with different people . . .'

'Where was this?' Laura interrupted.

'Mackay. And that's what was so great about the job. I was living on the coast. I went surfing and swimming every day. I felt free. Lee was working as a barmaid, and even though we were sharing a unit at the caravan park, we always did our own thing.

'Then, one evening just before Christmas, Dan, the bloke I was working for, shouted us both to dinner and drinks at the pub as a kind of Christmas bonus. That was the night everything changed.

'I believed we'd be together forever, but that was the mistake of youth, I guess. Lee was working, I was working, the weekends were full of good times, mates, the sea.' He shrugged. 'Bit like that Bryan Adams song you loved so much when you were a kid. What's it called? Something about lasting forever and being the best days of your life.'

'"Summer of '69",' she answered without hesitation.

'Yeah. Well, it didn't and they weren't, but that's what it felt like at the time.'

Laura noticed Sean hadn't eaten anything since his first mouthful. The food lay in front of him, untouched and cold.

She put down her fork and tried to work out how she was feeling. Normal, she decided. Safe in the knowledge her dad loved her and that whatever else this tale held it wouldn't affect her.

'Then, in 1977, Lee got pregnant. She was excited at first and I was too. I couldn't imagine anything making my life better than a baby! I suddenly felt like I was an adult, like I was about to be complete.

'It was then we talked about coming home to Nambina for a visit, but the morning sickness got to her. It was a terrible time. If she wasn't vomiting, she was lying on the bed with the blinds shut. She kept the house as dark as her moods and I couldn't do anything right. She'd snap and yell if I suggested she go to the doctor. I ended up researching morning sickness and what natural remedies there were. She had a distrust of Western medicine, so I tried to find natural things. Nothing worked.

'Oh, Laurs, she did suffer—the whole nine months, and I'm sure now that's where everything started to go wrong for her. She'd been so sick that, when you were born, she couldn't bond with you.'

'Was the birth easy?'

'Relatively. You were the most gorgeous baby I'd ever seen. I couldn't put you down. Just wanted to hold you all the time. But Lee didn't. She didn't really want you near her. I know now it was post-partum depression.

'When we took you home, she let me do all the normal things—bathing, changing nappies and so on. Obviously she had to feed you, but she was happy to let me do the rest. I *wanted* to do it.'

Laura heard a movement: Rip was stretching in his box. Even though she wanted to hear what was coming, she decided it wouldn't hurt to have something to cuddle, so she pushed her chair back and picked him up.

Sean continued to talk. 'Then one day she told me she couldn't do it anymore. Couldn't play happy families when there was still a life to be lived.'

Laura's gaze dropped to Rip and she patted his little head. He gave her chin a lick.

Sean must have sensed her apprehension, so he cut to the chase.

'That's when I decided it was time to come home. You were about six months old. Lee said she didn't want visitation rights and I could do as I pleased, so I did. I came back to Nambina, to Howie. You know the rest. We raised you together, until I met Georgie. You were four, then.'

He took a mouthful of his cold spaghetti and grimaced.

218

Laura returned Rip to his box. 'Here.' She held out her hand. 'I'll heat it up.'

He handed her the plate and she put it in the microwave and turned it on.

'Do you stay in contact with her at all, Dad? Do you know where she is?'

'No. That was never the deal. I guess we could try to find her if you want.'

But Laura was shaking her head before he'd finished his sentence. 'No. I wasn't asking for that reason. I was just curious.'

They were silent for a moment. Then the microwave pinged. Laura pulled out Sean's plate and set it on the table in front of him. He began to eat.

'How do you feel?' he asked after a few mouthfuls.

'I don't think I feel anything, Dad,' she answered. 'It's almost like it's a story about someone else, if that makes sense. Oh, I guess I had a few questions—those ones I asked when I first started school and realised our family wasn't the same as everyone else's. Nothing more than that.

'Talking about it tonight made me curious to hear how it all happened.' She shrugged, working out how to ask the question that had formed in her mind. With all this talk of other families, she had to tell her father about Meghan, she decided. She picked up Rip and gave him another cuddle before sitting down opposite Sean and settling the pup on her lap.

'Um, Dad?' she began hesitantly. 'Meghan Hunter threatened me at the show. To take Nambina away from us. I don't know how she could. Do you know?'

Sean was still for a moment before his face lit with anger.

'Bloody hell, that woman has got some nerve.' He glared at Laura, but she knew it wasn't for her. 'Not a chance, love. I gave up my right to inherit Nambina when we passed it over to you. The drawings we take every week are like a wage. There's no comeback. I can promise you there is no possibility that Meghan could get her hands on the property. None whatsoever. She's crazy!'

'Don't get worked up,' Laura said gently. 'I was only asking the question. She mentioned it once at the show and I've never heard about it again.' She broke off—Rip had widdled on her. 'Oh, Rip! Do you mind?' She got up and exiled him to his box before taking off her jumper. 'Anyway, now I know. And that's it, really.'

Sean eyed Rip. 'You may have just disgraced yourself, mate.' Then, looking back at Laura, he said, 'You know Georgie and I are here for you, Laurs. You should have told us sooner. We want to help you if you need it.'

'I know.'

༜

The next morning, Laura woke with a bubble of happiness inside her chest. She'd slept soundly, without dwelling on the conversation she'd had with her father. Maybe she would later, or maybe she wouldn't. All she knew was, she felt good.

She could hear Sean busy in the kitchen and smelt coffee. There was a short, sharp bark before her dad shushed Rip.

Throwing on her dressing gown, she went out and said good morning. Sean looked much more relaxed, she thought. It seemed to her that a weight neither of them had known was there had been lifted.

220

Laura bent down and rubbed her hands over the pup, then picked him up before heating up some milk and getting the Weet-Bix out of the cupboard. 'This'll have to do for breakfast until I get to town and find you some puppy mince,' she said to the dog. Once Rip was settled, she took the coffee Sean offered.

'So you never mentioned how long you were staying for,' she said, blowing on the steaming liquid.

'I'll head home tomorrow morning,' he answered, buttering a piece of toast. 'That'll give me a day and a half with Georgie. We've arranged to go to the beach down at Glenelg and have dinner there. I don't start back at the hospital until Tuesday morning. Want to take me for a drive a bit later?'

'Yeah, I'd love to. And you can come and see Random and the others. Boof thinks he's not my favourite anymore so he's got his nose out of joint!'

Sean swallowed his last bit of toast. 'Are you going to get out of your pyjamas? Come on, Laura,' he kidded. 'Is this how you run the farm?'

She threw him a look and flounced off to get dressed. Minutes later she was back. 'Come on. Tour time.'

They walked out to the ute together, the tiny pup running ahead.

They spent the day looking around the farm. Sean commented more than once how proud he was of what she was achieving.

'Why did you knock this bush down, though?' he asked as Laura showed him the new fence.

'I wanted it to be tidy and it wouldn't have been if I'd had to weave the fence in and out of it. Best to knock it down. I'll burn it later.'

Laura could tell he didn't agree with that, but it didn't bother her. Sean never questioned her—he asked so he understood, but he never questioned her decisions.

The evening was spent around the fire, eating dinner on their laps and, once again, drinking too much red wine. Laura learned that Poppy had started an arts degree after dropping out of a real estate course.

'She said it was too hard,' Sean said. 'Which disappointed me a bit. She does find it difficult to get out of bed in the morning and get to uni. Only because she's out so late, listening to bands in nightclubs.' He shook his head. 'It worries me, really.'

'But why? It sounds pretty normal.' Laura wondered why her father was so concerned. 'If you're thinking about what I did when I was twenty-two, you should realise you can't compare us. We're completely different people.'

'Which is part of what concerns me. You and Nicki were so focused on what you wanted to do. Poppy, well, she just seems to drift. Because she hasn't got something she's passionate about, it's easy for her to change her mind and get led in a different direction. She hasn't got any commitment; she changes her mind so often. If you don't have direction, it's easy to fall off the path.'

Laura snorted. 'Dad, the easiest way to get her to take some responsibility for herself would be to kick her out of the house and make her stand on her own two feet. After all, you had to do that and so did Papa. Most people actually have to work for a living, not bludge off their parents.'

He threw her an annoyed look. 'I wouldn't have spoken to you about it if I thought you'd react like that. Georgie and

I drummed it into all three of you: your sisters are your best friends. There's nothing stronger than blood, and one day Georgie and I won't be here. Be kind and compassionate, Laura.'

The subject was not mentioned again.

Laura told him about the fundraiser she was going to and mentioned that Tim had invited her.

Sean's eyes lit up. 'He was a nice bloke when you were all at school,' was all he said, although Laura could tell he was dying to ask more.

She wasn't going to say anything else. Tim's face kept coming to mind when she least expected it and little things reminded her of him, but she wasn't sure why. She'd told herself more than once in the last week that she'd sworn off men for good.

'And I think I might play basketball again this season,' she finished.

'That's a fantastic idea, Laurs!' Sean exclaimed. 'You were pretty good at it. And it's great to play sport. All those endorphins and contact with people.' He leaned back and looked at her. Laura could tell by his expression that he was happy with her news.

❧

Laura had a lovely weekend with her father, but all too soon Sean had to leave.

'Thanks for coming, Dad,' she said. 'I think it was just what I needed.'

'It was just what I needed too. Take care, my girl.'

'You too. Love to Georgie and Poppy.'

Sean got into the car and grinned up at her. 'You never

223

know what might happen if you make an effort with Poppy,' he said.

Laura rolled her eyes.

'Just try,' he said. 'For me.' He winked and put the car in gear. 'See you, Laurs.'

'Bye, Dad.'

They held hands for a moment, then the car moved away and their fingers slid apart.

Laura watched until long after the car had disappeared. 'Bye, Dad,' she whispered again.

Chapter 25

1940

It was October, which made for hot and unpleasant conditions in the shearing shed. But, for Thomas, returning to Mac's team had been like coming home.

The station they were working on, outside Port Augusta, ran nine thousand sheep over nearly a million acres. It was the first time Thomas had truly understood the term 'a sea of sheep'. The yards held nearly one thousand head. All he could see, every time he stuck his head outside, was low scrubby mulga bushes, red dirt and sheep. Always sheep.

When they were finally done, they hit the town, starting with the local show. Despite their best intentions, Mac and Thomas ended up gravitating to the sheep pavilion. They spent a pleasant few hours looking over the animals and wool, while the rest of the team sat at the bar and watched girls walk by.

They were discussing the pros and cons of a particular ram when a young lady came in carrying a basketful of white feathers. Everyone in the shed stopped and turned.

'Not again!' Mac muttered. 'Thought we'd moved on from all that.' He let out a hiss of breath then straightened and stood tall.

Thomas looked with curiosity at his boss. What did it mean? He wanted to ask, but everyone was so quiet and still, he was afraid to speak.

The girl walked around the pavilion and handed a feather to each of the younger men. Some blokes turned and left the shed before she reached them.

'What's going on?' Thomas asked out of the corner of his mouth.

'White feathers,' Mac answered, then accepted the one she handed him. 'Something they used to do during the Great War. The idea was to shame anyone who hadn't signed up to fight.'

Thomas accepted a feather from the young woman and looked down at it blankly.

The girl stopped to speak. 'I hope I've encouraged you all to join with the men who are already fighting for Australia and Britain. People who are prepared to die for your freedom. I have to wonder what you're all still doing here. Are you cowards?' She turned and left before anyone could say a word.

Thomas's mouth fell open. 'Cowards?'

Mac tossed the feather on the ground and stood on it. The other men did the same. 'That's what they think. But people like us, Thomas—farmers, food producers, manufacturers— we've all been told our work is vital for the upkeep of the armed forces here and overseas. The rest of us here at home need to be fed too. We have an exemption. We can join the army if we want, but our jobs are important here. She's probably got a brother or sweetheart over there or training to go.'

He shook his head. 'You know, I understand what she's going through. Families get torn apart during these things. I know of a family who lost all five sons in the last war. How do parents, and the ones left behind, recover from that sort of loss?' He cleared his throat and lit a cigarette. 'I wouldn't go if you paid me. Saw what it did to my father and how it affected the whole family. Nup. Not for me. I'll help class the wool for the uniforms and keep them warm.' He took a drag. 'I'm proud of those boys over there and have the utmost respect for them. But I couldn't do what they do. I *won't* do what they're doing.'

Thomas said nothing. A coward? He felt sick. Ernest forced his way into his mind. ''Fraidy Cat Tom' he'd called him.

Thomas had heard reports of the bloodshed in distant countries but, working in the bush as they did, news was scarce. Thomas didn't know of half the places the reporters spoke of. The war didn't seem real to him and it had never crossed his mind to become involved.

They left the rams and wool and moved out into the bright sunlight. The show's carnival atmosphere seemed suddenly subdued and, while their eyes were adjusting to the brightness, the sun, as if sensing the change, slipped behind a cloud. The children's laughter was as joyful as ever, but the men were now ashen-faced. Thomas heard snatches of conversation between them. 'She wouldn't know anyone's situation,' one snarled. 'I could be an army officer in civvies and she wouldn't know. It's wrong, that's what it is. Downright wrong.'

Thomas and Mac trudged across the dusty ground.

'I'll catch you up.' Thomas stopped to look at a poster showing a man in army fatigues.

Mac stood beside him and put his smoke to his mouth. He

regarded the poster impassively before looking at his friend. 'Wouldn't go getting any ideas, if I was you,' he said, turning to leave.

Thomas read the poster again. The soldier had his hands to his mouth, and he was calling out 'Cooee!'. Thomas had to admit it was enticing. 'Won't you come?' the soldier asked. At the bottom of the poster were the words 'ENLIST NOW!'.

Thomas thought of his father and his scorn. The anger Thomas felt was still just below the surface. He contemplated his mother and how he hadn't been able to save or protect her. He considered Howard and his brother's relationship with Ernest. Why was it so different to his own? Then he looked at the white feather still in his hands.

He turned it over slowly. Elizabeth popped into his mind. Strong, witty, lovely Elizabeth. Her last letter had encouraged him to come back to the station. To work as a jackaroo for a time. But they both knew it wasn't going to happen. Their friendship was just that. A friendship.

Elizabeth was a 'blue stocking'—highly intelligent and without regard for society's constraints. The way she turned the wool over in her hands and spoke so passionately about it . . . Anyway, Thomas knew there would never be anything more. Couldn't be anything more.

With one more glance at the poster, he let the white feather float to the ground and turned away. Without a backwards glance, he went to find his friends.

༄

'Another round, Herbie.' Thomas waved some notes across the bar. A cheer went up from his mates.

Gecko clapped him on the shoulder and held a foaming glass high in the air. 'Here's to Tommo,' he said drunkenly. 'And fuck all those white-feather givers.'

Another cheer went up.

'Well, I'll be. If it isn't the budding horseman from the shearing sheds.'

Thomas looked up from the bar with blurry eyes. For a long moment, he didn't recognise the man or any of his friends behind him.

'Ha! Can't remember me, eh?' The bloke rubbed the three-day growth on his chin and smirked. 'Something about a horse and . . .'

With embarrassment, Thomas suddenly recognised the man. It was Donnie, the jackaroo from Carpoole Station.

'Donnie,' Thomas said. He nodded, or at least tried to. His head wouldn't do what he wanted and flopped to one side.

'Can't hold your liquor either, shed boy?' Donnie gave a bark of unpleasant laughter.

'Piss off, you idiot.' Gecko stood and moved towards them.

Donnie spread out his hands as if in mock misunderstanding. 'What?' he asked. 'I'm just saying hello to an old friend. We could have a catch-up drink. Give him some tips on riding, you know?'

'You're no mate of ours. You never welcome us when we come to shear, so we won't be welcoming you to "have a catch-up drink".' Gecko drew himself up to his full height and stared down at Donnie with the glazed look of a man who's had too much alcohol.

'Yeah.' Thomas echoed Gecko's statement.

'I guess I won't be, then.' Donnie turned to leave. 'Ah! I

meant to ask: were you fellas given white feathers? Suit you lot, I reckon. Especially you, Thomas. Figure you're a bit of a 'fraidy cat. Like to stay away from all that? Not like us. We've just signed up, haven't we lads?' He turned to his mates for confirmation.

'Well, you just head off and get yourself shot at,' Gecko responded.

Thomas was so enraged at the echo of Ernest's words, he lunged at Donnie. The sound of fisticuffs reverberated throughout the bar. Gecko joined in, but not before Donnie's mates had come to their friend's rescue.

'Oi!' yelled the bartender as the other shearing team members moved to help.

Within minutes there was a full-blown melee in the bar. Thomas had never fought, had avoided it all his life, and he knew in the back of his muddled brain that he'd ended up in a situation he'd always sworn he wouldn't—drinking and hitting another human. But he was too livid to care. Someone had to pay for the anger he felt.

He was no quitter.

He was no coward.

Surely his life had shown that.

But as a strong hand grabbed the back of his neck and yanked him away from the brawl, he had a sneaking sense that perhaps Donnie and his own father were right. Maybe he *was* a coward. Maybe the fact he'd left Nambina didn't mean anything. Perhaps it didn't show he was prepared to move on and make something of himself. Maybe it just revealed that he was willing and able to *run*. Run away from things that were hard, things he wasn't prepared to stand and fight for.

Dimly, he saw a police uniform. 'You bloody idiots,' a gruff voice said. 'Save this sort of thing for the front line, if you can't behave yourself here. You're going into the lockup.'

~

Somewhere within the heavy stone walls of the Port Augusta police station, Thomas made a decision. He would enlist. He would go to the front line. Because, as much as he hated to admit it, he could see traits of his father within himself.

He'd let himself down and become what he'd sworn he would never be. In those few minutes, he'd actually become his father.

Ernest had accused him of having his mother's split personality. She didn't have anything of the sort, it was only what his father saw in her, but Thomas knew his own emotions could rise so quickly and fiercely that they frightened him.

That's why he never said much.

He never let himself think about things that hurt him.

He'd rarely had a drink—until today.

Perhaps the war was the best place for him. And with any luck, he'd be killed over there and he wouldn't have to come home and face it all again. Because home would always be here, waiting to confront him.

See? Thomas thought. *Knew you were weak.*

231

Chapter 26

2008

Rip turned in circles, trying to chew off his new collar. He sat down and shook his head a few times in an attempt to dislodge it, then once again chased himself around and around, his mouth open, tiny teeth trying ever so hard to grab at the leather.

Laura laughed. 'Sorry, little friend,' she said. 'That has to stay on.' She bent down and lifted the pup into the front of the ute, then climbed into the driver's seat.

She felt a little paw on her thigh. 'Nope,' she said gently, then, remembering she was training Rip, she repeated herself, more firmly this time. 'No, Rip. No. On the floor.'

She picked up the pup and put him back where he was meant to be. 'Time to introduce you to the girls and the sheep,' she said as she hit the ignition key. Hearing the diesel warmer click in, she turned the key. But she wasn't rewarded by the sound of the engine starting, just the tick of a dead battery. 'Bugger.'

Laura popped the bonnet and got out. Perhaps it was just a bad connection. She wiggled the terminals on the battery then tried to start the ute again. It was definitely flat. 'Bugger,' she said again. She'd have to bring the other ute over and do a jump start.

As she headed for the shed where the other cars were kept, she saw Robyn, still dressed in her pyjamas, come out of the students' quarters, with Will Scott following close behind. Laura pretended not to notice. How the girls spent their spare time was their business.

In the shed, she grabbed the jumper leads and, reversing out in the students' work ute, she drove it over to her own vehicle.

She worked quickly to connect the leads to both batteries. This time, she was rewarded with the sound of a revving engine.

Laura reached in and gave Rip an absent-minded pat as she walked past the window and opened the door. His high-pitched yap made Laura want to pick him up and cuddle him, but she knew she couldn't. Not if she was going to train him to be a great sheep dog. She'd pat him, be kind and loving, but she couldn't mollycoddle him. He'd have to grow up to love her and want to do anything for her, but he would also have to be tough, so he'd still keep working, no matter the weather or conditions.

'Sit down on the floor,' she commanded and gently pushed him onto the mat. Rip seemed to understand what was expected. With the heater going, it wasn't long before he was snoozing.

Laura drove the other ute back to the shed. Before climbing out, she leaned over to pop the glove box and pulled out the logbook. She wanted to check it was being filled in correctly.

She noticed Allie's writing in all the entries. It didn't matter that there was only one of them filling it out, she decided. At least it was being done properly.

Laura tried to return the book to the glove box but it was a tight fit and it took some effort to wiggle it back in. Something fell out and she grabbed it. It was a pouch of tobacco. Port Royal tobacco.

'Weird,' she muttered. As far as she knew, none of the girls smoked. She looked at it again. Perhaps it was Will's, although she knew there was no reason for him to be in the ute, which was for farm use only.

She regarded the packet again, then pushed it back into the glove box. It wasn't her business if the girls smoked occasionally. Just so long as they didn't do it in the ute, and it didn't smell like they did, so who was she to judge?

'Morning.'

Laura turned at the sound of Allie's voice. She opened her mouth to respond with 'good morning' but as soon as she saw the young woman's face, she blurted out: 'Are you okay?'

'Think I'm sick,' Allie answered. Her eyes and nose were red, her skin pale and hair greasy. She was till dressed in pyjamas, but her feet were bare.

'It looks that way,' Laura answered. 'How do you feel?'

'Pounding head, sore throat. Probably just a cold or a virus, but do you mind if I don't come to work today?'

'That's fine. I've got something that'll help your throat over in the house, if you want it.'

Allie shook her head. 'I'm just going to go back to bed to sleep,' she answered. 'Hope I'll be a bit better tomorrow.'

'Okay, then. Call if you need anything. Better put some

shoes on.' She looked over Allie's shoulder. 'The others just about ready?'

Allie shook her head. 'I don't know. I didn't want to infect them so I slipped out the back door.'

Laura glanced at her watch. They weren't late yet. 'I'll check on you later today, if you like.'

'No.' Allie's tone was annoyed. 'I'll be fine, Laura. Honestly. It's just a cold. Give me a day and I'll be better.' She turned to leave. 'Sorry, I just feel shitty. See you later.'

'Righto, then.' Laura moved away towards her ute. 'Hope you feel better soon.'

Rip had woken up by the time she returned. When she opened the door she was hit by the smell of poo and urine. 'Great,' she groaned. 'I'll have to get you toilet-trained fast, mate.' She lifted him onto the tray and went inside for a bucket of hot water.

'What an excellent start to a Monday,' she muttered to herself as she poured a liberal amount of sweet-smelling disinfectant into the bucket.

She heard Tegan's voice. 'I'm in the laundry!' she called out.

'Oh, Laura! He's so gorgeous!' Tegan appeared, holding Rip in her arms.'

'Very gorgeous,' Laura answered dryly. 'He's just shat and pissed all through my ute.'

Rip barked and Laura couldn't help but smile.

'Oh,' Tegan gushed. 'He's saying sorry, aren't you, my pretty one?'

Laura shook her head. It never ceased to amaze her that baby animals reduced adult humans to dribbling, baby-talking messes, herself included.

'Where did you get him?' Tegan asked.

Laura lifted the bucket from the sink and headed out the door. 'Dad brought him as a present. He came down for the weekend.'

'Well, I want one too!'

Laura gave a laugh. 'Yeah, until he chews your boots and craps in your ute!' She started scrubbing the mess while Tegan continued to goo and gah over Rip.

'Morning!'

Laura looked up to see Robyn approaching from the shed. 'Hi!' she answered and waited for Robyn to comment on Rip. But Robyn didn't say anything. She just reached out to pat the pup.

'So what's on the go for today?' Robyn asked. Her tone was clipped and she sniffed as she spoke.

'You're not getting sick too, are you?' Laura asked, giving the girl a once-over.

'I'm fine.' Robyn's tone suggested there was to be no more questioning.

Laura took the hint. *Fight with Will*, she surmised.

'I'd like to get the green-tag ewes in from Gum Paddock and give them a drench. I reckon we should run them through the dip too. Got any ideas why?'

She gently took Rip away from Tegan so they could concentrate on what she was saying.

'I noticed the ewes were a bit shitty,' Tegan said. 'I was out there on Friday after everything. You know, so they'd get flyblown fairly easily in this weather, I guess. It's certainly getting warmer.'

'Yep, you're right, Tegan,' she said. 'In a week or two it'll be perfect conditions for flies to cause problems if you don't think ahead and prevent them.' She paused. 'Now what about the shitty bums? Any ideas?'

The two girls were silent for a moment and then Robyn looked up. 'I saw a couple of dead ones out there last week, and some of the lambs look like they've got dirty arses too. Would they have worms?'

Laura pointed her finger at Robyn like a gun. 'Bingo!' she said. 'The lambs probably aren't doing as well as they could. Shitty bums often mean an upset tummy, which means they've had a change in their diet. But it can mean other things and worms could be one of them. Now, if mum isn't feeling so hot because she's got parasites, then she's going to make less milk because she's trying to save herself. Lamb doesn't get as much to drink, so starts looking elsewhere—green grass. Change of diet. Shitty bums. Flies. It all follows on.

'If we get rid of the worms, the ewes will start milking a bit better and hopefully the lambs will get a bit more to drink. They're a little too small to wean yet, so a drench for both mum and baby, then a run through the jetting race to stop any flies and we shouldn't have to touch these little fellas until it's time to start weighing them for the trucks. Any questions?'

Both the girls shook their heads.

'Great. Now, once we've done this mob, I'd like to start bringing the rest of the sheep through. It's definitely time to start the fly-prevention rotation. So it'll be mostly sheep work this week.'

'I'll get the ute,' Robyn said before walking off.

'And I'll set the yards up,' Tegan said, reaching forward to give Rip a final pat.

'Sounds like a plan.' Laura nodded her approval. 'What's up there?' she asked Tegan, inclining her head towards Robyn.

She shrugged. 'Been a bit off since yesterday evening. Not sure if she and Allie had words or if it was Will. Something like that. See? There are plenty of good reasons to be single!' She flashed a grin and Laura laughed with her.

'Oh, and while I'm thinking about it, which of you girls smoke?' Laura asked off the cuff.

Tegan stopped. 'Smoke? None of us. You said in the criteria you wanted non-smokers.'

Laura was convinced she saw the girl redden a little. 'I know I did,' she said, 'and I was sure you all were. But I was looking at the logbook in the ute this morning and a pouch of roll-your-own tobacco fell out. I'm not going to judge, although I'd rather you didn't,' she quickly added. 'And no one will lose their job, because I know you're not smoking in any of the vehicles, but I'd like to know who it is.'

Tegan shook her head emphatically. 'I've never seen anyone smoke. Even when we're at the pub. Did it have any tobacco in it?'

'I didn't open it,' Laura answered. 'Just put it back.'

'Honestly, I've never seen any of the others smoke,' Tegan repeated. 'I don't know whose it is.'

'Okay,' Laura said. 'Let's get these sheep. And you,' she looked down at Rip, who had fallen asleep in her arms, 'it's your first look at those furry aphids!'

☙

It was a busy week. In the end, Allie was off sick for all five working days. They managed to get everything done but, by

Friday afternoon, Laura was exhausted. Walking the last of the straggler ewes and lambs back to the paddock, she noticed, on the other side of the fence, her four rams grazing. They lifted their heads and regarded her solemnly. Laura smiled. It had only been a few weeks since Random's accident but already it seemed like ages ago.

Now Laura surveyed the gently undulating landscape. The colour of the lush grass was beginning to fade. It wouldn't be long before it turned golden and, a month later, summer would well and truly be upon them. She tried to estimate what sort of fuel load she'd have when summer's dry thunderstorms raced through, risking lightning strikes and fires.

Rip strained against his tight lead, anxious to get to the sheep. He was far too small to be able to get in the yards with the sheep yet—it would only take a ewe to knock him over and he'd break a leg or become too scared to work with the animals.

She whistled softly. 'Here, Rip, come behind.' Then she jerked the lead towards her so Rip knew she wanted him beside her ankle.

She held him firmly there for a few moments then said: 'Way back!' She let the lead loose. Rip, feeling freedom, took off until he reached the end of the tether.

A ewe, her lamb beside her, turned to stare at the pup. He gave a short, high bark and she stamped her foot in warning.

'Come behind, Rip,' Laura said.

The lamb took a step towards Rip and he froze, one paw in the air, the other three on the ground.

The lamb took another step and Laura stopped to see what would happen.

Another step, another step, until lamb and pup were almost touching noses.

Rip suddenly let out another bark and the lamb turned tail and scampered back to its mother.

Laura laughed. 'The last of the brave hounds!'

She turned when she heard an engine.

Robyn pulled up beside her. 'Need a ride?' she asked with a cheeky grin. Her mood had improved as the week had gone on, Laura noticed.

'Absolutely.' She tucked Rip under her arm and got in.

'Good job this week, I reckon,' Laura commented. 'We're all organised and the sheep will feel better for it.'

'The first mob we did are looking better already,' Robyn said. 'I went out there yesterday after we finished.'

Laura nodded. 'Yeah, I agree.'

Noticing Rip was trying to get up on the seat, Laura pushed him gently back down. 'I'm just relieved to get through the week without any more of you getting sick,' she said. 'It would have made for a hard slog if it had been just Rip and me.'

'If Allie *was* sick,' Robyn said cryptically. She put the ute into gear and drove off slowly.

Laura looked across at her student. 'What do you mean?'

Robyn shook her head, refusing to take her eyes off the road ahead.

Laura changed tack. 'Got plans for the weekend?' she asked.

'Will and I are going to Adelaide,' Robyn answered. 'I managed to get tickets to one of the musicals in town. I love theatre! I'm trying to get him interested too.' She stopped for a moment, glancing over at Laura. 'I'm really looking forward to it. Getting away for a bit.'

Laura tried to read what was behind Robyn's words. Something wasn't right with the students at the moment. The atmosphere had changed over the last week. The girls had once been friends. Good friends. Now all Laura saw were three girls who couldn't talk to each other or be around each other. Things seemed tense, even cold.

Laura decided to bite the bullet. 'Have you got anything you'd like to tell me?' she asked, looking sideways at Robyn.

Robyn raised her eyebrows but said nothing.

'You three used to be joined at the hip! Now it seems a little edgy between you all,' Laura pointed out.

'We're all fine.' Robyn brought the ute to a stop.

Laura stroked Rip's soft head. 'You know where I am if you can't sort it out yourselves,' she said. Getting out of the ute, she pulled the gate closed and latched it. She stood for a moment watching as the ewes fanned out, the lambs bleating as they followed their mothers.

'This time two weeks ago, we would have been beginning to think about it getting dark,' she called out to Robyn. 'We would have had jumpers on. We'll need them in an hour or so, but feeling the sun on my skin today has been beautiful!' She rubbed her bare arms and raised her face towards the last rays.

Robyn joined her at the gate. 'It's definitely been a beautiful day,' she agreed.

'Well, Rob,' Laura said, turning to her. 'I for one, wouldn't want to be anywhere else.'

Robyn studied the ground, then turned to Laura.

'Um, Laura?'

'Hmm?'

'I think Allie is into something bad.'

Laura looked at her.

'Like what?'

Robyn shook her head. 'I don't know. That's the problem. I don't have any proof, just a feeling. She's hasn't been sleeping—I know because I hear her up walking around. She's on the phone until really late—sometimes the phone calls don't come in until after midnight and I can hear her talking. It's just weird. And she's changed. It's been slow and gradual, but she's definitely different, somehow. Moody and grumpy.' Robyn shook her head. 'It's horrible in the house with her. This last week has been unbearable.' She stopped. 'And now I feel like I'm telling tales,' she said miserably.

'Not at all,' Laura said earnestly. 'If you're unhappy and worried about a friend, it's a good thing to tell someone. Let me say, there have been enough people suiciding around this area. No one in the district would ignore a problem with a friend. Their friends know them best. I just have to work out how to deal with it.' She paused. 'Has she got a secret boyfriend she's on the phone to, do you think?'

'You know who I think she's talking to? That lead singer from the band we saw a few weeks ago.'

'Is that a bad thing?'

'He looked like bad news, but I know you can't judge people by how they look. Sometimes the shaggiest, most tattooed person is the kindest.'

'What does Tegan think about it all?'

'She's trying to ignore it.'

They got back into the ute and Robyn started the engine. Rip woke up with a start, gave a yawn and then settled back down onto the floor.

'Do you think these nightly walks could be to help her go back to sleep?' Laura asked.

'I guess so,' Robyn conceded. 'But who would walk out in the freezing cold, pace outside and then try to get back to sleep? It would be more likely to wake you up.' Agitated, Robyn ran her hand over her hair. 'And Tegan told me you asked about the pouch in the glove box?'

'Yeah, I did.'

'It's Allie's.'

'Ah. You know, I haven't smelt smoke anywhere. She mustn't do it very often.'

Robyn looked at Laura for a long moment and Laura began to feel uneasy. 'It's not tobacco,' Robyn said finally.

Chapter 27

2008

Laura surveyed her clothes. The Baggy and Saggy Ball was on this evening and she still had absolutely no idea what to wear. She'd meant to make a trip to the second-hand store during the week, but had run out of time.

To make matters worse, she was in no mood to go—her mind was all over the place, careening back and forth between the plight of poor Jenny Spencer and the problem of Allie.

The evening before, when Laura had asked Robyn what she meant by 'not tobacco', Robyn had responded, 'It's weed.'

Laura had stayed silent, trying to find the right words to comfort Robyn and put her mind at ease. 'Okay,' she said after some contemplation. 'Leave it with me and I'll work out how I'm going to handle it. I have to be honest and tell you I've never had a problem with drugs at the school before. I'll need a little time to think about it.'

'I think you need to hurry, Laura, really I do. I don't think she's just doing weed.'

Laura had felt cold dread settle on her at that moment.

And then there was Jenny Spencer to think about. Here was Allie, her whole life in front of her, choosing to do drugs and muck it all up, while Jenny, through no fault of her own and with a young child in tow, had been cut down in the prime of her life with multiple sclerosis.

Laura gave up looking through her wardrobe in exasperation and went into Howie's room. She knew there were still some of her grandmother's clothes in the wardrobe. Even though Granny had passed away decades earlier, Howie had never properly cleaned out her wardrobe. Laura had never been sure why, but once he'd gone, she understood. It was the same reason she hadn't cleared his area of the house. It was her grandfather's and it was sacred. To leave it untouched meant he was still around in some way, watching over her.

She made her way down the long passageway that had once divided the house in two. Howie's office was off his bedroom on his side of the house and Laura lived comfortably in her half.

Now, Laura sighed as she looked around her Papa's room. It was just as it had been the day he'd died. She really didn't want to change anything yet. Her father had talked about clearing it out, but so far, every time he came to Nambina, there either wasn't time, or they avoided the topic.

She opened her grandmother's wardrobe. There were a few dresses still on their hangers, now yellowed and musty with age. She pulled out one that seemed in reasonable condition. It was black velvet dotted with large orange flowers, and had long sleeves and an empire waistline. The collar came high up under her chin.

'Oh, yuck!' she said, holding it up. It was hideous. 'You might be just about perfect.'

The phone rang in the kitchen and she ran to answer it.

'Laura, it's Tim. I'm just making sure you're not piking on me tonight.' His laughter rumbled down the line.

Laura grinned. 'I promise I'm not,' she said, tucking the phone between her shoulder and ear. 'I'll be there in—' she checked her watch, '—about an hour.'

'Good. Are you sure you don't want me to pick you up? I'm not convinced you'll make it. A lamb might need saving or a crop might need planting.' His tone was light and teasing.

'I'll be there. Golf club. One hour. See you then.' Laura quickly hung up on Tim's laughter. She hoped she'd alleviated his fears. And hers.

'Pull yourself together, Laura Murphy,' she chided. 'Allie will keep for a night.'

She returned to Howie's room to try on the dress. It was a bit big but she knew she had a cinch belt in her room somewhere. That'd fix the problem.

As she headed down the hall to the bathroom she thought, not for the first time, about how quiet her phone was these days. Back when she was younger it had rung constantly, and there were always messages. Now the only people who called were stock agents or family. She wasn't on any committees, didn't help out in the community in any way. Her phone for the most part stayed silent. And now she was about to throw herself back into the community. It felt strange.

She showered and dressed, then went to check on Rip, who was tucked up in the laundry. Finally she headed out the door, her gait unsteady in the unfamiliar high heels.

As she drove out, she couldn't help but look over at the students' quarters, where a lone bulb glowed behind a curtain. She'd seen Robyn leave as soon as they'd finished work the day before. Tegan hadn't been far behind, although she didn't say what she was doing for the weekend. That left Allie, she guessed.

It would be difficult living in circumstances like that, she thought. It was a wonder their work hadn't suffered. Maybe that was still to come.

When she drove into the golf club's carpark, she spotted Tim waiting outside. Even from a distance she couldn't miss his light blue trousers, orange shirt and purple jacket with leopard print lapels.

'Ah, so you didn't decide to save the world of agriculture tonight, then?' he asked as he held the ute door open. 'Wow. I have to say, that's, ah, an interesting dress.'

'Not saving anything today,' she answered. 'Thanks. It was my grandmother's. And that's a pretty spiffy jacket you've got there.' She froze as Tim leaned in to kiss her cheek.

'Hope you've got your purse ready to go,' he said, taking her arm. 'I hear that it's going to be a lot like Rotary—we're all going to get fined.'

'Sounds like fun,' she answered, not meaning it.

They went inside. 'Wow, whoever's organised this has done a great job,' Laura said. 'Look at the way it's been decorated— you wouldn't know it was the golf club!' Tree branches had been arranged in each corner of the room, while the tables were covered in white cloths and decorated with vases of native bush. There were linen napkins and sparkling silver cutlery, and hanging from the ceiling was a round hoop decked with flowers. The smell was country all over.

'Looks like a wedding, not a fundraiser, if you ask me,' Tim whispered in her ear. He took her hand and led her past the tables until they arrived at one on the edge of the room. 'Apart from the outfits!'

Laura looked around. There were people in brown flares, orange shirts and clothes that should have been consigned to the rag bag long ago. 'I can't believe there could be this much bad fashion in town,' she marvelled. 'Where's it been hidden all these years?'

'I think we all look rather dashing,' Tim said with a grin. 'Come on, let's sit down. None of the others will bite.'

Laura remembered the three couples already at their table. Suddenly she felt shy. *If only Catherine were here*, she thought.

Most of them were people she went to school with. Now they were married with kids. When had that happened? Where had the time gone? She and Tim were the only two out of the whole group who weren't hitched.

'Laura, do you remember everyone here?' Tim asked.

Laura nodded. 'Hello,' she said quietly.

'Great to see you again, Laura. Don't catch you very often.' It was Sarah, who was married to Jake.

'Don't get to many of these dos,' she answered, sinking into the chair Tim had pulled out for her.

'Drink?' asked Ken, who had his arm around Susan. 'I'm just on my way to get another round.'

'That would be lovely. A white wine if they have it.'

'Oh, they'll have it,' Katie answered. 'They've got every-thing here tonight, haven't they, Dave?' She turned to her partner.

Dave laughed loudly, his rosy cheeks giving the hint he may have had a couple of drinks before he arrived. 'I reckon they will, love. All profits from the bar are going to Jenny too.' He turned to Laura. 'So, how are you? We just don't see you out much anymore. How's the jillaroo school going?' He leaned forward, gazing at her intently.

Laura looked over at Tim before answering. 'Great, thanks. I've got three girls out there at the moment. They've already learned heaps and are showing more confidence than when they started, which is what I'm aiming for.'

'I think you're doing such a wonderful thing,' Susan said. 'I wish something like that had been around when I was leaving school. Used to hate going to the field days by myself, surrounded by blokes. Felt stupid asking questions in front of them and all that sort of thing. To be able to learn in a non-threatening environment would be fantastic.'

Laura felt a rush of pleasure and sat up a bit straighter. 'Thanks, Susan.'

'Yeah, but then you hooked up with me and I got to protect you and answer all those bloody endless questions you asked,' joked Ken. 'Drove me mad!'

Laura grinned as Susan batted her husband with her hand in protest.

The drinks arrived and they clinked glasses.

'Here's to us all,' Tim toasted. 'To healthy lives. And to Jenny.'

'Healthy lives and Jenny,' they echoed.

Laura looked around at the rest of the gathering and saw many people she knew. As she glanced behind her, her eyes locked with Josh Hunter's. He was sitting next to Meghan, deep in conversation with the woman beside her. Whether Meghan had noticed her presence, Laura wasn't sure.

Josh nodded at her and tried to hold her gaze.

Feeling uncomfortable, she was relieved when the MC commenced proceedings. Doug welcomed the crowd, then ran through the housekeeping before introducing the first act—a pantomime.

Laura laughed until her sides hurt, watching local men dressed as women and the villain sneaking, very obviously, across centre stage.

After the performance, the first course was served. Just as Tim offered her the salt and pepper, Doug appeared by her side, a microphone in his hand. 'Ladies and gents, I have it on good authority that we need to fine this young lady. My sources tell me she doesn't get out often and tonight is the first time we've seen her in ages.'

Heat raced to Laura's cheeks and she stiffened. Susan and Katie flashed her sympathetic looks.

'So, my good friends, what will we say? A dollar? Two?'

Calls of two dollars came from around the room and Doug waved a moneybox under her nose. Laura, hands shaking, reached for her bag, but was saved when Tim dropped the coin in on her behalf.

A cheer went up as Laura sank back into her chair.

'Don't let them get to you,' whispered Tim. 'Stand up and take a bow. Don't be a deer in the headlights.'

Flashing him a wide-eyed stare, she shook her head.

He raised his eyebrows and nodded. 'Come on. Be the Laura Hunter you were a few years back!' He took her hand and squeezed it.

Laura straightened her back, stood and gave an elaborate bow. Everyone clapped and some even wolf-whistled. Heart pounding, she sat back down again.

'It's always a bugger being the first one,' Jake commented between mouthfuls of his entrée.

Laura just nodded.

Chapter 28

2008

Laura walked out of the golf club bathroom and bumped straight into Josh Hunter.

'Excuse me,' she muttered, looking down and trying to sidestep him.

'Why are you ignoring me?'

'What?' she asked, eyes narrowed.

'I've been trying to talk to you all evening. Every time I make eye contact, you look away and start pawing at Tim-the-vet.' He crossed his arms and glared at her.

'Sarcasm doesn't suit you, Josh. It never has,' Laura snapped. 'I don't believe I have anything to say to you.'

'Can't we mend old fences? Laura, I've missed you and I've been thinking. We shouldn't keep a feud going on because of some misunderstanding. Life's too short.' He looked sad.

She stared at him, unsure where this was headed. 'As I recall, the last conversation we had wasn't a conversation at all. It involved you yelling at me while I was lying in a hospital bed. It's not a conversation I care to relive. So, no, I don't believe so.'

Josh sighed and ran his hands over his face. 'I'm sorry, okay. I was hurt and upset. I've been wanting to apologise for ages.' He grabbed her by the shoulders. 'I was wrong, Laura. I know that now. The last few months, well, it's been playing on my mind . . .'

'Months?' Laura pulled back and stared at him, furious. 'You've only thought about it in the last few months? It's been eight years, Josh. Excuse my language, but what the fuck?' She was seething.

'Laura . . .' Josh began again.

She held up her hand. 'No. I have nothing to say to you. It's been too long, there's been too much hurt, and nothing will fix that.' She stopped as she realised something. 'Is this because I'm here with Tim? Are you jealous? Well, mate, you lost the right to feel that eight years ago.'

She turned to leave, but he caught her by the arm again. 'Laura,' Josh repeated. 'Far out, woman, you're so pig-headed. Would you just listen to me?'

Now there was anger in Josh's eyes and Laura recoiled slightly. Their argument in the park that day came back to her. She shook him off and walked away. But something made her stop. A bubble of emotion she couldn't control made her turn back to him. 'And why the hell do you think I would talk to you after the way your sister threatened me at the show? Or are you going to tell me you didn't know about that? Ha! Unlikely. You were thick as thieves, telling each other everything. Believing what she told you, over me, even when it wasn't true.' She shook her head. 'You leave me alone, Josh Hunter. I have no interest in even being in the same room as you.' She turned again and fought the urge to look over her shoulder as she walked away. Was he still watching? She was sure he was.

Somewhere in the back of her mind, a little voice niggled. He did try and help at the show, she recalled. What had he been thinking then? Well, she didn't care. Pig-headed and stubborn were her middle names, and jealous, untrusting men didn't deserve a second chance.

Back in the function room she saw everyone crowded together. A roar of approval went up and she found Tim on the edge of the group crowded at the front of the room. She stood next to him and peered towards the front. People were throwing gold coins at a box.

'Closest coin is the winner, and winner takes all,' Tim said into her ear. He did a double-take. 'You okay?' he asked.

'Fine,' she answered shortly and forced a look of keen anticipation. 'What are they going to win?'

'A bracelet of some sort and a voucher to go for a spin in a racing car.'

Laura felt in her bag and came up with five two-dollar coins. 'It's for a good cause.' She pushed her way to the line where competitors had to stand. When it was her turn she began to throw the coins. The second coin landed on top of the box.

'That's the closest so far!' Doug yelled. 'Anyone else?'

No one else managed to better her throw. A few minutes later, Laura was named the winner and the rest of the crowd clapped.

CʃƆ

'Thanks for a lovely evening,' Laura said, fumbling in her bag for the keys to the ute.

'Sorry Doug picked on you first,' Tim said. 'I'm still amazed he actually saw you—I did get a table down the back.' He grinned ruefully. 'But that dress was just, ah . . . a standout.'

Laura smiled. 'At least I wasn't the only one. Poor Katie. Have you ever heard of anyone being fined for buying the wrong brand of tomato sauce? Nothing is sacred.'

'You can get fined for anything at these crazy shows. Let's hope enough money was raised for Jenny, though. I'm just pleased she was actually able to be here.'

They were silent for a moment.

Laura shivered. Tim took the keys from her hand and led her towards his car. 'It's cool tonight,' he said. 'Jump into my car, there's something I want to talk to you about.'

Laura didn't want the evening to end but she wasn't sure she wanted to get into the car with Tim. She gazed up at the sky to buy time. 'I never tire of looking at the stars,' she said.

'It's one of the things that's kept me in the country,' Tim said. 'That and the moon.' He paused. 'The ability to be able to breathe.' He opened the ute door for her. 'I don't think I'd make a good small animal doctor.'

Laura admired his long frame as he moved around the car and got in. Feelings she'd kept in check since Josh, forgotten desires, had re-emerged since Tim's appearance. She wasn't sure if it was because it had been so long or because she actually wanted this man.

She turned in her seat to look at him, her expression serious. Tim's eyes locked with hers and he reached out and touched her cheek.

'Oh!' She grabbed at his hand but missed. 'Your fingers are freezing!'

Tim burst out laughing and withdrew his hand. He held his fingers to his mouth and blew on them.

'That's a way to make an impression,' he said in between breaths.

Laura threw her head back and laughed. It felt good. The wine had made her feel mellow and here, in Tim's company, she felt suddenly happy.

'Are mine cold?' Laura wiggled her fingers at him. He took them.

'They're just about perfect.' They held hands in the dark. Laura could feel Tim's thumb running over hers and it sent little shivers down her spine.

'So, did you have a good time tonight?' he asked.

'I did,' Laura admitted. 'I really didn't want to go. I shun those sorts of events. I'm sort of happy with my own company, but I did enjoy tonight.' She paused, then said, 'You know what really surprised me? I found I had more in common with the people we went to school with than I realised. It might sound stupid, but I always felt I was on the outer back then. Like I never really fitted in. It's funny when you revisit that time as an adult. People and attitudes aren't the same as I remember.'

'We all grow up,' Tim said. 'People face different things in their lives that shape them, make them who they are. Thank goodness none of us are the same as we were in high school—self-absorbed, selfish teenagers!'

'Weren't we just?' Laura nodded. 'We knew everything and didn't have any more growing up to do.'

Tim nodded. 'So you think you might like to do it again?'

256

Laura pursed her lips. 'What?' she asked, teasing. 'Go to another fundraiser? Or grow up?'

Tim glowered at her. 'You know what I mean. Have another meal with me.'

She paused before answering, 'Yeah,' unsure where that one small word would lead them. 'Yeah, I would.'

He leaned towards her. 'You don't know how long I've been waiting to hear you say that.'

He touched his lips to hers and Laura could feel him smiling. She slipped her arms around his neck, but she pulled away soon after, feeling embarrassed.

'What's wrong?' Tim asked.

'Nothing. It's just been a long time.' She gently eased herself back to the other side of the car and tidied her hair. A mental image of Josh's face just after he'd kissed her intruded and she remembered their strange encounter that evening.

Why now? she wondered. Howie had explained everything to Josh, back when she was in hospital. Against her will, he'd tracked him down and made him listen. Josh had tried to see her, but she'd refused. The accusations had been too hurtful and to see him would have made it worse. That relationship ended, never to be revisited, in the hospital room.

Tim changed the subject.

'You know, as vets we see some strange things.'

Laura snorted. 'You think we don't in farming?'

'What's the funniest thing you've seen?' he challenged.

'Um, let me think. Oh, when Papa still had cattle, a calf was born with five legs. The fifth one grew off one of the other legs, so it wasn't sharing any major blood vessels or anything like that.'

'What did you do about it?'

'We put a rubber ring on it—you know, like the ones used when marking lambs? It just dropped off.'

'Yeah?' Tim sounded surprised. 'Was the animal still saleable?'

'It must have been. We didn't know which one it was after a while.'

The windows had fogged up so Laura rolled hers down a crack and breathed in the cold air.

'You know, I surgically removed a second penis from a crossbred lamb once,' Tim said.

'You're joking.' She was appalled.

'No, I'm not. It was growing out of his head.'

That made Laura snort. 'New meaning for the word dick-head, then. But you're making it up, I know you are.'

'I'm not. I'll show you the photos if you want.'

She could tell from the tone of his voice it was a promise.

'I can't even begin to imagine!' Laura laughed.

'You know,' Tim continued. 'I had a dog come in recently and I would have sworn he was hyped up on marijuana. After he started to come down he had the munchies.'

Allie immediately came to mind but she didn't say anything.

'It seemed a bit coincidental after Random's little incident.' Tim looked over at her.

'Whose dog?' she asked quietly.

'Can't really tell you that.'

'So what are you telling me?'

'I'm not sure. I just don't believe in happenstances.'

'Different drug,' Laura stated the obvious.

'Yes,' Tim drew out the word. 'But two animals drugged in our little town, within a few weeks of each other? See, that's where I have a problem.'

'Tim, I think you're grasping at straws, unless you know something more than you're telling me. Random was doped in Adelaide. Not here.'

'Hmm. I don't know,' he said finally, with a sigh. 'It was weird, so I wanted to get your opinion. It's probably nothing.'

'Okay, can you answer this? Did the dog come from anywhere near where I live?'

'Ah, yes.'

'Have you ever seen it before?'

'A dog hyped up? Yeah. A few times,' he admitted. 'But not for a couple of years.'

Laura nodded. 'I had one of my students come to me today and tell me that she thinks one of the other girls is smoking weed. Could there be a connection?'

Tim grimaced.

'I'm joking!' she said.

He shook his head as if it was all too confusing. 'Anyway, I'm on call tomorrow, so I'd better get a good night's sleep. I'll walk you back to your car.'

They got out and Laura's gaze shifted again to the stars above. She felt his hand on the small of her back gently propelling her towards her ute.

'Thanks again for a lovely night,' she said, smiling. In her heels she was almost as tall as he was, so he didn't have to bend far to kiss her.

'I'm planning on seeing you very soon,' Tim said as he pulled away.

'Good. But don't bring those photos,' she answered as she unlocked the door and got in.

As she backed out, she could hear his laughter. She waved again and drove off. As she did so, she caught sight of Josh's ute still down the far end of the parking lot. She narrowed her eyes, wondering if he'd been watching them.

Lying in bed later, Laura thought back over the snippets of information Tim had given her. She couldn't work out how there could be any connection between her ram and Josh's dog.

'Different drugs,' she muttered as she drifted off to sleep.

She dreamed of marijuana smoke curling through the trees. Animals were lying, dying, everywhere she turned.

Tim appeared, a wispy figure. He bent down next to one of the dogs, but she couldn't see what he was doing.

Then they all disappeared behind the sweet-smelling smoke of the drug and were gone.

Laura's eyes flashed open and she stared into the darkness, her heart pounding.

Chapter 29

2008

The sick feeling Laura had when she woke was still there. It had nothing to do with the amount of wine she'd drunk last night, and everything to do with Allie.

She was finding it impossible to think of anything else. Laura had to do something, talk to someone. Finally, she picked up the phone and dialled her father's house. But to her annoyance, Poppy answered.

'Hi, Poppy.' She paused, waiting to see whether her sister would recognise her voice. 'It's Laura,' she said when there was no answer.

'Laura,' Poppy answered flatly.

Remembering her dad's plea, Laura asked Poppy how she was.

'Fine. How are things down there in the sticks?'

Laura felt her anger flare. 'Damn it, Poppy, you can't help it, can you? You have to have a go at me every time we talk.'

'So-orry.' Poppy drew the word out, and Laura could

imagine her sister's mouth in a pout. She couldn't believe this woman was actually twenty-two. She acted like she was sixteen.

Laura knew she'd been completely different at the same age. Responsible, driven, with dreams, and ready to meet challenges head on. In contrast, Poppy seemed immature and lost—drifting, as her father had said when he visited, which, for a young person, wasn't good. It gave them more time and ability to get into trouble.

Laura took a breath. *Come on*, she chided herself. *You're the older one. Act your age.* 'But since you ask, everything's going really well down here "in the sticks". How about you?'

'Fine.' Poppy's tone was sulky now.

'Seen any good bands lately? Dad said you were going to a few when he was down here last.'

'Yeah, I like to go to the clubs. There's good ones and bad ones.'

Laura could hear the distaste in her sister's voice. It was as if she was forcing herself to have a conversation with someone who obviously wouldn't know anything about the Adelaide nightclub scene. How had it come to this?

She persevered. 'What's the best band you've heard in the last couple of weeks?'

'Like, as if you've heard of any,' Poppy scoffed.

'I might be a bit older than you, Poppy, but it doesn't mean I don't like good music or dancing or clubbing. I have done it once or twice before, you know.'

'Oh yeah? And where did you go?'

'I spent a bit of time at Lennie's down at Glenelg,' Laura shot back.

'Never heard of it.'

'I think it's closed now. Heaven was a bit of a hangout back then. I think that's what you guys call HQ, now.' Laura smiled at the memory. Josh had been by her side, sporting a mullet. Her own hair had been puffed out with hairspray; she may have looked like a witch. She remembered St Tropez coolers and Sambuca shots, ra-ra skirts and body suits that did up at the crotch.

Poppy's tone changed slightly. 'I don't mind HQ. Of course, it's not as happening as the Red Square. Good music there.'

'Bryan Adams was one of my favourite singers back then. But we used to dance to lots of great music. Michael Jackson, Mariah Carey. That's when the Spice Girls were huge too.' She laughed and sang the opening line to 'MMMBop' by Hanson. 'The music was between terrible and brilliant back then.'

'The Spice Girls?' Poppy's tone was laced with disdain. 'Hanson?'

'Oh, don't worry.' Laura was enjoying the memories. It beat thinking about Allie, anyway. 'They weren't my favourite's, but I didn't mind them.'

'There's a good band called Sinking Blizzard.' Poppy was suddenly enthusiastic. 'They're pretty rocky, with a huge sound. It's good stuff. They play at HQ. The lead singer's a bit of a dish, so they're not hard to watch.'

Something stirred in Laura. The name was familiar. 'Sinking Blizzard,' she said slowly. 'I don't know how, but I think I've heard of them. Maybe we could do it together some time?'

'Whatever.' Poppy's guard was back and Laura knew it was time to move on.

'I was looking for Dad. Is he around?'

'No, he's at work. Mum's here, though, if you want her.'

'That'd be great. Nice to chat with you, Poppy.'

The phone clunked down without another word.

'Bye, Laura,' she muttered to herself.

'Hello, darling.' Georgie sounded upbeat, as usual. 'How are you?'

At the sound of her stepmother's cheerful voice Laura felt a lump in her throat. Bloody hell, how could a mother and daughter be so different?

'Good and bad, Georgie.'

'Well, then, you'd better tell me what's going on.'

Laura heard Georgie sit down and pictured her in the bright warm kitchen of their Adelaide home.

'One of the students came to me on Friday and said she thinks one of the other girls is doing drugs.'

'Oh. A curly one.'

Laura gave a short, harsh laugh. 'Yeah.'

'What do you think?'

'I have no idea. At the beginning of the week, Allie came to me and said she was sick. She was complaining of a sore throat and headache and, you know, with the change of season and everything, I didn't think anything of it. There's a nasty virus going around town.'

'That could have been a hangover too,' Georgie observed.

'I guess so. I only went on what she told me. She didn't end up coming to work for the whole week. But I'd never have put whatever was wrong with her down to doing drugs. I don't know much about this sort of thing, but I'd have thought if she was smoking weed after work, it wouldn't affect her that much.'

'What I do know is, there's something going on with the girls. They're not getting along, for some reason.'

'So what differences have you noticed, or are you just realising something is amiss because you've been told it is?'

Laura paused. 'I think,' she said slowly, 'it's because I've been told. It's made me see something isn't right.'

'Ah.' They were silent for a moment. 'It's hard, isn't it?' Georgie said. 'I'm assuming you don't want to confront her in case it isn't true?'

'That's what's worrying me,' Laura confessed. 'Robyn was the student who talked to me. What if she is wrong, and I say something to Allie about it and it's not true? It would be terrible. There'd be a breakdown in trust and everything else that goes with that. Plus the repercussions between Allie and Robyn. Not that I would name her, but it's going to be pretty obvious that one of the other girls spoke to me.'

'Have you considered just watching and waiting?'

'That's the trouble, Georgie. I'm not sure I can. Robyn seemed to think Allie's doing something stronger than just marijuana. What if I leave it too long and something really bad happens?' Laura twisted the phone cord around her finger and looked out the window as she spoke.

She frowned. There was a ute coming up the drive.

'What a horrible position to be in, Laurs. You must be so worried.'

'I feel sick.'

'Well, darling, I can't tell you what to do.'

'I know . . .'

'But would you like to know what I'd do if it were me?'

'Yes!' Laura could now hear the approaching ute and she

looked out again. She bristled at the sight of the vehicle. Why was *he* here?

'If it were me, darling,' Laura heard Georgie say, 'I'd watch and wait. Listen and see if you can hear things you're not supposed to. A bit like a detective gathering evidence.'

Laura saw Josh get out of his ute and look around.

'Because then, if you do hear something yourself, you're not relying on hearsay. You're acting on truth. I know you don't feel like you've got much time, that you need to do something soon, so maybe just wait a couple of days. Think back to when she first started. See if you can remember how different she was then. Look at her skin, her weight, quality of work, personal hygiene. That sort of thing.'

'Georgie, that sounds like a plan. I'm going to have to go now. I have a visitor and I don't know what he wants.'

'Sure, sweetie. Let me know how you get on. I'll tell your father you called.'

Laura had been walking towards the door, but now she stopped at the sound of knocking.

'Bloody hell,' she muttered.

'Are you okay?' Georgie asked down the line.

'Josh is here.'

'Josh?' The surprise in Georgie's voice echoed Laura's.

'Yeah. Hey, Georgie? Thanks. I appreciate you listening and your advice. I'll call you later, okay? Love to Dad.' She hung up the phone and stood still. The knocking sounded again.

Swallowing, she pulled open the door and stood there, her face set.

'Hello, Laura,' Josh said with a half smile.

'Josh.'

'How are you?'

'Fine. How can I help you?'

Josh's poise faltered and he ran his hand through his hair. 'I told you last night. I wanted to apologise.'

'And I told you, I had nothing to say to you. Thank you for your apology. I appreciate you making the effort to come here but I have nothing further to say. So if you wouldn't mind leaving, please.' She started to shut the door but Josh reached out to stop her.

'Laura, if you'd just listen . . .!'

'What the hell is this?' Laura snarled, eyes flashing. 'Why, after all this time, do you want to talk about it? I've put it behind me. You made your choice back then by reacting the way you did. That means you don't get a second chance.' She blinked hard, emotions welling. 'Please, Josh, just go. I don't want to dredge up all the memories.'

'I want to talk now,' he insisted as he took a step towards her.

Laura was forced to look up at him. Josh had always been tall, but never before had she felt intimidated by him. She did now.

'Don't come in here,' she said, her voice shrill. 'I don't want you in the house. It's been too long. It can't be fixed. Just go.'

He stood and stared at her for a long time. Still feeling wary, she avoided his gaze. Finally he let the door go and turned to stomp back down the path.

Laura locked up and went to the window in the office to make sure he had left. She crossed her arms over her stomach, the way she had when she was first pregnant, like she was trying to protect the baby. Fat lot of good that had done.

'Why now?' she whispered into the empty room. 'Are you jealous? Or are you scheming with your sister? Do you really want to clear the air?' She found herself shaking her head. There had to be more to it.

಄

Later that evening Laura took Rip out for a walk and detoured past the students' quarters. Music sounded from inside.

Laura knew the other girls hadn't come home from their weekend yet and she toyed with the idea of knocking on the door.

Could she live with herself if she didn't act quickly and something happened to Allie? Laura was sure she couldn't.

Without thinking, she walked over and tapped lightly on the door. Allie opened it with a smile.

'Laura, hi. Oh you've got Rip! Hello there, little fella.' She knelt to pat the pup.

'Hi, Allie. I knew you were here by yourself. Just wanted to pop by and see how you were feeling.' She sniffed the air, trying to detect any foreign scents, but all she could smell was cleaning fluid.

'Much better,' Allie answered, still playing with Rip. She looked up at Laura. 'Sorry if I worried you. I just felt so terrible, I was having trouble being civil.'

Laura assessed the situation then gave Allie a large grin. Robyn must be wrong. 'No worries. I'm pleased you're feeling better.'

'Right as rain.'

They chatted for a while longer before Laura said goodbye, feeling greatly relieved.

As she opened the door into the house she heard a man's voice. Someone was leaving a message on her answering machine. She took her time getting to the office; she didn't want to answer it.

A nervous energy ran through her as she pushed the 'Play' button on the machine.

'G'day, Laura. It's, um, Tim.'

He cleared his throat. It was cute the way he sounded so nervous, she thought.

'Just wanted to say I had a great time last night. And, ah, was wondering if you wanted to come to the pub for dinner tonight? It might be too late notice for you, but I've just got off call. Anyway, give me a yell if you like. You've got my number.'

Laura sat down in her office chair and stared at the answering machine. Was it worth getting involved with another bloke? Last night, with an alcohol buzz and in good company, she'd decided it was. If he'd asked her last night, she'd have happily gone out with him again this evening.

However, Josh's reappearance reminded her just why she didn't trust men. They could cause too much hurt. It was much easier to just keep them at a distance. Friends, but nothing more.

She took her mobile phone out of her pocket and typed a text message: 'Sorry, can't meet tonight. Busy. L.'

She hit the send button and closed her eyes.

Chapter 30

2008

Laura surveyed the small paddock of barley. Robyn and Tegan were bent down beside her, assessing the crop.

She felt a surge of pleasure. The barley was growing well, albeit deficient in some trace elements.

When Laura had started the jillaroo school she knew she'd have to cover as many aspects of farming as possible, which would mean extending herself beyond what she was used to. And that would include cropping. Nambina already had a herd of ten cows and a bull, but while Howie had been alive there'd been little cropping done by a contractor. To seed, spray and harvest had been as steep a learning curve for Laura as it had been for the students she taught. But the effort had been worth it.

She turned to look down the laneway. They were waiting for Allie to arrive in the tractor, but there was still no sign.

Now that Laura was paying attention, she realised that, compared to when Allie started on Nambina in June, she was quite a different girl. Allie had been given several opportunities to prove herself over the previous three weeks and, more often than not, she'd made mistakes.

Laura was almost at her wit's end, but she was torn, too. She didn't want to let Allie go, frightened of what might happen to the girl if she gave up on her. She wished she knew what had changed in Allie's life. She wanted Allie to talk to her, to ask for help, but until she did, Laura felt her hands were tied.

A couple of times Laura had picked up the phone to ring Tim for his advice, but she'd hung up before the call connected. After she'd rejected his dinner date, he'd gone quiet, and Laura had decided that, maybe, if he was put off so easily, he could stay quiet.

When she'd said as much to Catherine in an email, her friend had yelled at her across cyberspace:

YOU ARE A STUBBORN, PIG-HEADED IDIOT. HE'S NICE. GET
OVER YOURSELF. Love C xxxx

Georgie and Sean had phoned to check on Allie's progress but neither of them had any further words of wisdom. There was little that could be done without proof, or Allie asking for assistance.

Now Laura watched as Tegan and Robyn walked out into the middle of the paddock and knelt down to study the plants again. Harry, the local agronomist, had been out the previous day to take the girls on a crop tour. They returned to report that the crop needed spraying with a couple of trace elements. Allie's job today was to fill up the fuel tank and the boom spray, add manganese and zinc to the water, get it mixed then bring it to the paddock.

The way Laura liked to teach was to have one girl at a time in the cab with her. She'd do a lap around the paddock and show the student how to use all the controls, watch for blocked jets and so on. Then she'd do the same with the other girls. Once everyone had had a turn, she'd hand over the controls to the first girl and sit with her, making sure everything was done correctly. Then it would be a repeat for the rest of the class.

It worked well and the one-on-one approach gave the young women the chance to ask any questions without embarrassment.

Robyn pulled a leaf off the barley plant and held it up for Laura to see. 'So it's this yellowness we're going to fix?' she called.

'That's right,' Laura answered.

Robyn nodded.

Laura dug down into the soil. 'See here,' she called. 'It's still damp at the roots, which is great. I haven't seen any evidence of frost damage so I reckon this crop has got great potential. Trouble is, you've never got it until it's actually in the silo.'

They turned at the sound of an engine. *About time,* Laura grumbled to herself without looking up.

Allie swung the tractor through the gate and into the paddock. There was a loud crunching noise.

Laura's head shot up. 'What the—?' She ran over.

Allie quickly pulled to a halt. The noise had been the sound of the boom spray hitting the gate.

Laura closed her eyes and tried to breathe calmly. This was a school, she reminded herself. You had to expect mistakes and accidents. The trouble was, this wasn't Allie's first mistake by any means. Laura had to admit she'd been half-expecting something to go wrong. In fact, she'd set Allie up to test her.

272

'I'm so sorry,' Allie said, her face white as she climbed down from the tractor. 'I was sure there was heaps of clearance.'

'It's fine, it's fine. But when you're coming through a gate, you must slow down and watch behind you. If you'd been a bit slower and seen what was going to happen, you could have stopped before any damage was done.'

Robyn and Tegan hung back, looking uncomfortable. They clearly knew as well as Laura that there was a problem with Allie's work. The previous week she had been refuelling the ute but left it and got caught up in the shed. The tank had overflowed, and litres and litres of expensive diesel had poured onto the ground. Before that, she'd been mustering a paddock and, even though Laura had told her there was a wire gate across the laneway, Allie had forgotten and driven right through it, wrecking the gate and breaking off one of the spotlights.

Now Laura inspected the damage to the boom spray. The jets had been torn off the bottom of one arm. She glanced over at the girls. 'I'm going to ring the machinery dealership and order the parts. Robyn and Tegan, can you head into town and pick them up?'

The two girls nodded but didn't speak.

'Righto,' Laura said. 'You guys take my ute and get going, and I'll give them a call. Just chuck me my mobile before you take off.'

Tegan and Robyn nodded silently and walked over to the ute, parked under a tree.

Laura ran her fingers along the boom spray and pulled off a couple of the smashed jets. 'I should have had some on hand,' she muttered, disappointed with her disorganisation. Finding a part number, she said to Allie: 'Can you get a pen and paper, please?'

When Allie returned from the tractor cab, Laura dictated the number. 'We need five of these. There doesn't actually seem to be any damage to the boom itself. It's just these jets, so that's a good thing.'

The ute pulled up beside them. 'Here you go.' Tegan handed Laura her phone through the window.

'Thanks. Hey, while you're in there, can you pick up a bag of puppy food from the merchandise store. Rip has just about eaten me out of house and home.'

The girls tried to smile and act like nothing had happened but it was forced. 'Sure,' Robyn answered before letting the clutch out a little too quickly. They were obviously keen to get away.

Laura turned back to Allie.

'I'm really very sorry, Laura,' the girl said. 'I wasn't concentrating.'

'But that's the problem isn't it, Allie? You haven't had your mind on the job for quite a few weeks now. There's been more than one accident. The overflowing fuel I can live with, even though it cost a lot of money. The other incidents . . .' She pursed her lips and tried to work out how to phrase what she wanted to say. 'I know there are going to be times that things get broken. That's to be expected on a farm, and especially on a teaching farm. I have insurance to cover these sorts of things. But what I don't like is knowing that you're not thinking about what you're doing. These accidents could be avoided if you were focusing.'

Allie looked at the ground.

Laura tried to give her a comforting smile to take away the sting of her words. 'Is there something on your mind? Something you'd like to tell me about?'

Allie shook her head. 'No,' she muttered.

'Well, then, you need to think about this. I can't have you making mistakes that put the others in danger. If you're a safety risk, you just can't be here.'

Allie's head snapped up. 'What? I love it here. You can't sack me! And I haven't hurt anyone. Diesel overflowing doesn't kill anyone.' Her voice sounded angry.

'But forgetting to put a tractor in park does.' There was silence. 'I'm not sacking you right now,' Laura calmly continued. 'I am *telling* you, you need to get your act together or I'll have to ask you to leave. Don't forget, you signed a contract. There's a safety clause in there.' She stopped, then rushed on, the emotion clear in her voice. 'Allie, you paid to come here. This is a teaching course, like going to uni, or TAFE, or some other type of educational institution. Do you really want to waste your money?'

Allie looked as if she wanted to argue, but didn't. Instead, she shook her head.

'If you were out in the workplace, you wouldn't have a job right now,' Laura finished.

'Okay.' The sulkiness was obvious.

Laura wanted to shake the girl. She'd been more than patient with her. 'So.' She lightened her tone. 'Let's move on, get the tractor back to the shed and fixed. We should still have time to get the spraying done before dark.'

Laura jumped up into the tractor and hit the key. Allie followed her up the steps and took the little seat next to her.

Laura frowned. There was an odour in the cab that she didn't recognise. She sat there a few moments trying to place the smell, then put the machine in gear and turned it towards the shed.

'I think it would be a good idea if you took the rest of the day off,' Laura said evenly. 'Have a long weekend, since it's Friday. Have a think about what I've said and front up again on Monday with a whole new attitude.'

Allie looked defiant but nodded. 'Okay.'

When they arrived at the shed, a ute was parked outside.

Laura felt Allie stiffen beside her. 'What the hell's he doing here again?' she muttered, her anger directed towards the man waiting near the student's quarters.

She shut off the tractor. Allie climbed out first. Then Laura got out and walked straight towards Josh.

'What are you doing? I've told you before, I don't want you here. This is the third time in as many weeks. I haven't changed my mind, so don't you think it's unlikely I will?' She turned to her student. 'You can head off. I'll catch you on Monday.'

Allie looked from one to the other and Laura saw a flash of relief cross the girl's face.

'Are you sure?' Allie asked.

'Very,' Laura answered.

Laura noticed that Josh's eyes followed the girl as she made her exit. When Allie was out of ear shot, Josh said, 'Why won't you let me explain what happened that day? Howie wouldn't let me through the door then and you won't now. Meghan brainwashed me into believing everything she said.'

'I can't understand why you feel the need to. It's reopening old wounds for me, Josh. Neither you nor Meghan have any idea what I've been through. Just think about it. I lost my unborn child, the father of my child and my best friend in one hit. You betrayed my trust the second you believed Meghan instead of me.'

Laura turned her back and walked away. 'And Howie didn't let you in because I told him not to,' she said over her shoulder as a parting shot.

She heard a car start and looked over to see Allie's dual-cab driving off. She'd obviously taken the long weekend option.

Shutting the tractor door firmly, Laura started it up and drove out of the shed compound. She didn't care where she was going, she just had to get away from Josh. She knew he wouldn't follow her.

When she spotted Josh's car driving along the main road half an hour later, she returned to the shed. Parking on the cement pad where all the maintenance was done, she went to get her tools. Then she started to remove the broken jets. She knew it would help to be busy, but she kept thinking about Allie and Josh.

Deep down, Laura was certain it was the drugs getting to Allie. She just had to catch her at it so she could get her some help. And as for Josh, well, she just wished he'd piss off. He was getting creepy.

Her phone rang and she answered it without looking at the screen.

'What's going on out at Nambina, then?' Tim asked by way of greeting.

Laura paused before answering. 'Just the usual. Work.'

'Right. Same here.'

Laura threw down the spanner she was holding and sank

onto the ground. She couldn't be bothered trying, so she let the silence stretch out.

'I should have rung before now,' Tim said finally. 'I sort of got nervous after you said you were busy a few weeks back.'

'What makes you think I'm not now?'

Laura listened as Tim blew out a breath. 'You can be so damn obstinate,' he said finally.

She drew in the dirt with her finger. 'Sorry,' she answered. 'I got cold feet.'

'And I got nervous, so that makes us a good pair, I guess.' He gave a short laugh.

Laura grinned. 'Yeah, I guess it does.'

'So, do you want to catch up?'

'I'm not sure.'

'Right.'

She knew she owed him an explanation. Each time she closed her eyes, she could see Catherine's email—the letters large and written in red: 'GET OVER YOURSELF!'

'Tim, I'm sorry. You don't know everything that happened between Josh and me, but that's why I'm not keen to get involved with *anyone*. I don't want to get hurt again. I *can't* get hurt again.'

'I don't want to hurt you, Laura. What I want to be is the man who helps you open your heart again. Let me know when you decide. But don't wait too long.' It was Tim who hung up.

Laura remained sitting on the ground, thinking about what he'd said. Eventually, she glanced down at her watch. It was time to get a wriggle on. The girls would be back from Mangalow very soon.

Climbing up into the tractor again, she started it up. She

hit the hydraulics to make the arms fold out, then opened up the armrest to get out the instruction booklet for the spray rig.

Inside, there was the pouch she'd seen in the ute a few weeks before. Staring at it, Laura suddenly realised what the smell earlier had been. Allie had been smoking weed while driving the tractor. Here was the cause of all her mistakes.

Laura breathed out and leaned back in her seat. Finally she reached for the pouch and opened it. Inside was some leafy green material. It was exactly as she'd expected.

'Oh, Allie,' she whispered.

Chapter 31

2008

'Tim, it's Laura,' she said quietly into the phone.

There was a silence.

'How are you going?'

Laura considered what he could be thinking. 'I, uh.' She stopped but Tim didn't say anything and she had a feeling he would wait her out. 'I need some help.'

'What kind of help?'

'It's Allie,' she said. 'She's doing drugs and . . .'

'Allie? One of your students?' Tim's voice rose a notch.

'Yeah. I found some weed in the tractor today.'

'What do you want me to do?'

'I don't know. I just . . .' Frustrated, she ran her fingers through her hair. 'I guess I needed someone to talk to. Catherine's overseas and Dad's at work. You're grounded and sensible.'

She couldn't mistake his sarcasm when he answered. 'Well, that must make me attractive, then.'

There was silence again.

'Could you come out?' Laura ventured.

'You know I can. See you soon.'

❧

'This could damage your reputation, your school, everything. Come on!' Tim urged.

'I know, I know. But I don't feel comfortable going through Allie's things without her permission.'

They stood on the stairs leading up to the students' quarters. Laura swung between anger and anxiety. Going through a student's personal space had never entered her head before. But when Tim arrived he'd confirmed that the green leaves were definitely not tobacco.

'She won't have left anything behind,' Laura argued. 'Allie's gone for the weekend. Surely she'd take her supply with her.'

'But we might find other evidence to give you ammunition to deal with this.' Tim stood firm. 'Come on. You asked for help. You wanted my advice. This is it! Let's go.' He propelled her towards the door.

Laura knew he was right. Everything she'd worked for was at risk. Her school, her farm—her *family's* farm!—her livelihood and everything she'd achieved in her life. No student was going to put that in jeopardy.

Laura opened the door purposefully and strode inside. She stopped. The place looked like a bomb had hit it. There was food on the bench, clothes all over the floor and empty Ruski bottles on the table.

Tim bumped into her.

'What the—?' Laura couldn't finish.

Tim looked around silently.

'The other girls have anything to do with this?' he asked.

'No,' Laura answered certainly. 'Not in a million years.'

'But they left after Allie?'

Laura was silent.

'Laura?'

'Yes,' she said quietly.

'Would you have expected them to clean it up?'

'Perhaps,' Laura said slowly, making her way through the mess to where she knew Robyn slept.

She opened the door and looked into a neat and tidy room which smelt faintly of the deodorant Robyn used. The bed was made and clothes hung in the wardrobe.

Next she looked into Tegan's room and found the same thing.

She gathered up some of the clothes on the floor in the living area and examined them. They were Allie's.

'You know what I think?' She turned to Tim, who was looking in the fridge.

'Nope.'

'I think they're sick of looking out for her. Trying to help her. Hiding the problem. These are all Allie's things.' She swept her arm around, indicating the mess. 'Look in their rooms. They're spick and span. Respected. Maybe they hoped I'd come in here, or maybe they're so sick of doing it all themselves, they've left it for her to clean up when she gets back. Tough love, sort of thing.'

'It's a possibility,' Tim agreed.

Slowly they started picking through the mess.

'I don't really know what I'm looking for,' Laura confessed, straightening up.

282

'Me either. Anything that appears out of place, I guess.'

'You know what? I'm going to start in her bedroom. The more I think about this, the more I'm sure she doesn't know the girls are on to her and Allie is still trying to hide her addiction.' She stopped and looked around, shaking her head. 'It's gotta be an addiction, doesn't it, Tim?'

He considered for a moment then nodded. 'I can only speculate, but it certainly looks that way.'

Laura closed her eyes. What a god-awful state of affairs. 'How do people end up like this?' she said. But she realised there wasn't a simple answer. From newspaper articles and current affairs shows she knew it happened all the time. Without warning. To 'good' families who walked with their kids every step of their childhood, and to families who didn't. To kids who had been offered everything, and to kids who'd been given nothing.

In Allie's room, Laura had to fight the urge to hold a hand over her nose. The unclean odour was powerful. Thick dust covered the dressing table and windowsill. The grimy sheets showed that the slide hadn't happened overnight. It had been going on for a long while. Photos on the dresser had fallen over and Allie hadn't even bothered to stand them up.

Gingerly, Laura pulled open a drawer in the dresser. Knickers and bras had been thrown in haphazardly, but a quick rifle through showed nothing out of the ordinary. The next drawer down was full of shirts but, again, there was nothing unusual. The wardrobe also held nothing of interest.

Laura turned to the bedside table. The first drawer contained cough mixture and a codeine-based painkiller, plenty of used tissues, pens, paper and a mobile phone charger. Something else caught her eye. She pulled out what looked like a grand-father's pipe. She sniffed at it. There was the unmistakable smell of marijuana.

She bent over and looked in between the table and the bed, and spotted the corner of an iPad sticking out from underneath the pillow. Reaching for it, she realised it was actually an iPod.

She called out to Tim, telling him what she'd found. 'But why would Allie have left it behind? Don't kids live their lives on these things?' she asked.

'Maybe she's got more than one,' he yelled from the other room. 'My thirteen-year-old niece has a really small one that she just keeps music on and another that looks more like a phone that she uses for watching movies and taking photos.'

Laura hadn't known he had a niece. She opened her mouth to say so, but looked instead at the device in her hand. She pressed the round button. The iPod lit up.

Laura's mouth fell open. On the screen was a photo of a topless Allie lying back on a bed, her lips in a sultry pout as she stared right at the camera. One arm was outstretched and partly out of frame. Her other hand rested on the curly hair of a man who lay across her body. His nose was on the dip between her breasts, a finger pressed to one nostril. There appeared to be something white on Allie's skin just where the man's nose was.

Laura zoomed in and gasped. Was he sniffing cocaine? She started to shake. Pressing the button again, she found where the photos were stored and tapped on the screen to open the files.

In another photo, Allie was leaning over a bed; Laura could

only see part of her face. The same man was behind her, his groin pressed up against Allie's bottom, his hands on her waist. He wore dark sunglasses, with what looked like a joint hanging from his mouth.

'Holy shit,' Laura muttered, appalled.

'What's up?' Tim appeared in the doorway.

Wordlessly, Laura held the worst photo out to him. Tim looked at it for a long time then whistled as he came to the same conclusion.

'Sex parties and selfies,' he said with certainty.

'I won't ask how you know that.' Laura turned away, so he couldn't see the look on her face. She'd been right to keep Tim at a distance, she decided. Obviously, if he knew about these sorts of things, he couldn't be trusted.

He gently grabbed her shoulder and turned her around. 'But I'll tell you, anyway. Just so you don't get the wrong idea. You have a habit of jumping to conclusions or lumping everyone into the same category, Laura Murphy. Are you listening?' He tugged softly at her ear. 'I've heard rumours of these parties involving, ah, how should I say it? Some of the younger people in the district. Everyone throws their knickers and jocks into the bowl and takes their pick. Then, so I hear, they get more adventurous. Taking photos, and other things. Pretty revolting stuff, really. Like I say, only rumours until now, but this pretty much confirms it. Believe me now?'

'How do you hear this stuff?'

Tim shrugged. 'You know how people like to talk in country towns. I see a lot of people. Hear a lot of things. Never repeat any of it, because you just don't know. I'm not about to ruin my business by spreading rumours.'

'I have never heard of anything like this. This shit happens in America, not here!' Laura was astonished and repelled at the same time.

'Laura, one thing I've learned by living in a country town is that anything and everything can happen. The wildest fiction is likely to be truth in the country.' Tim shook his head. 'So, sex *and* selfies. Not a good mix. She must have been out of it to do that!'

'Selfies?' Laura asked.

'You know—taking photos of yourself. It's all the rage these days with the kids. They post them onto Facebook or Instagram.'

He tapped at the screen. 'Do you know this bloke?'

'No.' She grimaced. 'So you're telling me that Allie isn't only doing drugs, she's somehow caught up in this sex party thing? Is it local, like really local?'

'To be perfectly honest, I hadn't heard anything about it for quite a few months—almost a year, probably—so I'd actually forgotten all about it. I'm pretty sure this is local, though. Even though the guy that Allie is uh, with, isn't. Look, here's another one. How many couples can you count here and how many do you know?' He held the device out to her. Laura took it with trepidation and scrutinised the photo. There, in the dark, she could make out two people. One was the slim figure of one of the local nurses she knew by sight. The other was a man. He was visible only from behind, and yet Laura couldn't help thinking the long legs and silhouette were familiar.

Laura's throat felt dry and her tongue stuck to the roof of her mouth. Wanting to be rid of the filthy photo, she pressed the button on the iPod again and took a breath. 'We'd better get on,' she mumbled, not looking at Tim. 'In fact, I just want to get outta here. Bloody *hell*.'

'Before we go, did you find anything else?' Tim asked.

'Oh yeah. This.' She opened the drawer into the bedside table and held up the pipe. 'And cough syrup and painkillers.'

Tim frowned. He picked up the prescription drugs and read the labels.

Deciding she couldn't give up the search now, Laura moved to the small table that served as a makeshift desk. It was covered with books and dirty clothes. She began to methodically sort through everything.

'Laura,' Tim said urgently.

She turned.

'You know what she's doing here?' He held up the painkillers and the bottle of cough syrup.

Laura felt numb. 'I don't think anything will surprise me now.'

'She's making her own drugs. Codeine, cough mixture and alcohol get you high. It's cheap and easy. There's scotch down here.' He held up a bottle that he'd found under the bed. 'She drinks it.'

'Oh.' Laura couldn't think of anything to say. 'She had a cold a couple of weeks ago,' she began weakly, but stopped as he shook his head.

Sighing, she went back to the job at hand. Soon she'd cleared the desk, but for some cigarette papers and the lid of a jam jar containing some type of small seed. 'Shit. Tim?' She handed him the jar lid.

Tim pressed his finger onto a seed and held it up to eye level.

'Marijuana,' he confirmed.

Laura then held up the cigarette papers. 'For rolling joints.'

'Far out, there are plenty of problems in this room, aren't there?' She shook her head, suddenly feeling an overwhelming sadness. 'Damn it, Allie was such a good kid.'

'She's going to have to go, Laura,' he said gently, confirming what Laura was already thinking. 'And I'm serious. This isn't good.'

'I know.' Laura's heart ached for the girl, and she thumped her fist on the table. 'What could have gone wrong in her life to make her turn to this? There was no indication when she came for her interview. Something must have changed.'

Tim reached out to hold her but Laura pulled away. She had to fix this.

'Right. I'll phone Allie and ask her to come in on Monday morning for a meeting. She can pack her things up and leave by lunchtime.'

'Good plan.'

They stood silently, Laura feeling a myriad of emotions. Betrayed, sad, angry, worried. This room was the final sign of a life that was self-destructing.

'I know what she's doing,' Laura said abruptly. 'These photos. They've not fallen over, she's turned them face down.' She picked up one of the frames. Laura recognised the elderly couple as Allie's grandparents. They were smiling proudly at the camera and in between them stood Allie, dressed in a school uniform. She was holding a prefect's badge.

'A year-twelve office holder,' Laura said as she handed the photo to Tim. She grabbed the next one. Allie with her sisters and mother on a beach. Three girls, young, lithe, carefree and covered in sand, beside their smiling mum. 'Do you see? She's embarrassed about what she's doing. She doesn't even want the photos of her family to see it. Look at her mum. So proud! And I know she raised those girls all by herself.'

It was sad, but it gave Laura some hope: if Allie knew what she was doing was stupid, if she'd just got mixed up in the wrong crowd, surely she could find a way back.

Desperate for clean air, Laura put the photo face down on the dresser again and headed for the front door.

'Jacob Collins,' Tim said, following her outside.

Caught up in her own thoughts Laura jumped at the sound of his voice. 'What?'

'Jacob Collins. You know, the Mount Gambier footy player. Do you remember, it was all over the local news for a while. So successful that he became the captain of the team. Won a heap of medals and accolade after accolade. But he still stuffed up. Hung out with the wrong crowd and got on to drugs. He lost everything for a time—the footy club said he couldn't play, then he lost his job. He went into rehab, then swore he was clean when he came out. Everyone gave him a second chance and he buggered that up too. He's got the most supportive family in the world and yet they haven't been able to help him.'

Laura nodded and turned to look at Tim. She noticed he was holding an envelope in his hand. 'What have you got there?' she asked.

Tim didn't say anything for a moment, just batted it against his other hand. He responded with his own question. 'Do you think it could have been Allie who drugged Random?'

'No.' Laura allowed herself a small laugh. 'That *is* ridiculous,

Tim. No matter what's happened to her, I'm sure she wouldn't hurt me.'

'This might change your mind.' He handed her the envelope.

Slowly she lifted the flap, took out the piece of paper inside, unfolded it and glanced at the handwritten words.

Here's what you need for the Adelaide show. Just crush it up and put it in one of the feed troughs.

Chapter 32

2008

Laura was at her desk updating the farm books, when she heard a car pull up. Rip started to bark.

'Yep, it's him,' she said to the excited dog.

They both walked out to the verandah just in time to see Tim unfold his long frame from his dual-cab ute.

Laura watched as his face split into a large grin and her stomach flip-flopped. She smiled back. She still marvelled at how this handsome man, who had been such a gangly teenager with braces and pimples, had this effect on her.

Laura knew she wouldn't have managed the last couple of weeks without his friendship. Which was all they shared, although she was aware he wanted more. He'd said as much the night before, when they'd eaten dinner together. She'd said something about everything being open to change and he'd responded that he was well and truly hoping that was the case.

Laura had kicked him under the table, but enjoyed the feeling of goosebumps on her skin when he touched her hand.

'Hey, good lookin'.' Tim opened the back of his ute and pulled out a bag of dog food.

'You're so clichéd,' she said, laughing.

Rip bounced up and down on his back legs and Tim bent down to pat him. 'I've brought you a present, young Rip,' Tim said as he dumped the food down. 'It's out of date, but there's nothing wrong with it. Does it smell good, my little puppy friend?' He reached into his back pocket and took out a small packet that he handed to Laura. 'This is out of date too, but only just. It'll still work.'

It was worm medicine for Rip.

'Thanks.' She put her hands on her hips. 'You didn't bring anything for me.'

'I brought your mail,' Tim said.

They went inside and he threw the bundle of letters on the bench.

'Any news on Allie?' Tim asked as he pulled out a chair and sat down at the table.

'I heard from her mum that they've put her into a rehab clinic in Adelaide. She isn't doing too well, from all accounts.'

Laura put the kettle on then stood at the sink, reflecting on the day they'd gone through Allie's room. The letter had been the clincher. So few words and yet so incriminating. The hurt Laura had felt had been instant and powerful. Tim had tried to take charge of the situation, but Laura, having looked after herself for so long, shunned his attempts. Seeming to know he was overstepping the mark, he'd retreated to the background, making cups of tea and, later, pouring wine, while Laura talked to the police and Allie's parents.

The police had taken the note with them to fingerprint.

They'd also confiscated the iPod and smoking implements, along with the cough syrup and the other substances.

In regard to the note, Detective Burrows had said it was unlikely they'd be able to prove anything. After all, the note didn't mention when, where or who.

It just happened to fit with the 'Random Incident'.

Laura was still none the wiser about who had sent the note.

When asked whether she wanted to press any charges against Allie, Laura had deliberated long and hard. In the end, after realising there was really nothing she could charge her with—Allie hadn't confessed to anything— she decided against it. 'I think that girl will have a hard enough time coming out of this hole she's put herself in,' Laura had said.

Detective Burrows had agreed. 'Once down there, it's difficult to get out, even with the best support,' he said.

'We can guess she was the one who drugged Random, but really, there isn't any proof. I think we should just let bygones be bygones. But I would ask one thing, Detective.' Looking the detective in the eye, she'd requested that the photos not be passed on to Allie's mother.

'I can't promise anything if we do get to the bottom of this and it comes to court,' he'd said, 'but I'll do my best otherwise.'

What had been harder to deal with was Allie's weeping mother. A single mum, Jackie had lamented that she didn't know where she'd gone wrong. Allie's sisters had been no trouble at all.

Laura hadn't been able to offer any comfort. She was still trying to work out how she'd missed the signs and if she could have made any difference.

Robyn and Tegan had been unsurprised and unmoved when they came home to find Allie gone. It was then that Laura understood how intensely they'd grown to dislike the girl. For them, it was a relief not to have her on Nambina. The only time they'd reacted was when Laura had recounted the story of Random at the show and the circumstantial evidence against Allie. They'd been stunned.

Tim broke into her musings. 'So am I going to get that cup of tea or are you frozen in time?'

Laura blinked and looked back at him. 'Sorry. Thinking about Allie.'

She poured the water into the cups, grabbed the sugar and milk then dumped them on the table before carrying the cups across and sitting down.

The silence was easy. It was one of the nicest things about their friendship. There wasn't any need for talking. They seemed in sync with each other.

'What are Robyn and Tegan up to?' he asked as he stirred sugar into his tea.

'Too hot to do too much today. I gave them the afternoon off. I think Robyn and Will were hoping to drive to the coast for a swim. Summer's supposed to start tomorrow but I think it's come early.'

'I wouldn't mind going to the beach,' Tim commented.

'I'll take the pool, thanks. Don't like seaweed and the way it can wrap around your ankles.' She took a sip of tea. 'I don't know why we drink hot liquid on hot days. Do you want water or something?'

'I'm good.' He drank his tea in silence before a sly look crossed his face and he put down his cup. He looked her in the eye. 'So are you telling me we've got the whole afternoon to ourselves? No students who'll come knocking on the door, looking for more jobs?'

She raised her eyebrows. 'Did you have something in mind?'

'I've always got ideas. The question is whether I can convince you?'

'Answering a question with a question.' Laura shook her head in mock disgust. 'Actually, now you mention it, I want to take you for a drive.' She pushed back her chair and stood up.

Tim looked disappointed but recovered quickly. 'I'm all yours.' He got up from the table and tipped the rest of his tea down the sink before following Laura out of the door.

Outside, Laura called to Rip, who bounded up and with one elegant bounce landed in the back of the ute. They climbed in and drove off with the windows down, the warm breeze drying the sweat on their bodies. The grasses had turned from a dull green to a brilliant wheat colour. Laura could see that there was a large fuel load in the paddocks, so much so she didn't expect to get away for Christmas this year. She was too worried about fires. Georgie and Sean had been on the phone, trying to make plans, but Robyn and Tegan would be heading home for the holiday. That meant Laura would have to stay put. She was sure that, if she asked, Tim would spend the day with her.

She slowed the ute to a standstill. 'Look over there.' She motioned towards a mob of sheep camped up on a dam bank.

Tim gazed in the direction she was pointing, but she could tell from the blankness on his face that he couldn't see what she could.

'Here.' She pulled a pair of binoculars from the glove box and handed them to him.

He peered through them for a moment.

'It's Random?' he asked.

'Yep!'

'He's working?' Tim asked.

'Yep again. I watched him serve three ewes within a matter of minutes this morning, before it got too hot. He's definitely back in the business of making babies!'

Tim hadn't lowered the glasses yet. 'No swelling, no signs of pain,' he mumbled more to himself than to Laura. She closed her eyes and leaned her head back against the seat.

'So what's your verdict, Dr Burns?'

'He looks really good, Laura. I couldn't have asked for a better outcome.'

'I reckoned the same, but wanted to get some expert advice.'

'Have you put the others to work? What about Boof and Mr Darcy?'

'Do you know, I think Boof is pining for Rusty?' Laura put the ute into gear and let out the clutch.

'The yard cat? It never ceases to amaze me how animals form really close friendships. It wouldn't surprise me in the least.'

Laura felt a familiar lump in her throat. A week earlier she'd found Rusty curled up asleep in a fleece left over from shearing. When Laura called him, he hadn't stirred. She knew then he wasn't sleeping. When she touched him, he was cold.

Reading her thoughts, Tim gave her knee a squeeze. 'He had a good life, eh?'

She nodded.

'Christmas pageant's on next week,' he said, changing the subject. 'Want to go?'

Laura looked at him quizzically. 'Can't say I've been to one since I was a kid.'

'Come on! They're fun. Kids on bikes, all the floats. And you get to sit on Father Christmas's knee. If you're really good, I'll give you a lolly to suck on.'

Laura's head whipped around. 'Are you Father Christmas?'

'The one and only.'

She laughed. 'Aren't you a bit underweight? But you'd be so good at that. So good!'

'Thank you,' Tim answered, stroking an imaginary long white beard. 'I thought so too. Now, back to the house, driver. I think a cold glass of something celebratory is in order! Random is in good shape.'

∽

Later that night Laura sat at the kitchen table drinking wine alone. She looked around the room and once again felt its emptiness. When Tim was around, the place seemed filled with laughter and friendship. Realisation dawned. She was missing him. Missing his company, his smile and conversation. *You'd better put those sorts of ideas out of your mind,* she told herself.

She thought of Catherine. Laura could see her friend, hands on hips, staring at her intently. 'Why?' she would ask her.

'Oh, go away,' Laura mumbled out loud. But she found herself asking the same question.

To distract herself, she flipped through the mail. One letter caught her attention and she slid her finger under the flap to tear it open.

The letter inside was from a law firm.

Her stomach flip-flopped.

Dear Miss Murphy,

We have been instructed to act on behalf of Meghan Hunter in establishing her interest in the parcel of land known as 'Nambina', location 486, Mangalow.

We have been able to ascertain that our client has a lineal relationship that we believe entitles her to make a claim on this land.

Further details will be provided in due course.

You can be assured that we are extremely confident of her position and entitlement.

The legal process to pursue this claim will be, of necessity, time-consuming and extremely expensive for both you and our client. We would therefore consider any offer you choose to make to satisfy our client.

All future correspondence and communication must be through this office. Direct communication with our client could result in action being taken against you.

We look forward to your response in writing within twenty-one (21) days of the date of this letter.

Yours faithfully,

Brendan Dark
Dark & Partners

Laura stopped breathing.

Chapter 33

2008

'How could this happen?' Laura wailed down the phone to her father. 'Lineal relationship?'

'Laura, calm down. I know this is upsetting, but . . .'

'It's beyond that, Dad! We could lose Nambina. What would we do without it?' Her voice broke and she felt like her heart was being torn from her chest.

'I can't see how it's possibly true,' Sean said. 'There must be some mistake. Or mix-up, or something. There's just no way.' His voice faded. 'Unless . . .'

'What?' The word came out of her like a bullet. 'Unless what?'

'Well, oh, I don't know. Let me think about it. You've only just told me,' Sean snapped.

Laura felt the floor begin to spin beneath her. She sank down against the wall and took deep breaths. She knew she was close to losing control and that wasn't going to help. They had to figure out what was happening, how it was happening, and how to stop it.

Laura could hear her father's short sharp inhalations over the line. He was upset too.

'How do I find out?' she asked. 'How can I prove they're wrong?' Her mind was racing, jumbled thoughts that she couldn't make sense of falling over one another.

'I don't know,' Sean answered. He made a sound of exasperation then said quickly: 'Birth certificates, obviously. We'll get her birth certificate.'

Laura crinkled her brow. 'We know who her parents are. Josh's dad and that stuck-up, toffy-nosed woman, Glenda, who married him.'

'Remind me of the history again,' Sean said. 'History will hold all the answers we need, I'm sure of it.'

'Josh's mum died while she was having him,' Laura answered. 'Mr Hunter hired a housekeeper because he needed someone to look after Josh. That was Glenda. She managed to get the old man to marry her—some people say she got up the duff on purpose. They had Meghan.'

'Ah, that's right. He was a lot older than her and died a few years ago. Cancer.' Sean said. 'Awful disease.'

'Hmm. Anyway, about three years ago Mrs Hunter-the-second left town. I think she moved to Adelaide or somewhere more cultural than Mangalow. I know she always reckoned we were second-class citizens down here. Not enough art and theatre for her.'

'That's strange, considering she started as a housekeeper,' Sean observed. 'I remember the story now.'

'Yeah, Papa always said that Mrs Hunter was too hoity-toity for her own good and she should remember how she came into money. Apparently, Mr Hunter worked really hard when he was younger. He got what he wanted through sheer determination and sweat.'

'Now, wasn't it Josh's aunty, the old man's sister, that Howie got into trouble with when he was looking through his rifle sights? Pretending to sight up a fence, wasn't he?'

Despite herself, Laura laughed. 'You're right! Howie always had a bit of a soft spot for her, I think. She was a widow but I don't know anything more about her.'

Renewed fear made her shudder and she gripped the phone more tightly. 'So, Dad, how do we fix this?'

'We hire our own lawyer and fight,' he answered with certainty.

'That was my first idea, too,' she said miserably. 'But I don't think I have the money. There isn't any extra cash around. The letter from the lawyers said it would be expensive for both parties.'

Her father let out a groan. 'We don't have any spare capital either. The hospital pays well and all, but we do rely on those payments coming from Nambina to keep everything running as it should and to pay the house off.' He paused. 'Would you consider mortgaging the farm?'

Laura was about to answer when Sean groaned again. 'Ah, the banks won't do that when they know there's court action hanging over it. Stupid suggestion.'

'I couldn't do it anyway, Dad,' Laura answered. 'The threat of losing this place to someone else is bad enough, but if something happened and I couldn't pay the loan back . . .' She gulped. 'Can't even think about it.'

'Look, I have to go to the hospital in the morning, but I'll see my boss and get some leave. I'll come down the day after and we'll work out a plan. We've got twenty-one days, haven't we?'

'Nineteen now,' she answered miserably. 'It's dated two days ago.'

'Well, then, we better get moving.' His tone was determined. 'Will you be okay by yourself until I get there?'

'I'll be fine. Tim's coming over tomorrow.'

'Good.'

They rang off. Laura still felt alarmed and incensed, but was calmer in the knowledge that her dad, as always, would be there and do his best to help her fix the situation.

⌇

Laura lay in bed, listening intently, trying to work out what had woken her.

Completely spent from the emotion of the day, she'd gone to bed before the sun's rays had disappeared below the horizon and had fallen into the deepest sleep she'd had in a long time.

Now she listened for any noise that was odd. The wind was rattling through the windows and the front door knocked against its frame. Nothing unusual there.

She had almost dropped off back to sleep when a soft tapping on the kitchen door startled her.

Now that was weird. She strained to listen. It sounded again.

There was someone knocking at the door.

Her eyes fell on the bedside clock. Who would be visiting at this hour?

Rip hadn't barked and Laura hadn't heard a car. Did that mean whoever it was had walked in? Memories of Josh's unwanted visits and Meghan's threats came to mind. Suddenly frightened, she slid out of bed and looked around wildly for a weapon, but she could find nothing.

Never, in all her time alone on Nambina, had she felt so scared and out of control—it had overtaken her so quickly.

Tiptoeing over to the window, she peered into the darkness and saw a man. He had a small light strapped to his head.

'Tim!' She sagged against the wall with relief. Hearing another knock, this time louder, she gathered herself and went to open it. As she crossed the dark kitchen, her anger rose.

She yanked the door open and stood there, her hands on her hips. 'What the fuck are you doing? You scared the bloody living daylights out of me!' Her voice was loud and harsh.

Tim pulled back, his ready smile dropping away and confusion taking its place. 'Sorry, Laura. I had a late call out this way. I wanted to come by and see how you were. Guess I should've rung first . . .'

'So you decided you'd creep in and scare me? Where the hell are your brains?'

Tim looked put out. 'I was worried. You sounded so down when you called. Didn't think you'd be in bed yet. Sort of assumed you'd be pacing the room trying to work out how to fix everything.'

Laura flicked the switch for the outside light. The moment the verandah area was illuminated, moths dive-bombed the lightglobe. 'Quick,' she said impatiently, motioning for him to come in. 'Before all the insects get inside.'

It was then she saw that Tim's jeans were dirty and he had traces of blood on his face. 'So, what call did you have?' she asked.

'Whelping bitch. Had the second pup stuck in the birth canal.'

'Right. You forgot to wash your face.'

Tim's hand automatically went to his cheeks and his fingers felt for the dried blood. He scratched at it. 'Sorry,' he said for the third time.

Laura's heart rate was returning to normal. 'No, it's me who should be sorry. I was a bitch just then.' She sighed and sank into a kitchen chair. 'I went to bed early. Did you drive in? I didn't hear a car. I was so tired I just went out like a light.'

'Yeah, how else would I get here? Walk? I don't think so. That's too much like exercise for me.' He grinned and squatted down in front of her. 'Sorry I woke you. And sorry I scared you.' He patted her knee. 'I was worried after you rang, then I got the call out this way. Thought it was an omen—like I was supposed to come and see you.'

'It's okay,' Laura said, putting her hand over his for a second, then taking it away. 'I think I'm overreacting to everything at the moment. I feel a bit out of control.'

'Understandably so. Did you talk to your dad?'

'Yeah. They'll be down in a couple of days.'

'That's good. You know, I've been thinking about the situation ever since you rang and I've got an idea.' He stood up straight.

Laura looked up at him, realising how pleased she was to have him here. She knew Tim would try and make things right. 'About what?' she asked.

'Would there be anything in Howie's office that might give you a hint? Have you looked? I mean, this house is so big. He lived on one side, you on the other. He might have known something and kept it hidden.'

304

Laura shook her head. 'Papa never hid anything from me,' she said with certainty.

'I'm not saying he did. He just may not have told you. I bet you never asked. And if you don't ask, often you don't get told.'

Laura stared at him. She didn't want to go looking in Howie's office until Sean arrived. 'What do you think I might find?' she asked finally.

Tim shrugged. 'I don't know. But I've been thinking about it non-stop since your call.' He began to pace the kitchen. 'Trying to work out how we can find information. I feel useless, Laura. I want to help but I don't know what to do. This is the best I've come up with so far. I can't bear to see you hurting, so let me in. You're so strong but I want to share the load. Let me give you the ideas I have, even if they're not very good.' He tried to smile but failed.

Laura held his gaze, thinking how much she liked it when he used the word 'we'. 'I'm not shutting you out. Not on purpose. I'm just so used to doing everything by myself. It's hard for me to stop thinking that way.'

'I know.' Tim came back to stand in front of her. He put out his hand to her and she took it. He pulled her up and looked into her eyes. 'I want to help, Laura.'

Laura looked steadily back at him, knowing he was genuine and it was up to her now. She took a breath. 'I want you to help too.'

They stared into each other's eyes. The only sound to be heard was the singing of the crickets.

Tim raised his hand and gently touched her cheek.

Laura covered his hand with hers. 'I like the way you used the word "we",' she whispered. 'It's got a beautiful sound to it.'

A ghost of a smile passed over Tim's face and he leaned down towards her. 'I'd be happy to keep using that word for a long time,' he said.

Laura opened her mouth to answer but before she could, Tim's lips were on hers.

⁓

Laura moved over to the window. The half-moon cast a soft light across the roof of the shed, which shone silver. She could see the dark outline of Rip's dog kennel to the left and the shearing shed and yards to the right.

She looked towards the boundary that separated Nambina from the Hunters' property. Laura couldn't see their house or outbuildings—they were too far away—but she could imagine them and wondered what secrets they held.

Against the moonlit sky she could make out the distant outline of the monstrosity that had housed the insane in the early 1900s. It was crumbling and decaying now, but on nights like these, Laura felt a tingling rush of cold run over her. She wondered about the lost souls who had been imprisoned there. What had happened to them all?

She shifted her gaze back to Tim. 'Who's out there?' she said softly.

Tim came and stood beside her. 'What do you mean?' he asked, staring intently through the glass. 'Can you see someone?'

'No.' She half-smiled. 'If I could see them, I'd know who I was fighting.'

'You're fighting Meghan,' he said.

'Yes, but who is Meghan?'

⁓

Laura watched through the open door as Tim unloaded two whiteboards, which looked like they would be at home in a small home office, from the back of his ute. He carried them across the yard one at a time and leaned them against the wall in the kitchen.

Laura was by the phone, the receiver in her hand. 'I'm not sure who to try first,' she said.

'Births, Deaths and Marriages. They'll tell you how to order the birth certificates.'

'But can anyone order anyone's birth certificate? I mean, won't I need identification or something?'

'Sweetheart, they'll tell you if you ring. I can't answer all the questions—I don't know all the answers.' He nodded encouragingly. 'Oh, by the way,' he said, uncapping a texta. 'I've taken almost three weeks' leave to help sort this.'

Laura's breath caught in her throat. 'Who's looking after the surgery?' she asked quietly.

'Called in a locum. Mate I went to vet school with. He's unemployed and happy to have something to do. He can ring me if he needs to, but he's a good vet. He won't stuff it up.'

'Thanks, Tim.' She looked over at him, wanting to convey how grateful she was, but he had his back to her and didn't turn around. In the end, she went back to the phone and looked up the number she needed.

While she talked to the woman at Births, Deaths and Marriages, she watched Tim draw lines down the first white-board and write headings:

Week One.

Week Two.

Week Three.

Then under each heading he drew seven lines. Day One, Day Two and so on.

Laura hung up. 'What are you doing?'

'I talked to Detective Burrows today,' he said, still writing, 'and this is how they solve crimes. They use boards. They write every piece of information they get up here, brainstorm it and see if anything stands out. That's what we're going to do. And on this board here—' he pointed and grabbed a red texta, '—we'll write the family tree.'

He started by writing 'Meghan' in large letters at the bottom of the board. Then he wrote 'Josh (half-brother)', 'Glenda (mother)' and 'Mark (father)'. The lines he drew to connect them were wobbly, but Laura could see what he was doing. He was going to take the family tree back to where Meghan believed she had a link to the Murphys.

'Do we need one for us?' she asked. 'A Murphy family tree, to see if we come up with the same link?'

'Not at the moment. I think we should just focus on Meghan and see where it leads.'

There was a knock at the door. Tegan and Robyn came in. They stopped when they saw the activity.

'Headquarters,' Tim confirmed with a grin.

'For what?' Tegan said slowly, glancing from Tim to Laura.

'Ah.' Laura looked at both girls, wondering how much to tell them. They were part of it, she decided. 'I got a bit of bad news last night. Meghan Hunter has made a claim on Nambina.'

She filled them in quickly and answered their questions. 'What would be really great is if you could keep an eye on the stock and things outside for me while we focus on this. It's only for a couple of weeks.'

'Eighteen days,' Tim broke in. 'We're on a countdown.'

'How come?' Robyn asked, and Laura told her about the letter and the deadline.

'Don't you worry about anything outside,' Robyn said. 'We can handle it. If we've got any questions or problems we'll come and ask you. But let us know if we can help in here in any way. Meghan's a stuck-up bitch.'

Laura was at a loss for words when she heard that, but Tim laughed. 'Good judge of character,' was all he said.

Laura found her voice again. 'Great. Just come and ask if there are any hassles. The farm still needs to operate—it can't just stop. So, this morning, could you do a stock run? Go into every paddock, check the troughs, fences, stock. Make sure everyone's happy. Thank goodness the crop isn't ready to be harvested yet.'

'Righto. We'll report back,' Robyn said. They trooped out.

'Can you take Rip with you?' Laura called after them. 'He needs a run.'

'Okay.' Tegan's voice floated through the air.

'What did the B, D and Ms say?' Tim asked, his texta poised to write.

Laura looked at her notes. 'I can't get them—the certificates, that is. Well, I can if I can get Meghan's permission, but since I'm not allowed to contact her, it's unlikely that'll work.'

'Ah.' Tim looked slightly crestfallen. He put the cap back on the texta.

'Why don't we put up what we know?' Laura asked.

'That's all I know,' Tim answered, indicating what he'd written. 'Do you know the names of Meghan's grandparents?'

'No-o-o,' she said slowly. 'But I wonder who in town would?'

Tim brightened, and he grinned. 'Someone in the old folks' home, I reckon.'

'We can't just go barrelling in there,' Laura said. 'I don't know anyone.'

'But I do and I can. Great Aunty Ruby lives there. She's a terrible gossip. She might know something.'

Laura brightened. 'If you're comfortable asking her?'

'Course I am. I visit her every time I'm passing.'

Laura gave Tim a once-over. There was a lot about this man she didn't know, but she liked what she was finding out.

'I know, I know,' he said, as if reading her mind. 'I'm a good nephew. And such a catch!'

She rolled her eyes.

'Do you want to have a look in Howie's office first?' Tim countered.

Laura screwed up her face. 'I wanted to wait for Dad to help me. I know I need to, but I sort of feel like I'm intruding, and I wouldn't so much if Dad were with me.'

'He's not going to be here until tomorrow. What if the answer is just sitting there? Intrude or lose the farm. Your choice.' Tim folded his arms across his chest and stared at her.

She frowned. 'I take back all the nice things I was just thinking about you.'

Tim continued to stare.

'Oh, all right,' she said, her huffiness apparent.

She walked to the end of the sunroom, pulled open the door that led into a passageway and called over her shoulder. 'You'd better come with me. I don't really want to do it by myself.'

The part of the house that held Howie's office and bedroom seemed cold, despite the heat outside. Laura shivered. She could feel Howie here, smell his deodorant and aftershave. She was probably imagining it, she told herself. Her last trip down here was to look in her grandmother's wardrobe for the Baggy and Saggy dress. That hadn't bothered her—she hadn't gone through personal papers or diaries. She hadn't been looking for secrets. But this was different. It felt like prying. Overstepping the boundaries they'd had when they'd lived together.

Howie had always welcomed her into his office when she was a child. However, as adults, they'd both needed their privacy and had usually talked in the sunroom or the kitchen. There'd been little need for Laura to visit Howie down here, so she hadn't.

She bypassed Howie's bedroom and went straight to his office. Hearing Tim behind her, she felt reassured.

She felt a lump in her throat as she touched Howie's desk, her fingers tracing the old furrows and nicks. She sat down in the worn fabric chair. As a child she'd sit here and swing herself in circles until she was dizzy. Then, as her head spun, she'd lean all the way back until the chair was in a reclining position. It had been a pleasant sensation—she'd always felt safe in her grandfather's office.

'It's crazy, isn't it? We all know we can't take anything with us when we die but it's not until after someone has actually gone that the people left behind realise how true it is. I mean, all these things he always used. The letter opener, the pen, even the envelopes he bought that he didn't get to use. He wouldn't have known he wasn't going to get to use them. But they're all still here and he's not.'

Her voice caught and she felt Tim put his hand on her shoulder. She made a decision then and there. 'You know what?' she said.

'What?'

'Once all this shit is sorted with Meghan, I'm going to clean out the office. I'm going to clean the clothes out of the wardrobes. I know I can't hang on to the past. If I'm going to fight Meghan and win, I need to have a future. All this stuff is from the past. It's history. It can't be changed because it's already happened, but I can make the future better. It can have a different outcome, because it's still undecided.'

'Howie will never disappear from your life, Laura, because you hold him in here.' Tim tapped at his chest and then his head.

'Yeah,' she said quietly, putting her own hand on her chest. 'Yeah. In here.'

Tim turned her around, pulled her to him and kissed her.

Laura felt her energy renew. 'Okay, let's do this.' Tentatively, she pulled open the top drawer. A neat and organised display of pens, liquid paper, paper clips and other office paraphernalia lay where it had been last used. Nothing important in there.

The second drawer yielded as much as the first. In the third drawer she found a stack of old Adelaide Agricultural Show programs and a postcard.

The postcard had been sent during the war and showed a picture of London.

'Dear Howard,' she read aloud for Tim's benefit. 'Howard? I never heard anyone call him that!' Momentarily she was thrown.

'See?' Tim said. 'Already we're discovering things about him you didn't know.'

Laura continued to read. 'Your brother spoke briefly of you during our time together in air force training. I wanted you to know that Thomas was shot down over the English Channel. I'm aware you were estranged, but he did speak of you fondly. It is only fair that you know what happened.'

The postcard was signed Michael Cooke.

'Dad was right,' she said slowly. 'Thomas was killed in the war.'

Chapter 34

2008

Over a cup of tea at the kitchen table Tim and Laura studied what they'd found in Howie's office. It wasn't much.

The postcard.

The pile of Adelaide show programs.

And a photo of two boys and their parents.

On the back of the photo was scrawled in a feminine hand: 'Ernest, Jessie, Thomas George and Howard Ernest. Christmas, 1930.' The boys looked uncomfortable in ties and starched pants.

Laura guessed the boys were ten or twelve years old. She was intrigued to see her Papa as a youngster. It was one of only a handful of photographs she'd ever seen of him. Even though it was a faded black and white picture, she could see the familiar pattern of the face she loved. She looked at it for a long time before handing it to Tim.

'Geez, Thomas looks like his mum, eh?'

Laura took the photo back for another look—she'd been too interested in Howie.

'He does,' she confirmed. 'But look at the similarities between Papa and Ernest,' she pointed out. 'The family genetics are strong there as well.'

She reached for the show programs and rifled through them until she found the one for the year Howie had won. Flicking through it, she realised there wouldn't be any announcement because it had been printed before the judging.

Beside each of the classes was Howie's familiar scrawl. 'Jackson's two-tooth wether should win.' And: 'Goyder's team impeccable.'

She put the programs aside. 'What now?' she asked. 'There's not much here that's useful.'

'No.' Tim was tapping his fingers on the table. Laura knew it was something he did when he was thinking. He stood up abruptly. 'Let's go for a drive and see Aunt Ruby.'

∽

The woman on reception smiled when she saw Tim. 'Hello there. Here to see Ruby again?'

'Yep, we are,' he answered, ignoring the curious stare she gave Laura. 'Is she playing bingo in the lounge today, Janice?'

'No, it's morning tea in the gardens. Bridge this afternoon.'

'Right. I'll find her.' He pushed a swinging door and motioned for Laura to follow him. 'Bye,' he called over his shoulder. Quietly he muttered to Laura: 'You've given her something to gossip about, anyway! I've never brought a woman with me before.'

Laura barely heard him; she was trying to ignore the hope that was building inside her. These people would know so much about the past. Would they know anything about Meghan's family? Would they *remember*? Why hadn't she come up with the idea herself?

On the drive there, she and Tim had discussed what they knew, which was very little, about Meghan's mother, Glenda: how she'd come to meet Mr Hunter, whether she'd been born in the area. Laura had suggested she hadn't been. 'If she'd grown up here, she wouldn't have had the opportunity to develop those tastes,' she said. Tim had agreed. They'd realised they didn't know much about the Hunters, either, even though the family was local.

'Here she is.' Tim nodded towards a tall lady sitting on a bench under a leafy tree. Laura's step faltered as she studied the elderly woman. Her long grey hair was knotted in a bun, kept in place with a net. Her dowdy clothes and solid walking shoes were out of place among the flowery tops of the other ladies and the plaid shirts of the men. She was sipping tea from a cup, a saucer in her other hand. Beside her was a walking frame.

'Why's she here?' Laura whispered.

'Just not safe in her own home. Had a couple of falls and broke her hip last year. Aunty Ruby was lucky to come out of it alive. Got pneumonia. "Lucky Lady Ruby" we call her.' He waved his hand to get his great aunt's attention and Laura saw a thin smile cross the elderly woman's face.

'Hi, Aunty Ruby,' he called as he strode towards her. Bending down, he gave her a smacking kiss on the cheek. 'How are you today? It's lovely out here in the sunshine.'

'But too hot for my liking,' Ruby huffed. 'Who's your friend?'

316

Laura put out her hand.

'This is Laura, Aunty Ruby. She's Howie Murphy's grand-daughter. Laura, this is my Aunty Ruby.'

'Hello,' Laura said.

Ruby ignored her outstretched hand. 'Great Aunt, actually,' Ruby corrected. 'So, you're the baby Sean brought home from Queensland?'

'Yes, that's me.' She let her hand fall to her side.

'I've heard good things about you. About time Tim brought you to visit. Now, tell me, what's happening on the farm? So help me God, if only I were up and able I'd be back out walking the paddocks of my father's property.'

On safer ground, Laura launched into a discussion about Nambina in particular, and the district in general. Ruby asked informed questions and tutted at the story of Allie's misadventure with the sprayer and tractor.

'Oh, I miss all of that. Stuck in here, with all these . . . these . . .' She waved her hand. '. . . people. Don't know what it is about ageing men, but they all smell. Bit like the old rams in the ram paddock. Ugh!'

Laura bit her lip, trying desperately not to laugh, but Tim had no such qualms.

'I guess we know you're not chasing any of the blokes then, Aunty Ruby,' he said, still chuckling.

Ruby turned back to Laura and spoke in a hushed tone. 'I still get the *Stock Journal*, you know. Read it from cover to cover every Thursday. It's like my bible. I know the nurses laugh at me behind my back, but I don't care. I love it.'

'I like reading it too,' Laura said. 'Lots of good information for farmers and station owners alike.'

After a pause, Tim said: 'Aunty Ruby, we've got a question for you.'

'Oh yes? Needed a reason to come and visit, did you?'

'Absolutely,' Tim said with a wicked grin on his face. 'I wanted you to meet Laura.'

'And what else?'

'We were wondering about the Hunters.'

Ruby sat back in her chair and eyed Tim and Laura. 'What about them?'

'How long have they been around here?'

'Now, are you talking about Mark's family?'

Laura nodded, knowing that was Josh's father's name.

'Poor devil. Cancer got him. Younger than me, he was.'

A couple of other residents hobbled past. 'Jack!' Ruby called out. 'Jack!' She raised her voice when he didn't turn. 'Deaf as an old post. Jack! Come over here. These young people are asking about Mark Hunter. You'd probably remember him better than I would. You'd have seen him at the markets.'

Jack turned at the sound of her voice. 'What's that, Miss Ruby?' he said, a smile revealing white teeth.

'They're asking about Mark Hunter.' She spoke clearly and loudly.

'Ah, Mark Hunter. Top bloke. Yes.'

'Then come and sit down.'

Ruby turned to Laura. 'False teeth,' she whispered, raising her eyebrows. 'And he's *definitely* an old ram.'

'Remember his dad, so I do. Been around here for generations,' Jack said as he shuffled over and settled next to Ruby. He tried to scoot a bit closer, but she moved away and placed her walker between them.

318

Laura glanced at Tim, trying not to giggle.

Tim cleared his throat. 'How many generations have they been here?' he asked.

'What's that, lad?' Jack cupped a hand to ear.

'How long have they been farming here?'

'Let me see. There was Mark and his father, and *his* father before. I'd say at least three generations. Excellent farmers too, mind you. A bit conservative, but good nonetheless.' He turned to Ruby. 'I used to see him riding to school. He was a bit younger than me. Only reason I took any notice of him was because he was a bit of a daredevil on horseback.'

'All of us who were on farms rode to school, Jack,' Ruby said in a cutting tone. 'And we all liked to have a bit of a play around. Give the horses their head.'

'The good ol' days.'

She pointed a finger at Tim. 'That would make the Hunters fourth generation, then. Mark's young son manages the place now, doesn't he?'

'That's right.'

'Do you remember Mark's second wife?' Laura asked carefully.

'Unfortunately, yes,' answered Ruby bluntly.

Laura was liking her more and more. 'Goodness, nobody seems to like her,' she said in a singsong tone.

'Oh, she wrapped Mark around her finger good and proper,' Ruby said. 'Came in as a housekeeper and wiggled that tush of hers. I remember the gossip it caused.'

'She had a very nice tush, from memory,' Jack interjected.

Ruby gave him a withering look. 'It was tragic, Mark's wife dying in childbirth. Wouldn't happen these days. But it did.

Of course, Mark couldn't cope by himself. He couldn't run a farm and bring up a child at the same time.'

Laura wanted to ask why not. Her father had. But he'd had Howie, she reminded herself.

'And he was grieving, poor man, and men *are* the weaker species.' Ruby continued as if reading Laura's mind. 'When that woman turned up, she had her heart set on one thing, and she worked until she got it.'

Jack nodded in agreement. 'Wasn't long before they walked down the aisle and brought another little one into the world.

'She was a bit too good for us down here.'

'Where did she come from?'

'Well, I don't rightly know,' Jack answered.

Ruby shook her head. 'She was English, wasn't she?'

'No,' growled Jack. 'Course she wasn't. Reckon she would have had to come from the city somewhere. She had a posh way of talking. And boy, could she dance.'

'So she wasn't married when she came here?' Tim asked.

Ruby looked over at him and frowned. 'No, dear,' she spoke slowly. 'She married Mr Hunter. Mark.'

'Would you remember her maiden name?' Laura asked, suddenly breathless.

Jack snorted. 'We're gettin' a bit long in the tooth, young lady. My memory's not what it was.' He tapped the side of his head and grinned ruefully. Laura returned his smile. She liked this man and it was clear he was sweet on Ruby, even though she wouldn't have a bar of him.

'Speak for yourself, Jack Williams,' Ruby said loudly. 'I remember her name. It was all rather curious, when she turned

320

up. It was the same as Mark's neighbours and it caused some talk among the townspeople. It's the same as yours, love,' she turned to Laura. 'It was Murphy.'

Chapter 35

2008

Tim and Laura didn't talk much on the drive back to Nambina. Laura was visibly shaken and confused. She just couldn't fathom how Glenda's name could possibly be Murphy. It seemed bizarre.

Before they'd said goodbye to Ruby and Jack, Tim had the foresight to ask them if they knew of Thomas Murphy and what became of him. Neither of them did.

Then, as they were leaving, Ruby had grabbed Laura's arm. 'When you come back and visit me, you might tell me what this is all about.'

Now Tim reached over and held Laura's hand. 'I know you're very special,' he said above the noise of the engine. 'And I shouldn't degrade you to the commonness of, say, a "Smith", but Murphy is a name that is heard a lot. She's probably no relation at all.'

Laura continued to stare straight ahead. 'You said you don't believe in coincidences,' she answered flatly.

When they arrived at the house, Sean's car was parked outside. Laura could smell a roast cooking. Her family had arrived early.

Georgie came to the door to greet them. 'Hello, darling,' she said with a gentle smile. 'How are you holding up? What a horrible thing for Meghan to do.'

Laura was so grateful to see her stepmother, she couldn't speak. Georgie hugged her and stroked her hair, just as Laura remembered her doing when she'd fallen over at basketball or taken a scrape in the schoolyard.

'Where's Dad?' she asked eventually.

'He's inside, in Howie's office. He probably hasn't heard you arrive.' Georgie turned to Tim. 'Hello, Tim. It's been a long time.' They shook hands.

'Hi, Mrs Murphy. Good to see you, even if it isn't under the best circumstances.'

Inside, Laura was surprised to see Poppy sitting at the kitchen table.

'Hi, Poppy. Do you know Tim?'

'I've heard of him. Hello,' Poppy answered sullenly.

'We decided we'd bring Poppy with us,' Georgie said before Laura could ask. 'She needs some time away from the city.'

Laura stared at her sister with growing fear. She'd seen that look before. Poppy looked exactly like Allie had: tired, pale, dull eyes.

'It's good to see you here,' Laura said, clumsily trying to hug Poppy, who still hadn't got up from the table. 'I'll go and find Dad.'

She left the room as Tim started to write everything they'd learned on one of the whiteboards. Laura could hear Georgie

323

talking to him about his vet practice. For a moment, she stood in the passage leading to Howie's part of the house. She was glad her family were here. When it mattered, they always were.

In the office she found her father bent over the filing cabinet. He was surrounded by papers. Tears pricked her eyes—how she wished she could stop being so emotional. It'd be better if she could stay angry and rant and rave, but the tears kept threatening to come and it made her feel weak. 'Dad.' She uttered the word in a strangled tone.

He shot up from the floor and crossed the room in two steps. 'Laurs,' he answered, folding her into a bear hug. 'Oh, Laurs.'

They stood like that for the longest time, until Sean, still holding her, pulled back to look her in the eye. 'I'm so sorry this is happening,' he said. 'We'll beat them, though. You have my word.'

'How can we, Dad? Tim and I have just been talking to his great Aunty Ruby. She told us Glenda's maiden name was Murphy.'

The surprise was plain on his face. 'What?'

Laura nodded. 'That's what she told us.'

Sean sighed and rubbed at his head. 'I never knew! Well, that's thrown a spanner in the works.' He turned and indicated the mess of papers. 'Good Lord!' He let fly with an expletive, then said: 'You and Meghan may be cousins!'

Shock filtered through Laura. 'Bloody hell.' She looked around wildly, not knowing how to react. 'Cousins?' she repeated, as the words began to sink in.

'I've been looking for anything in here that might help us—birth certificates, death certificates, diaries, something. I haven't found anything yet.'

324

Laura flopped into the chair and leaned back, tired of the whole thing already. She told him how she and Tim had been through the office in the morning and what they'd found.

'It looks like you were right, that Thomas went to war and was killed. We found a postcard from one of his air force mates saying he'd been shot down. It's out in the kitchen.'

They were silent for a few moments before Laura ventured to say: 'Don't take this the wrong way, but I think Poppy has a problem.'

Sean nodded sadly. 'I know she does.'

'She looks just like Allie did.'

'That's why we've brought her. To get her away from everything up there. Need to give her something to do, something to make her feel useful. See if we can get her back.'

Laura just nodded. 'I'll do what I can.'

Sean's face was filled with pain. 'I know you will.'

ও

Georgie pushed back her plate and looked around the table. 'It sounds to me like we need to concentrate on Glenda's side of the family. Work out where the connection is.'

'It's got to be through Thomas,' Laura said.

Tim shook his head. 'As I said before, Murphy's a common name. Doesn't have to be through him at all.'

Laura threw him a dismissive look. 'It's too coincidental,' she said.

Sean sat silently. Laura was sure he looked like he wanted to say something but couldn't find the right words. 'Dad?'

'Hmm?'

'You've got something to say?'

325

He looked beaten but started to talk. 'This is just an idea. But Ernest was free to leave his farm to whoever he wanted to, wasn't he? Yes, all this happened during the time when it would have usually gone to the eldest son. As Thomas wasn't around, Howie got it. But that doesn't mean Howie couldn't have verbally promised it to someone else, does it?'

'What?' gasped Laura.

'I'm not saying it happened, Laurs, but I can't work out why Meghan would think she had a claim. It's the only reason I can come up with.'

'Papa wouldn't have done that, Dad. He wouldn't hurt me like that. Or you.'

'If it was a verbal promise, but there was a will that stated otherwise, the promise won't hold up in court,' Tim said.

'I know all of that,' Sean said. 'He may have made it before either of us were around. I'm wondering if that's why she thinks she's got some sort of claim, though. Somehow, someone promised something to Glenda, her being a so-called Murphy, and now she's getting Meghan to claim it.'

The silence around the table was so heavy Laura couldn't bear it. She wanted to scream and hit out and cry. But that wasn't an option. They had to fight, and giving way to emotions would only blur her thinking. Her mind was whir-ring. Suddenly she brightened. 'I've got an idea!' She looked at Poppy. 'Are you good with computers?'

Her sister snorted. 'Yes, of course.'

'Isn't there some computer program you can use to draw up a family tree? I've seen them advertised on TV. "Heritage Families" or something? Could you have a go at using it?'

'I'm sure I could figure it out. Shouldn't be too hard.' Poppy looked perkier than she had on the first day. Out of the corner of her eye, Laura could see Sean smiling with approval.

'And do you know what I'm going to do?' Laura said. Everyone waited. 'I'm going to Adelaide. I'm going to find Glenda and pay her a visit. I can't go near Meghan—the letter states that, but it says nothing about extended family. I'll find her and ask her who her father was.'

'Oh, Laurs, do you think that's wise?' Georgie asked, concern etched on her face. 'I'd imagine she knows exactly what her daughter is up to. I can't think she'll welcome you with open arms.'

'I don't care.' The anger was back now and, thankfully, it was overwhelming the worry. 'It's my farm. Or ours. Even if there is a blood link or a promise, they're not entitled to it. They haven't worked it, they don't know its moods or love it the way I do. The way Papa did. And Dad, if what you told me about Thomas is true—and that's where the connection is—well, he obviously didn't love Nambina, either. He walked away.' She saw Tim nodding in agreement.

'That's all true, Laura,' Tim said. 'But a court of law may not see it that way.' The voice of reason.

'I'm not lying down.' Her eyes flashed.

'I can't imagine loving something so much,' Poppy said quietly before seeming to shrink in her chair as everyone looked at her.

'It's a matter of principal,' Sean said to no one in particular. 'Would you like me to come with you?' He asked Laura.

She shook her head. 'No. I'll do this by myself.'

'How will you find her?' Georgie asked.

'Someone around here will have to know.'

She felt Tim touch her arm. 'It's completely unethical for me to tell you this, but her bills go to a post office box in Adelaide. She must still pay the accounts for Meghan and Josh. I won't tell you the address, but I can tell you where to go to watch for her.'

Everyone looked at him.

'That'd be brilliant,' Laura breathed.

❧

As Laura negotiated the city traffic, she practised what she'd say to Glenda when she opened her front door. All the sentences started with 'bitch', but she figured that wasn't the best way to get a positive response. She'd have to keep working on it.

After finding the street she needed, she parked along from the post office and fed enough coins into the metre to cover four hours. Realistically, she knew Glenda may not even collect her mail every day. She might collect it after hours. Laura just had to hope.

Needing a coffee, she quickly crossed the road to a café and ordered a takeaway. She kept looking behind her, fearful she'd miss Glenda. Returning to her ute, she set up watch. While Laura hadn't laid eyes on Meghan's mother in years, she remembered her only too well, and was confident she'd recognise her, unless Glenda had changed dramatically.

People came and went, inserting their keys and grabbing items from the boxes. Smartly dressed businessmen and -women walked quickly to nearby offices; school kids loitered outside the newsagent. The pavement was continually busy. All the activity reminded Laura of ants building their nests before the rains came.

Cars rushed past and occasionally an irate horn sounded. It made her dizzy, but she tried to see every driver as they stopped at the lights, tried to canvas the whole area in case Glenda arrived and she missed her.

By her third coffee in as many hours, Laura was getting jumpy, and was beginning to regret her decision not to bring someone with her. Then a silver Mercedes glided to a stop at the traffic lights. She watched as the driver flicked on the indicator, pulled into an empty five-minute parking spot and climbed out.

Laura recognised the casually stylish woman immediately. Glenda walked to the mailboxes, took out her letters then returned to her Merc.

Laura's heart was pounding as she started her car and waited for the woman to drive off. Once she did, tailing her was difficult. Laura hadn't really thought it through, assuming that following a car was as easy as it looked in the movies. She found out very quickly that it wasn't. Once, when the Merc ran an orange light, Laura thumped the steering wheel, certain she'd lost her. She caught up at the next set of traffic lights and, grinning, yelled a loud, 'Yes!'

The traffic had thinned by the time Glenda made a series of turns through residential streets lined with impressive homes that oozed affluence.

Laura knew she needed an element of surprise, so when Glenda turned into a paved driveway and she saw the garage door open, she kept driving past. She didn't want Glenda to see her at all.

Parking a few streets away, Laura walked quickly back, trying once more to work through her opening lines.

When she arrived at the house, she stopped, intimidated. The place was large. Painted white with black awnings, it radiated status, looking exactly like the sort of abode rich people *should* have. Momentary fear was quickly overtaken by anger.

Walking up the driveway, she pressed the bell and waited. Within moments, she heard the clicking of heels on tiles.

The door opened. The two women stared at each other for a moment. Glenda's mouth fell open in shock. She began to close the door.

Without thinking, Laura put her arm up to stop the door closing and pushed forward. 'Hello, Mrs Hunter,' she said. 'I was in the neighbourhood and wanted to say hi.'

'You shouldn't be here, Laura,' Glenda said stiffly.

'Maybe. But I needed to ask you some questions. And it's very hot out here. Do you think I could come in and have a glass of water?'

The indecision on the woman's face was almost laughable, but Laura was confident Glenda's good manners would prevail. They had every other time Laura had had anything to do with her—it seemed an instinct as strong as breathing for Meghan's mother.

'Of course,' Glenda answered with trepidation. She waved Laura into a lounge room and towards a white leather lounge. 'I won't be a moment. I'll get you that drink.'

As Glenda's heels clicked down the hallway, Laura looked around. One of the walls was covered with photos. Some were old black and white prints; others were more contemporary. She saw one of Josh and Meghan at school. Meghan's hair was up in a ponytail and Josh's was parted and swept to the side.

She stepped up to the wall to study the photos more closely.

At one end was a black and white one of two teenage girls and their parents. Looking more closely, Laura felt sure that one of the girls was Glenda. She turned her attention to the man. His face was deeply lined and saggy, as if life had beaten him down many times. Could it be Thomas? Surely not, she told herself. He'd died in the war. She studied the photo again. Could there be a resemblance to the boy in the photo she'd found in Howie's office, she wondered.

To find out, she needed to get the picture back to Nambina to show her father, but she couldn't just take it off the wall, she realised. It would leave a gaping hole and Glenda would notice immediately. Beginning to panic she glanced around, wondering if there was something she could replace it with.

Her mobile phone vibrated with a text message and she pulled it out. It was from Tim asking how she was getting on. Of course! Hearing Glenda's footsteps approaching, she quickly tapped on the camera icon and snapped a couple of shots of the photo.

She was putting the phone back in her pocket when Glenda walked through the door. 'Thank you,' Laura said, accepting the water. She took a sip, playing for time and wondering what to say next.

'I don't think I can help you in any way, Laura,' Glenda said coldly.

'You know what Meghan's up to?'

Glenda nodded reluctantly. 'I'd appreciate it if you would leave.'

'Is your maiden name Murphy?' Laura stared hard at the woman and saw something flicker in her eyes. Disdain? She couldn't be sure.

'Oh, yes, Laura. That is definitely my maiden name.' The words hung in the air before Glenda indicated the front door.

'What was your father's name?'

'I don't have to answer any of your questions. I'd like you to leave.'

Glenda's attitude confirmed Laura's suspicion that the woman had information worth having. 'I'm not going down without a fight,' Laura told her. 'Meghan will regret taking me on, I can promise you.' She put the glass down and walked towards the door.

'Is that a *threat*? Are you threatening me or my daughter? Because if you are . . .'

Laura interrupted her. 'No, Mrs Hunter, it's not a threat. It's just how it is. A fact. Thank you for the water.'

The door banged behind her. Laura walked back to her car, looking over her shoulder every so often to see whether Glenda had followed her. She breathed a sigh of relief when she climbed inside the ute and locked it.

Her heart was still racing as she pulled out her phone and checked the snaps she'd taken. Looking at the photo again, she was certain one of the girls was Glenda as a youngster. But as for the man? If it wasn't Thomas, who was it?

☙

The house was in darkness when she arrived home. She went to bed but couldn't stop thinking about her encounter with Glenda Hunter. Too wired to settle down, she gave up and flicked on the bedside lamp. Grabbing her mobile phone, she studied the photo again. But nothing jumped out at her. Sighing, she rolled onto her back and stared at the ceiling.

Finally she got up and went out to the kitchen. She switched on the kettle for a cup of tea. While she was waiting for the water to boil, she picked up one of Howie's old show schedules. It was dated 1952. She flicked through it.

On the fifth page she saw it. Howie had circled the words in red. 'Judge: T.G. Murphy.'

Chapter 36

1952

Thomas sat and leaned back against the warm tin of the shearing shed. He turned his face towards the dying sun and breathed deeply. In his mind he could hear the tin ripping and the static calls over the radio. He could feel the fear from that day eight years earlier. But that was all he could remember. No matter how hard he tried, his memory of those few days after the crash were gone.

'Daddy! Daddy!'

Thomas dragged his eyes open, irritated.

A little girl ran from the stables towards him, a pannikin in her hand. She held out the cup.

He looked at it blankly. 'What about it?' he asked.

'I milked a cow!'

Her smile was as wide as the cow's arse, Thomas thought, but it didn't touch his heart. He knew it should, but it just didn't. 'Good on ya.'

The smile faded and the little girl cocked her head to one

side. 'Drink, Daddy?' She offered the cup again.

'Not now. I'm busy. You run along like a good girl. Your mother will be calling for you.'

'You're sleeping.'

'No, I'm thinking. Now, off you go.' Thomas shut his eyes again.

When he heard her leave, he tried to think about the telegram he'd received two months earlier. To judge the wool classes in Adelaide would be an honour, but could he do it?

Within seconds his mind had returned to the crash. Reliving it every time he shut his eyes made him anxious and angry. It made him never want to close his eyes again. But shutting his eyes locked out the sight of his own decay. He was damned if he did and damned if he didn't.

Some days he found it hard to believe he'd been shot down. Despite all his training and quick rise through the ranks, his Spitfire had been caught over the English Channel. His attention had wandered for just a second and, from nowhere, a dark shape had appeared under the belly of the plane. A German Focke-Wulf; it banked and fired.

The call over the radio had come a fraction too late. 'Tally-ho! Bandits on the approach,' another pilot in his squad had yelled. Thomas had felt the impact before he had time to locate the enemy. He remembered struggling to get the plane under control—he'd only been winged. He'd turned the aircraft around and checked left, then right. He saw another plane from his own squadron sweeping beneath him, and seconds later the black smoke of the German plane as it trailed into the sea.

Thomas remembered glancing down and seeing a ship on the brilliant sapphire water. The sun caught the waves, throwing sparkles of diamonds into the air, almost blinding him. It was a rare English summer day, when everything looked and felt beautiful. And up in the freedom of the sky, it was easy to forget you were in a war zone. Easy to forget until Thomas looked below again and realised the ship didn't look right. As he'd taken another swoop around, he'd seen the ship's bow was too low in the water. Bodies floated in the water, some still struggling.

He'd directed his eyes skyward, into the abyss of blue, and had tried not to think. The plane shuddered again—he'd been hit.

Something had snapped inside him. He could end it all now, and no one would know how he'd done it. Just another casualty of war.

He turned the rudder and flown downwards. He wished he'd been taken ages ago. Thomas understood in that moment that Ernest had been right about one thing and wrong about another. Thomas was weak, all right, but not like his mother. He was weak like *Ernest*, and that was why he *wanted* to die. He'd been drinking too much, fighting with people. Angry. It had to stop and this was the way he'd do it.

As the water grew nearer, Thomas had patted his pocket, which contained Elizabeth's last letter. She was to be married. Thomas increased the throttle. And Mac? Oh, that's right. Mac wasn't there anymore, either. He'd let them both down.

'Murphy! *Murphy!*' The crackling radio had broken through Thomas's reverie just as the window shattered. His blood spattered the window. Another hit.

He'd flicked his radio to transmit and said one word: 'Ejecting.'

The last thing Thomas remembered was floating through the air momentarily before the iciness of the water and the relief it was all over. Then again, if he'd been truly determined to die he would have stayed in the cockpit as the plane sank.

He opened his eyes. The sun had disappeared. *See?* He tortured himself. *Even when you decide to not think about it, you still do. You're hopeless.*

He stood and stretched. He felt the familiar ache in his leg from when it had caught in the parachute. He rubbed at it and started down the track towards the house. Elsa would have tea cooked.

Being sent back to Australia had done nothing to help his state of mind. Once again, he'd failed. There was nothing to come back to, either. Elizabeth was married now, so their friendship and letters had stopped. Thomas had felt her loss keenly. Other than Mac, she'd been his only friend. And Mac? Thomas felt his heart ache as he trudged towards the house. He would need extra rum tonight. Extra rum to take all the pain away. Extra rum to hide the hurt and make him forget.

If he was lucky, Elsa would let him have his way with her, once the girls were asleep. Between sex and the rum he'd slip into oblivion, remembering and feeling nothing.

He pulled open the flimsy screen door then let it slam behind him. The girls were sitting in an iron tub. Elsa was pouring tepid water into it.

The faces of Leanne and her sister, Glenda, lit up as he walked into the room. 'Daddy!' they shouted in unison.

Thomas narrowed his eyes. If only they knew. If only they knew. Disregarding them but for a curt nod, he poured himself

337

a drink. He ignored Elsa's wary look. He was just like Ernest now, but he would never hit the girls. He stomped out to sit on the verandah.

'I've cooked a rabbit stew for tonight.' Elsa appeared in the doorway. 'Do you want it now?'

'No.'

She left him alone. He'd been lucky, he supposed, when he'd met Elsa three years earlier. He'd been on the train from Sydney to Melbourne, headed to Portland, even though his grandparents had both passed on and the farm had been sold. He didn't really understand why he wanted to go there, but something had pulled him in that direction. He'd inherited some money from the sale of the property. Maybe he just wanted to see what the place looked like now it had a new owner.

Elsa had been sitting opposite Thomas on the train. They'd nodded at each other but made no conversation for the first few hours. When she took out her sandwiches, he'd glanced over and wished he'd remembered to pack some food. She'd seen his look and offered him half of hers.

'Thank you,' he said.

'Have you been overseas fighting?' she'd asked, gesturing towards the strapping on his leg.

He nodded and bit into the bread and mutton.

'Where are you headed?'

'Portland. I have family there. You?' He wasn't sure why he'd lied to her. Maybe he hadn't wanted to seem needy. Alone.

'I'm going to Melbourne,' she answered. They had talked a lot after that and she'd told him of her family and how they had a little farm on the outskirts of Dubbo. And now, at the tender age of twenty-two, she was a widow.

They'd promised to keep in touch. And while still on the train, Thomas had formulated a plan. He didn't end up going to Portland. Instead, he caught another train to Adelaide and then ventured further north to a little town called Mount Bryan. He'd been there once with Mac and knew it was a renowned sheep-growing area.

Soon he'd bought a parcel of land not far from town, using his small inheritance and a returned soldier's subsidy he'd received. Then he wrote to Elsa, asking her to join him. A month later, she arrived.

At first, he'd built up his sheep numbers, but the memories of his childhood and the war never left him, and he found himself turning to the bottle more and more. The nights he spent at the local pub were punctuated by fights and more grog, and the sheep and the work took a back seat. Thomas wasn't interested in anything but numbing his feelings of inadequacy and anger.

As time went on, Elsa had withdrawn. If he was honest with himself, he couldn't blame her. He hadn't turned out to be the husband she was expecting and she hadn't had the sort of life he'd promised her.

Thomas didn't know whether Elsa knew of the women who offered services behind the pub's back wall, but they were women who didn't mind how rough he was with them. He liked rough. It made him feel powerful and dominant. How a man was supposed to be.

Now he looked out across his land. The full moon cast a pearly glow. The whiteness of the tree trunks stood out in the faint light and he could see a mob of sheep grazing towards the fence he'd put up two years ago.

He should be proud, he told himself. Proud he'd got his own parcel of land. Proud he'd started his own merino stud, and lived up to Mac's expectations.

Ah, there was Mac again.

Mac's disappointment had been obvious when Thomas told him of his decision to go and fight.

'I told you. It's not a job for you, Thomas.'

'I gotta go, Mac. There's nothing for me here.'

'Nothing for you . . .? What?' Mac had been incredulous. 'What have I been training you for? You've got your wool classer's stencil now. You can class, be your own boss. How can you say there's nothing here for you?' The bewilderment on Mac's face had registered with Thomas but he hadn't known what to say. Hadn't known how to thank him for everything and make him understand that he had to go. It was the only way to save himself from becoming his father.

Mac had walked away without saying goodbye.

Now Thomas felt in his pocket for Elizabeth's last letter. He carried it in his notebook and kept it with him to remind him of his loss. Of his mistakes. He took it out, and just looked at it, not wanting to open it; the paper was so fragile. He knew its contents by heart so he didn't need to read the words, blurred by the cold water of the English Channel.

My dear Thomas,

This letter contains both sad and joyful news. I hope you will bear with me while I give you the good news first.

I am to be married in four months. Glen is a lovely man

who Father introduced me to at the last show dinner. He is steady and practical, with a love of sheep. We are building a small hut on the station and will live there after we're married. It's certainly a time of great excitement and anticipation.

It's with a heavy heart, however, that I write to tell you of the death of Mr McDougall. Your friend and mentor, Mac. Father told me he contracted tuberculosis last autumn and didn't see the end of winter. He is buried in Adelaide.

And now, dear Thomas, this must end. Our friendship and letters. I'm sure you understand it would be inappropriate to keep up this correspondence once I am married.

With every best wish I can muster,

Elizabeth

There it was. In one fell swoop, everything Thomas had held dear had been snatched away.

He looked out across the moonlit paddocks again and folded the page. Then he drank deeply. He felt the urge to hurt something. He went inside. The girls were asleep.

Elsa was by the stove, darning a sock. She glanced up as he entered the room. He strode across the wooden floor and grabbed her by the arms, pulling her to him. He sucked at her neck and let his hands bite into her buttocks. He ignored her struggles—he knew she wouldn't scream or cry out for fear of waking the girls. Forcefully, he pushed her to the floor and tore at her clothes. As she struggled to get away, he felt himself harden. Seconds later she stopped resisting him and went limp. Thomas slapped her face.

'Come on, darlin',' he whispered harshly in her ear. 'Fight me. You know you want to.' He grazed his teeth over her now bare nipple and yanked at it roughly. He narrowed his eyes as he felt her stiffen. She would be biting her lip to keep from crying out, he knew.

'You bastard,' Elsa snarled in a low voice. 'I hate you. I *hate* you.'

Thomas barely heard the words because he had entered her and had forgotten everything else.

Chapter 37

2008

Laura had stared at the show schedule for a long time. She'd tried to tell herself that the T.G. Murphy listed as a judge in the schedule could be someone else, another Murphy who just happened to have the same initials. She *wished* this was the case. But it seemed a long shot, and Laura found herself repeating Tim's line: 'I don't believe in coincidences.' And why would Howie circle the name?

She'd thought the postcard had confirmed that Thomas died in the war and therefore hadn't fathered any children. But now it appeared that the information contained in the postcard could be wrong. If Thomas was alive and judging at the Adelaide show in 1952, it suggested he'd survived the war, and may well have married and had a family.

At first light Laura tried to ring Tim, but he didn't pick up so she had to wait until Sean woke up before she could tell anyone about these revelations.

After giving it some thought, Sean agreed that the judge

could well be from a different Murphy family—after all, those initials could stand for any number of names. But Laura wasn't convinced, and there was no doubt that Georgie and Sean were as shocked by the discovery as she was. And when she finally told Tim he couldn't disguise the concern in his voice.

However, after a morning in the paddock her view had changed completely. Now she barged into the kitchen, calling for Sean.

'Dad? Are you here? Dad?'

Poppy came out of the office. 'They've gone to town to get food,' she said. 'You've got nothing to eat here.'

'Damn!' Laura stormed past her sister in the direction of the office. Poppy followed. 'Where's Tim?' she demanded.

'He hasn't got here yet.'

She threw herself onto the chair and slammed her hands onto the desk.

'What's wrong?' Poppy asked tentatively.

'I don't know what I'm doing,' Laura said, raising her hands in frustration. 'All I seem to be doing is *proving* that Meghan is related to us, and how the hell is that going to help my cause? It's stupid.'

Poppy, hesitating in the doorway, didn't say anything.

'The lawyers must have some type of evidence that we're related or they wouldn't have sent that letter. Surely they wouldn't just fire off something like that on a whim.'

So what if the photo on Glenda's wall proved that Thomas was Glenda's father? It simply put her in a weaker position.

She peered up at Poppy, who looked uncertain. Then Laura caught sight of the computer screen. A Facebook page was open there.

'What are you doing?' she asked.

Poppy shrugged. 'Just checking Facebook.'

'Oh. How did you go with the family tree stuff?'

'Not too bad. I've worked out how to use the site, but it doesn't help unless you've got the information to put in or someone else has done a family tree and you can draw on their info.'

'Why are you helping, Poppy?' Laura asked suddenly. 'You don't like me.'

The girl was silent.

Laura looked back at the computer and her eyes focused on an image in her sister's timeline. She leant closer, squinting.

'Who's that?' she pointed to a man with his arm around Poppy. Just for a moment she'd thought she recognised him.

'A friend.' Poppy came forward and moved around the desk. With a click of the mouse the screen vanished.

Laura let it go.

'Hello?' Tim's voice echoed through the house.

'In the office!' Laura called. Pleased he'd arrived, she got up and went to meet him. She hadn't seen or talked to him since she'd got back from Adelaide.

'Come on, let's go for a drive,' she said and walked out past him. 'I need to talk. And I've got to get outside.'

'You've just come inside,' Poppy muttered as Tim dutifully followed her.

'How'd you go in the city?' he asked as he drove towards the middle of the farm. Nearby was an outcrop of rocks with large gum trees where Laura did her best thinking.

'All I've done is prove they're related to me. What a stupid thing to do!' Her anger hadn't diminished.

Tim frowned. 'How d'you mean?'

'Glenda had this up on the wall.' She took out her phone and held up the photo. 'I'm sure that's her.' Laura jabbed a finger at one of the girls. 'This one must be a sister. But the man—I don't know if it's Thomas or not. He hasn't aged very well. If it's him.' She barely drew breath. 'And this photo proves what I found out last night. Thomas was alive in 1952, because he was judging at the Royal Show.' She crossed her arms angrily, not knowing which way to turn.

Still driving, Tim glanced sidewards at the image on the tiny screen. 'Reckon you should put that onto the computer and blow it up a bit so we can see it better.'

'But it's not really going to help, don't you see?'

He parked under the cluster of trees and reached for the phone and looked again. He handed it back.

'You know what I think, Laura?' He got out of the car, walked around to her side, opened the door and pulled her out. Then he kissed her and held her to him.

'What do you think?' she asked.

'I think you've got to know what you're fighting. That's why you need to know if or how you're related. Be it through Thomas, or some other means, you need to know. If you gather all the info and go to a lawyer with it, it will decrease his fees and he can advise. That's why you need to keep doing this. You asked that first night, who is Meghan Hunter? Well, you've got to find out.'

Laura tipped her head back and looked at him. 'When did you get to be so wise?'

'I was born that way.'

He led her over to a shady tree and they sat down under it. Laura relished being outside in the fresh air.

'And by the way, you're not fighting me, so stop being so cranky.'

'My brain feels like it's stuffed with cotton wool,' she complained. 'I can't think straight.' She closed her eyes and enjoyed the sensation of Tim's strong arm around her. 'Smells like hay.'

'It's a beautiful day,' he agreed.

They sat listening to the sounds of the farm. Birds singing, the rustle of leaves in the breeze, a soft buzz—of flies, not bees, Laura thought.

She sat bolt upright. 'That's who it is,' she said, turning to Tim.

'What?'

'The bloke in the photo with Poppy! It's the same guy.'

Tim picked a piece of grass and chewed on it. 'I'm lost. You'd better explain.'

'When I went into the office, Poppy was checking her Facebook page. There was a photo of her with a man. I *knew* he looked familiar but I couldn't place him.' She slapped her thigh. 'I just figured it out: it's the same guy as the one in that filthy photo Allie had on her iPod. The sex party one. Bloody hell, how . . .?'

Laura broke off, understanding what it meant. 'She looks like Allie did, Tim. I told Dad and he agreed there was a problem. Bloody drugs. How do people get mixed up with them?' She reached for his hand. 'We've got to stop her. Help her.'

'It's the skin and dull eyes,' Tim said. 'I wonder . . .' He paused and looked at her. 'How's this for an idea? We see if we can get a copy of that photo from the police and leave it lying

347

around for her to see. If she's working in your office you can leave it on the screen or something. It might give her pause. Just make sure your father doesn't see it.'

Laura nodded. 'That's a good idea, but would they do that? I'm not sure they would. Far out, what else could go wrong?'

'Nothing else. You've got enough to handle at the moment. But how about I make you forget it all for the time being?' He leaned forward and kissed her again.

❧

'Dad, I need to have a chat. Can we go somewhere private?' Laura spoke in a low tone, glancing around to make sure Georgie and Poppy were out of earshot.

Sean nodded. 'How about we talk in Howie's office?'

Laura followed her father down the hall. She needed to talk to him about Poppy. And there was something else, something that had been in the back of her mind since she'd received the letter from Meghan's lawyers.

Once inside the office and with the door closed, Laura took a deep breath and jumped straight in. 'There are two things I need to talk to you about.'

'Sure.'

'Okay, first one.' She recounted the conversation she'd had with Tim earlier, about whether proving Meghan was a relative would be to their detriment or their advantage. 'Tim thinks it's to our advantage to know who and what we're fighting,' she said.

Sean nodded. 'I agree with Tim.'

'But on top of that, I've been thinking. Papa asked us to look after any of Thomas's descendants, didn't he? As much as it hurts, we probably shouldn't be fighting at all. We should just cop it on the chin.'

Sean shut his eyes for a moment. Laura knew the look on his face—he was thinking hard.

'I hear what you're saying, Laurs. And yes, you're right. But we still need to ascertain that they *are* family before we hand anything over. So what we're doing is the right thing. And Tim is spot on about needing to know what we're fighting. I'm sorry, Laurs, but I'm not just going to believe some lawyer who writes a letter. I wouldn't have thought you would, either.'

'Yeah, I understand that. But Dad, if they are family, and I think they might be, we're going to have to give them something. That's what Papa wanted and we can't go against his wishes. Even if he's not here. He gave us so much.'

'The Hunters have plenty,' Sean answered, the disgust plain in his tone. 'They don't need what we have, even if they are our relations. Stand up for yourself, Laura. I don't understand where this is coming from. It's certainly not what you said the night we arrived. You swore to fight it.'

Laura took out her mobile phone and showed him the photo. 'This is what I found at Glenda's house and this is why I think we're family.'

Sean stared at the photo for a long time. 'Can we make this bigger?'

'Tim suggested we put it onto the computer, but I'm not sure how. I was going to ask Poppy to help.'

'Let's do that. I want to see it bigger.'

'Okay.' Laura stopped, unsure how to start the next conversation. 'Um, Dad? Speaking of Poppy? I saw a photo on her

Facebook page. Of her with a guy.' She went on to tell Sean exactly what she'd seen and how she knew who it was.

'I don't know who he is, but I reckon he's one hell of an unsavoury character.'

'It's strange that Poppy should know someone that Allie knows.' Sean sounded sceptical.

'But if they're both into drugs and the club scene, and they both know this guy—which obviously they do because there's photographic evidence—maybe he's the common link. After all, Adelaide is pretty small. I don't think it would be that unusual for them all to cross paths. Maybe he's the drug supplier or the one who's got them into it in the first place.'

Laura stopped. She had her own theory, but she couldn't tell her father until she was sure.

Sean wearily rubbed his eyes. 'Let's not worry about that right now. Poppy's here with us and she's safe. Once we've got you sorted, we'll sort her,' he said.

Laura nodded uneasily. 'Okay. I'll go and ask her if she can do something with the photo.'

❦

Poppy transferred the image to Laura's computer in no time. With a few clicks of the mouse, she opened the black and white photo and enlarged it, then printed a couple of copies for good measure. Everyone gathered round to look at it. Georgie was holding the photo of a young Thomas to compare it with.

There was a reflection in the glass, but it didn't affect the quality of the image too badly. The photo seemed to have been taken on a farm. Laura couldn't see any resemblance to Nambina though. The mother looked nervous, as if she really didn't want to be standing still, while the man stared unsmilingly and dead-eyed into the camera. The two girls were the opposite of their parents, their carefree expressions obvious.

'I think I can see some similarities,' Georgie began. 'But, gee, he hasn't aged at all well, has he?'

'War can do that to you,' Sean said. 'He might have seen things no human should. It ages people, turns them to drink, changes their personalities, sometimes.' His voice sounded strange and Laura glanced over at him. He was still staring at the photo. 'Forget him for a moment, though,' Sean continued. 'I'm interested in the others. In fact, I'm sure I know one of those girls.'

They were all looking at him now.

'How?' Poppy asked.

'It's Glenda, Dad,' Laura said impatiently.

'No, Laurs, not her, the other one,' Sean said patiently.

Laura's breathing turned shallow and her heart thumped. Somehow she knew he was about to drop a bombshell. 'What about her?' she asked.

Sean looked across at Laura. 'I think it's Lee,' he said. 'Your mother.'

Chapter 38

2008

Laura couldn't take it all in. She was staring at a photo of her mother?

Georgie gasped. 'That's too weird,' she said.

Tim reached over and grabbed Laura's hand while Poppy silently gazed up at her father.

Sean was still staring at the image.

Laura finally managed to speak. 'Are you sure?'

Sean's answer was almost inaudible. 'Yes.'

'And the other girl in the photo is definitely Glenda?' Georgie had to be sure.

Laura answered this one. 'Yeah, it is.'

There was silence as they considered this latest revelation.

'And we have a mum we don't know anything about and a dad who is potentially Thomas?' Tim's usually calm voice had taken on a high pitch.

Still the shell-shocked family didn't move.

'Who am I?' Laura muttered finally.

Poppy suddenly bent over the keyboard and took charge. 'We need to find her. This Lee,' she said. 'What was her last name, Dad? I'll see if she's on Facebook or Twitter.'

She hit a few keys, typed in 'Lee' then looked at her dad for the rest of the information.

Sean's face had lost all colour. He blinked at Poppy as if seeing her for the first time. 'I, ah . . .' Georgie went to stand beside him. She put her arms around his waist and he grabbed on to her like he was hanging on for dear life.

'Dad?' Poppy's voice was a mixture of fear and no-nonsense. 'Dad, what was her name?'

'Creedon,' he answered finally.

'So not Murphy?' Laura was even more confused.

'No. She wasn't a Murphy. She was Lee Creedon.'

As quickly as he spoke, Poppy typed it in. There were only three hits for Australia and as she clicked her way through the names, Sean shook his head to all the photos. The other twenty-four were overseas profiles and Poppy skimmed through these ones cursorily. 'I doubt that Lee is overseas,' Sean said with certainty. 'When we split up, she was content to bum around the Queensland beaches. It's unlikely she's changed.'

'Everybody changes,' Georgie said. 'You just said as much.'

Sean shook his head. 'I don't think Lee will have, not to that extent. She was like a kid when I first met her and she had no intention of ever growing up. She's probably become a hippy or something.'

'Let's try Google,' Poppy said. 'That's so weird,' she muttered to herself as she clicked on different links and read through the newspaper articles she found. 'A name like Lee Creedon should be fairly common, but there are hardly any hits.'

'Try a different spelling,' Tim suggested.

'Or Leanne,' Laura said. 'There's lots of different takes on Lee.'

'You're right. Lee with an "a" on the end instead of an "e". So L-E-A,' Poppy said.

But those two combinations didn't produce any hits on Facebook either.

'If she's a hippy type,' Georgie said slowly, 'maybe she doesn't use her name. Did she ever call herself Rainbow or something ridiculous?'

Laura saw a spark of memory on Sean's face. 'Try L'creed.'

They all watched the screen. There was one hit.

Poppy took a breath and clicked on the name. The profile downloaded.

'It's not a normal page,' Poppy said after a quick look through. 'It's a fan page.'

'There's a difference?' Laura asked.

'Yeah, with a fan page you're not actually friends with anyone, people have to "like" your page to see your posts. Lots of bands and famous people have them.'

'That's her.' Sean's voice echoed through the room.

'How do you know?' Georgie asked. 'There isn't a photo.'

'I don't know. I just do.'

'Okay, let's see where she's living and what's she's up to,' Poppy said. 'Hopefully her security settings aren't too high.' She scanned the information and Laura leaned forward, looking at the picture of the woman who had given birth to her but not wanted her. Her stomach felt like there were a million butterfly wings inside it.

'Basic Info,' Poppy read. 'Birthday: 31 August, but no year.

Gender: female. Relationship: open relationship. Living: Airlie Beach, Queensland. No mobile number or landline.' She looked up at them all. 'There is a Skype link.'

Nobody moved.

'Have a look through her timeline,' Tim instructed.

Poppy scrolled down. The page was full of inspirational quotes and optimistic affirmations layered over beautiful photos. Not once did a photo of Lee appear.

'Definitely her,' Sean confirmed. 'She loved that sort of thing. I need to think about this.' Sean disentangled himself from Georgie and left the room.

'Well, I don't,' said Laura. 'One thing I do know how to do is Skype. Can you send her a request, Poppy? I'm going to call her.'

'You don't need to send her a request. Look here, she must take calls from anyone. "Call for positive reinforcement. No video, just voice."'

'Well, call,' Laura urged.

'Are you sure?' Poppy hesitated.

'Laura, you don't want to think about this a little more?' Georgie asked in a soft voice.

Laura shook her head. 'No. Call.' She turned to Tim, who was watching her with concern. 'What?'

'You can't go back, Laurs. Once you've made contact, you just can't.'

'But she'll be able to answer all our questions.'

'She might not want to talk to you.'

Laura stopped and squared her shoulders. 'Well, we won't know until we try. Come on, Poppy.'

Poppy clicked on the call icon and they heard the Skype ringtone.

Laura motioned for Poppy to get off the chair and took her spot. She stared intently at the screen as the others slipped quietly out of the room.

'Hello?' The voice was low and husky.

Laura found she was stuck for words. 'Ah . . .'

'How can I help? Would you like some positiveness in your day?' the woman prompted. 'Are you sad or fearful? I can help relax you with wonderful words.'

'Lee? It's, um, your daughter. Laura.'

There was dead silence and, for a moment, Laura wondered whether the call had been disconnected. Suddenly a video box appeared in the bottom corner of the screen. It showed a woman with a headscarf around her head and beautiful, glowing skin. A cat was sitting on a desk to the woman's right; to her left could be seen the soft light of a candle.

'Can you turn on your video, so I can see you?' Lee asked.

Laura fumbled with the mouse and finally managed to click on the camera icon.

They stared at each other but didn't speak.

Lee reached out. Her fingers bumped the screen and it wobbled. 'How did you find me?' she asked.

'Dad found you.'

'You're beautiful. Everything I imagined you'd be.'

Laura felt self-conscious. 'Thank you. You're nothing like I imagined.' She tried to smile to soften her words.

'How did you imagine me?'

'I don't know, really. I never really thought about you much until recently, and even then I didn't have a picture in my mind. You were a sort of shadowy figure from my dreams that I couldn't pinpoint.'

'Now you know.' Lee leaned back in her chair. The cat jumped onto her lap and Laura fought the urge to reach out and try to pat it. 'I've wanted to get in touch with you, Laura. But I didn't know how you'd receive me. I did a pretty terrible thing when I left you with your father. What sort of mother leaves her child?' She ran her hand over her face. 'I've wanted to apologise, to explain, but something always held me back. And now here you are. Tell me about you. What do you do? Where are you?'

Laura felt the sting of tears and she tried to smile. 'I had a wonderful childhood. Dad was brilliant and so was Papa. I don't regret anything about my upbringing, so please don't worry.' She went on to tell Lee about her life and Nambina. The school she ran, and Tim. She was surprised at how comfortable she was with this woman. How easily the words flowed.

'What about you?' Laura asked finally.

'Not much to tell, really. I live in a caravan. I walk on the beach every day and spend hours looking for quotes on the internet. I've had breast cancer, you see. I'm in remission now, but I know the reason I survived was through positive thinking. There are so many sad people out there and if I give them something encouraging to hang on to, I've done a good thing. I help someone who needs it and, in a way, I help myself.' She smiled. 'I get many, many calls a day, often the same people ringing back. I love having the contact and making a difference, but very much at arm's length. I'm a solitary creature. I like my own company. Except for you, Bonkers.' She scratched the cat's ears.

'Lee, I actually got in contact for a reason. I'm wondering if you can help me.'

Lee looked back at the screen. 'I can try.'

Laura held up the print of the photo. 'Do you know any of these people?'

Lee looked through the video camera and frowned. 'None of them have rated a mention in maybe thirty years. Why do you want to know?'

'My neighbour, Meghan, is Glenda's daughter and they've put in a legal claim on Nambina. They want to take it away from me. They're saying they're related to us.'

Lee didn't say anything.

'Who are these people?'

'Look, Laura. I need to think about this, okay? I've loved talking to you, catching up on your life. But this is opening up a whole other can of worms for me. Things I've made myself forget. That I never wanted to remember. I'm going to need a bit of time before I talk to you about this.' There were tears in her eyes.

For a second Laura felt terrible. 'I'm so sorry, Lee. I didn't think about how it may affect you. All I could think of was how it was affecting me and that I needed an answer.'

Once the words were out, her frustration returned. This woman held the answers. Lee could dash Laura's hopes and break her dreams, or she could stop what was happening. Why couldn't Lee answer her questions now? She tried to pull herself together, then heard Lee say something.

'Sorry?'

'I'll Skype you back.'

'Soon?'

'Soon,' Lee confirmed. 'Give me a week to get myself together so I can talk to you about this.'

358

'Well . . .' Laura broke off. What a whirlwind the last couple of hours had been. Another couple of hours or days wouldn't hurt, she told herself. *But there's not much time*, another little voice reminded her.

'So it's goodbye for now, but not for long.' Lee wasn't going to change her mind. She tried to smile but Laura could see the photo had shaken her deeply. 'Remember me to your father. He's a good man.' With that, Lee disappeared from the screen.

Laura tried to think, tried to make sense of what had just happened. But it was so monumental she was overwhelmed. She needed space and air. And a bloody big paddock.

She got up from the desk and went out into the kitchen where everyone was waiting for her. Nobody said anything; they just looked at her expectantly.

'She's going to ring back in a week,' Laura said with no emotion. 'We just have to wait.'

The atmosphere in the room relaxed a little.

'How,' Sean cleared his throat. 'How was she?'

Laura looked at him for a moment. 'She's had breast cancer. That's why she's doing this positive thinking thing.'

'Sounds exactly like something she'd do.'

'She said to be remembered to you.'

Sean nodded and looked over at Georgie. He reached for her hand and squeezed her fingers.

'I'm going for a drive,' she said.

'Want company?' Tim asked.

She smiled. 'If you like.'

⁓

Once she was out in the paddock, Laura felt like she could breathe again. But with so much information to take in, so much emotion and so much shit being dragged up, her head was spinning. The letter had arrived only a week ago, and yet so much had changed, especially her! She was questioning who she was and why she was here.

Tim stopped the ute under their favourite tree and they got out. Rip bounded ahead of them. He stopped and peered into the grass before barking.

'No, Rip!' Tim shouted urgently.

Rip came running back and Tim went over to where he'd been sniffing the ground.

'Sleepy lizard,' he called, sounding relieved.

Laura crinkled her brow. 'What did you think it was?'

'Could have been a snake. There have been five bites since my locum has been at the practice,' he answered.

Laura felt a shiver of anxiety. 'I didn't even think.'

'I don't think we need a sick dog on our plate as well.' Tim smiled lopsidedly at her.

'No bloody way.' She stretched and Rip tried to put his paws on her chest, but he was still too small to reach. They landed on her stomach instead, and Laura staggered slightly. She let herself fall into the dry grass.

Rip bounced on her and tried to lick her face.

'Get off,' she said, pushing him away playfully.

Rip quickly found another scent and followed it for a little way. A fly buzzing past his ear distracted him and he snapped at it before flopping in the grass. They watched as he rolled onto his back and scratched it by wiggling from side to side.

'Oh, to have your worries, Rip,' Tim said, sitting down

next to Laura and putting his hand on her stomach. Laura covered it with hers and he leant forward to kiss her. 'You know,' he said. 'I think I love you.'

Laura arched her eyebrows. 'Think?' she said, a sudden happiness flooding through her.

'Know, actually.' He kissed her again, slower this time. Then he gently lay next to her and peppered light kisses down her neck. Laura closed her eyes, concentrating on nothing but how good it felt.

They both started as a cold nose sniffed one face and then the other.

Tim groaned. 'Good interruption, Rip. You're worse than a kid!'

Despite everything, Laura laughed. 'Mustn't do anything rude in front of the children,' she said.

'I could tie him up.' Tim looked at her hopefully.

'Nah, I've got some things I need to tell you first.'

'Sounds interesting.' He sat up and looked at her.

'Thank you for being here throughout all of this. It's crazy what's going on.'

'I wouldn't be anywhere else,' Tim said. 'I mean that. I love you, Laura, and I want to be here for you.'

'I love you too.' She took a breath. 'And because I do, I need to tell you what happened between Josh and me ten years ago.'

He shrugged. 'I don't need to know, Laura. It was so long ago and I don't care.'

'Maybe not, but I think I know why Meghan is doing this. Just let me tell you, okay?'

'Only if you think you need to.'

She took a deep breath and recounted the story of the day Howie had handed over Nambina to her, and how, only days earlier, she'd found out she was pregnant and had still been reeling from the news. How she'd tried to tell Josh, but every time she opened her mouth, something stopped her. She spoke of Meghan's diagnosis and the way Josh had acted so jealously in the park. With halting words, she told him how she'd been hit by the ewe and the incident at the hospital.

Laura watched as Tim's eyes widened in disgust. 'She spat on you?'

'Well, on the floor, as she was leaving.'

'What the hell? That's a bit over-the-top, wouldn't you say?'

Laura shook her head. 'Probably not for her. She'd just been told she couldn't have kids and she honestly thought I'd just killed one on purpose.'

Laura felt the sun hot on her back. Tim was looking down at the ground.

'So that's it. Meghan assumed I'd had an abortion, either because it was another man's baby or because I was career orientated. And she managed to convince Josh of the same thing. Papa did eventually clear it up with them but, as far as I was concerned, the damage had been done. I don't remember a lot about the hospital, but Papa told me later the doctor said that, because the baby hadn't actually miscarried, it was unlikely it'd come out by itself. That's why they did a D and C. They had to clean the uterus properly.'

Tim reached for her hand.

'Hang on,' she said. 'I haven't finished yet. It's about Josh. He's jealous, you know?'

'Of what? Us? We've only just got it together.'

362

'We know that, but he doesn't. His first contact with me in eight years was on the night of the Baggy and Saggy ball. It's the only thing I can think of to explain his strange behaviour.'

'Why, what's he been doing?' Tim asked, straightening up, his face tight.

'He keeps coming around. Saying he wants to talk, to work things out. In eight years he never once tried to do that, so it's a bit of a joke he's saying that all of a sudden. But it's only been since he saw me with you.'

'He'd better not visit while I'm here.' Tim's voice rumbled deep in his throat. 'He might get a bit more than he bargained for!'

Laura laughed, and it felt good.

Tim took her hand and squeezed it. 'I love you,' he said again.

Chapter 39

1952

The previous year, Thomas had bought a flatbed truck to cart bales of wool to Adelaide for sale at the wool store. He also used it to pick up all the farming and food supplies from town. Today he was driving the loud, rattling vehicle to Adelaide.

When he first bought the Dodge, he'd been pleased with how high above the ground he was when he sat behind the wheel, and how much of the neighbours' property he could survey as he drove past. The dashboard was modern and he could see how fast he was travelling and the temperature of the engine. It even had a radio. The speaker was attached to the roof behind his ear, so he could hear it clearly above the noise of the engine. But it was the bench seat that had been the deciding factor. So far it had proved hard on his bum during long trips, but it made a firm bed and he liked that. The women he had been with in the Dodge couldn't get away from him.

Now he swung the truck into the main street and continued

on his way to the Adelaide Show. He was pleased he'd agreed to judge such a prestigious event. Thomas knew he'd be well received and looked after, for the invitation had come from the head steward himself, and he'd seen how Mac had been treated when he judged. Thomas remembered John Banks fondly. After all, it had been John's good memory that had resulted in Thomas finding his grandparents. And from there, everything had fallen into place, just like dominos. The money and land he had today had come directly from that happy coincidence. Yes, Thomas decided, John would be happy with what had transpired since he'd seen him last.

He thought, then, of the hours before he left home. He'd gone without so much as a word to Elsa but, in a rare show of affection, he'd hugged the girls and promised them a present on his return. They'd jumped gleefully all over him. As he climbed up into the truck and the girls had waved, Elsa had stood at the door, her face frozen. He knew why he felt so little for them; never once had he wished he could change that.

Three hours later he turned his truck onto Greenhill Road and drove towards the showgrounds. Howard crossed his mind. Did he ever attend the show? Was there a chance he might see him today? Thomas decided he didn't care. Howard very rarely came to mind these days. The visit to Nambina had freed Thomas from the torment of caring for his little brother.

He parked on the edge of the showgrounds and made his way to the merino pavilion. At the door, he stopped and tried to control his breathing, which had become heavy. His heart raced and he craved a drink. 'Too many memories,' he muttered, entering the shed anyway.

The familiar smell of sheep and wool hit him. His anxiety

level rose, but he forced himself onwards. He hadn't expected to react this way. Just another sign of weakness, he thought.

'Can I help you?' A man with a white coat and clipboard appeared and looked him over. Thomas opened his mouth to answer but, quickly giving himself the once-over, he realised with horror that his clothes were shabby, his boots grubby. Mac would be horrified if he could see him now, in more ways than one.

'Clothes maketh the man,' Thomas muttered to himself. He squared his shoulders and looked up. 'I'm Thomas Murphy.' He held out his hand to the man, who shook it gingerly.

'How can I help you?' the man asked.

Thomas was tongue-tied. This wasn't how it had been with Mac. Everyone had known him. Respected him.

'I'm here to, um, judge the wool. The fleeces.' He stumbled on the words, and he felt his face redden. He looked around and fidgeted.

The man consulted his clipboard again.

'Right. I see. You're not required yet. Not until two this afternoon. Could you come back at the allocated time, please?'

Thomas looked around, hoping to spot John Banks.

'Is John Banks here? He's an old friend, and I'd like to see him.'

The man's face changed. 'I'm sorry. You obviously haven't heard. He passed away last week. In his sleep.'

Thomas felt as though he'd been punched. The last link with his old life. Gone. Snuffed out.

'Are you all right?'

'Uh, yes. Fine,' Thomas stuttered. 'I hadn't heard. I'm sorry.'

'He was a ripe old age, so I'm told. He obviously had a good innings. I'm taking his place.'

Thomas wanted to hit the man. It was so easy to hand out off-the-cuff sympathy when you didn't know the person who'd died. He eyed the steward, frustrated.

'I see,' was all he could manage.

'Good. Well, I have things to organise. As I said, we'd appreciate it if you would come back at your allotted judging time. It makes the shed too crowded if people come early.' He nodded to Thomas and walked away.

Glancing at his watch, Thomas saw it was eleven o'clock. There was time for a drink. A rum would definitely hit the spot.

Without another glance, he left the shed and showgrounds and went in search of a pub.

Three hours later, and with more than one rum under his belt, Thomas walked back in with a swagger.

His confidence was up after winning twenty quid in a poker game with a bartender. Thomas hadn't used his shuffling and card skills in many years, but when the man put a deck on the bar, Thomas couldn't resist.

The bartender had won a few rounds until Thomas got on a winning streak. He'd lost track of how many games he'd won and how many drinks he'd had. In the end, he'd had to promise he'd return so the bartender could have a chance at winning back his money.

Now, the man who had greeted Thomas at the pavilion in the morning handed him a clipboard and pen.

'And your name was?' Thomas asked.

'Ken Britton.'

'Ken, I've been around wool longer than you've been alive. Don't you go getting all high 'n' mighty with me, like you did before. I was trained by the best judge this side of the black stump, so I reckon I've earned my place here, no matter how I dress or speak.' He nodded and left the man spluttering an apology.

As soon as Thomas felt the wool between his fingers, he closed his eyes. He was home. He rubbed the fibre, feeling its softness. There was a little grit in this piece, but that was okay. He lifted it to his nose, smelt it, gazed at it.

Why was it, when he was here, that the wool held such a pull for him, he wondered, but when he was at home it just all seemed too hard?

Elsa kept the farmyard and house running well, but it was his job to do the outer paddocks and the stock. His sheep were high quality. Good breeding and great structure. He could make a really successful business if he wanted to. But he didn't want to.

The problem was, he just couldn't move on, he knew. He still felt dissatisfied with his life—he'd been dealt the unkind hand, after all. He'd lost his mother, his father had abused him, his brother had forgotten him. What a great family.

His mind turned to the girls. He knew he was doing the same thing to them as his father had done to him. It was the cycle repeating itself, but he felt powerless to stop it. Or too weak to try. And on top of the hurt he'd suffered as a child were dark memories of the war. Only alcohol made his life bearable.

'Excuse me, Mr Murphy?'

It took Thomas a moment to realise someone was being

spoken to. He glanced around. A pimply-faced youth stood at his shoulder.

'Mr Murphy, I'm here to scribe for you.'

'Are you now?' he asked humourlessly. 'Can't write the numbers down myself, huh?'

The youth looked embarrassed. 'You'd been standing at this exhibit for a little while. I think Mr Britton was worried about you.'

'Well, you tell that half-arsed steward that I'm perfectly capable, thank you.' Thomas lurched forward to the next box and picked up another piece.

Somehow he knew this was how it would be for the rest of his life. Always being judged by others. Staggering, half-drunk, from one memory to the next. Poker games and hard, violent sex.

The more he pondered it, the more he wanted to live like this, because to return to the normal world of living would mean having to confront his past and his problems, and he had no intention of ever doing that.

Yes, Father, he thought, as he scribbled down some comments on the judging card. *I'm the image of you. Just call me Ernest. But I'm actually not, am I, 'Father'? I can't blame you like I have been. Dorothy told me who I really am in her last letter. And all this is because of me.*

He spat on the dusty ground and banged his fist into the display bin in front of him.

Chapter 40

2008

It had been a nail-biting week of long, stressful days and restless nights. Each time they heard the familiar sound of the Skype ringtone, everyone would rush to the computer. But it was always Nicki, calling for an update. Laura hadn't had the heart to tell her sister that, every time she rang, Laura's heart thumped and she began to shake. It underlined exactly how much Nambina meant to her. The fact that her family were standing beside her through it all meant she also now knew how much it meant to them. Even if they didn't want to live here, they weren't going to see the farm torn away. It made her feel incredibly grateful and deeply touched.

Now Sean and Laura were seated in front of the computer with Skype open. Today was the day.

'Ready?' Laura asked.

'Yep.'

Laura bit her lip and checked her watch. It was the prearranged time. There would be no going back.

The video flashed up. There was Lee sitting at her desk. Once again Bonkers was there, this time draped round her shoulders.

Her mother looked more relaxed than the last time they'd spoken.

'Hello.' Lee's husky voice came across the airwaves but as she shifted in her chair, the screen froze.

'Hello,' Laura tried. 'Damn,' she swore. An error message had popped up, saying the connection hadn't been fast enough.

Poppy stuck her head around the corner. 'Okay?'

'Connection isn't worth shit,' Laura said.

'Try without the video. After you establish the link, bring the vid back up again.' She disappeared.

Laura followed her sister's instructions.

'Hello, Lee?' she tried again.

The disembodied voice came through the speakers. 'Hello. There you are. How are you?'

'We're fine,' Laura answered. 'Dad's here with me. I wanted him to hear everything you say.'

There was a short pause. Then Lee greeted Sean.

'Hi, Lee. It's been a long time,' Sean answered.

'It certainly has. What are you doing with yourself?'

Sean gave a quick account of himself. When he'd finished, Laura tried the video again. It worked.

Sean and Lee regarded each other for a moment. 'You're looking good, Lee,' Sean said. 'Sounds like you've had a tough time.'

'Nothing I couldn't handle.' She smiled and shifted her gaze to Laura. 'I enjoyed talking with you last week, Laura,' she said. 'I'm sorry I couldn't discuss my childhood with you when we first talked. I'm sure it made you angry and frustrated.'

Laura gave a small smile of acknowledgement.

'That photo dragged up so many memories for me—things I haven't remembered in years. Events I didn't *want* to remember. That's why I needed time for my head to clear. To be able to talk unemotionally about it with you.'

'I'm sorry you've been dragged into this,' Laura answered.

They stared at each other for a few moments before Lee dropped her gaze. 'Okay,' she said. 'Okay.' She took a deep breath. 'I grew up on a farm in South Australia. Near a little town called Mount Bryan. Nothing there but a pub and a couple of houses. Apparently, Father managed to get a "soldier settlement" block there. He produced fine wool merino sheep, although I think Mum did more of the work than he did. He didn't ever seem to be around much. And I'll be honest, I loved the times when Father wasn't home. Mum was a gentle soul. A hard worker and high achiever, but very placid and kind. She got on with whatever needed to be done. It wasn't until I was older that I realised Mum withdrew whenever Father turned up. He was often drunk and . . .' She stopped and took a shuddery breath. 'He was hideous. There's no other word for it.'

Not wanting to push her, Laura nodded and Sean looked down at his hands. Laura noticed he couldn't keep his fingers still—they were tapping out a silent rhythm on his leg.

'My older sister left to work as a maid for one of the larger stations, further north. Glenda left when I was about nine. That photo you have was when she came home for Christmas once. It was the only time she returned after she left. Mum should have gone when the violence started. But, of course, a marriage breakdown in those days was frowned upon. Women didn't have anywhere to go, or any means.' She broke off and took a sip of water.

Laura felt sad for Lee—the difference between Lee's childhood and her own was stark. She wanted to hug her mother, to tell her she was sorry.

'Thomas's violence escalated as he drank more and as time went on.'

Laura took a sharp breath and felt Sean stiffen beside her. 'That was your father's name? Thomas?' Laura asked.

'I'll get to that. But the short answer is yes.'

Sean and Laura looked at each other and Laura felt herself grow cold.

'I was fourteen when I walked into the shed and found him raping my mother.' Her voice dropped, became very quiet. 'At the time, I didn't know what he was doing. Mum saw me over his shoulder. Somehow I knew, I just knew, I couldn't let him see me. Something in her face told me it wasn't right, so I ran. Mum explained to me afterwards it was just what he did, that she put up with it. He gave her a home when she didn't have one and he'd provided for, and never hurt, her daughters.

'That same day he left to drive to Adelaide as he did once a month. I don't know what he did down there, but my guess is he used to gamble. He never came home. I remember it clearly. He'd promised us a present when he came back. That was unusual. I can still see him climbing into the truck he had, driving down the track and Mum becoming herself again. That night we had a special dinner. We laughed at funny things we'd seen out in the paddocks that week and talked about Mum's vision for the new drop of rams—she knew so much about farming, but Father never asked her opinion or let her help when he was home. It was one of the most pleasant evenings I can remember at that place. At some point during that evening, while we were talking and laughing, Father was stabbed in a brawl. It happened at an illegal gambling den in someone's cellar. It took some time for the police to find us and let us know. The relief I felt was immense. I know I shouldn't have felt like that, but the tension and fear he put into us all was horrible. To be honest, we couldn't have asked for a better outcome—please don't be shocked or judge me when I say that. If you haven't lived through it, you can't possibly understand.' Lee took another sip of water and absent-mindedly stroked Bonkers.

Laura could hear the cat purr and wanted to pat him too. She missed Rusty.

'Mum sold the farm but it was in so much debt she didn't come out with anything. She moved back to New South Wales to live with her sisters. As for Glenda . . . well, she and I were so different, we didn't make contact for years. It was really only through Mum's pushing that I went to Mangalow and tried to see Glenda. She was working for a man whose wife had died and, like me, wasn't keen on having anything to do with the past. That meant not having anything to do with me or Mum.'

Lee looked at Sean. 'That was when I met you, Sean.'

'Afterwards, I really didn't want to have anything to do with any of them. Oh, I wrote to Mum every so often, but I was desperate to forget that part of my life.' She sighed. 'Selfish, I guess, especially since I didn't suffer the violence, not the way Mum did, but it still affected me. Mum was much better off when she shifted back with her sisters.'

'So,' Sean began slowly, 'Thomas Murphy was your father. How come your surname is Creedon? Did you change it so you wouldn't be found?'

Lee smiled. 'Creedon's my real name. I wouldn't have taken his name for all the Crown Jewels of London. After Mum married him, she decided it would be a good idea to change our names to his, to make him feel like we were his kids, but it never worked. As soon as I was able to, I found out who my real father was and changed my name back. But Glenda never bothered.'

Laura started. 'What?'

'Thomas wasn't my real father. He wasn't Glenda's real father. Our father was Graham Creedon. Mum married Thomas Murphy after we were born. She'd been widowed. We aren't related to either of you.'

Laura blinked. She understood what Lee had just told her, but she suddenly felt removed from everything. Still, if what Lee had told her was true, then everything Meghan was trying to do wasn't possible.

'How . . . Um, why . . .' Helpless, Laura turned to Sean. 'So they can't take Nambina away from us? Why did the lawyers send that letter?'

Sean shook his head. 'I honestly don't know.'

Laura burst out laughing. 'So we're free? There's no come back on us?'

'Actually, Laura, I can give you another piece of news, too,' Lee said before disappearing for a moment. When she returned, she was holding a yellowed page. 'After my mother died, this was found among her things. Glenda didn't want anything so one of my aunts packed up a few of Mum's personal belongings and sent them to me. I'll read it to you, if you like?'

'Sure! Whatever.' Laura couldn't contain her happiness.

'Dear Thomas,' Lee began. 'Please forgive your grandfather and me for not telling you this while you were staying with us. At the time we didn't think it would serve any purpose, but in hindsight, perhaps it might have.

'When your mother's fiancé died, she was devastated. You know the story of how she came to marry Ernest.

'Thomas, have you ever wondered why your second name is George and not Ernest? Usually the first-born son is given the name of his father. And so you were.

'Your father was Jessie's fiancé, George Constable. That horrible excuse for a man, Ernest, isn't your father. I hope this knowledge brings you some peace, for I believe it explains why he treated you the way he did.

'I'm sure you can understand the situation Jessie was in. She didn't tell us she was pregnant. If she had, we would have helped her, but she chose to make her own decisions and her own choices.'

Lee stopped to look up at Laura.

Laura shook her head. It was another bombshell, and all too much.

Lee continued to read. 'My dear Thomas, with your grandfather's passing, I am the only one who knows of this and I had to tell you. I hope it will help you understand your atrocious childhood.

'Be safe and strong and know you are loved. Your grandmother, Dorothy.'

Lee paused for a moment before speaking again. 'You know, I think it made it worse for him.'

'Knowing he wasn't Ernest's son?' Sean frowned.

She nodded. 'Yeah. I would hear him talking when he was drunk. He used to ramble and rant, saying he was just like Ernest now and Ernest had been right. It must have been terrible to discover, not only that the man he'd assumed was his father was not, but that he'd become the mirror image of that man. To go from thinking the violence and drinking was in his genes, to finding out it wasn't, that he'd *chosen* to become that way, well . . .' Lee shrugged. 'That would have been a bitter pill to swallow.'

There was a loud barking. Laura looked out the window. Robyn and Tegan had returned from town.

'Laura, that's why I had to leave you.'

Laura's head whipped back to the screen. 'Sorry?'

Lee chewed at her bottom lip. 'I was scared I might be like him,' she said finally. 'I knew he wasn't my father, but I had grown up in a household that didn't value people. There was abuse, violence and arguments. I have a really bad temper. Really bad. I couldn't risk that for you.'

'Oh.' Laura couldn't think of anything to say.

'You know how they say the abused becomes the abuser? I worried that would be me.'

Sean spoke up. 'You're very strong to be able to say that, Lee. Thank you. It makes a lot more sense now. I never understood why. Put it down to post-natal depression.' He stopped and looked at Laura. 'I can say it means a lot to both of us, knowing that.'

Laura nodded.

Lee sighed. 'Well, I don't know about you, but I think I need to go for a long, long walk. It helps me clear my head.'

'Me too,' Laura said. 'I can't think indoors!'

Sean grinned. 'You girls might be more alike than you think.' He looked hard at Lee. 'I know this has been difficult. But we can't thank you enough. You've given us the missing pieces we needed.'

'You're more than welcome. Thank you for getting in contact.' She turned to Laura. 'I've never stopped thinking about you, you know.'

Then they said their goodbyes, promising to keep in touch.

When Lee had hung up, Sean blew out a sigh. 'Didn't see any of that coming.'

'Me either.'

Poppy stuck her head in. 'Can I use the computer, please? Like, now?'

Laura got to her feet. 'Sure. I'm outta here.'

'I'm going to find Georgie,' said Sean. 'Think I might take her for a drive and explain everything to her.'

'She's a rock, Dad. Just amazing. Love her to bits.'

'Me too,' Sean answered.

✂

Tim was cleaning the barbecue when Laura got back from the shearing shed, where she'd spoken to Robyn and Tegan, inviting them to dinner that evening.

'Hello, you,' she said, swinging her arms around his waist.

'Hello back,' he answered, stopping his scrubbing in order to kiss her.

'You hear all the news?'

'I did. And I think Poppy has some more for you.'

'Let's hope it's a little less dramatic than everything else that's happened today.'

'I think it's the icing on the cake,' he said mysteriously.

Laura went inside. On the kitchen table was a newspaper article that Poppy had printed from the computer.

Laura picked it up and went to find her sister.

'What's this?' she asked, walking into the office.

'It's the answer to why the Hunters' lawyers went off half-cocked,' Poppy said.

Laura began to read. When she'd finished, she punched her fist into the air. 'We got you, you fuckers.' She picked up the phone.

Chapter 41

2008

The dinner table at Nambina was full, and the mood had turned from solemn to celebratory. This time it was Laura who commanded everyone's attention. 'Thank you,' she started. 'Thank you for all being here, for supporting me and Nambina. I know what this land and Papa's legacy mean to us all now. Even you, Poppy.' She gave her sister a cheeky grin. 'I rang the legal firm of Dark & Partners this afternoon and informed them there was no substance to Meghan's claim. I explained this to them in small words.' She grinned.

'After much bluster, they were forced to admit they hadn't done their research properly. In fact, they're apparently being sued for firing off letters and making claims without checking them properly first. Thanks again to Poppy for that piece of information. So we've turned a full circle. Papa has gone, but we're here. Nambina stays in the family.'

A cheer went up.

'Here's to Nambina and the future.' Laura raised her glass.

'Nambina and the future,' everyone repeated.

Rip started to bark and the gathering turned to look out the window. Laura sucked in her breath. Meghan was getting out of her car.

'What the hell?' Tim asked, half-rising. 'Leave her to me.'

'No.' Laura held up her hand. 'She's mine.' She put down her glass and headed out to meet her former friend.

'We need to talk,' were Meghan's first words.

'I have nothing to say to you,' Laura answered.

'Maybe you should just listen. You have to know that, even though my name was used, it wasn't me who put that lawsuit in place.'

'Why would I believe that?' Laura looked hard at Meghan.

'It was Josh.'

Laura didn't move. 'I don't believe you.'

Meghan gave a sharp bark of laughter. 'No, you wouldn't. No one would. Josh is everyone's favourite, isn't he? Everyone thinks I'm a stuck-up bitch who doesn't care for anyone. Well, if people only knew what Josh was . . .'

'Meghan, you're not making any sense.'

'Who do you think supplied Allie with the drugs to put in your ram's feed?'

Laura blinked at the change of subject.

'Who do you think got Allie hooked on drugs and took her to all those parties? She was his eyes and ears here. Into Nambina. To what you were doing. He's obsessed with you, Laura. It started slowly—he took his time accepting what had happened. I mean, you guys were good together, but as the years went by, he didn't change. There was obviously something else going on in his mind. He'd never actually talk about you, he just watched. But since he saw you with Tim at the Baggy and Saggy ball, his slide has been massive. He's managed to hide it from everyone else except us—Mum and me. His room is covered in photos of you from when you were together. And photos he took that you probably didn't even know about. You don't believe me? Look at this.' She pulled a folded page from her back pocket and handed it over. 'His jealousy is abnormal, Laura. If he can't have you, he doesn't want anyone else to. He can't be happy, so you can't. That's why he concocted this idea of trying to take Nambina away from you. He knows it's your life, that this land is everything to you. If you've fallen in love and really begun to move on, he somehow wants to stop you.'

Laura looked at the piece of paper in her hand and slowly unfolded it, irrational fear shooting through her. She recoiled. It was a photo of herself, driving the ute along the boundary fence. Robyn was sitting beside her. The image was so clear and close, Laura could see her own sun-damaged skin. How had he been so near without her seeing him? Him and his bloody camera!

'That doesn't prove it was him,' she said, though the doubt was beginning to filter through. She gave the photo back. She was confused and still desperate for Meghan to be the cause of all this. After all, it was Meghan who'd told the lies, convinced Josh and started the downward spiral for them all.

'I have proof,' Meghan said. 'It's in his bedroom. He's the drug supplier for the whole town. Hell, he supplies me, which is why he's got a hold over me. If I don't want to do something he withholds my speed. That's why I threatened you at the show. He told me to, and I needed a fix.'

Meghan continued, her eyes wild. 'It was easy to hate you,

382

Laura. You had everything I wanted. A good man, a baby due. A family who loved you wholly and completely. You were taking what I wanted away from *me* because you were taking it from *Josh*. I knew I couldn't have kids, but I'd decided I'd make a fantastic aunt. I knew I could live my life through you and Josh. Then, without warning, you were at the hospital. The word was going around you'd had an abortion.' She gave a harsh laugh. 'Good old Mangalow and its gossip mongers. Realistically, I know that couldn't have happened. You have to have counselling and so on to have a procedure like that. But suddenly what I wanted had gone. That's why I convinced Josh. It wasn't hard. He'd always been possessive of you, although I'm not sure you ever saw it.' She sighed. 'You have no idea what it's been like living with him these past years. It's Laura, Laura, Laura. The only thing that gives him relief is the drugs. Then he got mixed up in these sex parties, and the rest is history.'

Laura's eyes widened. 'Damn,' she said. 'That was him in the photo that Allie had, wasn't it? I knew I recognised the features. I couldn't believe it would be him, so I ignored it.'

'I don't know what photos you're talking about, but if they had anything to do with drugs or these parties, it would have been Josh. He's the one who organises everything. And if Allie was at those parties, she would have been with a guy called Terry. Josh made sure he had her just where he wanted her. That she couldn't get away from his influences, and Terry helped with that.'

'Who's Terry?'

'The lead singer from Sinking Blizzard. He and Josh were boarding-school buddies.'

'Fuck . . .' It didn't take Laura long to connect the dots. Poppy was mixed up with that bloke too.

'I came to tell you, Laura, because the lawyers have been in contact. Josh knows it's all fallen through. I'm frightened about what he might do.'

'You need to go to the police,' Laura said sharply. 'I can't do anything. It's all hearsay to me.'

'I know.' She looked down miserably. 'I'm sorry I'm so weak. I'm sorry I let him control me. Especially when I knew you didn't have an abortion. I was still so angry with you for not talking to me, not trusting me.'

'Go to the police now, Meghan,' Laura urged. 'And you need to get some help.'

'Will you come with me?'

'No.' Laura paused. 'I'll ask Tim to take you, if you want.' It was the least she could do to acknowledge the friendship they had once shared.

ⅎ

'Poppy, I need to talk to you.'

'Why?'

'Just come down here.' Laura led the way into her bedroom and sat on the bed, patting the spot beside her.

'You're most of the reason we worked out where Lee was,' she said to her sister with a smile. 'That deserves really big praise!'

Poppy half-smiled but looked wary.

'You know the band called Sinking Blizzard? I think you talked about them on the phone one day.'

A smile split Poppy's face. 'Yeah. They're the hottest thing around Adelaide at the moment. Awesome music.'

'They played down here a couple of times too.'

'Seriously? Did you go?'

Laura shook her head. 'But Robyn, Tegan and Allie did. Allie got quite friendly with the lead singer. Terry, I think his name is.'

Poppy's face lost its smile and she crossed her arms. 'What about it?' she asked.

'Oh, Poppy, don't you see what you're mixed up with? He's supplying drugs to people, going to sex parties. You're so much better than that. You've got the world at your feet, a family who love you. Please, please don't go down that path.'

'For your information,' Poppy said haughtily. 'I already know all of that. Including that I'm better. I haven't taken drugs for five weeks and I haven't seen him in as long. Yeah, I got caught up in the hype and excitement. But not now. So don't tell me what's good for me or what I am. You don't know me that well.'

Poppy stomped out of the room, leaving Laura feeling more hopeful that her sister might be getting back on track. She'd still word up her dad and Georgie, she decided, but maybe Poppy had got out before she was hooked. She hoped so.

☙

When Josh was charged with stalking, possession with intent to sell and having sex with underage girls, it was the talk of the town. But the Murphys of Nambina weathered the storm calmly.

'Crazy!' Laura had said. 'No one would have known. He was so uptight and straight in public.'

Tim shook his head. 'I hear all types of gossip in the surgery. But there was never one word said about Josh that I know of. How he kept everything under wraps is beyond me.'

Laura put her arms around him. 'Now we've got to get the crop off. And then Christmas! It's only a week away! This year has just flown.'

'And I have to get back to work.'

'I'm pleased Meghan has managed to get into rehab,' Laura mused. 'I think she'll be okay in the end. Glenda won't let anything else happen. I'm going to meet the new manager Glenda has installed tomorrow. Hopefully there can be a decent relationship between the two farms again.'

Tim swung her around until she was sitting down. He plonked down next to her. 'So what are your plans?'

'Crop off, graduate these girls in another five months and start all over again with a new bunch. I've learned a lot from this group, so I'll be better at it next time.'

'Got time for a wedding?' Tim asked as he drew in the ground with a stick.

Laura looked at him. 'Wedding? Whose?'

'Well, ours. Had an idea we might, you know, get married.' He sounded unsure of himself.

Laura pushed him back and kissed him. 'Tim Burns, you always know the right thing to say.'

Chapter 42

2009

Laura was woken by a tapping sound. Tim's face appeared around the door.

'I'm not supposed to see you before the ceremony,' she whispered.

'I know, but you can't miss this sunrise. If you're quiet, no one will know.' He grinned cheekily at her, and she felt her heart race.

She glanced at her wardrobe to make sure her wedding dress was out of sight. Tim could break all the rules he liked—except seeing the dress, she decided.

Throwing on a pair of jeans and a T-shirt, she gathered up the pile of letters on her dressing table and tiptoed out to the kitchen. Tim had disappeared—she guessed he was waiting in his dual cab.

'Where are you going? It's still dark outside.'

Laura started and turned around. Catherine was standing with her hands on her hips and a curious look on her face. Her hair was messy and her cheeks were lined with crease marks from the pillow.

'Um . . .' Laura felt her face grow red. She'd been caught.

'You're incorrigible! What about all the traditions?'

'He hasn't seen the dress,' Laura said defensively.

Catherine flapped her hands. 'Go on, then. Meet Tim. I won't tell anyone. Just bring me a coffee when you get back.'

Laura flashed her a grin and turned away. She stopped and went back to hug her friend. 'It's so good to have you here.'

Catherine returned the hug. 'Off you go or you'll be late for your own wedding. Only a farmer would time the ceremony for ten in the morning.'

There was the sound of footsteps on the verandah. Tim appeared in the doorway, holding a thermos cup of coffee. 'Come on, Laurs,' he hissed, gesturing with his one free hand. 'Ah, Catherine! Good morning to you.'

Catherine waved as Laura ran out the door. Outside, she started to laugh wildly. 'I feel like I'm sneaking off without Dad knowing,' she said. She spun around in the cool morning air, her head back. 'I'm so excited. So *happy!*'

Tim handed her the cup. 'Come on,' he hurried. 'We'll miss the sunrise.'

Rip had materialised in the back of the ute. Laura gave him a quick pat and they were off.

'Where are we going?' She took a sip from her cup. 'Oh, you've brought the coffee from town? Did you drag one of the ladies at the deli out of bed to make it for you?'

'No. I made it myself. Now, we're going to the old asylum.' He leaned across and kissed her, keeping his eyes on the road. 'I needed to spend this morning with you.'

Laura smiled and put her hand on his knee. The rest of the trip passed in contented silence.

At last Tim turned off the road and pulled up near the crumbling building. It had been abandoned years before and was now inhabited by pigeons and rabbits.

They got out and, leaning on the bullbar, sipped their coffee as they waited for the sun's first rays to show.

'How did you and Sean go at cleaning out Howie's rooms?' Tim asked, still staring towards the horizon.

Laura took another sip and felt for the letters in her pocket. 'Okay. We got rid of all the clothes—who knows what they'll do with them at the second-hand store. I certainly can't see anyone buying them!'

'Might be useful for another Baggy and Saggy,' Tim said with a grin.

'That's about all,' Laura agreed. 'We kept a few things— things that need to stay with the house because they're part of Nambina's history. You know, like his records and books. The paintings on his wall can stay there too. I don't want to shift them. It would look strange not having them there.'

'History is important,' Tim agreed. 'But it'll be nice to have the use of those rooms for kids.'

Laura didn't say anything. Her emotions had gone a little crazy last night, when she and Sean finished carting the final boxes out to the back of her ute. She knew something had finished, but at the same time it hadn't. Howie would always be with her. In her heart and memory. He'd helped shape and teach her. He couldn't be lost, no matter what changes she made to Nambina. But the physical history would teach the generations to come. The generations she and Tim would create.

Laura wished Nicky and Poppy felt the same way about Howie as she did. At the last bridesmaid fitting two days before, she'd tried to explain her love for him to them. The sad fact was, however, he hadn't been a great part of their life—the part they could remember, anyhow.

The heavy-heartedness that had taken over halfway through yesterday, when she had discovered the old letters, came back. She dug into her back pocket. 'I found these in Papa's suit. They were in the inside pocket of his jacket.' She handed them to Tim. 'These made me think about what could have been,' she said. 'How the choices we make can take us on different paths.'

Tim put down his cup and opened one of the letters. As he did, a shimmer of red hit the clouds. The new day was on its way. In the pale light of sunrise, Tim began to read.

Dear Thomas,

Dad said you'd been here to Nambina. I wish I could have seen you. I've been wanting to write to you for so long, but didn't know where you were. I guess there is still every chance this letter won't find you.

Thomas, you hurt Dad really bad. For a while I was angry with you for that. I know all of the times he hurt you, you took it without saying a word, so I can sort of understand what you did.

He's old and all the whiskey has made him sick. He hides it well, since he's stopped drinking. The doctor has just said there's not much they can do.

Thomas I need you to know I'm sorry. Sorry for not standing up to Dad when he started hitting you. I was pleased it wasn't me so I kept my head down and stayed out of the way. I was happy to let you take the beatings.

Once you left, I was sure he'd start on me, but he didn't. Dad stopped drinking. Just like that. He sort of became a different person. A much happier one. We started to make a friendship—a good one, and I enjoyed it. I felt like he'd chosen me to be the son he loved and as much as I didn't understand why, I wasn't going to question it. I didn't want to be abused the way you had.

So I let it go. I basked in his attention once you left. When I look back now, I know I was wrong.

I need to apologise and know that you've read this letter. Know that somehow you might consider forgiving me.

Dad died two weeks ago. Would you come home, Thomas? To be brothers and friends? Workmates and partners?

I won't ever give up hope you'll come home at some stage in your life. The offer will be there until I die.

Your brother,

Howard

'Wow,' was all Tim said. He started to open the second letter.

'They're all the same,' Laura said. 'They say exactly the same thing.' She reached for the envelope. 'Look here. They were all returned to him.'

'Not known at this address,' Tim read out loud. They were silent again, thinking of all that had happened and about all the 'what ifs'.

'Life's a bit like those *Choose Your Own Adventure* books we read as kids, except you don't get a second chance at it,' Tim said. 'If you make a bad mistake you've either got to admit it and fix it, or live with it forever.' Laura slipped her arm around Tim's waist as the sun broke over the horizon. 'That's what Thomas did. I reckon he thought he'd be the one to make a better life for himself by leaving but it didn't work out that way. Somehow, it was Howie who ended up with the life Thomas wanted.'

She looked out across the landscape. The grass had turned from brown to green over the last two weeks. Laura had planned it that way, scheduling the wedding for May so she could be married on Nambina when everything was green.

Which reminded her: today was her wedding day! The house would be coming to life now, she guessed. Poppy would be making coffee; Lee would be making fresh juice while she chatted to Nicki. Sean and Georgie would be at the kitchen table, making final arrangements for the coming day. In the students' quarters, Tegan and Robyn would be planning their outfits.

Allie hadn't responded to their wedding invitation, but Laura still hoped she might be there today. Laura was keen to see how her former student was getting on.

The clouds were glowing a dark crimson now. A new day was here.

'It's our turn to make greatness happen here, Laurs,' Tim said after a while. 'We can leave the ghosts and stories from way-back-when right here. We'll just tell them when they're needed again.'

Laura turned to him and tilted her head back. 'I like that idea.'

Acknowledgements

Although we spend much time, while writing, by ourselves—more likely than not a dog (or cat) at our feet—authors never write a book alone. A truer sentence was never typed!

Mae Flynn, for all your hard work and encouragement.

David and Nicole Swan from Swan's Vet Services in Esperance. Your dedication to vet students and their practical learning inspired me to dream up Laura. Hopefully she's half as good as you guys! Thanks for your encouragement, support and answers, no matter how silly the question.

Bob and Jean Fisher, who answered my endless questions about shearing teams and woolsheds back in the '30s and '40s—your eyewitness accounts were incredibly helpful.

Sally van de Walter, Sarah Peck, Rebekah Herden and all the girls (and guys) who were involved in the hilarious Facebook conversation about nightclubs, bands and clothes from the early '90s, just after we left school. Thanks for the laughs and memories!

Louise Gray for all the merino show information and stories.

All the Facebook fans who were involved in choosing the animal names in *Crimson Dawn*.

Alecia Hancock—great job.

Robyn—for being there.

Louise, Jude, Sarah, Amy, Marie and all the other incredible people at Allen & Unwin. Thank you for all of your hard work in making my books the best they can be and continuing to give me these wonderful opportunities.

Gaby, once again, your calming influence and gentle guiding hand have kept me at the top of my game. Heartfelt thanks.

Cal, for the whole kit and caboodle—love you to bits.

The people who hold my heart and I theirs—Anthony, Rochelle and Hayden. Mum, Dad, Nicholas, Ellie and Elijah, Susan, Nathan, Ned and Lexy. Sharon and Ron.

Catherine Marriott, who has been nothing short of an inspiration since I met her and on whom the character of Catherine is very loosely based. Thank you for allowing me to use some of the words from your speech. Maz, the energy changes when you walk into a room.

A massive, massive shout out to those who read the words within these pages. I'm in debt to you, because it's you who keep my dream of writing alive. I delight in your messages and interaction, be it through email, Facebook, Twitter or letters. It's only through you that my books can live. I hope Laura's journey entertains you.

If I have inadvertently forgotten to mention someone here, I'm very sorry and thank you for your help.

Isaiah 41:13